SG·1

THE BARQUE OF HEAVEN

Jack looked around, through the little clouds of his breath condensing in the still, frigid air. Maybe this niche in the tunnel walls would offer a few moments' respite. No movement showed in the passage they had just raced through. Ahead, another tunnel angled away into the darkness, offering at least somewhere else to run.

His team gathered near him, faces turned toward the tunnels and watchful for any hint of pursuit. Carter balanced on her left leg as she scanned the darkness, denying the ache in her right ankle, twisted on the treacherously slick rock. Teal'c faced the opposite direction, alert as ever, yet his utter weariness could be seen in his slumped shoulders and slowing movements, his skin an unhealthy grayish hue.

Daniel was leaning against the dank wall, the façade of stubbornness on his face slipping as surely as his body was sliding down the uneven rocks, his lungs now emitting little more than a distressed wheeze. His left fist was still firmly planted on the pain below his ribs.

Jack shifted, vainly trying to ease the muscles knotted along his spine and the stabbing pain that had been his constant companion for what seemed like his entire life.

How the hell did we end up like this?

Movement flickered in the corner of his eye—Carter's hand coming up and signaling they were about to be discovered.

He sucked in a gasp of cold air, reached over and grabbed a fistful of Daniel's shirt, help off in Teal'c's wake—plung

Within seconds SG-1 had nal rock showing no trace of

STARGÅTE
SG·1™

THE BARQUE
OF HEAVEN

SUZANNE WOOD

FANDEMONIUM BOOKS

An original publication of Fandemonium Ltd, produced under license from MGM Consumer Products.

Fandemonium Books, PO Box 795A, Surbiton, Surrey KT5 8YB, United Kingdom
Visit our website: www.stargatenovels.com

STARGÅTE
SG·1

METRO-GOLDWYN-MAYER Presents
RICHARD DEAN ANDERSON
in
STARGATE SG-1™
AMANDA TAPPING   CHRISTOPHER JUDGE   DON S. DAVIS
and MICHAEL SHANKS as Daniel Jackson
Executive Producers ROBERT C. COOPER   MICHAEL GREENBURG
RICHARD DEAN ANDERSON
Developed for Television by BRAD WRIGHT & JONATHAN GLASSNER

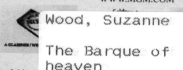

ISBN: 978-1-905586-05-9   Printed in the USA

I would like to thank the following people:
Heather, for all those brainstorming sessions
and beta reading.
Judy B, for her grammatical expertise and
generous assistance.
Jill, for leading the cheer squad.
The Duzites, for their support and helpful hints on
how to maim people.
Rowan, for sharing her medical knowledge.
Mum and Dad.
Molly, for all those 'Just another five minutes, then
we'll go for a walk'.
And
Michael Shanks, for being Daniel.

This story takes place in Season Three, following the episode "Deadman's Switch".

ANOTHER DAY, ANOTHER PLANET

"And we bid you welcome to P-three-R-seven-seven-niner, where the weather is a balmy eighty-four degrees. Today's special for our campers includes palm trees, a babbling brook, lots of weird grassy things and a honkin' huge sheep." Jack O'Neill broke off his travelogue to give the colossal statue nestled in the valley before them a quick glance over. He clapped his hands together and continued, "As an added bonus, the management is delighted to announce that the Tok'ra will *not* be joining us on this mission, thus ensuring three days of uninterrupted fun in the sun."

Jack settled his shades over his eyes and snugged his cap firmly into place as he continued to scan the area around the Stargate. Teal'c was likewise on guard for potential hostiles. Carter maneuvered the loaded FRED down the platform steps and around Daniel, who was already filming the structures before them.

"I don't remembering buying the monologue package for this trip," Carter's voice floated up to him.

"Regrettably it appears to be supplied free of charge, Major Carter," Teal'c replied. "Whether one wishes it or not."

Their colonel feigned wounded feelings and skipped down the stone steps. "Of particular interest is our collection of big ol' moldy buildings, designed to capture the interest of any archaeologist worth his salt." Jack clapped Daniel on the back with enough force to break into his archaeologist's reverie.

Daniel lowered the camera slightly and his gaze flicked to Jack for a second before being dragged back to the wonders before him. "Wow," he muttered.

"You're welcome." Jack loftily took the credit and launched back into tour-guide mode. "So, we trust you all enjoy your stay and remember—take your trash with you when you leave." He waved his MP5 expansively at the surrounding landscape. "Fan out, people."

SG-1 moved away and began to take a proper look around. Jack circled behind the Stargate and glanced through the ring at the V-shaped valley that widened from where he stood to stretch for nearly two kilometers. Scrubby bushes and mounds of tufted grass dotted the arid soil. To the right of the Stargate he noted the brown waters of a river meandering through palm trees and large rocks; a backup water supply was always welcome. Turning from the empty land behind the platform, his gaze settled on a wide stone causeway that led directly to where the colossal statue of the ram-headed beast crouched, impassively guarding the entrance to an equally massive, many-columned temple.

Behind the temple rose a familiar sight: an enormous pyramid, built of the same pale stone as the statue and temple, and large enough to serve as a landing platform for a Goa'uld mothership. Warm breezes wafted over the team, bringing the crisp, hot scent of desert sands from beyond the surrounding rocky hills. Tiny birds twittered and darted through the grasses along the river while larger hawk-like birds coasted on air currents high above. Nothing else stirred; there was no movement among the buildings, no Jaffa coming to challenge the intruders.

Teal'c halted fifty meters along the causeway, scanning the area and absorbing what he saw with practiced ease. "This place appears deserted, O'Neill," he called out, voice carrying distinctly in the warm air.

"Clear, sir," echoed Carter, a hundred meters off to the left.

O'Neill finished his own sweep. "Well, what do you know? Tok'ra intel that's actually right for once. Okay kids, have at it. Teal'c, you and Daniel go check out that statue." He grinned as Daniel, who had been impatiently inching sideways while waiting for the all-clear, took off up the causeway at a trot, Teal'c striding along behind.

Jack ambled over to the DHD, identified the lone unfamiliar glyph as the point of origin and dialed up the coordinates for Earth, the immediate check-in with Base now SOP since their little problem on Ernest's world.

Seven symbols locked, Jack pressed the center crystal and—nothing. He frowned, quickly checking the symbols were correct. They were, the point of origin the only unfamiliar glyph, and the corresponding symbols were locked on the inner ring of the Stargate. After a few moments the glowing chevrons winked out.

He glared at the DHD and tried again, pressing each symbol firmly: Auriga, Cetus, Centaurus, Cancer, Scutum, Eridanus, Point-of-origin. The inner ring of the Stargate spun, chevrons clunked as they locked, and Jack leaned on the big red activation crystal with deliberate force. Nothing. He pressed again, this time with both hands, but the wormhole refused to establish. Once again the symbols winked out, leaving a cold foreboding to crawl up his spine.

Looking up, Carter's name on his lips, Jack saw the major already headed toward him.

"Problem, sir?"

"Can't open the wormhole, Carter," he replied. "Chevrons are locking, but no cigar."

Carter dropped her pack to the ground and whipped out a diagnostic tool. She popped the access panel on the DHD and hooked up to the crystals inside. "Power readings are all within acceptable parameters, sir." She stowed the tool and rose. "Mind if I give it a try?"

O'Neill stepped back, uneasily scanning the area. "Please, prove me wrong, Carter." He looked along the causeway to see Teal'c staring back at them, already alerted to trouble by the lack of activity at the Stargate.

Carter hit the symbols for the address to Earth, methodically pressing each panel and muttering its name. She depressed the activation crystal and got nothing. The chevrons around the Stargate glowed cheerily in the sunlight but the

Stargate itself remained merely an empty ring. After a minute, the lights winked out and the DHD shut down.

"What's the likelihood of this happening two missions in a row? If Aris Boch is lurking somewhere…." Jack swiped his cap from his head and scrubbed at his hair. He smacked the radio on his vest and barked, "Teal'c, Daniel, fall back to the 'gate. Wormhole's not opening."

Jack watched for a moment as Daniel and Teal'c turned and retraced their path along the stone causeway, then looked down to see Carter again on her knees with her head nearly inside the access panel.

"Anything, Carter?" He knew he should probably give her more than a minute to come up with a solution, but still….

"Hoo boy. Take a look at this, sir." She sat back on her heels, her face scrunched up in a mix of worry and interest.

Casting another glance around the empty valley, Jack dropped to one knee and peered inside the DHD. His knowledge of the inner workings of the alien machines was enough to tell if one was in working condition or not. The usual set of crystals was present; their color and arrangement all as they should be. What was not usual was a spidery-fine network of filaments, concealed behind and attached to the control crystals. Alien and very out of place, they glittered blackly sinister in the sunlight.

"The DHD is accepting the coordinates we enter and they're lighting up on the 'gate in the correct sequence, but my guess is this is stopping the wormhole from initiating," Carter said.

"Whoa, what the hell is that?" Daniel's voice floated over Jack's shoulder as he and Teal'c arrived and bent to peer inside the DHD.

"Good question. Teal'c, you seen anything like this before?" Jack asked, twisting around to squint up through the sunlight at him.

"I have not, O'Neill." Teal'c's eyes tracked the path of the black tendrils. "They appear to be connected to the crystals that are responsible for controlling power and transmitting coordinates to the Stargate."

"That can't be good," remarked Daniel.

"Indeed. It is not unknown for some Goa'uld to tamper with the DHDs for their own purposes."

Jack straightened up and snapped open the cover of his chrono. Twenty minutes on-planet already. "Well, we've missed our check-in. The SGC should be dialing in any minute now. Carter, you'd better work out if you need any extra gear from home."

"Yes, sir. The piece that was missing from the DHD on PJ6-877 is still here. I don't think we can blame this on Aris Boch." She bent her head back inside the pedestal and began to talk quietly with Teal'c about the placement of crystals.

Daniel moved to stand next to Jack. The valley spread out before them in silent majesty. Against an indigo sky, the limestone surface of the pyramid, buildings, statue and causeway gleamed brilliantly in the sunlight. A gold capstone on the pyramid blazed in an ostentatious display that impressed even Jack. Beside him, unable to examine these wonders closely while their present problem remained unresolved, Daniel pulled out his camera and began to film.

Five, six, seven chevrons locked—and no wormhole. Jack turned away from the silent valley to see Carter and Teal'c duck behind the DHD to worry at the controls once more. Six attempts to dial out and they were none the wiser. The Stargate shut down with a disappointed whine, then almost immediately the chevrons began to light up again with another attempt. They glowed brightly for close to a minute before winking out with a mocking snap.

Stranded.

No way out.

Jack stalked back to his team.

"Anything?"

Carter glanced up at him, squinting against the sun in her eyes. "Sir, it looks like the black filaments are disrupting the connection between the coordinate verification mechanism and the wormhole activators."

Daniel appeared at Jack's shoulder, shielding the glare from her face. "Is it just Earth's address that it blocks? Maybe another address will get through."

Jack shrugged and gestured with his MP5 at the DHD. "Go for it, Daniel."

Pocketing his camera, Daniel stepped up, and after a moment's thought dialed the coordinates for the Alpha site. Symbols lit, chevrons locked — but no gushing splash of event horizon answered his call.

He tried again, this time Cimmeria. Nothing.

Argos. Zip.

Oannes. Squat.

Orban. Diddly.

Planet of the Naked White Bald Guys. Bupkiss.

One last one. Nada.

"You dialed the address for Chulak, Daniel Jackson?" queried Teal'c.

"Chulak?" Jack echoed. "What, you think we need another challenge right now?"

"Well, I wasn't planning on going through if it worked, Jack. I just thought maybe the DHD has been tampered with to recognize only Goa'uld worlds," Daniel pointed out. "I guess not."

Jack allowed him that and sighed in frustration.

"Perhaps if we were to dial the Stargate manually, we could bypass the mechanism on the DHD." Teal'c's suggestion broke through the strained silence.

"It's worth a try, sir," added Carter as she stood up.

Fifteen minutes of back-wrenching labor later they were no closer to an answer.

"I don't get it, sir," complained Carter as they all stood sweating in the sun. She accepted the canteen offered by Daniel and swallowed a long, cool drink of water. "If the filament is stopping the DHD from sending the coordinates to the 'gate, we should still be able to dial out manually. We've done it before without a DHD."

Jack's next question went unasked when the first chevron on the Stargate lit up with a reassuring clunk.

"Yes." Long, determined strides had him in front of the MALP, ready to make contact with the base. The seventh chevron locked and the gush of the wormhole brought a sigh of relief from them all. Within seconds of the event horizon stabilizing, the camera on the MALP was tracking around, moved by unseen hands and accompanied by the welcome sound of General Hammond's voice, issuing tinnily from the speaker.

"SG-1, this is Hammond, please respond."

"SGC, this is SG one niner. We read you, General."

"Colonel, you missed your first check-in. What's your status?"

"We've got a bit of a technical hitch, sir. We're secure, no hostiles, but there's some kind of... thing attached to the DHD controls. It's preventing us from opening the wormhole. Carter?" Jack motioned her forward and stepped aside.

Carter swiftly filled the general in on what they had discovered so far. "Also sir, there's a box of tools in my lab marked 'Offworld diagnostics'. Could you arrange for it to be sent through?"

"It's on its way, Major. Colonel, apart from the equipment Major Carter has requested, is there anything else we can do from here?"

"We're good for the moment, sir. We'll have a look around the buildings here, see what we can turn up. If it looks like we're going to have an extended stay, we'll need extra supplies."

The thought of spending days or weeks in this empty place didn't exactly fill him with cheer, but things could be oh, so much worse. If all else failed they could get the Tok'ra to scare up a ship and come get them. Speaking of....

"Sir, this entire mission was the Tok'ra's idea. They came up with the address, they asked us to head a mission to check out this place for some old base of Ra's, and yet at the last minute they're suddenly 'unavoidably detained by political matters' and it's 'don't wait for us, we'll catch up with you'." Jack waved sarcastic quotation marks in the air as he spoke.

"Understood, Colonel. We'll contact the Tok'ra and see if they can shed any light on the situation." Jack could just picture the look on Hammond's face. *"Heads up, people. Sergeant Siler has Major Carter's requisition."*

They moved back, unnecessarily, as a large plastic crate popped through the wormhole, propelled by a push along the grating of the SGC's ramp to slide gently to a halt on the stone platform a whole world away.

"We'll dial in again at 1400 hours and on the hour after that. Good luck. Hammond out."

The Stargate disengaged, leaving the four looking at each other.

"You think the Tok'ra set us up, Jack?" asked Daniel.

"I'm just saying it's a mighty big coincidence."

"Well, they were right that this planet was once used by Ra," Daniel countered. He turned, waving an arm at the looming statue. "That's a Criosphinx. The ram's head design is a typical feature of smaller sphinxes on Earth that were dedicated to Amun, or Ra. Also, there's a design above the entrance to the temple that could well be a Wadjet — The Eye of Ra. I'll have to get closer to be certain, though."

Jack scowled, unwilling to give up his main suspect just yet. "Well, Miseanu said she and the rest of the Tok'ra would be joining us at 2000 hours. I'll reserve judgment until then." He looked over his team, glad once again that he had a wealth of knowledge and experience to call upon instead of a grunt of Marines.

"Carter, Teal'c — see what you can do about disconnecting that thing from the DHD. Daniel, let's you and I take a walk and find out what's so damn fascinating about this place."

The causeway led them directly to the statue. A fat, yellow sun beginning its afternoon descent glared hotly on the limestone structures before them. Daniel, reveling in the heat, had already shed his BDU jacket and Jack followed suit, rolling the jacket and clipping it on to the back of his vest as they both gazed up at the sphinx.

Ninety feet high into the sky it reared: the huge, powerful haunches and body of a lion coiled under the head of a ram; its wicked, curled horns tapered to razor fine points capped in gold and framed a fine-boned face that seemed more than passingly familiar.

"Is that…?" Jack cocked his head to one side, considering.

"Yes. Yes, I think it must be," Daniel replied absently, transported in an instant back to the first time he had met Ra—haughtily majestic, surrounded by half-naked, scalp-locked children—himself overawed, impressionable and vindicated, and having the most amazing time of his life with a dangerous and unpredictable Jack by his side.

"Wonder how the kids are doing?" Jack mused fondly.

Daniel knew Jack was remembering his delight at finding the children had abandoned Ra and were wandering bewildered in the back corridors of the Abydos pyramid. The Abydonians had accepted the lost ones into their lives and homes like the precious gifts they were. "Probably still getting up to all sorts of mischief," he said, quickly bringing the camera up to his eyes. "After a lifetime of total obedience to Ra, they really let loose once they felt safe. Kasuf and the elders used to shake their heads and bemoan the 'shocking nature of youth'." His voice was soft with memories and just a hint of sadness for his lost life in Nagada.

"Nice to know some things stay the same, no matter what planet you're on."

Goa'uld script filled Daniel's viewfinder, translations automatically springing to his lips. "'Kneel ye before Ra, mightiest of gods, all who come before him'."

Jack made a face and walked on along the sphinx's side. "As Teal'c would say, Dead False God."

The causeway continued on from the rear of the sphinx—a

hundred meters walk to a short wall enclosing the temple. Inside stood a forest of thick columns supporting a roof of massive stone slabs that soared high over their heads. Walls, columns, roof: all were heavily carved and painted in vivid reds, greens, blues and golds, the bright white of the stone barely managing to peep through in places. Dotted around outside the temple were small open-sided stone shelters, each consisting of a roof and four supporting pillars. In the background rose the pyramid, almost incandescent in the sunshine and dwarfing even the stunning height of the temple.

Jack winced as a reflected shaft of sunlight lanced through his glasses. He looked over at Daniel, his complaint dying as Daniel stared up, delight and awe spreading across his face, his mouth open, unable to find any words to express what he was feeling.

"Jack," Daniel finally croaked out. "Do you see?"

"I'm seeing it, Daniel, I'm seeing it." There was a beat of silence, then Jack sighed in defeat. "Okay, what am I seeing?"

Daniel drifted forward a couple of feet, arms gesturing expansively around him.

"Jack, this is Ancient Egypt. These buildings, the sphinx, the — the pyramid; this is how the temples and monuments in Egypt looked, thousands of years ago when they were first built." He turned to flap a hand at the pyramid, its crown a blaze of light. "The limestone covering, the gold capstone — they're the same features many of the great pyramids initially had, particularly at Giza... where the Stargate was found." Daniel trailed off as yet more evidence of the Goa'uld's interference in human history slammed home.

"The Abydos pyramid is brown," Jack remarked, derailing Daniel's train of thought.

Daniel stared at Jack. "Abydos was only ever home for slaves who worked the naquada mine. It was functional. This," he turned back to the colorful glory quietly waiting before them, "it's too decorative." Brow creased in thought, he waggled a finger at him. "This is significant, Jack."

Jack's eyebrows rose skeptically. "Exactly how so?"

Daniel turned and began striding swiftly towards the temple, armed with camera, notebook and the eager anticipation of a puzzle to be solved. He called back over his shoulder, spurring Jack into a jog to catch him up.

"I have *no* idea."

Teal'c paused in his fourth circuit of the perimeter around the Stargate platform, the silence heightened by the soft susurration of the foliage growing along the river bank, gently moving in the warm breeze. A pleasing place, were it not for the lack of a ready exit.

His eyes roamed over the Stargate, then focused through the ring on Major Carter's legs stretched out in the dirt, the rest of her body obscured by the squat mushroom shape of the DHD, as she patiently disconnected the black filaments from the operating mechanism.

Teal'c brought his gaze back to the Stargate itself, standing silent and mysterious as it had surely done for many thousands of years. The gray naquada surface showed no sign of wear; harsh sun, sand-filled scouring winds, rain and even time itself had failed to tarnish its simple elegance. The inner track with its thirty-nine symbols nestled snugly in the outer ring, waiting for the next command to open itself to the universe beyond.

The chevrons gleamed under the bright sun, each as recognizable to Teal'c as old friends; a lifetime of using the Stargate network had brought familiarity and no little respect. He absently noted each glyph was correctly depicted. Nothing appeared untoward, except... tiny black filaments snaking out of the sand piled around the base where the ring disappeared into the platform's support.

Teal'c dropped to one knee and gently brushed the sand away. Tendrils of black wound up out of the surface of the outer ring itself and led into an oval object melded onto the flat side of the Stargate.

Straightening, Teal'c reached for his radio. His open mouth

closed as the speaker crackled to life with O'Neill's voice.

"Major, Teal'c? Report."

"Sir, I'm halfway through disconnecting the device on the DHD. Another twenty minutes and we should be able to give it another go," Major Carter's voice rang out, echoing slightly in the quiet air.

"Good job, Carter. T?"

"O'Neill, the Stargate perimeter is still secure. Also, I have just discovered another device attached to the Stargate itself."

Major Carter popped her head up from behind the DHD. "Really?" She scrambled up and jogged over to him.

"Oh, swell," sighed O'Neill. "Well, we're heading to the temple. Check in every thirty minutes. Out."

"Acknowledged, O'Neill." Teal'c shifted aside to allow Major Carter access to their newest problem.

"Oh, boy."

Teal'c acknowledged her look of exasperation and the two of them got down to work again.

Daniel led Jack, circling the temple cautiously. Built to the same gigantic proportions as the sphinx, it towered into the clear blue sky, rows of columns shouldering the burden of the thick slabs of granite forming the roof.

Behind the first building, a covered walkway led to a walled court. With a leap and scrabble they peered over the top of the wall to see inside. Amid exotic shrubs and tall palm trees stood five slender obelisks, all with markings etched deeply into their white stone and golden capstones. At the opposite end of the garden, another walkway led into an even larger building, this one with solid, bare walls. They dropped down and completed their circuit around the building.

"Before we go in, I want to recon that pyramid," Jack said. "It looks deserted, but we need to check it out regardless."

Reluctantly, Daniel pulled himself away from the beauty of the temple and followed Jack along the causeway to the pyramid. Although it seemed close by, its size made judging distance difficult, and it was a long, fifteen minute hike in the heat before they set foot on the ramp leading up to the only visible entrance. Fighting back a sense of déjà vu, he walked next to Jack, past the two obelisks standing sentinel at the foot of the ramp, up to the vast portico at the top which was flanked by two thick pylons. Stale, cool air drifted from the dark entrance.

They quietly edged through the opening and were enveloped by darkness. Pulling off their sunglasses, they peered into the shadows of a bare, pillared hall. Like Khufu's pyramid on Earth and Abydos's own, the stone walls bore no inscriptions. The first hall gave on to a second, then a third, until finally, they found themselves standing in a chamber.

The beams from their flashlights picked out the closed iris of a ring transporter on the ceiling, but nothing else. This room, too, was bare. For a brief moment, Daniel's mind overlaid another scene—hand-woven curtains between the pillars, rumpled bedding behind them, smokeless fires burning cheerily, the scent of bread and meaty stews filling the air, the chatter of people, happy and at peace. But that had been another time, another world, and this room was just empty.

"Let's go." Jack looked at him for a moment, then headed back the way they had come.

Daniel nodded, pushing down the grief that threatened to surface inside him, and silently followed.

Back at the main entrance to the temple, Jack slowly led the way into the forest of stone, cool darkness once again swallowing them. The further they advanced down the central path, the more he felt the sense of immensity; the vast weight of stone above seemed to press him down to insignificance. Each column they passed revealed another avenue stretching away in broken shadows. Shafts of sunlight slanted down through small gaps between the rows, each ray illuminating the decorations on the pillars in brilliant flashes of light. Painted scenes of Ra crushing his enemies, being worshiped and feted by his adoring people wrapped each column, some figures reaching twenty feet high and still dwarfed by the overall height of the pillars that disappeared in the gloom some hundred feet above them.

Jack flipped on his flashlight and followed Daniel as he meandered around, his muttering loud in the stifled silence.

"Incredible… workmanship… outstanding… 'Mighty is he'… obviously the written word is permitted here… 'great task'… 'will be proven'… oh, look at that!"

"Daniel?"

"Jack, this is—wow—a treasure trove of information about Ra."

"Well, nice as that is, does it say why we're stuck here?"

Daniel walked past him and plunged further into the darkness. "I'm sure we'll find some answers, Jack. I'm going to have a look in the courtyard."

Jack ambled along behind, always keeping Daniel in sight. For a moment Daniel's body was silhouetted against the sunlight streaming through the open doorway, then he was out in the walled garden, staring up at the row of obelisks.

Daniel half-turned as Jack stopped beside him, unable to completely tear his eyes away from the beauty before him.

"The Ancient Egyptians believed the obelisk was a shaft of light sent from the sun god," Daniel said quietly. He leaned backwards, trying to capture the fine details in the camera's viewfinder.

"Yeah, I've always preferred Asterix, myself." Jack pushed through the reedy grasses toward the covered walkway at the opposite end of the garden.

"Very funny." Daniel caught up to him then fell behind once more, attention captivated by figures on the third obelisk.

Jack stepped into the second enclosed building, his footsteps echoing on the polished granite floor. No columns here, just a vast hall, empty but for an alabaster altar and a gilded throne set upon a platform at the rear. The flashlight's beam played along the walls, chasing dust motes drifting in the still air. There were no carvings here, no drawings or pictothings, but ownership of the place was announced quite emphatically by the enormous golden Eye of Ra hanging above the throne.

Jack flipped it the bird and turned away. Rejoining Daniel in the courtyard, he said, "There's nothing in there, just a big ol' chair and an Eye of Ra thingy."

"Really?" Daniel's brow creased in thought.

"Got anything?"

"I think so." Daniel tapped the carvings before him. "This mentions a test. There was something similar on the columns inside." He broke off to stare at the plants bending gently in the breeze. "What does this remind you of?"

"Uhm," Jack huffed and searched for inspiration. "Really bad falafel I had in Alexandria one time."

"*Jack*. Think about it. We have a pyramid. We know the Goa'uld used pyramids to land Ha'tak ships. We have a sphinx guarding the way from the Stargate, loudly proclaiming this planet belongs to Ra. We have shelters and kiosks spread all over the place and we have a huge temple, just waiting for a lot of people to come and pay homage to their god."

Daniel took a breath and gestured at the assortment of structures around them.

"There are no dwellings, no places for common folk to live and work. No kitchens, no food gardens, no pottery workshops; nothing to show people lived here. This—this is all temporary. It's a fairground."

"*A fairground?*"

"Well, maybe not a fairground but a place where some kind of significant event occurred. Ra and his people came, they did… whatever, and they left. Probably on a regular basis."

"And this event could be linked to the Stargate not opening?"

"That's what we'll have to find out."

Jack stepped back as Daniel dropped his pack to the ground and set to work.

As darkness swallowed the light and heat of the sun, Jack called for a meal break and debrief. They sat together along the top step of the Stargate platform, eating MREs and watching the sun be sucked below the horizon in a final, protesting blaze of fiery red. Jack set aside his empty meal container and attacked the packaging of his pound cake.

"Okay, kids, where are we at?" he asked.

"I have extended my perimeter patrols to the top of the hills on both sides of this valley, O'Neill." Teal'c paused to squeeze more hot sauce onto his beef franks. "There is nothing to be seen in either direction, other than sand dunes. We appear to be secure here."

"Good to know, Teal'c," nodded Jack. "Carter?"

"Well, sir, I disconnected the filaments from the DHD, but without them the power supply completely disappears, both on the DHD and the Stargate. Reconnect them and the power flows through but no outgoing wormholes will form. Frankly, I'm stumped." Carter glared at the cheese and crackers in her hands as she spoke.

"Could we get a wormhole going with an external power source?"

"Possibly. We don't have anything with us that would come close to the wattage we need. The prototype naquada reactor back at the base might generate the required amount of energy, but it's not fully tested yet. I think lightning is out too. We could ask the general to send through some truck batteries, but without an engine to keep them charged I don't know how long they'll last."

"What about Teal'c's little pal down here?" Jack disposed of his cake with economical bites and gestured at the small device almost hidden in the shadows at the base of the ring. Shaped in a half-oval of highly polished black stone, it was no more than ten inches wide.

Carter rose and walked around the ring to stand frowning down at the device. "This is even stranger than the device on the DHD, sir. I can't detach the filaments connecting this to the Stargate at all; they're sunk right into the material of the ring and I can't cut through them. There are no writings of any kind, only nine gemstones inset along the outer rim, and eight of them are glowing."

Daniel finished off his bean and rice burrito and moved to stand beside Sam for another close look. "What's the panel in the center for?" he asked.

"Beats me, Daniel."

"Think a little C4 would dislodge it?" Jack suggested.

Carter blanched and Daniel stared at him. "Well, it might be an idea to get a little more information before you start blowing stuff up, Jack."

He shrugged, not discarding the option. "So, what have you got for us, Daniel?"

"Well, we have plenty of inscriptions to work with from the hall of pillars and the obelisks in the garden, but they're all scattered fragments, not a continuing text as I would expect."

"Do these passages give any information about what took place here, Daniel Jackson?" Teal'c asked.

Daniel dug out his notebook. "Maybe, possibly… not. I'm not sure, actually." He sped on before Jack could offer a comment. "For instance: 'Mighty is the power of Ra.' 'He commands all before him.' 'On bended knee will supplicants come before the Greatness of Ra.' 'The Trial of the Moons will receive only he who is worthy.' 'Greatly will the successful one be welcomed by Ra.' The phrase Trial of Moons is mentioned several times. I really need more information before I can make a proper assessment, but I'm sure there are more clues there. We'll find the answer to this."

"Daniel's right, sir. With a little time we can work this out," added Carter.

Jack swallowed a little gloat of pride in his team. How easy it was to keep up morale when they did it all for him.

"Perhaps there may not be as much time available as we would wish," said Teal'c, squatting in front of the device on the Stargate.

Not counting Mr. Pessimism, of course.

"Teal'c?" Jack leaned over sideways to get a better view.

"Eight of the nine gems are illuminated. It would seem to indicate a countdown of some kind."

"With one to go until—what?"

"Maybe it goes the other way, sir. Eight more to go before...," Carter made a gesture halfway between uncertainty and something blowing up.

"Sweet." Jack pulled a face. "The SGC is due to dial in any minute now, so...."

Right on cue, the Stargate churned to life once again and Jack moved to the MALP to give their report to Hammond.

It sounds like this situation may take some time to resolve, Colonel, Hammond said. *"Quarter Master is assembling additional supplies, enough to see you through for a month. Also, SG2 is on standby in case you need extra manpower. We've had no reply from the Tok...."*

The Stargate snapped off, aborting the general mid-sentence.

"What the hell?"

"Uh, I'll check it out, sir." Carter scrambled to the DHD and resumed rummaging through its innards.

"This might be coincidental, but the 'gate cut off at the same moment the sun disappeared." Daniel gestured past the ring at the horizon and the fading glow from the now vanished sun. "I was watching it."

The chevrons on the Stargate reactivated. Six, seven red crystals glowed brightly but the wormhole failed to engage. After a minute, they winked out, then sprang alight once again. To no avail.

"It would appear that we may indeed be stranded here," Teal'c said with doom-like calm.

"Okay. Teal'c, you and Daniel head back to the temple, see what you can find. Carter, let's see what we can do with this thing."

Several hours later, Teal'c was strolling slowly through the temple, a powerful flashlight playing over the disjointed phrases and sudden declarations carved into and painted all over the pillars. As he passed, Daniel Jackson shifted restlessly inside a circle of battery-powered lamps, near the temple's central row of columns. Many inscriptions, in the familiar dialect of the Goa'uld, praised the 'god' Ra, proclaiming his beneficence and majesty in a way only sycophantic priests desperate to gain the favor of their god could. This temple bore little resemblance to those erected in honor of Apophis, where the writings, praises, prayers and appeals began to the left of the entrance and ran continuously around the walls until they ended at the opposite side of the doorway.

The haphazard method of inscription here was confusing and causing no small problem to Daniel Jackson as he searched, translated and attempted to piece together a puzzle without knowing where or how many pieces there were.

"Huh." Daniel rose and rubbed circulation back into his cramped legs.

"Have you discovered something, Daniel Jackson?"

Daniel waved his notebook at the inscriptions before him. "I don't know whether it's by design or not, but all of the useful information I'm finding is down around floor level. Everything above six or seven feet high is just the usual worship of Ra. Also, Ra seems to have used a greater percentage of Ancient Egyptian words mixed in with the higher-Goa'uld dialect than we've seen on Apophis' worlds, or other Goa'uld worlds for that matter."

"Is this significant?"

"Well, it seems to indicate his ties with Ancient Egypt were deeper, perhaps longer, than those of other System Lords. Which doesn't really help us, per se. This however, does."

Daniel Jackson lifted one of the lamps up close to a passage carved into the stone just above his head. Teal'c glided closer as his voice rose into the echoing darkness of the building.

"'Go ye forth by set of the ninth new moon. Great shall be your journey. Great shall be your reward. With smiling eyes will Ra look down upon you as you complete your task.' Actually I think 'trial' would be more accurate." Daniel glanced over his shoulder. "Teal'c, do you recall hearing anything about a trial or test held by Ra? Did Apophis ever conduct anything that sounds like this?"

"The business of Ra's domain was always strictly guarded. Those outside his rule were never privy to any of the workings within his court, Daniel Jackson. Nor did Apophis seek to test his followers. If they did not meet his expectations, they were… disposed of."

"Oh. Well, there's more."

Teal'c followed Daniel as he stepped over the lamps and headed further into the gloom.

"Over here, where we've got Ra depicted in his solar boat or barque, sailing through the stars and smiting a mighty snake, it says, 'Journeyers go forth to give humble service to Ra, Mighty God of the Sun', and so on. Also, 'Each solar year will see the Gate open once only to the worthy'. Similar passages are all over these pillars, Teal'c, referring to the Stargate only opening once each year."

"The purpose of the mechanism inside the DHD," Teal'c surmised.

"Yes." An excited smile crept over Daniel's face. "Which means there is a way to open the Stargate here."

"O'Neill will not be happy to stay on this planet for an extended period of time."

"No, no he won't. Why don't you tell him while I get back to… uh… you know?" Daniel flashed Teal'c an innocent smile and sidled back into the shadows.

Teal'c blinked in surprise at having been so neatly maneuvered by his young friend. He stood gazing ruefully at the column and the image of a serpent thrashing in its death throes at the hands of Ra, and offered up a prayer to the true gods that all Goa'uld might suffer the same fate.

Reaching for his radio, he announced, "O'Neill. It is I, Teal'c."

Sam shared a grin with the colonel at Teal'c's unique call sign. While he talked to Teal'c, she headed back to the

Stargate for another look at the mysterious device attached to it. Immediately she saw that in the time they had been working on the DHD, the display on the device had altered.

The center panel now showed what looked like a quarter moon, risen above the flat base and moving up along the arch of the half-oval panel. She glanced up at the night sky and, sure enough, a moon had risen behind the pyramid—a thin quarter moon in the same relative position as that shown on the device. With foreboding, Sam noted the ninth gem on the device had begun to glow a pale green. Worse, after six more failed attempts, the SGC was still unable to establish an incoming wormhole, and at 2000 hours the chevrons had lit up again—presumably the Tok'ra attempting to keep their appointment. She sighed and gazed up at the stars: bright, unfamiliar constellations studding the deep velvet of the night sky, twinkling over their heads with utter disregard for their plight.

Nearly an hour later all four of them were searching the temple for some clue to open the Stargate. In the night sky, the moon was moving quickly toward its zenith, indicating a relatively short cycle. Another piece of the puzzle had been discovered—a passage carved into the lintel over the entrance to the throne room: 'By the Grace of the Name of Ra will my journey begin.'

For ten minutes now, Daniel had been muttering to himself, the words floating out of the darkness as he examined the pillars.

"The name of Ra... name of Ra... Ra's name... name... *name... RA!*"

Jack was on the verge of telling him to put a sock in it when Daniel suddenly shouted, "Of course! Jack!"

Jack swung around and was promptly blinded by the beam of Daniel's madly swinging flashlight coursing across his face.

"What?"

"I know what the names are." Daniel ran past him at full tilt, flinging explanations over his shoulder. "It's obvious! Don't know why I didn't think of it sooner, but they're written right there on the statue in the Abydos cartouche room."

He vanished into the obelisk garden and shot past Carter, with Jack and Teal'c hot on his heels. "Now I come to think about it, it was also on the Horus figure behind the ring device on Ra's ship. I haven't thought about that in ages, probably because he was trying to melt my brain at the time."

Daniel skidded to a halt before the altar in the throne room.

"I sometimes wonder if he succeeded," Jack muttered as he stalked after him.

Daniel glanced at his teammates ranged behind him, a small grin on his face. "Watch this."

Dropping to his knees, Daniel flung out both arms and dramatically declared, "Praise to you, Ra Triumphant. Lord of a million years, Eternal child of morning, He who stands above and apart, Shining one, The one who is first and last, He who is without equal. May you guide me to the path of the sun."

Silence covered the four like a suffocating blanket.

The sight of Daniel on his knees, praising the name of a Goa'uld, made Jack share a frown of unease with Teal'c.

Suddenly, a faint hum resounded from the direction of the altar.

"Listen." Carter's voice was hushed with expectation.

A beam of golden light shot up from the center of the altar, quickly spreading into the air above their heads. Diffused light coalesced into symbols—address glyphs. Seven of them.

"That's it!"

"Somebody write them down," Jack barked.

Teal'c was mouthing the names of the glyphs, as Daniel filmed the display while still on his knees. The light show snapped off, leaving them spot lit by their own flashlights.

"Okay, I got Mic and Sculptor," Jack started.

"Andromeda and Triangulum," added Carter.

"Gemini, Aquila," Daniel said, reading from the display in

the camera.

"The point of origin is a pyramid shape with a crescent moon above it," finished Teal'c.

"Way to go Daniel." Jack pulled Daniel to his feet and clapped him on the back. "I give you a ten for execution and eight for presentation."

"Only eight?"

"A little too dramatic for my taste, but, hey."

An hour later the moon was sinking rapidly toward the dark earth. Jack stood on the wall surrounding the courtyard, eyeing the horizon behind the pyramid where a silvery line foretold the sun's imminent arrival. A chilly breeze plucked at his clothing, bringing alien scents of desert and emptiness.

He lowered himself to the ground and strode into the temple to round up his team.

"Okay, kids, gear up. Dawn's breaking, and I want to be at the 'gate when the sun comes up and that countdown crystal thing runs out."

Daniel and Carter were packed and ready to go, and they still looked fresh and alert despite working through the night. Teal'c helped Carter with her pack as Daniel quickly scrutinized one last pillar.

"It's possible the SGC will be able to dial in during daylight, sir, though why, I can't work out just yet."

"I'm hoping so, Carter. Things could get a little tight if we have to start foraging for food."

"You intend for us to remain on this planet, O'Neill?"

"Best scenario, T. Even if the SGC can't get through to us again, they know where we are and I'm sure Hammond will get Jacob to scare up a ship and come get us eventually."

"What about the address we found, Jack?" Daniel hefted his pack up and Jack helped clip it to his tac vest. "We've compared it to all of the ones we know by heart, and it doesn't match any, even the hundreds Teal'c has used. Of course, that doesn't mean it's not on record in the SGC's database."

"We'll keep it in reserve, but if this planet is the jumping off point for some test of Ra's, then I don't think we want to be going anywhere the SGC can't find us. Hammond's expecting us to stay in our mission area, and here we'll stay."

"The Tok'ra sending us here now is pretty coincidental, isn't it?" Daniel muttered as they followed Teal'c out of the temple and onto the causeway.

"My, what a suspicious mind you have, Doctor Jackson." Jack couldn't have agreed more with the direction of Daniel's thoughts. He was looking forward to having a little chat with the Tok'ra operatives responsible for sending them here when SG-1 got back.

"We may find that we are able to connect to Earth from the Stargate on the planet to which this address leads, O'Neill," Teal'c commented.

"Or we could end up in the middle of a planet full of not so friendly Jaffa," Carter said, looking at the bright side.

"Charming," Jack grunted. He glanced up at the sphinx as they passed by, avoiding its stone eyes that seemed to follow their progress.

"So, what could the purpose of this 'test' be?" Carter asked.

"Probably to select hosts," Daniel said bleakly.

"All the more reason to stay right here," Jack pointed out. "For now, we'll establish camp by the 'gate; keep close in case we need to evacuate in a hurry."

By the time they returned to the Stargate, the ninth gem on the device was glowing a solid green. As a further contingency plan, Jack swiftly copied the address found in the temple into a brief report and buried it at the base of the DHD, then scratched 'SG-1' onto a rock to point the way for any potential rescue team.

"The moon has set, O'Neill," called Teal'c, standing on the Stargate platform and gazing through the ring at the now empty sky.

Long moments passed.

The sky behind the pyramid brightened swiftly from gray

nothingness to a golden-hued pale blue. A flock of birds broke from cover near the river, making everyone jump. Then the sun itself became visible, slightly to the left of the pyramid and framed between the valley walls; it was enormous and brilliantly fierce. Rays of light streaked up into the sky, a trumpeting herald of the new day.

"Oh, wow. Guys, look at the pyramid," Daniel uttered in awe.

Fire seemed to fill the capstone—a deep angry red-gold of refracted sunlight.

"I wonder if it's hollow?" Carter stepped back a pace, marveling at the sight as Daniel captured it on camera. Teal'c moved down the steps to stand near them, all four mesmerized as fiery light shot out from the capstone, over the roof of the temple and wrapped around the head of the sphinx, infusing the eyes in its Ra-face with a menacing gem-like glow.

"Er…," Daniel trailed off uneasily. "That's not natural."

"Yeah. Heads up, people," Jack said, automatically bringing his weapon up. "Carter, why don't you try dialing Earth one more time?"

"Yes, sir." She hurried to the DHD and punched in Earth's address. "No go, Colonel."

A bone-shuddering tremor rippled through the ground under their feet. A split second later amid a deafening boom, a tall, slender pillar shot up out of the sand in front of the sphinx. Before the team's astonished eyes another pillar exploded from the ground twenty feet away, followed by another and another, arcing in a circle around the Stargate and DHD and back to the sphinx.

There was a moment of silence—sand drifting back to earth and startled birds taking flight the only movement.

"Defensive positions," Jack snapped out, dropping to one knee and raising his gun. Daniel and Teal'c spread out to flank him, while Carter went for the high ground, hunkering down by the MALP on the platform behind them. "Teal'c, you got any idea what this is?" His voice sounded unnaturally loud in the quiet.

Teal'c's reply was drowned out by a snapping sizzle of electricity as an energy field popped up between each pillar, effectively corralling the team inside.

"These appear to be automated defensive posts, O'Neill." Teal'c appeared at Jack's side. He primed his staff weapon and crouched, alert and ready.

"Looks like my old buddy Ra didn't want anyone changing their mind about going on this trial thing," Jack replied as he eyed the pillars for weak spots.

Almost in response to Jack's comment, something exploded up out of the ground only two feet away from him, showering dirt and grass everywhere. The dawn light glinted off a small mechanical orb as it soared into the air. A bright blue beam lanced out from it and swept over each of the team.

"I think we've just been painted, Colonel," yelled Carter.

"I think you're right, Major."

Jack ratcheted the safety off his weapon, but the orb was already moving—faster than any of them could aim—zeroing in directly on Daniel.

"Daniel! Down!"

Daniel dived for cover behind the DHD, his pack shifting awkwardly over his shoulders as bullets from Jack's gun zipped over him. His hand slapped at the back of his right leg as he was struck. "*Ow.*" He rolled to one side, trying to keep the fast-moving orb in sight.

"Daniel?"

"I'm okay," he yelled, hand coming away bloodless from his leg. "I think."

A squawk from behind the MALP announced Carter had been hit too. "Sir, whatever this is, I don't think it's a weapon," she called out.

The orb whizzed over Jack's head. He fired instinctively, but missed by a mile. "Son of a bitch!" A sharp stinging pain flared in his shoulder.

Jack spun in a three-sixty degree arc, unable to keep up with it as Teal'c was zapped in the butt. As fast as it had arrived, the orb disappeared back into the ground leaving only a puff of dust in its wake.

"What the hell was that all about?"

Teal'c leaned over and prodded at the small cut on Jack's shoulder.

"See anything, T?"

"I cannot. The wound seems to be closing over."

Jack shared an uneasy glance with Daniel.

"Creepy." Daniel scratched uneasily at the gash in his thigh.

"These wounds may have been caused by the insertion of a tracking module," Teal'c continued. "Such things are favored by the Goa'uld when hunting those they consider a threat to their rule. I believe we should leave this place, O'Neill."

Jack scanned the buzzing force-field surrounding them. "I just wish we knew what we might be heading into, Teal'c. This whole setup sucks."

An earthy chuffing sound drowned him out as more objects shot up into the air. Five, ten, dozens of them. Whirring up from the ground came scores of glittering, golden objects, slowing to hover with silent and malicious intent.

"Crap." Jack stepped out in front of Daniel, weapon raised. "Now what?"

"They're shaped like the Eye of Ra," Daniel said, his gaze riveted to the menacing cluster.

As one, the miniature Eyes swarmed towards them, tiny objects launching from their centers.

"Scatter!" Jack bellowed.

Everyone dodged as small but powerful explosions ripped the ground at their heels. All around the space they were confined in dirt, rocks and burning grass erupted in choking clouds. Teal'c turned and launched stream after stream of staff-fire into the attackers, destroying many of them. Yet still they came, splitting like flocks of birds around the danger, reforming and hurtling after Jack and Daniel. Over their heads, Carter sent sprays of bullets into the flying Eyes, but it seemed for every one that fell, three more appeared.

Jack rolled to his feet, emptying his magazine at the closest mini-bombers. "Daniel, dial that address. Carter, get ready to send the MALP through." He reloaded and fired again, coordinating with Teal'c to cover their teammates and their vital gear.

Carter loosed another burst at a group of Eyes targeting Daniel, then ducked to one side as the wormhole roared to life. As soon as it stabilized, she hit the controls on the MALP and sent the bulky machine lurching toward the Stargate.

Daniel dashed toward the FRED and slammed his hand on the controls. It jerked forward, churning steadily to the platform. He kept pace behind it, edging backwards and was only a few feet from the steps when another explosion nearby threw him to the ground. He rolled into a crouch, flinching from the concussion and the thunderous hammer of weapons' fire over his head. Jack glanced at Daniel, saw he was up and moving, and continued firing.

Slowly, keeping pace with Teal'c, Jack fell back, the mini-bombers obviously herding them toward the Stargate. Spinning in a circle, trying to keep a bead on a particular group of attackers, he had an instant's snapshot of Carter silhouetted against the blue of the event horizon. For a split-second she was there, then through the smoke Jack glimpsed the soles of her boots as she was thrown backward into the vortex. A billowing cloud of smoke and debris flew out from the MALP; charred and bent metal showing where one of the little bombs had scored a direct hit.

"Sam!" Daniel scrabbled up four steps through acrid smoke. Another bomb exploded on the edge of the platform, spraying him with stone shrapnel and sending him sliding back down the steps.

"Go, Daniel, *go*," yelled Jack.

Daniel clawed his way up the rest of the steps. Three large strides and he flung himself headfirst into the rippling event horizon.

Teal'c fired a near-continuous stream of blasts at their attackers, he and Jack covering each other in their retreat up the steps. The FRED had reached the top of the platform but was stalled behind the smoldering MALP. Jack broke off the battle and threw his weight at the machine, pushing it far enough into the wormhole for the vortex to take it and suck it away, the FRED following along like a giant wind-up toy. He spun around and picked off several more Eyes heading toward them. All over the area in front of the Stargate the ground was littered with craters and burning, broken metal.

"Teal'c, go," Jack croaked, smoke catching in his throat.

Teal'c backed into the Stargate, still firing until the event horizon swallowed him up. Jack threw himself sideways into the wormhole, then the cold grip of the vortex was spiriting him away to the unknown.

GATE ONE

Hour of Trembling

Daniel exited the wormhole as he had entered it: headfirst and at high speed. He hit the stone platform, rolled, overbalanced on the edge and bumped and slid down a dozen steps. Dazed, ears ringing from the battle still raging on another planet, he got his hands and knees under him, the pack on his back hanging heavily to one side.

He looked around wildly, aiming for more targets, but the Eyes of Ra had not followed and there were no people in sight, not even Sam. Frantically he looked for her. There, on the opposite side of the steps, by the corner of the platform, a still, pale hand was just visible on the ground.

"Sam!" Daniel scrambled toward her, hoarsely coughing smoke from his lungs

Sam lay sprawled on her side, propped up by her pack. She was conscious, blinking dazedly, her breath catching in little coughs. Her face, hair, hands and clothing were singed and smoke-blackened.

"Sam? Can you hear me?" He thumped to his knees beside her.

"Urgh." She coughed again and tried to focus on him.

A slurp and a clank above their heads heralded the arrival of the MALP. It barely cleared the wormhole before seizing to a halt, black smoke still billowing from the fried batteries. Directly behind it, the FRED churned through under its own power. It clipped the track of the MALP as it passed; one tread left the stone platform and gravity took hold, pulling the MALP down to crash in a heap not a meter from Sam's boots.

Afraid the thing might explode again, Daniel flung himself over Sam. Moments later, Jack and Teal'c shot out of the Stargate in a hail of debris and dove for cover. After agonizingly slow seconds the vortex swept away into nothingness, leaving them shaken, panting and searching this new planet for danger.

Before Jack could call out to them, Daniel raised his head. "Are you okay?"

"Fine, Daniel." Jack moved down the steps. "What about you? Where's Carter?"

Sam managed a faint "I'm good, sir."

"The MALP exploded in her face," Daniel turned back to Sam. "Easy. Don't move. Let me check you." Gently, he felt her limbs and torso. There were no breaks, no open wounds or suspicious swellings. He was relieved to find no burns under the smoke stains. "Did you hit your head?"

"Bit," she mumbled.

He ran his fingers though her hair, finding a cut on the base of her skull. She hissed in pain.

"Ouch, sorry." Daniel dug out the small first aid kit from his vest. "It's not bleeding too much. Any headache, dizziness, nausea? Did you pass out?"

"No," Sam croaked. "Just"—she coughed—"got the wind knocked out of me. Ow." She batted a hand at him as he wiped the cut with disinfectant.

Daniel felt his hands shake as adrenalin drained out of him. Despite Sam's protests, he dressed the wound neatly.

Teal'c appeared at Jack's side, having completed a circuit of the Stargate area. "We appear to be secure here, O'Neill," he reported. "The supplies on the FRED have suffered no harm, however the MALP is significantly damaged."

Jack looked at the machine, lying on its side, wisps of smoke curling up from it. "Better it than one of us. Okay, let's see if we can dial out of here. Carter, take five." He cut off her abortive attempt to stand as Daniel repacked the first aid kit.

This new destination certainly appeared different from the

previous planet. It was a high alpine meadow, where thick green grass and clusters of delicate flowers bent under a cool breeze. Spindly trees — brilliantly colored in warm autumnal tones — were dotted all over, and in the distance mountain peaks circled high around them. A line of small stone columns, over a dozen of them, stretched away from the Stargate, ending where the slope disappeared downhill.

Jack watched as Teal'c punched in the address for Earth on the DHD but, as before, the chevrons on the Stargate lit up and the wormhole refused to engage.

"Well, crap."

Jack stalked back to the platform, leaving Teal'c to try several more addresses.

Carter was on her feet, pale and squinting through what looked to be a hell of a headache, as she let Daniel gently wipe the soot from her face.

"DHD's not responding," Jack said. "How are you doing, Carter?"

"Got a head like the morning after graduation, sir. Just waiting for the pills to kick in, then I'll be good to go." She gingerly slid her sunglasses on.

"Rest up while you can, Major. Daniel, why don't you come exploring with me?"

"Sam, are you sure you're okay?" Daniel guided her down to sit in the shade of the platform. "Can I get you anything?"

"I'll be fine here, Daniel. Thank you." She caught his hand and gave it a reassuring squeeze.

"Keep your radio open, Carter."

"O'Neill, there is another device attached to this Stargate."

Jack looked up at Teal'c, who was prowling around the Stargate while Daniel set Carter up with water, food and first aid kit. "Same as before, T?"

"It is very similar, with the addition of a countdown in time as the Goa'uld measure it."

Jack was up the steps in a flash. Teal'c pointed out the numbers clicking down above the depiction of an empty night sky.

"How long?"

"Eleven hours, six minutes."

"And then what? More of those flying things trying to blow us to pieces? We don't have enough ammo to hold them off in a prolonged fight."

"It is a possibility. Perhaps if we are able to leave this world before the countdown ends, we will avoid a repeat of what has just occurred on P3R-779."

"Sounds like a plan, T. Okay boys, spread out. Let's see if we can find a way off this rock."

Jack headed right, Teal'c left, and Daniel was drawn to the row of stone pillars, which, after a short hunt, proved to be the only man-made structures in the meadow. He stopped in front of the first one, immediately captured by the Goa'uld script carved from top to bottom and covering the surface completely. He circled the pillar; reading, translating, absorbing.

"Oh."

Swiftly he moved on to the second, then the third, muttering the odd word to himself.

"*Aqai.*"

"*Tekem.*"

After reading the fourth stone chapter, cold dread was congealing in his stomach. "Oh, boy." He tilted his head toward the radio on his shoulder and clicked the call button. "Guys, you'd better listen to this."

"Right here, Daniel," Jack's voice breathed in his ear, making him start. "Sorry," he said, almost managing to look guilty. "What'cha got?"

Daniel glared at him and led the way back to the first column where he paused, gathering his thoughts which were straying wildly through the fields of conjecture.

"These are ben-bens," he began.

"Not obelisks?" Jack butted in as Teal'c returned to join them.

"No. Obelisks are taller, like Cleopatra's Needle. Ben-bens are more often used to record messages, historic events or, as in this case, instructions. This first one is mainly just praising Ra for his wonderfulness." Daniel flapped a dismissive hand at it and moved to the second ben-ben, Teal'c and Jack trailing. He keyed the radio again so that Sam could hear.

"This is where it gets interesting. It commands those who have come to give their devotion, their lives, their souls if you will, to Ra, to tremble in fear at the task now before them.

"Now, we know that P3R-779 was the starting point for some kind of trial. From what this says, anyone wishing to enter the highest levels of service to Ra must embark upon a journey of 'great and hazardous ordeals' and if found worthy at the end—by which I'm taking it to mean they're still alive—they will be rewarded with a place of service to Ra, to 'journey forever at his feet in the Barque of Heaven'."

Jack looked extremely skeptical, but Teal'c was intrigued, intently reading the carvings himself.

"Who in their right mind would sign up for something like that?" Jack demanded.

"Most probably they would have been Goa'uld of low birth seeking to further their rank by attaining a trusted position within the House of Ra," Teal'c answered. "Ra was the supreme leader of the System Lords for many thousands of years, O'Neill. Even holding a minor clerical position within his domain would confer much higher status upon an ambitious Goa'uld than would the same position with any other System Lord."

Jack gave an exaggerated shudder. "Power hungry Goa'uld. Why does that not surprise me?"

"Does it say where this journey leads to, Daniel?" Sam's voice crackled over the channel.

"Well, they don't give specific details." Daniel moved on to the third ben-ben. "Ah, it says here, 'you will journey through thirteen gateways and on each world will you prove yourself worthy of servitude to Ra'."

"Thirteen?" Jack was outraged. "Forget it. Just skip ahead to the part that says how we get out of here."

"Jack, I don't think it's that easy. Um, it says that 'by passing through the Temple of Departures, the supplicant has shown his acceptance of the conditions of the Trial.' That has to be the temple on P3R-779. Once the first step on the journey has been taken, the Trial must be completed. Failure to leave each planet in the allotted time will result in the supplicant being banished to 'forever contemplate his dishonor'."

"And I'm betting that thing on the Stargate has something to do with all this?" frowned Jack.

Daniel crouched down by the base of the ben-ben and recited, "'By first moonset after arrival must the supplicant depart or be forever lost to those who knew his name'."

"The device attached to the Stargate must measure the time before moonset," Teal'c said.

"Carter, can you get up there and give us a reading?"

"Already on it, sir." There was a short pause, then, *"It's showing twenty-five point seven marks."*

Teal'c did a quick calculation. "Ten hours, eighteen minutes."

Jack set the stopwatch on his chronometer. "Okay, so if we don't go through the 'gate on time—what happens? Can we stay here, rig up something to get it working? Are we going to get attacked by those flying things again?"

Daniel moved on to the next ben-ben, the script revealing more and more about the depth of trouble they were in.

"Okay, there's a lot about the glory awaiting the successful supplicant—basking in the splendor that is Ra—ah, here we go. 'Those bearing the seed of the god's possession shall be confined to the Trial of Moons until welcomed into Ra's embrace; only then shall they be allowed to walk the path of servitude amongst the stars. The supplicant who does not journey to the next planet within the Trial before moonset will be condemned to eternal confinement on the planet of their failure. The unworthy shall never again leave the Trial of Moons, or they shall perish by the Mark of the God that swims within their blood'."

"*'Mark of the God'.*" Sam's unease carried over the radio. *"Then those first hits we took, they weren't targeting us, they were implanting something in us."*

Jack's gut curdled into a cold lump of anger. "So that means…?"

"The devices injected into our bodies must stay within a certain proximity to the Stargate and must not be taken through the Stargate after moonset, otherwise the elements within will combine into an explosive compound, in the manner of the device implanted in Cassandra Fraiser." Teal'c's deep voice filled the stunned silence. "I have seen similar methods used to confine prisoners to penal outposts. The results of any attempted escape were always fatal."

"So that rules out leaving here by ship, always assuming we could contact the Tok'ra," Carter said.

"Indeed it does."

"But, we'll be alright if we go through the Stargates of the Trial, providing we 'gate out before moonset. The markers will be deactivated at the end," Daniel said.

"Thirteen 'gates, Daniel. Anything could happen. Besides, Ra is dead, so he won't be waiting at the end to flip the off-switch." Jack paced angrily in a tight circle.

"Well, maybe that's automated too. Everything we've encountered so far has been. And who knows, maybe these things have a time delay. Stay too long and you blow up anyway." Daniel subconsciously scratched the closed wound on his thigh, then caught himself and shoved his hands in his pockets.

Jack pulled a face at him. "There's a cheery thought. What else do we need to know?"

Daniel shuffled around two more of the ben-bens before pausing to stare up at the crown of the final pillar. "'Only to the worthy will one's destination be revealed. By the name of the Herald will the Gateway be cast open'."

"That's it?"

"That's all there is, Jack. I assume that means the address to the next planet is hidden somewhere around here." Daniel retraced the inscriptions with his fingertips. "'By the name of the Herald'," he mused. "Teal'c, Sam, is it possible the Stargate is controlled by a spoken password?"

"I have not encountered such a mechanism, Daniel Jackson."

"I doubt it, Daniel." Carter sounded strained and a little breathless over the radio.

"Carter, you're supposed to be resting," Jack sighed.

"I am, sir. I'm just having a look at the DHD."

Jack flung out his hands in a silent plea to the universe in general and strolled a short distance into the meadow. He glared up at the mountains in the distance, towering toward the sky in unforgiving majesty, all bare, jagged rock and snow covered crests. Daniel's theory was compelling and if Jack decided to hold the team here to search for a way home, they may not have too long before the elements turned against them. Judging by the riot of flowers in their meadow here, this part of the planet was nearing the end of its warm season. Any extended stay could find them trapped in a fierce winter they were ill-equipped to survive. Hell, even their kit was summer-weight desert camos.

"There's another device in the DHD," Carter's voice came over their radios, amplified across the grass. *"Same as the one on P3R-779, but it has an extra attachment. It looks like an audio pickup — the readout is oscillating to the sound of my voice."*

Daniel turned to gaze at Sam by the DHD. "Do you think it could control the activation of the Stargate?"

"We'd need to test it to make certain, but it could do that, Daniel."

"So we need an address and a password to activate the 'gate, and even if we do find them the only planet we can travel to

is the next one in the Trial?" Jack scowled at the far-off panorama, then turned to look at his team scattered amongst the
leavings of a long-dead alien.

"Looks that way, sir."

"This whole thing was a setup from the get-go," Jack stated,
his anger forced him into motion and he strode back through
the grass. "Tok'ra chick shows up with a previously unknown
'gate address, promises weapons galore and *hey*, we have to
go right *now* because she has something really important to
do later, and gee, what a shame, 'General Carter is out on
assignment' and can't be contacted. Then what's-her-name is
delayed at the last moment, promises to catch up, and wonder
of wonders, that's the last we see of her."

*"But sir, the Tok'ra have dealt openly with us so far. Do you
really think they would intentionally lead us into a trap?"*

"No disrespect to your dad, Carter, but we still don't know
a whole lot about them. Who's to say they don't have hidden
agenda or double agents in their ranks?"

"But why would they go to such lengths to get rid of *us?*"
asked Daniel, still closely inspecting the information on the
ben-bens. "The Tok'ra have always seemed to be pretty dismissive of us."

"Why indeed?" echoed Jack. He returned to the boys and
led them back to where Carter sat by the DHD.

"Perhaps the underlying motive is the bounties offered for
our capture," Teal'c said. "Aris Boch appeared to consider
them sufficient reason to detain us, and he fully intended to
trade us to the Goa'uld."

"But, then surely someone would have been waiting to take
us prisoner on P3R-779. All they've really achieved is isolat-
ing us," Carter said.

"It could be they were unaware they would not be able to
dial in to P3R-779 once the sun had set."

Jack let out a frustrated snort. "Now that does sound like
the Tok'ra intel we're used to. Okay, let's find the address and
this password we need. I want to keep our options open—this

doesn't look like a good place for an extended stay. Carter, have a look at the MALP, see what you can scavenge off it."

"Yes, sir."

Daniel watched Jack and Teal'c move out through the meadow, finding nothing but trees, flowers and steep grassy slopes dropping away on all sides. He touched the inscriptions again, reveling for a moment in their ageless beauty and wondering, as always, about the craftsmen who had plied their tools so skillfully and with such art. For long moments he stood at the end of the line of ben-bens, staring hard, absorbing the mathematically precise line of them marching out from the dead center of the Stargate—as if pointing the way....

He turned on his heel and strode rapidly toward the end of the meadow where the hill dipped sharply downwards. As the gradient steepened dramatically, Daniel sat on the grass, cautiously inching ahead. Heels digging into the earth and legs beginning to shake from the strain, he was rewarded with the sight of a narrow ledge cut into the underlying rock. He straightened his legs, hoping not to slide any further, and spoke into the radio.

"Guys, I think I've found something."

"Daniel? Where are you?"

"Down the slope, straight on from the ben-bens," he replied breathlessly. "Be careful, it's pretty steep." Gravity took hold of him and he began to slide slowly, yet inexorably toward a gaping expanse of nothingness.

"Daniel! Hold on!" Behind him, he heard Jack shuck his pack and weapon and start down the hill, feet skidding on the lush grass.

"Jack, it's okay," Daniel said, his voice betraying the tension building in him. He looked over his shoulder toward Jack, but this only served to displace his center of gravity and speed up his slide.

"There's a...."

His boots hit thin air.

"Oh, boy."

His rump left the ground and he was falling, hands convulsively clutching clumps of dirt and grass.

"Daniel!" Jack was shouting frantically now. "Teal'c!"

"Ooof."

Daniel landed on his butt, scraping hands and arms on the rocks as he dropped six feet down to the narrow, rocky ledge. Gingerly he got to his knees, and keeping his back to the chasm, clawed his way upright, just managing to peer up over the edge to the hillside above.

"Jack, there's a ledge here," he said to O'Neill's boots as they bore down on him.

Jack flipped himself onto his stomach mid-slide, whipped out his knife and rammed it into the soft soil, stopping his own descent just as his boots left the earth.

"Daniel Jackson!" Teal'c hollered from the top of the hill.

"Teal'c, I'm okay," Daniel yelled back. Looking up at Jack, he winced slightly at the glare coming his way.

"Dammit, Daniel."

"Sorry." He reached up and guided Jack down to stand next to him.

"Don't make me ask why you're down here."

"This ledge has been hand-cut," Daniel replied, as if that was a valid reason for throwing himself off a cliff. "It must lead…." He darted a quick glance to the left and right. "Oh. Nowhere. That's odd."

Jack heroically restrained himself from commenting. "Oh, Teal'c?" he called out in that tone Daniel knew was a warning to tread carefully.

"I am here, O'Neill."

"Go get some ropes and the climbing harness from the FRED, will you? Better yet, bring the whole thing. It can pull us out of here."

"I shall do so immediately." There was a pause, then Teal'c added, "Do not go anywhere, O'Neill, Daniel Jackson."

Jack gently rested his brow against the cold rock and

closed his eyes. "Jaffa humor and disappearing archaeologists. Great."

Daniel dropped his pack at his heels and took one cautious step closer to the edge. He knelt and inched closer, searching for the answer he knew must be there.

Vertigo swept over him in a nauseating wave. The mountainside fell away into a rocky gorge thousands of feet below, and the void caught him with a sickening fascination. Resolutely he focused on the rocks a few inches from his nose, lay down on his stomach and slithered forward to peer straight down.

"Jack? Hold my legs will you?" He hoped Jack didn't pick up the shakiness he felt in his voice as he hung his head over the edge, one hand keeping his glasses in place, the other clutching the rocks by his side in a death grip.

"What? Why?"

Daniel heard Jack's boots scrape on the rock as he turned.

"God, what are you doing? Are you *trying* to give me a heart attack?" Jack grabbed his legs and hauled him back to safety.

"No, wait, there's something down there." Daniel stubbornly wriggled forward again, looking for the shapes that had caught his eye.

"Do I have to remind you of your little problem with heights?"

"Oh, no. I'm well aware of it, thanks," Daniel said, groping around for another anchor. Jack grabbed his hand and snagged his belt for good measure.

"Thank you."

"What can you see?"

"There are carvings down here, glyphs, and it looks like... like the whole side of the mountain has been carved into something."

"Why on earth would anyone put a statue down there? Or on *this* planet for that matter?"

Daniel shimmied another six inches out over the precipice, his hand cleaving to Jack's like a limpet. This was not what

archaeologists were supposed to do—he was a whiz at crawling down hot, airless holes or being cramped like a pretzel in
caves or tombs, but hanging like a kite over the edge of oblivion? No.

"C'mon Daniel, if there's something there it can wait for
Teal'c to get back with the climbing gear."

"Hang on, Jack. I've nearly got it."

Another wriggled-out inch brought a line of Goa'uld script
into focus. "*Sejem sesher hereh*.... What the...?"

He scrutinized the carved rock, twisting his head to get it in
perspective, breathing in shallow gasps around the rocky edge
cutting into his ribs. He followed the line of the rock up and
out on either side, and suddenly what he was seeing coalesced
from graceful carved planes and odd angles into a single entity
of monumental scale.

"Oh, he's got to be kidding," Daniel croaked in disgust. "Of
all the egotistical...." He twisted halfway onto his side and
tugged on Jack's hand. "Pull!"

Jack heaved on Daniel's hand and BDUs and slid him back
to safety. For a moment they sat together on the ledge, backs
against the rock, staring out at the vista before them and rubbing life back into hands squeezed white by their mutual death
grip.

"Daniel Jackson? O'Neill? Do you need assistance?"
Teal'c's voice drifted down to them, filled with concern as he
listened to their acrobatics.

"We're fine, T. Just Daniel doing a little exploration," Jack
called. He slid a glance at Daniel. "Please tell me you got
something worthwhile out of that?"

Daniel's eyes stayed fixed on the panorama before them as
he began to articulate his thoughts. "There is a line of script
just below us that reads, 'From the mouth of Ra, god of all
he surveys, will the opening of the Gateway be given'. Below
that, there is something carved into the side of this mountain.
Judging from the proportions that I could see, it's monumental, and if the pieces rising up on either side of it are the horns I

think they are, it is probably a representation of Ra as the ram-headed god. I think we'll find the address and password we need by the mouth of the carving."

He closed his eyes. The thought of going down the face of the mountain made his stomach churn.

"Could you see a way down?" Jack asked quietly, watching him.

"No. No, the scale of this thing, it's enormous. Jack, we're sitting on top of Mount Rushmore." Daniel stared at Jack, willing him to understand. "I don't know how I'm going to do it," he admitted finally.

Jack raised his eyebrows, surprise turning to perception as he realized what Daniel was contemplating. He smiled and patted Daniel's leg. "Well, that's okay because I'll be the one going over the edge."

"Jack, you can't. You can't read any of the glyphs. You won't know what to look for." He tried not to show the relief and denial warring inside him.

"This is why we invented digital cameras with wide-angle lenses and notebooks. I'll record it all and you can translate it up here."

"But...."

"Daniel." Jack cut through his objections. "I trust you implicitly to translate any kind of squiggles we find, and you've done your basic training and refreshers admirably, but you haven't done the high-angle climbing course and the years of refreshers that I have. This is what I'm trained for. Let me do my job."

"Oh." Daniel struggled not to cave too quickly. Lost. "Okay."

Sam pulled off her jacket in the warmth of the sun and slid it under her backside, cushioning the lowest step of the Stargate platform where she sat. Scattered at her feet were the disassembled remains of the MALP. She stretched the sore muscles of her back, a remnant of her expeditious arrival. At least the headache was down to a dull throb. Taking another sip from the canteen, she watched Teal'c driving the FRED down to the end of the meadow to retrieve Daniel and the colonel.

Maddening to have to sit here while the others had all the fun — but she knew the importance of tending to injuries quickly in the field. Something big was looming, and she needed to be in peak condition to face it.

She surveyed the charred hunks of metal, the extendable sensor arm sticking up like a disembodied limb. The battery was fried, as were the optical array which had been active at the time the bomb hit the MALP, along with the atmospheric sensors. The casing and treads were torn and charred, useless now. What was left was a disappointingly small collection of electronics, and — vitally — the communication array, still live and useable.

Looking down the meadow once more, she saw only Teal'c busy with the ropes. With the faint but comforting sound of her team's voices in the distance, she set to work.

They padded the edge of the rocks with a sturdy tarpaulin to protect Jack's line as he made ready to abseil down the mountain. Braced on the precipice, Jack dropped the rope bag down behind him, and did one final check on the karabiners.

Satisfied, he looked up at Daniel, standing on the ledge with an anxious grimace on his face that practically yelled the man was uneasy being there, but was too stubborn to stay with Teal'c. Jack wore a vox mic, the pair to Daniel's that would enable him to talk to Daniel hands-free. He looked further up, at Teal'c planted in the grass as strong and immobile as one of the ben-bens. He gave them both a nod, received a solemn acknowledgement from Teal'c and a jerky wave from Daniel, flexed his knees and launched himself backwards into the air.

He covered the first twenty foot drop in three exhilarating bounds. Damn, but he'd missed doing this.

The carved rock Jack landed on stretched out a good hundred feet to either side of him and arched forward into a curve.

He stepped over the carvings, stopping for a quick practice run with Daniel's camera. A large patch of grass had sprouted in a dip in the rock and he elected to descend there, giving his rope a bit more protection from chafing.

"Descending now," he said, the sound of his voice activating the microphone.

Short bunny hops took him down the rock, worn smooth by uncounted years' exposure to what had to be some nasty weather. Thirty, sixty feet before he hit the first real contour—an inward dip of cavernous proportions. Jack rappelled slowly down another twenty feet before his boots hit rock once more. He stared up at the convex mound in the center of the cavern, liberally sprinkled with old birds' nests. It took a moment before he realized it was an eye, exotically shaped and still bearing some traces of gold and blue paint.

He continued down in short, careful hops. To his left the rock rose in a graceful slope—what had to be the biggest nose he'd ever come across. Another fifty feet passed on the rope markers before the curves of the rock changed into the swell and gape of an open mouth.

Jack locked off and dangled, taking a good look around.

"I'm a hundred and fifty feet down. Looks like you were right about Mount Rushmore, Daniel."

"Is it Ra, Jack?"

"Can't tell for sure but I'm guessing yeah. Floppy ears, pointy horns, crossed eyes. Looks like that statue behind the ring transporter in Ra's throne room."

"Okay, well the address should be near the mouth. Can you see anything?"

"There's a long pointy thing hanging off its chin."

"That's a beard, Jack."

Jack rappelled down, past the cold stone lips to a smooth blank chin.

"Nope, nothing there. Going down the beard."

Several bands of faded gold paint slid past and then—there they were. Goa'uld characters carved deeply into the stone beard.

"Bingo."

"Really? What's it look like? Is it an address?"

"Gimme a minute," groused Jack. He pulled the digital camera out of his pocket, carefully attaching the wrist strap to a d-ring on the vest. He braced his feet on the rock and started snapping shots, able only to fit one glyph in the viewfinder at a time.

"We've got a line of Goa'uld writing," he said, then slid a few more feet down to a Stargate address carved inside a cartouche. "Write these down: Norma, Hydra, Lynx, Canis Minor, Equuleus, Mic, and point of origin is three small circles set at forty-five degrees to a larger oval."

"Got it," Daniel replied.

Jack looked back up at the line of script. Beneath him the mountain fell away in a jagged jumble of broken rocky valleys and pinnacles. He pulled out the notebook and began sketching the symbols.

"I'm going to read out this writing too, just in case. I'm hoping it's the password."

"Jack, just copy it and come back up," Daniel said quickly.

"Believe me, Daniel, I plan on doing just that. Still, a little insurance never hurts. Ah, there are five symbols, first one looks like a shepherd's crook."

"Is the loop on the crook short or long?"

"It goes halfway down the length of the first side."

"That's a fold of cloth then. Next?"

"An arm, hand pointing to the left."

"Forearm. Got it."

"Third looks like a line twisted into three loops with the ends at the bottom."

"Twist of flax. Go ahead, Jack."

"Then there's a bird, not much of a tail. Looks like a puffin."

Daniel snorted a laugh over the radio. "I don't think there were many puffins in Ancient Egypt or anywhere Ra might have been. It's a quail."

"Looks like a puffin," Jack pushed off from the rock face for a better view.

"Trust me, it's a quail. Any others?"

"Last one is a loop, fat at the top, the two ends drawn together with a small oblong over them at the bottom. I still think it's a puffin."

"Seal cylinder. That's all there is, Jack? And, it's a quail…."

"That's all she wrote."

"Come back up now."

"On my way."

Jack tucked the camera and notebook securely into his vest pockets. One final look around for missed carvings revealed nothing on the rock, but something past his dangling feet caught his eye. Using hands and feet to steady his body, he looked down, staring hard.

He moved further down, a harder task now as the wind began to pick up; cross-directional updrafts pushed at him, threatening to send him spinning, and flapping his clothing madly.

There—nearly a thousand feet below was a splotch of color against the rocks, fluttering in the wind. Cloth? He tilted his head and the thing resolved into human remains: broken bones and weathered clothing. As he brought his line of sight back up the mountain, he picked out another pile of bleached bones, and then another, shattered long ago on the uncaring mountain. Empty eye-sockets stared up at him accusingly. It would seem not everyone attempting Ra's Trial had come prepared.

"Oh, my."

"Jack? Are you alright?"

"Fine and dandy. On my way up now."

Jack turned his thoughts to the task at hand. He attached the étrier and began the arduous climb.

While Jack took a breather and a well-earned drink dangling in front of the carving's eyeball, Daniel looked up from the notebook balanced on his knee as he sat cross-legged on the ledge. Squinting into the orange glow of the setting sun, he checked for the thousandth time that the rope had not suddenly unraveled or snapped. The rope was intact and, for the moment, still as Jack hung securely below.

Too far below for Daniel's liking.

He cleared his throat and yelled up to Teal'c, who stood guard over the ropes securing both Daniel and Jack.

"I've translated the word Jack found. Assuming it was a quail and not a puffin, it reads *'Sahu'*, which means the Oversoul."

"And what, pray tell is that supposed to mean?" Jack's grunt floated over the radio as he inched his way upward once more.

"It, er, well… actually, I don't know. I'm guessing it's the password we need to unlock the DHD, but in reference to the Trial its actual meaning could be anything."

"The Oversoul may be a reference to one of the names of Ra," Teal'c called down. "Goa'uld System Lords take great delight in pretentious appellation."

Daniel let out a snort of laughter. He settled back against the cliff and began to pack his gear away.

Jack was getting to the hard part of the climb now, where the rope ran taut and close to the curve of rock forming the statue's headdress. With an undignified scramble, he pulled himself up onto the top of the carving.

"Okay, I'm up on top of Fred's head here."

He took a moment to stretch his back and leg muscles, relishing the burn in them. Methodically, he reeled in the climbing rope, re-coiling it into the drop bag.

"Oh. Hi!" Daniel's head popped over the ledge above him.

"Hey."

Apparently satisfied Jack was in one piece, Daniel retreated to his place at the back of the ledge. Jack began the final leg of his climb, easier now with the natural surface providing extra foot- and hand-holds. He paused as he reached Daniel's ledge.

Daniel was already at the edge, offering a firm grip to haul him up. They gathered up their gear and let the winch on the FRED guide them up the grassy slope to join Teal'c.

Jack accepted the canteen offered by Teal'c. He took a long swig of water, then keyed his radio. "So, Carter, how are you doing back there?"

"I'm good, sir. Head's clearing. I've stripped the MALP down—I think I might be able to jury-rig the transmitter to send a message into space. If I use the batteries from the FRED we just might get a signal strong enough to reach one of the Tok'ra listening arrays. It's a long-shot but you never know."

"Good work, Major."

"Are we to understand that you intend us to continue on traveling through the Stargates of this Trial, O'Neill?" Teal'c asked.

"I'm thinking we don't have too many options at the moment, T. There's no ready cover or food or water source here. If we stay, we might be forced a fair way away from the Stargate in search of supplies. We don't know how far we can go before these nanothings kick in and besides, I'm guessing the winter up here will be pretty nasty.

"I think it's best we keep moving. We'll leave a message at each Stargate in case another team does manage to get through, but I'm betting our best chance is to go through the 'gate. We may find Ra's technology has broken down along the way and we can dial home, or we might find a more suitable planet to establish a long term camp, see if Carter's doohickey can make contact with the Tok'ra."

Teal'c inclined his head in agreement with Jack's assessment. "It should prove a most interesting journey."

Jack consulted the countdown on his chrono. "Five hours, forty minutes till zero hour. Food, some shut-eye and then—we shall see what we shall see."

Exactly five hours later, SG-1 stood before the Stargate platform, geared up and ready to move on. The moon hung brightly above their heads, so close its craters were clearly visible. In its bluish light, Teal'c had instructed the others on how to read the moon-clock, converting the Goa'uld marks into standard Earth time. They had the Stargate address and the password required to activate the wormhole, both carefully copied by Daniel into four notebooks. A message, sealed in a sample bottle and detailing all they had discovered, was buried at the base of the DHD, signposted by the small '*SG-1*' carved into a rock half buried in the ground.

The moment of silence was broken by Jack clapping his hands together.

"Well. Here goes nothing. Daniel, if you will?"

Daniel entered the Stargate address and pressed the center crystal. The chevrons glowed expectantly around the Stargate. Clearly and precisely, he spoke the password.

"*Sahu.*"

The vortex surged obligingly out, once more opening the way to the stars.

"Huh." Jack was impressed. He cast a quick glance around the meadow. No pillars or Eyes of Ra appeared to chivvy them on their way. Great.

"Teal'c, take point."

Teal'c marched forward into the wormhole, his whole body alert and primed for action, with Carter behind him guiding the FRED. Daniel exchanged a glance with Jack, then followed her through.

Jack gripped his weapon and stepped into the Stargate, welcoming the familiar cold tug of the wormhole as it whisked him away.

With no living bodies in proximity to the platform, the Stargate shut down. Silence descended over the lonely mountain meadow, its monuments, its graves, and its secrets.

GATE TWO

Prevailer with Swords

They stepped out of the wormhole onto a snow-covered circle of flagstones. Slender pillars surrounded the paving. Beyond stood the DHD, and behind that a vast, white field framed by leafy trees, grown twisted into elegant lines under the snow's weight. At the far edge of the clearing, almost hidden by the trees, stood buildings; five, six long peak-roofed huts, smoke curling from each into the cold, still air.

"Jack, there are people here," Daniel said, his breath frosting. He pointed to the huts as doors opened and figures began to pour out.

Before anyone could react, a glowing red force-field snapped up between each of the pillars, effectively trapping the team on the paving.

"This barrier is resistant to our weapons, O'Neill," Teal'c declared.

"Son of a…." Jack aborted reaching for his gun and pulled his knife free. Teal'c and Sam followed suit, a small show of defiance in the face of what appeared to be an entire company of Jaffa.

Within a minute the Jaffa reached them, many looking surprised and expectant at the team's appearance. Heedless of the cold, they all wore sleeveless vests and bore an Eye of Ra tattooed on their upper arms. A tall warrior, his bearing clearly unaffected by his age, which looked to be greater than Bra'tac's, stepped forward. His forehead was unmarked but he too wore Ra's brand on his right arm. Daniel stared at it for a moment before the memory clicked into place; the Jaffa on Ra's ship had been branded in the same manner.

The man held his gaze for several seconds, then scrutinized

each member of SG-1, evidently pleased with what he saw. "Welcome, supplicants of our Mighty Lord Ra. Welcome."

At a brief go-ahead nod from Jack, Daniel stepped forward with a tentative smile. "Hello, I'm Daniel Jackson. My friends and I are explorers — travelers. We're not actually supplicants of, uh, Ra."

"All who come through the Chappa'ai are bound by the laws of our Lord's Trial," the Jaffa replied. "Whether you come singly or with companions, such as yours, you have shown your desire to be known as supplicants, young one."

"No, you misunderstand me. We were, well, forced into going through the first Stargate of the Trial," Daniel persisted, pressing as close as possible to the heat of the force-field. "We have no desire to complete the Trial. We just want to go home."

The Jaffa's expression darkened. "Your change of heart brings shame upon you and disgraces the honor bestowed by participating in the Trial." He looked around at the warriors ranked behind him. "We shall wait until the remainder of my men have returned from their training exercises. You will use this time to reflect and recognize the honored position you hold as supplicants seeking our Lord's favor." He scowled at Daniel.

"Uh, what exactly happens when we're finished waiting?"

"You shall be tested, individually, and we shall judge your worthiness to continue the Trial."

The man turned away but Daniel strode along the barrier, anxious to keep him talking. "Wait, please. How will we be tested?"

At Daniel's question, the Jaffa's expression lifted a little and he moved closer to examine each of the four. He paused, staring hard at Teal'c. "Jaffa — trusted child of Apophis — do you renounce all allegiance to the god of the night, mortal enemy of Ra, sun god?"

Teal'c considered the question carefully and as always, answered truthfully. "I do."

The Jaffa inclined his head in a respectful bow. His gaze moved on to Sam, holding eye contact with her for an uncertain moment. Stepping back, he addressed them.

"Your task is, with your own choice of weapon, to engage in mortal combat with the chosen of Ra. Should you prove your worthiness by surviving, you shall be granted the Keys to the Gateway, and continue your quest."

"Mortal?" Sam's whisper hung on the cold air.

"Wait a damn minute, what do you mean by *mortal?*" Jack bellowed over her.

"We shall begin with the woman. Our brother Jaffa shall follow, next the loud one, then the boy."

Daniel's eyebrows lifted in indignation.

"Victory shall be achieved upon the death of either suppliant or challenger," the Jaffa ended simply. He clapped his hands, sending his men scurrying in all directions.

"Should'a stayed on the mountain," Jack muttered.

Daniel remained by the barrier, watching as one group of Jaffa set to clearing the snow from a large area near the tree line. Off to the left of the team's imprisonment another group erected an elaborate tent and could be seen carrying all manner of goods inside. Between the area being swept clean and the shimmering force-fields, a long table was settled into the snow. Upon this table, two Jaffa arranged the wickedest assortment of weapons he had ever seen.

Jack and Sam prowled the confines of their prison, testing the barriers for weak spots but finding none. Teal'c sought out the moon-clock then moved over to Jack and spoke quietly.

"The device registers fifteen hours and thirty minutes until moonset, O'Neill."

Jack nodded, his attention captured by the activity beyond the barrier. "What the hell are they doing?"

The team of sweepers had completed their task, revealing a circular stone area almost twenty meters in diameter. With a loud crack, the stone suddenly split right across the center, the two halves sliding away to reveal a wide arena made of gleaming black slate. The Jaffa swiftly formed ranks along either side of the table. For long moments, silence stretched thin between both groups.

Worried, Daniel turned away. "They can't be serious, can they? A fight to the death?" He looked at Teal'c, hoping for some insight that would get them out of this. Teal'c returned the look bleakly while Jack continued to stare belligerently through the force-field.

"There are too many for us to attack in a group," Teal'c replied. "Without the Stargate address and password we are unable to leave this world. Our best chance may well lie in single combat."

"But surely, if we tell them Ra is dead, they'll see there's no point in making us go through with this," Daniel objected. He took in the stony set of Teal'c's face with a sinking heart.

"I do not believe we will easily change their minds, Daniel Jackson. All Jaffa are trained from a very young age to believe utterly in the power of their god. That these men are still here, following their orders years after Ra's death, speaks highly of their training and devotion."

"But you overcame your training, Teal'c," Daniel said. "You realized Apophis wasn't a god and rejected him. Maybe some of these men feel the same way about Ra."

Teal'c lifted a brow in consideration. "Perhaps. I was fortunate to have Bra'tac as my mentor and guide to the truth. These warriors may not be so lucky, and to insist their god is not a god may serve only to incense them and provoke more violence toward us."

"You think we should fight, T?" Jack turned around, lines of concern etched in his face.

"I do, O'Neill. When one or two of us achieve victory in our battles, we may be in a position to assist our teammates."

"Well, if I'm first, I'd better warm up." Sam shed her jacket and handed it to Daniel. He clenched his fingers in the material and watched her start a routine of warm-up stretches.

"Sam... Jack, we can't let them do this."

"Not a lot of options, Daniel. Teal'c's right, we get a couple of us outside this barrier, we might have a chance."

"But we have to try talking to them," Daniel insisted. "This is wrong. Sam…."

"I'll be okay, Daniel. At least they aren't making me wear a dress this time." Sam grinned and threw him a wink before launching into a series of push-ups.

Daniel quietly watched Sam prepare, not wanting to believe they were so suddenly in a life or death situation. He saw her close down into that military mindset: shut off the feelings, close out the conscience, get the job done and survive to worry about it later, and he admired and envied her for it. He knew she could win this fight but she shouldn't be forced into such a situation in the first place. None of them should. Uncomfortably, Daniel became all too aware of himself. Sure, he had the skills. Hours and hours of drilling by Jack and Teal'c and the SGC trainers ensured that, but to intentionally set out to kill another person? Self-defense not withstanding, he had to admit it would be easier to throw himself into death's path to save someone he barely knew than to resign himself to deliberately taking another person's life.

Finally, the Jaffa in charge reappeared, accompanied by three others. All were stripped down to pants and boots with thick metal greaves covering their forearms. They seemed heedless of the cold and stood in the limber stance of professional fighters. At a gesture from his leader, a younger man stepped forward, pointed what looked like a small, black remote control at the field and pressed a series of buttons. A white light enveloped each of the weapons borne by the team and in a flash they were gone; MP5s, staff, zats, knives and Berettas were suddenly in a pile on the other side of the forcefield.

"Hey!" Jack leaped forward, nose reddening from the warmth generated by the barrier. "We don't want any part of this Trial."

The leader ignored him and addressed Sam. "Our men have

returned from their training. You shall commence your Rite of Combat now and prove your life worthy to be given in service to our god."

Teal'c moved up to Sam and stared gravely down at her. "Major Carter, it is unlikely these Jaffa have had to engage a woman in combat who does not possess a Goa'uld or a symbiote. They will not expect you to have the level of fighting skills that you do. They will, in all likelihood, underestimate you. Use this to your advantage."

"I will. Thanks Teal'c."

Jack left off glaring at the Jaffa. "Major." He fixed her with an uncompromising stare. "You can do this. Remember your training."

"Yes, sir." Sam stood, shaking her arms and legs, pushing the adrenaline through them.

"Go get 'em, Major."

"How...?" The Jaffa with the control box adjusted something and suddenly Sam was standing on the far side of the force-field. "Oh."

Grimly, Sam pulled herself to attention and snapped off a salute at Jack. She nodded sharply to Teal'c, met Daniel's gaze with a soft smile, then allowed herself to be escorted away.

As Carter made her way to the weapons table, Jack drew Teal'c back from the force-field, out of Daniel's earshot.

"Teal'c, any ideas here? You think we can take these guys?"

"You and Major Carter are highly proficient in hand-to-hand combat. Both your own methods and those I have taught you will serve you well. Jaffa rarely fight in ways outside the bounds of their training. I believe the three of us shall prevail."

Teal'c shifted his gaze and Jack followed to look at Daniel, standing with arms crossed, his whole body radiating concern for Carter.

"Jaffa honor scholars, don't they?" Jack asked quietly. "Would they expect one to fight to the death?"

"Scribes are honored with the same regard as priests in Jaffa society. They would be well protected and not expected to take part in any battles. However, if the purpose of this Trial is to gain advancement within the court of Ra, then I fear that all who come here are put to the test, regardless of their vocation."

"If we told them he's not a fighter, do you think they'd make an exception?"

"Perhaps. They may also view him as vulnerable."

"Christ." Jack scrubbed a hand through his hair.

"It is possible the victor of each fight will be placed in the tent the Jaffa have erected." Teal'c gazed at the brightly colored tent, clearly mulling over possible strategies.

Jack was right behind him. A lot of things had been carried into the tent during its set-up. "It's outside the force-field."

"That it is. As will be ourselves and Major Carter. We may be able to come to Daniel Jackson's assistance should he require it."

"Well, it's a start at least," Jack conceded, beginning to walk slowly back to Daniel. The main priority was to keep the team together, preferably uninjured, and then they could concentrate on escaping the planet.

"Daniel Jackson is a resourceful and capable man, O'Neill."

"I know, Teal'c. I know."

They returned to the barrier and stood either side of Daniel, eyes fixed on Carter.

"Choose. Your opponent shall be likewise armed."

Sam drew a calming breath and let her gaze wander over the assortment of deadly weapons before her. There were swords of varying length and width, all razor-sharp and brightly polished. Clubs, batons, daggers, knives, what was probably a version of brass knuckles, odd multi-jointed chain and stick affairs, something that looked disturbingly like a nail-studded mace; the selection, and their potential for harm, was chilling.

She fixed on a gleaming eight inch knife, sharp and efficient. She picked it up, testing the weight. It sat snugly in her hand, not too heavy and perfectly balanced.

Sam looked up at the commander and nodded. He nodded back, seeming pleased with her selection.

"Jaffa, kree!"

One of the fighters stepped forward. Not the biggest, thankfully but certainly capable-looking. His muscles gleamed under a coating of oil. He picked up the partner to her knife, inclined his head solemnly and turned, leading the way to the arena.

There had to be nearly sixty Jaffa arrayed around the stone border. Sam followed her opponent into the center, where they stood, each sizing up the other. She felt her focus narrow, blocking out everything beyond the man in front of her.

He stood only a couple of inches taller and probably had fifty pounds on her in weight. His chest was bare but a light chain-mail wrap covered the vulnerable symbiote pouch; his trousers were a thick material, topped by a flap of chain-mail at groin level.

Sam pulled her forage cap off and resettled it backwards. Her BDU jacket was done up and she felt prepared, tension zinging the blood through her veins.

There was no preamble, no flowery speeches to get the proceedings started, just an expectant hush in the crowd. A gong rang out.

The Jaffa tensed into a crouch, body flexing, hands spread apart. Sam began to circle, her weapon held wide, ready to strike. The Jaffa lunged with blinding speed. Sam twisted away, feeling the knife rip through her jacket sleeve. Her knife flicked as his arm withdrew, leaving a score of blood along his bicep.

Circling each other, they lunged and feinted, knives connecting with skin and clothing, glancing off out-flung arms. They fought silently, breath consumed in exertion. The Jaffa's size was deceiving, and he moved with the speed and grace of a panther.

Sam sucked in her gut as his knife made another attempt to disembowel her. She twisted away, slashing her weapon across his bare back, flinging up an arm to block his return blow. He feinted again, she followed for a fraction of a second and he got under her guard, scoring a long cut along her hip.

Letting the contact carry her down to the ground, she tucked her shoulder in and rolled, coming up behind the Jaffa, and in one fluid movement slashed with everything she had at his unprotected knee. Off balance and bellowing in pained rage, he fell, landing awkwardly on his side.

Now driven by pure instinct, Sam leapt on him without a moment's hesitation. Even as he was pulling himself up she kicked out at his hand, sent the knife spinning away, and reached over his shoulder. Her blade found his neck and with one sickening heave, she jerked it straight across his throat.

The warrior fell limp with a small gurgle of air escaping his lungs. Dead. So very dead.

Sam rolled away, coming to her feet and scanning the Jaffa surrounding her. None made a move toward her. The gong rang out again. The commander rose and beckoned her to him.

Instead, heart hammering in her chest, Sam turned and forced herself to really look at the man on the ground. At the death she had caused. His handsome face found a place deep in her memory, likely to stay there for a very long time. She bowed to him in respect, one soldier to another, then turned and made her way out of the arena.

A young Jaffa, eyes wide with admiration, presented her with a small stone plaque, into which was carved a Stargate address and presumably the password in Goa'uld script. He turned and escorted her to the tent on the other side of the clearing.

Sam glanced at her teammates and gave them a thumbs-up before entering the tent. Inside she found pallets and cushions to rest on and tables laden with food, drink and bowls containing herbal-smelling substances. The warrior left her alone.

With slow, deliberate movements she picked up an empty bowl, dropped to her shaking knees and proceeded to throw up what felt like every meal she had ever had.

"Is she okay?"

Jack stood as close as he could to the force-field, straining to see clearly through the rippling red energy. Carter's thumbs-up answered Daniel's question and filled him with relief. They had watched the fight, their view partly obscured by the spectators, with helplessness gnawing at them. Now the Jaffa were headed toward them again.

Teal'c shed his vest, jacket and empty holster. He stood calmly anticipating the fight to come, confidence a near-visible aura around him.

"So. T." Jack found the words sticking in his throat. He hated — *hated* — this, sending his people off into danger with no backup, without even a good reason for risking their lives; even Teal'c, who had more years and experience than the rest of them put together.

"Fight the good fight," he said lamely.

"I shall, O'Neill. I bid you good fortune in your own battle."

A faint smile flickered across Jack's face.

"And you, Daniel Jackson." Teal'c looked intently at Daniel. "Remember the skills O'Neill and I have shown you. You are quick of mind and supple of body. Keep moving at all times, be unpredictable. Give your enemy little opportunity to strike you. Use your natural skills to confound them and strike with intent at the first opening." His voice softened with emotion. "Be well, my brother."

Daniel shut his mouth with a clack of teeth. "I will, Teal'c. Good luck."

Daniel extended his hand and Teal'c gripped it, shifting to the forearm clasp of warrior-brothers. He repeated the gesture with Jack, then turned to face the waiting Jaffa. In a flash of light he was outside the barrier and striding toward the weapons table.

Watching him go, Jack patted Daniel's shoulder.

"C'mon. Warm up with me."

The array of weapons brought a jumble of memories flooding into Teal'c's mind: happy days of apprenticeship, training with friends in mock battle, seeing those same friends' lives thrown away for the vanity of their 'god'. Almost instinctively he reached out and picked up a sturdy *bashaak* staff, four feet in length. Simple. Unadorned. Deadly in knowing hands.

His opponent stepped forward and picked up the matching staff, thickset face sneering dismissively.

Teal'c glowered contemptuously at the man. He stalked into the arena, impatient to begin.

The Jaffa facing him was the largest of the four challengers, yet still many years younger than Teal'c himself. The gong pealed, echoing flatly off the snow-blanketed ground and trees.

The challenger sketched a haughty bow to Teal'c, barely this side of polite acknowledgement between warriors of equal rank. Which they were not.

"You reject the service of your god to seek succor at the feet of Ra Almighty, Jaffa?"

With an eerily graceful twist, the Jaffa launched through the air, staff cracking hard into Teal'c's, and dropped lightly to his feet.

"Apophis was not my god." Teal'c answered the move in a dazzling flip, using the staff for support, his foot connecting most satisfyingly with the other's head. "Apophis is no god at all. He is in fact dead." His voice rang clearly through the silence of the spectators.

"Hah! No wonder you abandoned your duty and sought service with the one god who rules all!" The challenger uttered an incoherent howl and flung himself at Teal'c in a whirlwind of feet and staff.

Teal'c dodged, rolled, and delivered a solid strike with his weapon. The Jaffa's staff landed bruisingly on his back, but Teal'c spun away, retaliating with a backhand swing that nearly broke the man's arm.

"You fight well," he growled. "You should use your skills to make a better path for yourself in this life."

His opponent threw himself to the ground, sliding into Teal'c and sweeping his legs out from under him. Teal'c crashed onto his back. He blocked the incoming staff, jerked his legs towards his chest and flipped back onto his feet.

His opponent was unimpressed with Teal'c's advice. *"Hassac,"* he spat. He swung his staff at Teal'c with such force that Teal'c felt his thumb break as he deflected the blow.

"Death is the reward of the ignorant." The old saying came softly to Teal'c's lips. He knew words would never change this man's devotion to a false, dead god.

He dropped into a cartwheel, hands brushing the stone paving for bare seconds. His feet impacted with the challenger's face who was sweeping forward in his own attack. Cartilage and bone shattered, bright blood glittered through the air. As the man fell, Teal'c surged on, never breaking his momentum. He raised the staff and brought the blunted end down on the base of the Jaffa's skull.

The challenger was dead before his body crashed to the ground.

Teal'c stiffened into a formal salute, the staff tucked tight along his arm. "You died well, *cha'til*."

He looked up at the silent witnesses, his chest heaving. Once again the gong resounded through the crisp air. Teal'c allowed himself to be escorted toward the tent where Major Carter waited, the stone tablet of victory in his hand.

More difficult than the battle just fought, he strove to raise his eyes and allow himself one final glimpse of his two comrades, yet to endure their own struggle for life.

"Teal'c!" Major Carter looked up as he entered the tent, and he felt the grim lines of his face soften as he saw her.

"Major Carter. Are you well?"

"I'm good, Teal'c. Just the one cut that's hurting. The rest are minor."

Teal'c knelt at her side, inspecting the wound through the tear in her pants and reaching for a bowl on the table containing a particularly pungent paste. "There are only two guards in attendance. We must hold ourselves ready to assist O'Neill and Daniel Jackson."

She winced as he slathered the substance over the wound, covering it with a thick bandage.

"I'm ready."

Keeping one eye on Teal'c as he headed for the arena, Jack took Daniel through a series of stretches and exercises, feeling his own muscles—taxed from his little mountaineering jaunt—burn in protest.

"Daniel?"

"Yeah?"

"You're going to be able to do this, aren't you?"

Daniel paused in mid sit-up. Slowly completing the movement he glanced carefully at Jack's worried face. Disconcerted, he looked down at his own feet.

"I know what's at stake, Jack," he hedged. "I think so. I hope so." He sighed, honesty seeping out as always. "I don't know."

Jack finished his push-ups and faced Daniel. In the background, a roar rose from the spectators around the arena. They both turned, catching a glimpse of Teal'c flying feet-first through the air.

"I have to know you will do this, Daniel."

Daniel opened his mouth but Jack cut him off.

"You've got the training, the knowledge. Use it. We're not going to get any second chances here, Daniel. It's kill or be killed and I sure as hell don't want to see you killed. Again."

"Well, I don't want to die, Jack. If it comes down to that, then I will do my best to... you know. But I still think we should try to talk to them, tell them Ra is dead."

"You think a bunch of Jaffa is going to be happy hearing their entire way of life is a lie and the god they serve has been dead for years? They'll just say sorry and let us go home?"

"It's worth a try, isn't it?"

Jack let out a frustrated gurgle, leaned over and grabbed two fistfuls of Daniel's jacket, bringing them nose to nose.

"There is no try. There is only *do*, Daniel. You go in there, kill that guy, come out alive and for once value your own life more than some guy who's spent his whole life killing nice people like you."

Daniel's eyebrows bobbed up and down as he blinked at Jack. "You kind of sounded like Yoda there for a moment," he said mildly.

Jack let Daniel go, patting the rumpled jacket back into place. "Yeah, well, apparently he was always right too. Just keep in mind, Daniel, that Sha're and Skaara are still out there, depending on you to find them."

Another roar from the arena brought them to their feet.

"Carter and Teal'c, they need you too. And if you think I'm gonna keep going through the 'gate without you, you're wrong," Jack persisted. "So if you won't do it for yourself, do it for us."

Jack stared into Daniel's eyes for a long moment, saw doubt chasing reason. It was the best he could hope for. He slapped Daniel's shoulder lightly and they rose to move back to the force-field. Moments later another great cry rose up from the spectators, this time joined by the gong signaling the end of the contest.

Teal'c appeared soon after, striding tall and proud toward the tent. He glanced at them briefly before being ushered inside. Jack sighed. Two down, two to go. And they now had half their team outside the force-field.

"Okay." Jack turned to Daniel, trying to ignore the thud of blood pounding through his head. He plucked Daniel's glasses from his face and tucked them in a pocket, then reached out and started zipping Daniel's jacket as he spoke. "Keep this done up, it'll help protect you. Pick a weapon you're comfortable with. Try and bring him down quickly, keep moving all the time."

He was on the verge of babbling when Daniel caught his hands, his grip warm and steady.

"Jack, I'll be okay. Look after yourself. Please."

The Jaffa were already there, standing expectantly on the other side of the force-field.

"I'll see you soon," Jack said quietly.

"You will." Daniel nodded encouragingly. "Good luck."

The beam whisked Jack away, a thousand things he wanted to say churning inside him.

Glaring at the Jaffa around him, Jack marched so swiftly toward the weapons table they had to scurry to keep up. There was an anger building in him, fuelled as it often was by injustice. The Jaffa's rigid one-dimensional devotion to a dead god and their eagerness to throw away lives in pursuit of that devotion were stoking a rage that would soon only find release in violence.

None of the weapons offered sufficient savagery to match what he was feeling.

His opponent stepped up to the opposite side of the table: muscled, of indeterminate age, face haughty and cruel. The epitome of every uniformed thug Jack had ever met in a lifetime of combat. He pointedly turned away to stare at the Jaffa leader. There was intelligence in that face, wisdom born of years, reminding him vividly of Bra'tac.

"I don't suppose we can dispense with the weapons and just do this bare-handed?"

The old guy seemed surprised, but considered the question carefully before answering. "It is not against the rule of Trial to fight without weapons. If that is your choice, so be it."

Jack's adversary clapped his huge meaty hands together and all but ran for the arena. Jack kept his attention on the old Jaffa.

"What do your rules say about allowing someone to cede the fight because they were brought here against their will?"

The Jaffa's face closed down in refusal, but Jack pressed on. "Your society reveres scholars, scribes, doesn't it?"

Confused, the old warrior nodded slowly.

"Well, that man back there behind the force-field is one of the most learned scholars you'll ever meet. He speaks many different languages, knows more about your history than you do. Why would someone like that risk their life in a trial like this?"

"For the highest honor of serving our god." The stock answer came out right on cue.

Jack sighed, frustration forcing him to ignore Teal'c's earlier advice. "Now see, that's another thing you don't know. Your god is dead. Blown with his ship to little, itty bits that are still floating in orbit around Abydos."

Leaning in till they were almost nose to nose, Jack cut off the Jaffa's indignant denial.

"You wanna know how I know that? Because I'm the one who blew him up. Sent a big old bomb up through the rings as he was taking off. The whole planet saw the explosion. Your 'god' has been dead for three and a half years. How long has it been since you had contact from off-world? How many more lives are you going to waste here?"

The Jaffa stepped back, his face twisting with fury. "Lies... blasphemy... *sacrilege*. You shall engage in combat and your untruths will not aid you." He turned on his heel and stalked toward his waiting men.

Jack yanked his forage cap off and shoved it into a pocket. "Fine."

He strode into the arena without a backward glance. Murmurs were silenced as the watching troops came respectfully to attention. The gong rang out and the Jaffa facing Jack rushed him with a gleeful bellow.

Jack let the man get within spitting distance before sidestepping and delivering a straight-fingered jab to the hollow between the man's collarbones. The Jaffa went down with a horrible choked rasp.

Turning slightly, Jack sought out and held the commander's gaze for a significant moment. Beside him, his challenger staggered upright. Thickly muscled forearms wrapped around Jack's neck, cutting off oxygen, but Jack felt only a cold clarity in his mind. One goal. Achieve it now.

Jack raised his right leg and shredded his boot heel down the long nerve running the length of the man's thigh: agonizing and terribly effective. The Jaffa screamed, his legs collapsing under him, overloaded nervous system shrieking in pain. Before he was even halfway to the ground, Jack twisted around and rammed the heel of his left hand up under the man's chin, sending shards of broken jaw up into the brain. A quick twist snapped his neck and the body thudded to a heap on the ground.

Stunned silence settled over the watching Jaffa. Jack straightened up and walked out of the arena less than two minutes after entering it, the gong sounding belatedly behind him. He didn't look at the body; he needed no more faces joining the ones already shelved in a dark corner of his memory. He pulled out his cap and rammed it back on his head, yanking the bill far down over his eyes.

The trophy tablet was thrust at him and he took it, his eyes pinning the elder Jaffa.

"You have to stop this. Now." Jack's voice came out in a shaky hiss.

The Jaffa gazed at him, a little doubt showing on his face. Nonetheless, he indicated toward the tent and Jack was led away. The moment he was in the tent, Carter and Teal'c were at his side. A swift glance told him they were whole and functioning.

"Where are we at?" he snapped.

"There are only the two guards out front, sir. Seems they're not too concerned about us once we've passed the test," Carter said.

"We have cut an exit in the back of the tent, O'Neill," Teal'c continued, brandishing what looked like a sharp dinner knife. "With most of the Jaffa concentrating on the arena, we should have no difficulty disabling those on the fringe and recovering our weapons."

Adrenaline still pulsing through him, Jack gave a feral smile.

"Good work. C'mon, let's go get Daniel."

Jehen'u watched, emotion stripped from his face, as Ninan's lifeless body was taken away. *You died well, Jaffa.* Pride surged through him at the honorable death his young warrior had received, thus ensuring his reward with the god in the afterlife.

It had been a long and worrying time since the last suppliants had faced the challenge of his Jaffa, time during which — cut off as they were from the rest of their Lord's planets — Jehen'u had begun to fear disaster may have overtaken Ra. But those thoughts were, of course, wrong, blasphemous even, and these new arrivals proved the affairs of their god went on as usual. And yet, the words of the third suppliant repeated with annoying persistence in his head. They *were* lies, although Jehen'u could not find a reason why the man would say such things. No. They were lies. All the same, it would be good to have their supply shipments resumed, too. He left the Arena of Honor and walked toward the containment field.

He nodded, pleased his initial assessment of the four new suppliants was proven correct. The young man who had spoken first — his accent strangely old-fashioned — had not seemed too willing to face his Lord's Trial; indeed his claim that he and his warriors wanted no part in it had made Jehen'u feel shame for him. But, when faced with the truth of his situation, the boy had acquiesced. The concerned looks darted the man's way, even by the woman, had confirmed this youngster was the leader in this little group — no doubt a newly matured godling seeking position with the greatest god of them all. His protectors were an odd group, to be sure: one of Apophis' Jaffa, a one-time first prime, now switching allegiance to one who would carry him to serve with a much worthier god; the older man, that one was pure warrior, lean body honed by years of fighting, a good man to have as protector; and the woman, near as quick and deadly as the man, obviously devoted to protecting the young lord. Neither she nor the man were Jaffa, not an unknown occurrence, but unusual.

He halted a pace away from the force-field, his blood stirring at the challenge ahead. Young the godling may be, but he should prove to be a worthy adversary, worthy enough to face Jehen'u himself. He waved a hand and the field was dropped. The young lord took a moment to realize it was gone, wrenched his gaze away from the tent his warrior had just entered and focused on Jehen'u. Blinking, he cautiously stepped forward and nodded at Jehen'u and his escort.

"Hello. My name is Daniel Jackson."

It was Jehen'u's turn to blink in surprise. Without the force-field's interference, he could sense now that this young man was just that—a man—not one of the gods, young or old. Nevertheless, it was too late to assign another warrior to face this man and it was still fitting that he, as fourth prime commanding this outpost, be the one to challenge the leader of the supplicants.

"You will come. Select your weapon." Jehen'u turned away, swiftly revising his assumptions about his chosen opponent.

"Okay, but if I'm going to fight you can I at least know your name?"

The Jaffa halted, staring at Daniel Jackson in bewilderment. "Why do you wish to know my name?"

"Because, in my society, it is polite to get to know someone a little before trying to kill them," he said with an apologetic smile.

What an odd thing to say. Jehen'u looked at him closely, then relented. "I am Jehen'u, son of Kelnat, Fourth Prime in charge of our Lord's Rite of Combat."

The young one bowed his head politely. "I am Daniel Jackson, son of Melburn and Claire, scribe, translator and peaceful explorer, from the planet Earth. I'm pleased to meet you."

"Why?"

"Why am I pleased to meet you? Because I am always happy to meet new people, to find out who they are and how they live."

"You are a spy?"

Daniel Jackson's eyebrows rose. "No. No, I'm not a spy. I'm an arc… scholar. I study how people lived in the past."

"What use is that?" Jehen'u asked, intrigued in spite of himself.

"Because, only by knowing the past are we able to avoid repeating its mistakes in the future. It's how all societies learn and grow," he replied, watching Jehen'u carefully.

Opening his mouth to say something, Jehen'u found no appropriate words and shook his head. "Enough. Come. Choose your weapon."

He led the way toward the weapons table, his opponent trailing. So, the battle was not to be with one of the gods. Well and good. The human must still be a formidable warrior to merit the concern and protection of such companions as those he had.

Daniel Jackson inspected the choice of weapons. "Jehen'u, we don't have to do this. We did not intentionally embark on this Trial. We came here by mistake, really."

"So your companions have said. Choose your weapon."

The youngster sighed. He fingered a short, slender sword thoughtfully. "Did they also tell you… never mind." He picked up the sword, testing the delicate balance between blade and grip.

Jehen'u picked up the sword's partner, saluting Daniel Jackson with it. "A fine weapon. You have chosen well."

There was hesitance in the human as he examined his weapon, seeming to pay more attention to the carved hilt than the polished, lethal blade. *He fears*. The thought stole through Jehen'u, planting the foundation for deeper concerns. All warriors had fear in them — those who did not lived short lives and did not die well. But all warriors learned how to conceal their fear, push it deep inside until it turned into a fire that fuelled the desire to survive.

Unsettled, he led the way to the arena, Daniel Jackson a step behind and immediately beginning to talk.

"Over three and a half years ago the Chappa'ai on our planet was, well, rediscovered and we got it to work. We only had one address so we dialed it up and went through."

"You were searching for your god then."

"No, not at all. We knew nothing about the Goa'uld or Jaffa. We were just exploring. We ended up on Abydos. We met the people there. They were… very nice. We were distressed to find they were being used as slave labor in the mine. You see, on our planet, slavery is regarded as cruel and unlawful."

They moved between the rows of spectators and onto the black slate arena. Jaffa surrounded them and Jehen'u walked proudly to the center. Two large bloodstains were clearly visible on the surface. Jehen'u turned to face Daniel Jackson, bringing his sword up in a readiness salute.

"The second day we were there, Ra arrived. He landed his ship on the pyramid." Daniel Jackson tore his eyes away from the bloody pools and nervously looked at Jehen'u, but kept his sword hanging point-down by his side. "How long have you served Ra, Jehen'u?"

"In my twelfth year I entered Ra's service as an apprentice, and for one hundred and forty-six years my duty has not wavered," he replied proudly, wondering when this chattering boy before him would realize he was expected to fight, not spend the day gossiping.

"Wow, that's very commendable. You must have served in many different positions in that time. Did you ever actually meet Ra?"

"For sixteen years I served in our Lord's personal guard,

before being rewarded with this post." Jehen'u swallowed the inevitable pang of regret that he had not succeeded in rising to a rank higher than Fourth. He repeated the signal to commence the combat, but again, Daniel Jackson started to talk.

"So you would have spent time on Ra's Ha'tak ship?"

"I had that honor."

"The one with the ram-headed statue behind the ring transporter? The huge throne room with the long billowing curtains and pillars everywhere?" Daniel Jackson asked eagerly. "The throne was flanked by two huge Horus statues, their wings outstretched, and behind the throne were two incense braziers."

Jehen'u eyed him speculatively. "Such words do describe our Lord's vessel," he admitted. "Enough, we must begin." He brought his sword down in a sweeping, testing arc, expecting the boy to follow suit.

Daniel Jackson danced back out of reach and kept talking, his hands and sword flapping through the air in emphasis. "There were children, all ages, not wearing very much. He kept them close to him. They were his personal servants, even helping him bathe and dress. And cats! Huge, brindled cats all over the place."

I may be wrong about this one. He is not as powerful as I thought. He may even be the opposite. He does not engage me in battle. Is he a coward?

Confused, Jehen'u prowled toward his opponent who again backed away, all kinds of emotions flittering across his features. "How could you know this?"

"Because I've been there. I met Ra. I talked to him face to face."

Anger fuelled Jehen'u's lunge at the boy. His sword flashed in a glittering arc through the air. "No servant who does not belong to his personal retinue has ever been gifted with the sight of our Lord's true face."

Daniel Jackson ducked and danced back, his own sword gripped tight but only half-raised in defense. Above them, the gong belled flatly across the snow.

I have made an error.

Jehen'u swung again. With a grimace the boy deflected the blow, the sword handle twisting in his grip with the force of the strike. He grabbed it with both hands and sidestepped away.

This 'fight' insults me. He is no more than a chattering boy. My men shall lose all regard for me. They see now, I have chosen the weakest opponent. The others were strong, honorable warriors. I shall face a challenge when this day is finished. My misjudgment has undone me.

Not really listening to the human's babble, and resolutely ignoring the niggling doubt that it would be dishonorable to win such an unequal fight, Jehen'u attacked, driving Daniel Jackson back and back with a succession of solid blows. Yet, still the boy avoided any aggressive moves and chattered on and on.

"Ra was very young, very beautiful. He had long black hair which the children pinned up when he bathed. His eyes were dark brown, but sometimes they would glow bright white. He was slender, moved very elegantly." Gasping against the shock of the strikes but, apparently undaunted, Daniel Jackson continued to rattle on. He evaded another sweep of Jehen'u's sword and kept bouncing around the arena, leading him in a bizarre, frustrating dance.

"He had a device on his hand that he used to shred the brain of anyone who displeased him."

As Jehen'u's sword swept over his opponent's head, the boy dropped into a crouch and craned around, trying to keep the weapon in view while he struggled back upright. To Jehen'u's mounting exasperation, the boy continued to talk.

"You know I'm speaking the truth, Jehen'u. We were prisoners on his Ha'tak. We were exploring on Abydos when Ra came in his ship. We were captured and brought before him."

Jehen'u's sword whistled toward him again. Desperately, the young man blocked it, wincing as the blow reverberated up his arm.

"Ask yourself this: why would prisoners who had been captured and beaten by Ra want to go through this Trial to serve him?"

"Your reasons for seeking the blessing of our god are no concern of mine."

Jehen'u swung wide, forcing Daniel Jackson to skip sideways. He halted, not even breathing hard and tracked the young man with his eyes. Movement flickered beyond the sweating, still-talking boy: a brief flash of pale brown behind the ranks of Jehen'u's men. He swatted at Daniel Jackson, kept him moving and continued to watch. *There.* A glimpse of pale hair and sand-colored clothing. It was the woman, out of the recovery tent and skulking behind the lines of his warriors.

Jehen'u toyed with his opponent, sending him dancing in a circle with wide sweeps of his sword, not bothering for real contact as he searched for the other two. Sure enough, the first prime and the older man were sliding through the snow, crouched down but maneuvering with intent, no doubt to rescue this burbling weakling.

Why should they bother so? His opponent was no fighter. Did he have worth that would warrant such risk when the three had already won their freedom? A scholar, the older one had said. They had value in certain circles, but to deserve such devotion from warriors seemed wrong... then again, his own people did protect the weaker ones of their society, the women, children, those of great age.

Confusion and annoyance mounting in equal measure, Jehen'u swung his attention and sword at Daniel Jackson, delivering a series of hard, well placed blows. After eluding the first, the boy surprised him all over again by suddenly returning the attack, parrying each strike with graceful strength and skill. He handled his weapon well and Jehen'u found a force of determination in those dazzling eyes that once again confounded his assumptions. This man was no weakling. He had the skills of a considerable warrior, but chose instead to wield his tongue as a weapon.

Why?

Jehen'u backed off his attack and began to listen properly.

Slowing as the assault died off, Daniel Jackson dragged air into his lungs. His hands were white with the pressure of his grip on the sword and his clothing bore several slashes from Jehen'u's attacks. He stumbled away as Jehen'u stalked toward him. Instantly, the boy's tongue started again.

"Okay, answer this then. How long has it been since you last heard from anyone in Ra's empire? Have your supply shipments stopped? Have any other supplicants come through the Stargate on the Trial recently?"

"It has been three years and three months since we last received supplies," Jehen'u admitted reluctantly. "And you and your companions are the first to engage the Trial in four years."

Ugly realizations began to build in his mind. Not wanting to confront them, Jehen'u lunged, but pulled the blade down at the last second. Daniel Jackson countered, missed by a sword's length, then froze, the tip of Jehen'u's sword pressing lightly on his groin. The spectators cheered at the prospect of at last seeing blood shed in this odd duel.

Daniel Jackson gamely pressed on, flinching only slightly at the pressure of the sword. "Ra's empire has disintegrated," he said quietly, earnestly. "I'm sorry, Jehen'u, but Ra died on Abydos three years ago. His death upset the balance of power amongst the System Lords and there have been many battles to try and gain dominance. For a while, Apophis was in control but he suffered heavy losses and was caught and killed by Sokar." He gasped as the sword pressed a little harder. Jehen'u was impressed with the young man's courage as he held still, fighting the instinct to pull away.

"You are free, Jehen'u. All of your men here are free. Unless you want to seek service with another System Lord, you can go home, be with your families. No-one else has to die here."

Shock rippled through Jehen'u, echoed by a murmur from those Jaffa closest to them. *A god cannot die.* The thought came automatically, but even so, it was filled with doubt. He had misjudged this young man twice, assuming him the strongest, then the weakest. Now he did not know what to think.

"You and your men are trapped in this Trial as surely as we are, Jehen'u," the soft voice persisted.

Past the panting man, Jehen'u saw the woman rise from concealment, her weapon reclaimed and aimed squarely at his own heart. A flicker of brown to the other side told him the other two supplicants were prepared to fight to the death. For the life of this young human... or for the truth?

And he was not.

There was no honor in this fight. He could dispatch the boy, no, man, with a flick of his wrist, but it would be no worthy victory. After a lifetime of dutifully following the orders of his god, Jehen'u knew, this time, he wished to follow the honor of his heart. He snatched the blade away so abruptly that a little yelp escaped Daniel Jackson.

Jehen'u turned to his men and bellowed, "Jaffa! Kree! This combat is postponed. Return to your quarters."

Stunned, the Jaffa slowly obeyed and moved away from the arena. Suddenly, commotion erupted within three different sections of the crowd as the supplicants were discovered. Jaffa milled uncertainly together, until Jehen'u shouted them on their way.

Daniel Jackson closed his eyes in relief, backed away and headed shakily out of the arena toward his people, keeping a reasonable distance from Jehen'u and his sword. "Hi guys. I'm okay, actually. You don't need to, um...." He indicated the round object in the older one's hand. It was unfamiliar to Jehen'u but seemed to be a weapon.

His protector's eyes raked Daniel Jackson from head to toe. Sighing, he secured the weapon. "Keep you from being turned into a eunuch?" he finished bluntly.

Jehen'u ignored them and walked up to the first prime. "The b... young man says that Ra and Apophis have perished. Does he speak the truth?"

"Tec'ma-te, upon my honor as a Jaffa, his words are the truth," he replied gravely, offering the honorific of Master.

"I'm sorry, Jehen'u," Daniel Jackson began.

A slashing motion of Jehen'u's sword cut him off. "You will leave here now."

"What?"

"Swell. Thanks a bunch. Be seeing you," the loud one interrupted. He indicated for the first prime and the woman to head for the Chappa'ai, snagged a handful of Daniel Jackson's clothing and began to tow him along.

"Wait, Jack... Jehen'u, if you believe me, then can you tell us if there is a way out of this Trial?"

"There is not. You must complete your quest."

"There's a surprise," came a loud mutter.

Jehen'u trailed them to the Chappa'ai, dismissing his shamefaced troops who were supposed to have been guarding the tent.

"Well, what about you?" Daniel Jackson persisted. "If the Stargate only leads to the next planet in the Trial, do you have any way of getting home?"

"We do not. This planet has been our home for many years. It shall continue to serve as such."

Daniel Jackson's protectors swiftly repacked the equipment vehicle they had brought with them and had raided in their attempted rescue. Jehen'u's eyes met the young man's gaze.

Daniel Jackson walked over to him and gravely presented his sword, hilt first. "If we make it through the Trial is there someone, somewhere we can contact, let them know you are here?"

Jehen'u regarded him solemnly, a small smile tugging the corner of his mouth. He would like to see his home planet once more. "Should you find yourselves on Dashani you may find the Jaffa there disposed to bring a ship to collect us."

"Dashani? Dashani. I'll remember. Thank you, Jehen'u"

"Go before my Jaffa realize I have lost all my faculties."

Daniel Jackson nodded and shivered, now clearly feeling

the cold air. He joined his people who smiled at him, pleased
with his survival, although they did make him carry his own
equipment. The loud one attached a heavy sack to Daniel
Jackson's back and thus prepared, they clustered around the
first prime as he dialed the coordinates and read the password
from his tablet.

"*Semetu.*"

The Chappa'ai belched to life. The first prime bowed
gravely to Jehen'u and stepped into it. The woman guided
their machine forward while Daniel Jackson gave a tentative
smile and nod of farewell before following her. The loud one
sketched a salute and hopped quickly into the vortex.

The Stargate snapped off, and Jehen'u found himself alone
in the deserted, snow-covered field, a sense of change looming
over him, his maturing symbiote shifting in its pouch.

GATE THREE

Destroyer of Fire

The cold nothingness of the wormhole resolved into warm, breathable air as Teal'c emerged from the event horizon. Even before his eyesight had cleared he extended a leg to take that first step, and found himself falling. He caught a fleeting glimpse of water underneath him and then he hit the surface, sending up a huge, briny splash.

Dark water closed over his head. He sank until reflexes kicked in and he struggled for the surface, his pack and staff weapon weighing him down and his broken thumb throbbing with the strain. He broke the surface, twisting around to find the Stargate, just in time to see the FRED emerge and perform a perfect nosedive, its weight dragging it straight down. Making a mental note of its position, Teal'c swam to one side. Seconds later Major Carter emerged and fell with a squawk and a frantic wriggle.

Paddling to the spot where she had disappeared, Teal'c extended his staff down into the water and moved it about, hoping to locate her. It bumped against something solid, then was pulled downward. Left hand stroking steadily to keep his head above water, Teal'c pulled the staff up and Major Carter followed, gasping and spitting out water.

"Teal'c? What...?"

His answer was cut off by Daniel Jackson's arrival, whose momentum carried him out several feet before he dropped in an ungainly flail of arms and legs, his yelp of surprise swallowed by the water closing over his head.

O'Neill tumbled out of the wormhole seconds later, unable to do anything but hit the water in a stunning belly flop.

"Ouch." Major Carter winced in sympathy, treading water

and trying not to drag Teal'c down.

Daniel Jackson shot gracelessly to the surface, head stretched back to suck in great gulps of air. O'Neill popped up right in front of him, spitting water and curses with equal abandon.

"Sonofabitch! What the hell happened to the ground?"

Teal'c cranked his head around as far as he could; there was little to see but water stretching in all directions. The Stargate seemed to be perched on thin supports just above the surface; the DHD also sat on stilts. The usual platform was obviously missing. Further away, what looked to be roofs or pillars extended from the water. There was no dry land in sight.

"We must remove our equipment," he said.

Together they struggled back to the now-deactivated Stargate, finding a small foothold on its supports. Major Carter heaved herself up and draped over the ring like a sack of wet laundry. Teal'c hooked an arm next to her and looked anxiously back at their teammates as they splashed and spluttered their way over, weapons and waterlogged packs doing their best to drag them under.

Daniel surged up onto the ring, throwing one leg over to sit side-saddle. Major Carter wriggled around to face him. They stared at each other, a pair of drowned rats with water streaming off them. They grinned.

"Glad I cut my hair," she said, shoving wet strands of hair off her forehead.

"Me too," Daniel admitted wryly.

Teal'c handed his staff to Major Carter and levered up to sit behind her. O'Neill aborted heaving himself onto the ring and launched back through the water, swimming several furious strokes to recover his floating forage cap before splashing back to the Stargate. He hoisted himself up behind Daniel Jackson, shaking his head like a wet dog.

They sat there for a time in bemused silence.

"Well," O'Neill said finally. "This is different."

"There are no people in sight," observed Teal'c.

Daniel, shading his eyes against the sun's reflected glare, stared intently at the few structures showing above the water; here and there the skeletal limbs of trees reached forlornly to the sky. "Whatever happened here, it happened a while ago," he said. "The trees are all dead."

"Found the moon-clock, sir."

Teal'c twisted around, peering down at the rear of the Stargate. The device sat snugly attached to the outer ring, just above the water level.

"How long have we got?"

"Twelve hours twenty-seven minutes, O'Neill." He extended a hand to Major Carter, assisting her to straighten up without sliding off into the water.

"Okay. We can't stay here. We'll need to salvage what gear we can, get some food and I think we could all do with some rest after our little encounters back there." O'Neill glared at the water splashing cheerfully around his boots. "And I really need to pee."

"The roof over there looks intact, Jack." Daniel indicated a U-shaped pitched roof surrounding the top of a fat obelisk, some hundred meters away. The water lapped lazily at its eaves with all the motion of a land-locked lake: no visible swell or currents.

Teal'c peered into the murky water below them. "Before we depart, I shall determine the depth at which the FRED lies." He handed the staff to Daniel Jackson, carefully shrugged out of his pack and passed it to Major Carter. He slid back into the water, drew in several deep breaths and upended. Powerful strokes pulled him down. Unerringly, his sense of direction led him on the path the FRED had taken, until a dark shape resolved into one of the containers strapped to the back of the machine. Teal'c groped along the length of the drowned vehicle, counting containers and testing the bindings over them. Satisfied all was secure, he pushed off and rose to the surface.

"The boxes are all still intact. The vehicle lies only three meters below. We should be able to salvage as much as we can carry." Teal'c pulled himself back up onto the ring and Major Carter helped him gear-up.

"Thanks, T." O'Neill clapped his hands together, his enthusiastic look unconvincing. "Okay, everyone up for this?"

A shrug, a nod and an inclining eyebrow were not exactly the ebullient responses he had been hoping for, but Jack was happy to take what he could get. "We'll do this slowly. Keep together. If you feel yourself getting a cramp, or anything, yell out and drop your gear. Watch out for undercurrents and snags, particularly around the buildings." Jack looked intently at his team, then nodded. "Let's go."

One by one they slipped into the water. From surface level the building seemed a lot further away. Like ducks in a row, Jack led his team through the cold water. He and Carter had their already soaked MP5s strapped to the top of their packs, Teal'c's staff was likewise secured. Their packs, clothing and boots caused a serious amount of drag, but their steady breaststroke kept them moving slowly toward their goal.

Just like Basic.

Jack paused at the halfway point, treading water while he turned to check on the others. Carter stroked steadily up to him, spouting out little jets of water with each exhalation. She nodded and churned past, not losing her momentum. Daniel, a few feet behind her, ploughed strongly on, his training in this very maneuver serving him well. Jack sent him on with a tilt of his head and waited for Teal'c to come abreast. The Jaffa cruised through the water like a submarine running on the surface, smoothly powering along with barely a ripple left behind. Jack grinned and paced alongside him, mind flashing back to the skeptical look on the Academy swim instructor's face when he'd shown up with Teal'c and Daniel. Daniel had proved to be a strong swimmer and, after a few pointers on technique, Teal'c had taken to the water like the proverbial fish—out-distancing them all by the end of training.

Jack spat out a splash of saltwater and slowed as they

neared the slim haven of the rooftops. He led them to the low eaves of the roof that hung only inches above the water's surface, where they rested for a few minutes, lungs heaving and muscles burning.

"Carter, you first."

With a shove from behind by the three men, she hauled herself up onto the terracotta roof tiles. One by one they released their packs and passed them up, then pushed, pulled and scrabbled to join her.

"Oy." Jack flopped bonelessly onto the warm tiles. They all stretched out, flat on their backs, streaming water and quite spent.

"We need to find the address and password," Daniel said after a while.

"Well, I hope they left it somewhere obvious, or we're really up a… lake without a paddle," Jack grumbled.

"There appear to be carvings on the obelisk." Teal'c was sitting up, looking annoyingly undaunted.

"Food and rest break first," Jack ordered, rolling to his feet and pulling Carter, who had been on the verge of dozing off, to her feet.

They spread out along the ridge of one wing of the roof, stripped down to their skivvies, the warm afternoon sun reinvigorating their bodies. Clothes, boots, and all manner of gear from their packs were scattered over the tiles to dry. They broke down and cleaned their weapons; Teal'c's staff and the zats proved their superior alien design to be unaffected by the dunking. MREs were broken out, heated and devoured, while the far side of the roof was declared the latrine and duly christened by Jack.

Jack turned away from another survey of the drowned buildings surrounding them. The lonely peaked roofs and bare tree limbs were desolate in the unnatural quiet. But for the lapping of small waves against the building and the soft rustle of wind over the water, there was no sound to be heard.

"What's all this?" He nudged several piles of rolled cloth

and small glass vials spilling out of Carter's pack.

"Teal'c and I helped ourselves to the medical supplies while we were waiting in the tent, sir," she replied.

"Nice."

"That reminds me, thanks for coming to the rescue, guys," Daniel spoke up.

"Any time, Daniel." Carter smiled at him.

Jack shook his head, still amazed at how Daniel had bamboozled the guy into letting them go. Perhaps there really was a deity that guarded the path of loquacious archaeologists. *Might pay to light a candle for it, just in case.* "Waste of a good ambush," he groused. "I might have known you'd talk your way out of trouble."

"Well, it seemed worth a try." Daniel squinted at Jack with a little grin.

"Words are a most formidable weapon, Daniel Jackson," Teal'c said softly. "You wield them with the skill of a master warrior."

Daniel's grin widened. "Thank you, Teal'c."

"Carter, how's that cut doing?" Jack asked.

She put aside the BDUs she was in the process of sewing up and looked down at the thin red stripe along her hip. "It's fine, sir, just stings a bit. Actually, I think a dip or two in the salt water here will help it heal."

"Okay. Let's get moving. Teal'c, you feel like some diving to get our gear?"

"I do, O'Neill."

"Alright. Carter, you help Teal'c with the salvage while Daniel and I look for the 'gate address."

Fed and somewhat refreshed, Teal'c and Sam slipped into the water and swam back to the Stargate. Sam clambered up onto the inner ring and began securing a number of pack straps and short ropes to the pillar support underneath her.

Armed with his knife, Teal'c took several deep breaths and submerged. Sam watched anxiously as his bare feet disappeared. For almost two minutes the water lapped undisturbed, then Teal'c resurfaced a couple of meters out, blinking water from his eyes and inhaling deeply. She knelt up on the Stargate and extended her hand, pulling him over to her.

"Teal'c? How did it go?"

"Extremely well, Major Carter. I have our rations." He brought up his right arm and the long container holding three day's supply of MREs came into view.

"Oh, great." She grabbed one of the ties and secured the box, leaving it to hang half-submerged from the supporting pillar. "Horrible as they are, they beat foraging for food." She looked at him uncertainly. "I feel like a lemon sitting up here while you do all the work. Are you sure you don't want some help?"

"I will be more at ease knowing you are up here protecting our equipment. It would not do to have it sink once again."

Sam gave him a rueful grin. "True. Good hunting."

Teal'c inclined his head and disappeared under the surface once more, sleek and powerful as a seal.

Sam shifted on the inner track of the Stargate. Not the most comfortable place to sit, though the afternoon sun was pleasantly warming and a gentle zephyr rippled the water around her. Looking up into the sky, she realized what she had been missing — birds. There were no birds wheeling through the air, none diving after fish, if indeed there were fish. The absence of wildlife made this lost city even more desolate and alien.

Gazing around, she counted only seven structures visible above the water. Most had the same terracotta roof tiles as their resting place. Looking over to their temporary base, she saw Daniel and the colonel perched on an eave above the roof's inner courtyard, obviously discussing the obelisk in the center. They stood up and moved a little further along the roof. Daniel turned her way, saw her watching, and waved. She waved back. Daniel eased himself carefully into the water, followed by the colonel. Together they swam to the obelisk and began to investigate.

Sam kept a wary eye on them, turning back as Teal'c

brought more and more containers up to the surface. Survival gear, spare clothing, ropes, scientific equipment—she fervently hoped that one in particular had remained water-tight as it held the salvaged communications unit from the MALP.

Next up was the ammo case, its weight threatening to challenge even Teal'c's massive strength. Sam got up on her knees and leaned precariously over the water. She grabbed a handle, looped two ties through it and secured it to the pillar.

Teal'c took a few minutes to rest, then returned to his task. The silence of the place seemed to swallow Sam. She found herself humming just to fill the emptiness. Sitting there on the Stargate in her underwear, warm air ruffling her half-dry hair, the splashes and voices of her teammates close by—it was just another day in the life of a galactic explorer.

Jack followed Daniel carefully through the water, alert for undercurrents or weird alien octopi ready to suck them down to a soggy grave. The surface remained mostly calm, if slightly choppy. The obelisk was a huge, squat affair, rising only three meters above the roof, but four times the girth of the obelisks in the garden courtyard on P3R-779. Each side was heavily carved with Goa'uld script and the side facing out of the courtyard toward the Stargate sported a large sun-disk symbol of Ra.

Daniel pushed away from the obelisk, floating on his back to get a better view of the carvings at the top. With his glasses—retrieved from the pocket Jack had stashed them in—firmly secured around his neck with the cord from Jack's sunglasses, he read the lines of script down to where they disappeared under the water. That side covered, he paddled around to the next side to read, then the third and fourth, with Jack gliding behind him through the cold water.

Shivering in the shadow of the obelisk, Daniel led the way back into the sun before sharing what he had learnt.

"There's no address or any passage resembling a password in sight, Jack. But," he pointed a dripping finger at the Eye of

Ra symbol, "up there is one of those Ra-is-wonderful lines so I think we're in the right place."

"There are carvings under the water-line."

"Yes. Ra may have flooded this place on purpose."

"Sweet. Can you work them out by touch?"

Daniel nodded. "The glyphs all follow the same structure, so it won't be like trying to read someone's handwriting. I should be able to make them out. The difficult part will be the address. If I miss part of a symbol it'll be invalid."

Jack grimaced at the thought of being stuck on this watery nowhere for any length of time. "We've got some lightsticks on the FRED, but I don't know how much use they'll be in this silty stuff."

"Well, maybe hold those in reserve for a final check. I'll find what we need first, transcribe it and see if it fits."

"If you're going under, I want you on a tether," Jack said. "There's no knowing what kind of snags are down there."

He swam to the roof and retrieved a long roll of thin cord he'd had in his pack, then splashed back to Daniel. Reaching around Daniel's waist, he deftly secured the line.

"One yank," he said. "Any reason. If you're in trouble, just one yank on the line and I'll pull you up. Okay?"

"Yes." He pulled his glasses off and handed them to Jack who strung them around his own neck. Daniel paddled back to the obelisk, hands reaching out to trace the carvings where they were swallowed by the lapping wavelets. He looked up, positioned himself under the Eye of Ra—the most likely place to find the address—then took several slow, deep breaths and sank under the water, fingers playing over the stone before him.

Visibility was limited. Daniel could make out the shadowy shape of the obelisk but any detail on the stone was impossible to discern. The salt water, though less potent than Earth's oceans, stung his eyes. He ran his hands down the carvings, following the declarations about the munificence of Ra that ran down from the Eye.

Starving lungs forced him to the surface. Daniel kept his eyes centered on the carvings in front of him, marking his place to prevent himself drifting. Jack hovered close by, ready to assist.

Down he went, again and again, fingers finding and reading the familiar Braille of hieroglyphs. The signs, so little changed from their Ancient Egyptian roots, were as visible under his fingertips as if he were gazing at them in bright sunlight; the viper, flowering reed, water ripple, bread loaf, bolt, foot... on they went, revealing their long hidden secrets. And there, words formed in a different pattern — no grandiose praise, but a name.

Daniel clawed his way into the air for the sixth time, spraying water out of his mouth, lungs heaving, eyes trying to blink away bright oxygen-deprivation spots.

"Daniel?" Jack was next to him, one hand on his arm anchoring him.

"Found... a name," he said between wheezes of air.

"Knew you would. Don't rush it, we've got time enough."

Daniel closed his eyes briefly, concentrating on breathing. When his head started to spin from too much oxygen, he submerged once more, the rough scrape of stone under his fingers leading him unerringly back to the name. Opening his eyes, he peered at the symbols, barely able to make them out, but needing visual confirmation. The name was short but unmistakable; set at the end of the other carvings, the stone below and to either side lay disturbingly blank.

A tug on his waist brought him back to the surface, mind and body moving sluggishly as the cool temperature of the water began to leech his strength.

"Got it, Jack," he sputtered. "Got the password — *Ashebu*."

"Attaboy." Jack patted him on the shoulder. "C'mon, ten minutes rest out of the water."

Noting the passage on the obelisk above the name, Daniel allowed Jack to usher him back to the roof. He accepted a boost up onto the warm tiles, where he flopped, limp as a landed fish, soaking in the welcome gift of the sun.

Teal'c floated, ten feet down, one hand anchored against the slight pull of the current, the other gripping his knife as he sawed through the swollen ropes holding down a container full of tents and sleeping bags. The rope finally parted and a mini-avalanche of boxes slid to the floor of the lake. He released another small exhalation of air. Deep within its womb his larval Goa'uld thrashed its displeasure at being forced to sustain his system for such an extended time. Teal'c ignored it, pleased the evil inside him was being of use to his team.

He took hold of the box's handle — his broken thumb almost healed now — and pushed off, rising effortlessly to the surface. Towing it to Major Carter, he steadied it while she secured it to the supports. He let go and it hung just below the surface with the other recovered containers.

"How are you holding up, Teal'c?"

He looked up at the major. "I am quite well, thank you, Major Carter. There are four smaller boxes yet to be retrieved. I regret however, I will not be able to salvage the water tank."

Major Carter nodded. "No, thirty gallons, we'd never carry it. We'll just have to forage for fresh water on the next couple of planets. At least we've got enough purifying tablets in our supplies to last months. We'll survive."

"Indeed we will."

Teal'c rested for a few moments more, the ripple of wind over the water the only sound to be heard.

Jack squelched up next to Daniel and sat appreciatively on the tiles, listening to Daniel's breathing. Over on the Stargate he could see Carter and Teal'c, likewise taking a break. A good stack of salvaged gear already bobbed near them.

He let his gaze drift over the eerie remnants of the city. Nothing stirred apart from the water lapping against rooftops. The sun was well on its descent to night-time; by his reckoning only one or two hours of daylight remained.

Daniel, battling not to fall asleep, finally rolled over and crawled up the roof to his pack. He pulled out his notebook, kept reasonably dry in its plastic baggie, and carefully recorded the name he had found. After digging out a power bar and canteen, he slid back down the roof to Jack and shared the food and water in silence.

Sitting with eyes closed, face turned into the sun, Jack could almost hear Daniel thinking.

"Jack, do you think we'll find a way out of this?"

Jack tilted his head at Daniel, seeing worry in his usually optimistic friend. "Sure we will. What, you don't think we can beat the Goa'uld at some game they set up hundreds, thousands of years ago?"

"Well, the fact it has been running for uncounted years must be an indication of how difficult it is. We have no way of knowing what's coming next. The previous planet…."

"We'll handle whatever they throw at us, Daniel. Just remember, we stick together and we can take on all comers. It's what we do." He stared at Daniel intently, seeing his words sink in. "C'mon, let's get this done."

Jack rose to his feet, this time securing Daniel's tether to his own waist. They slid back into the water, the cold a shock against their warmed skin. Daniel once again submerged beside the obelisk and Jack resumed counting off the seconds, eyes tracking Daniel's air trail. He was down over ninety seconds and Jack was on the verge of dragging him up when Daniel shot to the surface, a meter away from where he went down.

The look on his face spoke volumes.

"What?"

"It's blank — to either side and underneath the name — there's nothing else carved on the obelisk."

Before Jack could marshal a response, Daniel was gone again; upending, white shorts flashing in the sun before powerful kicks from his legs drove him deep into the water. Jack glided after him, following the tether stretched taught between them. Daniel finally surfaced at the far corner of the obelisk, swam back to the center and dived again. Another minute dragged by before he came up once more, at the other corner, anxiety creasing his salt-irritated eyes.

"Nothing. Jack, it's only nine or ten feet down. The obelisk is resting on bare earth. There's nothing."

"Has it been broken off, eroded by the water?"

"No. The stone is smooth, polished even, like this." Daniel reached up to run a hand along the polished border of the carvings above his head. "If it had eroded, there would still be traces."

"Okay, maybe it's on one of the other sides. Take a breather, Daniel. I'll do the next side."

Jack swam past Daniel, around the corner of the obelisk. He traced his hands down the stone, following the carvings to where they ended eighteen inches under the water. He filled his lungs and sank, fingers roaming the polished surface all the way down to the silt it rested on. He bobbed back up for air, then repeated the maneuver along the length of the stone to the far corner. His questing hands met nothing but cold, slick stone.

Jack came up gasping air and blowing water out of his nose, Daniel's anxious face only a foot away from his. Silently, Daniel rounded the next corner and proceeded to examine the third side. Jack took over at the next corner, groping his way along the fourth side and finding no answer.

Back at the first side he had examined, Daniel trod water, eyes searching the carvings above him. "This doesn't make sense. It should be here."

"And yet—no address. Where else would they put it?"

Daniel twisted around, as if expecting to see another stone monument he had missed. Apart from the Stargate and DHD there were only drowned buildings in sight. If it was hidden inside one of those....

"The whole point of this Trial is for people to find the addresses and move on. It would be somewhere safe, where storms and age wouldn't erode it."

"So it must be here."

"Yes."

"But it's not."

"No."

"So, where is it?"

"Aakhut Shetat."

"Bless."

"Thank you. Actually, it's the line carved above the sun disk." Daniel shoved his wet hair off his forehead and backstroked a little to get a better view, dragging Jack along on the tether.

"Which means?"

"Revealed to you the Secret Horizon."

"Ah. And? So?"

"The *Aakhut Shetat*, the Secret Horizon. It's from the Egyptian sacred astronomy, meaning the chamber or temple where the god resides."

"Somewhere hidden?"

"Possibly."

"And can be 'revealed to you'?"

"Perhaps."

"By…?"

"Ashebu."

"What?" Jack scowled at Daniel, sure that his gentle prodding had been coaxing Daniel in the right direction, only to have him skew off at a tangent.

"The password, *Ashebu*. It means Flame Dweller."

"Okay. That helps us how?"

For a moment Daniel stared blankly at Jack. He glanced back up at the disk carved near the crown of the obelisk. "The sun god—Ra—flame dweller… maybe it's hidden behind the sun disk?"

Jack shrugged as best he could while treading water. "Worth a try, Daniel."

Daniel looked up at the panels of glyphs carved below the

sun disk. "Okay, ignoring the random passages into which they translate, if we focus on the hieroglyphs themselves... running from top to bottom, they hold no special meaning—but, oh... clever. It's hidden in plain sight. There's a line of symbols running from right to left through the passages to form the words 'Secret Horizon'."

Jack followed Daniel's gaze up the side of the obelisk. Naturally, they were out of reach.

"Jack, help me up."

A lot of fumbling and splashing later, Jack was attempting not to drown while boosting Daniel six inches out of the water.

"*Ah–khet,*" Daniel said softly. "The glyphs are giving slightly when I push them. *Shet–At–Neter.*" From above came a grinding sound, echoed below by a gurgle as Jack went under. Daniel wriggled out of his grip and slipped into the water, pulling Jack back into the air.

"It worked!" Daniel indicated the sun disk, pulling apart like an opening flower. From inside the revealed cavity, an oval piece of stone was ejected, glancing off Jack's head before disappearing into the water.

"Ow!"

They both scrabbled madly to catch it before it was lost. Daniel snagged it, held it up to the light, and was relieved beyond words to find the much needed address carved into its surface.

Jack glared at him, rubbing his abused head. "Are you done?" he enquired.

"Yes. We've got it, Jack." Daniel beamed happily at him.

"I'm so glad," Jack muttered.

Daniel splashed back to the roof, eager to warm up and dry out, towing Jack behind him like an overgrown, cranky buoy.

Half an hour later, Sam returned with Teal'c. Colonel O'Neill and Daniel pulled them out, offering compact towels and power bars to help restore some body heat.

The team hunkered down along the eaves of the roof, surveying the salvaged boxes tethered around the Stargate's supports. Teal'c's Herculean effort had retrieved everything from the FRED: tents, sleeping bags, spare tarps, food, ammunition, clothes, survival gear, Sam and Daniel's tools.

"Way to go, T. Thank you." Colonel O'Neill slapped the solid muscle of Teal'c's shoulder and stood.

The sun was only a half-hour or so away from sliding under the watery horizon and its warmth was noticeably waning. They had a little less than five hours yet before moonset.

Dressed once again in their dried clothes the four worked quietly together, repacking provisions and gear, bearing witness to the spectacular sunset and the rise of a huge, brilliantly white moon that cast such effective light that their flashlights remained unused.

Daniel sat next to Sam, methodically writing up his notes while she worked on the MALP's comm unit. After a couple of sidelong glances, he spoke cautiously. "Sam, you're okay, aren't you?"

She smiled at him briefly, then bent her head over the electronics in her lap once more. "I'm alright, Daniel."

"It's just…." Awkwardly he touched the slashes in her jacket, legacy of the knife fight. "It can't have been easy."

Easy. The knife slipped in very easily, actually. Sliced through cartilage and tissue like cutting a cake.

"It wasn't. It had to be done. It's over now," she said shortly.

More dead eyes to haunt me in the night.

"How do you cope with…." He flapped a hand in search of words that would not hurt.

"I guess you deal with it a little bit at a time, Daniel," she replied softly. "You don't dwell on it, but you don't forget either."

And I'm so very glad you don't have to deal with it, too.

Daniel's hand squeezed hers, an offer of the sympathy and support she relied upon.

"Ahh." The colonel returned from a trip to the latrine, plunked himself down next to them and fished out his shaving kit. Slightly below them, Teal'c sat drifting into kel'no'reem, like a big, placid, golden Buddha.

"So, you're not going to miss this place when we leave, sir?"

"Are you kidding, Carter? All this water makes me pee every ten minutes. Give me dry land any time." He grinned wickedly as Daniel darted a disconcerted look at the water they had been swimming in together.

Sam choked back a laugh, then stood and moved higher up the roof to stand sentry, listening to the men talking below her.

"So, Daniel, what's the deal with this Barque of Heaven?" the colonel asked.

"Uh, well, in mythology it was one of the names for the solar boat in which Ra traveled the night sky, or the underworld. The Ancient Egyptians saw the setting of the sun each day as a death, if you will. Ra traveled through the dark of the underworld each night, battling serpents, facing challenges and passing a number of gates until he was reborn as the sun in the dawn of the new day."

A flicker of white caught Sam's eye. She turned but saw nothing more threatening than the water around them. A brief chill prickled her neck, then it was gone. Shaking her head, she walked slowly along the spine of the roof.

"Serpents, huh?" Suspicion filled the colonel's voice as he turned Daniel's words from their historical context to a whole new meaning.

"Yes."

"Challenges and…?"

"Gates." Daniel finished for him, staring over at the Stargate.

"Seems Ra took the mythology a bit too literally," Sam called down.

"Yeah."

"Teal'c, you ever heard mention of this Barque?" the colonel asked.

"I have not. Many System Lords bestow grandiose names upon their biggest vessels. It is possible this is the name of Ra's premier Ha'tak."

"Uh, oh." Daniel turned back to look at them, eyebrows bobbing with concern.

"How many Ha'taks does a System Lord have?" Sam asked.

"Oh, there's a joke in there, somewhere," the colonel muttered.

"To my knowledge, Apophis had only two such vessels. However, the resources at Ra's disposal were legendary. It is quite likely he had several at least."

"So, the one we blew up over Abydos might not be this Barque of Heaven."

"If this Trial does terminate within a Ha'tak, I do hope that is the case."

"Sweet. Get some sleep, Daniel. Carter, I'll relieve you in an hour."

Daniel put away his notes and secured the waterproof bags in his pack. He stretched out, head pillowed on his pack, and pulled a space blanket over his shoulders. The colonel followed suit and Sam settled down to guard duty.

Four hours of sleep in shifts, followed by a rationed hot meal, saw them preparing to enter the cold, briny water. With uniforms this time stowed in their packs, the team was shivering in the cool night air. One by one they slipped into the water and under the moon's waning light, headed for the Stargate.

Teal'c swam with Daniel Jackson to the DHD while O'Neill and Major Carter bobbed in position to one side of the vortex's path. With one hand anchoring himself to the DHD's supports, Teal'c boosted Daniel up the side of the pedestal to where he could cling precariously to the decorative sweeping side panel. He dialed the coordinates, meticulously checking the symbols from the stone tablet he had hung from his neck in a macramé of cord.

When the chevrons were glowing, he voiced the password.

"Ashebu!"

Obligingly the Stargate burst to life, the blue light of the vortex reflecting on the lake's surface. Together they hoisted their packs, gear and weapons up into the wormhole. As soon as the last box was gone they began the equally difficult task of hauling themselves out of the water and into the event horizon.

"Teal'c, can you get yourself up and through the 'gate on your own?" O'Neill asked, one hand plunged into the open wormhole.

"I can, O'Neill."

"Great. Give me a boost up."

Teal'c obliged and with several helping hands pushing, O'Neill was up and slithering into the Stargate's cold embrace. Major Carter followed next, then Daniel Jackson propelled by a solid shove from Teal'c. Left alone, Teal'c surged up out of the water and plunged head first into the Stargate.

For a couple of minutes the wormhole remained open, the moonlight shining brightly off its surface. Eventually, the motion sensing capability of the event horizon tripped the power connections and the wormhole collapsed.

The water smoothed out and the Stargate sat alone under the beauty of the moon's light.

GATE FOUR

Cradle of Asar

Their awkward entry into the wormhole ensured an equally undignified exit, although Jack found that entering the vortex headfirst gave him a much stronger impression of actually flying than just walking through it. Such fanciful thoughts ended abruptly, when Carter slid out of the Stargate and collided with him as he was struggling to his feet. She bowled him over like a ninepin and they both crashed over their boxes of equipment, piled in a jumbled heap just beyond the event horizon. Daniel rolled out of the Stargate next, nimbly dodged any collisions and came to his feet with graceful aplomb. He sidestepped just in time to avoid Teal'c who slithered out, head-butted the MRE container and, bringing his knees up, rolled sideways over another box.

"Well, that was fun." Jack, finally on his feet with MP5 gripped firmly, started scanning the surroundings.

Arid, scrubby land stretched away from the Stargate platform, breaking up into ancient, eroded watercourses that cracked the land like the smile lines on his old grandpa's face. The world seemed poised on the cusp of night, the afterglow of a set sun fading rapidly into the horizon to the right of the Stargate. Two moons, one a deep yellow and the other bright white, had already started on their nightly journey.

"Oh, wow. Look."

"Carter? What?"

She was staring up at the beauty of the night sky; darkening velvet studded with thousands — millions — of stars, many burning with a hot blue or golden gleam seldom seen in Earth's skies.

"Whoa, now *that* is something." Jack craned his head up and over, trying to take in the magnificent panorama. "Hey! Well, I'll be… looks like we've got an old friend."

The others turned as he pointed to his discovery. Perched in the sky, just over the rim of the Stargate, sat a very familiar constellation.

"Orion." Daniel smiled in recognition. "Hello, old friend. It's a lot closer and upside down, but it's the same configuration."

"That it is. And there," Jack's finger traced up to a much brighter, blue-white star at the bottom of the saucepan, "is Rigel. Which means my old buddy Beetlejuice is right down… there." He pointed out the dimmer reddish glow of Betelgeuse at the opposite end of the constellation from Rigel.

"I'm not so sure, sir," Carter said quietly. "This planet would have to be in direct alignment with, and relatively close to Earth, for a star formation to appear the same in both skies"

"Well, I'm willing to suspend belief this one time, major."

"Nothing's coming out on the camera." Daniel said. "The Ancient Egyptians knew Orion as the home of Osiris. It was a constellation that bore good omens."

"Perhaps the blessings of Orion will bestow good luck upon our journey," Teal'c mused quietly.

Somewhat comforted to have a — possible — familiar friend above them, they turned back to the Stargate. Daniel scrambled through the ring, finding the moon-clock in the gloom.

"Fifteen hours, twenty minutes till moonset."

Jack completed his second three-sixty survey; nothing stirred within sight, but with the ground so broken up and buried in deep shadows there were any number of hiding places in the dried out creek-beds that snaked past their position.

Need a new metaphor, O'Neill.

A light wind wafted past their wet bodies, ruffling his chest hair and sending them all shivering despite the warmth of the air. Returning to the bottom of the platform steps, Carter and Teal'c completed their own recon and traded a rueful glance at their appearance.

Jack felt oddly proud that they both still looked capable and somewhat lethal despite their lack of clothes. Daniel's lean body made him appear quite the soldier, belying the impression of the affable anthropologist his baggy BDUs created.

"Alright, we're clear," Jack decided. "Let's get some clothes on before we catch pneumonia. We'll secure the gear, bury it near here somewhere. We can't drag it all around with us and I don't like leaving it visible."

It was an order followed gratefully as they rubbed themselves down and slid into dry clothes. A depression in the earth behind the Stargate provided a burial site for the excess equipment, hidden under a tarp liberally covered with dry soil and stones. Their packs, already filled with as many essentials as possible, rested heavily on their shoulders. Jack tried the DHD, not expecting any response but still annoyed when Earth's address refused to lock.

"So. Where do we go from here?"

Teal'c and Daniel were sharing binoculars, staring at a small rise in the landscape, nearly a kilometer away, but easily visible in the double moonlight.

"Jack, I think there's something man-made up there," Daniel announced. "At least it doesn't look natural. Might be worth investigating."

Waving the team on their way, Jack fell in at the rear. Teal'c led them over the broken ground, following dried streambeds, scrambling up and down crumbling banks. Small, gnarled bushes with spiky leaves snagged at their clothing as they pushed past.

Twenty minutes into the trek Jack paused on the bank of a wadi, his gaze following the fantastic shadows thrown up by the jagged landscape. Then, with shocking force, something hit him hard on the back of the knees and he was down, rolling into the creek bed in a cloud of dust. He hadn't even stopped sliding when a figure launched itself at him, landing on his chest in a barrage of snarls and spittle.

Jack brought his weapon up with lightning reflexes, jamming it under the chin of his attacker. *Was this a person?* Hands flailed at his face, long tangled hair whipped at his eyes. He pulled the MP5 back a couple of inches and let fly a good solid crack at the face. It swung away under the force of the blow then back again, features twisted with rage and something much darker, not wholly sane.

A woman?

Her hands closed around his throat and squeezed viciously. Again he thumped the gun stock into her face, producing nothing more than a feral smile. Dimly, through the blood pounding in his ears, he could hear his team shouting but his attention was riveted to the woman's face above him and the eyes that glowed: hotly, hideously white. A jolt of pure fear lanced through him.

No!

Steely fingers pressed on the hinge of his jaw, forcing his mouth open. The woman's mouth was gaping and something moved sickeningly in its recesses. Jack gurgled in panic, bucked and twisted for all he was worth but the woman remained plastered to him like a limpet. The head of that *thing* emerged past her teeth, fangs bared and frill extended. Faster than thought, it shot from her mouth, body covered in its already dying host's blood.

Panic blanked Jack's mind. Eyes squeezed half-shut, his hands still ramming the gun into her throat, he barely saw the large dark hand fly out of nowhere, grab the Goa'uld a scant inch from his clenching mouth, and haul it away.

The woman collapsed on top of him, her dead weight pinning his arms and her dusty hair in his face. The fingers pressed bruisingly into his jaw went limp. Above him the shouts of his team were drowned out by a sickening reptilian squealing. Then the body was gone and he shot to his feet, fear-fuelled adrenaline making it hard to focus on what was happening around him, and still that damnable noise....

"Sir!" Carter's voice finally registered.

"M'okay. Okay...."

Carter was right in front of him, concern written plain on her face, one hand gripping his arm. Daniel was a pace behind her, horror making his eyes huge in the moonlight.

"Jack, you're bleeding."

He frowned at Daniel, not feeling anything amiss.

"Sir." Gentler this time, Carter wiped something under his chin. It came away bloody. "I think the tail got you."

His stomach flipped into knots and it was only by sheer will he didn't dump his last MRE on her boots. Finally the squealing penetrated once more. A few deep breaths brought him back to his senses. His eyes tracked to Teal'c, standing several feet away, one arm extended, fist wrapped like steel around the thrashing body of a Goa'uld.

Heedless of the cuts the scaly body was inflicting on him, Teal'c met Jack's eyes. Slowly, deliberately, he squeezed his fist until the Goa'uld hung lifeless. To make doubly certain of its death, he grasped the head in his other hand and a quick yank separated it from the body. Teal'c tossed the pieces to the ground in disgust. He accepted a medicated wipe from Daniel and fastidiously cleaned away the blue blood.

Jack swallowed against a chill of revulsion that swept up his spine and over his scalp, standing every hair on end—a sense memory, perhaps, of that awful second awakening in Hathor's cryo-chamber. He shook off the images and snapped back into action, bringing his weapon up and joining his team in scanning the area for any further threat.

Nothing stirred across the broken landscape apart from a swooping bird, catching insects on the fly in the night warmth. Jack left Teal'c and Carter on watch and turned to the woman's body. He grimaced as Daniel, already kneeling next to her, straightened her limbs and worn clothing.

Daniel closed her staring eyes and brushed the tangled hair away from her face, revealing a young, once beautiful woman, clearly ravaged by deprivation. Softly he spoke a few words over her, the lilting Abydonian tones of his prayer doing much to sooth Jack's ruffled nerves.

Finished, Daniel stood up and looked at Jack. "Are you okay?"

"Yeah. Where the hell did she come from?"

Daniel shook his head and it was Teal'c who answered. "Judging by the amount of dirt on her clothing, it is possible she concealed herself in one of these gullies, lying in wait for us."

"She must have been trapped here for a long time, to be desperate enough to jump Jack like that," Daniel mused. "Which means she failed the test or couldn't find the address for the next planet."

"I thought Goa'uld could survive four hundred years or so before needing a new host," Jack said, slapping the dirt from his clothing.

"But the Goa'uld would need a new host body to escape this planet. One with nanocytes that would let it get through the 'gate before our time here expires," Daniel replied.

"Swell. Move out and keep sharp." Jack settled his cap back on his head and wrapped his fingers around his MP5.

Denied the time to bury her, Daniel bent and gently covered the woman's face with her tattered shawl, then fell in line behind Carter.

The Goa'uld lay discarded in a torn, congealing heap.

With the two moons lending ample light, the journey was completed in watchful silence. Viewed close-up, the object spotted by Daniel and Teal'c was revealed to be a sphinx statue, considerably smaller than the first one discovered on this mission, but still impressive; it crouched on a small hill, ram-headed face gazing at the now vanished sun.

"This has been here a long time, centuries even. The material might not even be native to this area," murmured Daniel, running his fingers lightly over the faded red stone.

"Ra certainly seemed to like his sphinxes," Sam commented.

"In Ancient Egypt the sphinx was regarded as the living

image of the sun god. I guess it's no wonder Ra took it as his physical representation, or if the carbon dating on the cover stone from our Stargate is anything to go by, Ra probably initiated the use of the sphinx to honor the sun god and the practice continued after the rebellion. In fact, the word sphinx is derived from an Ancient Egyptian formula that transliterates as *Shesepankh*, meaning living image of a god or king."

Daniel paused beneath the finely carved face, camera rolling under its small spotlight, carefully scrutinizing the surface of the statue for any clue to its purpose. Sam shadowed him while Jack and Teal'c stood back, on guard.

"Actually, given the Stargate was found at Giza, it's possible the Great Sphinx is a relic from Ra's time on Earth. Geologic evidence dates its construction somewhere between seven and ten thousand years ago, despite archaeological evidence to the contrary." Daniel snuck a look at his audience and felt quite gratified he still had the attention of two. Jack's focus was elsewhere; he had drifted further out to a higher rise, on recon.

"Is not the head on the Great Sphinx a representation of one of the kings of the Old Kingdom, Daniel Jackson?" Teal'c asked as he prowled around the base of said statue's smaller cousin.

"Khafre, yes it is, Teal'c. But the head is noticeably out of scale with the body and shows none of the water erosion the rest of the structure does. Conceivably it could have been damaged in the uprising that ousted Ra from Earth, and Khafre came along a few thousand years later and had the image of his own head added on." Daniel tried to temper his enthusiasm as he reveled in this rare opportunity to voice his theories.

"Wow," Sam smiled. "That will make quite a paper for your peers to digest one day."

Daniel huffed a laugh. "I think my peers have just heard it, Sam."

"So, any ideas on this?"

"Yeah, a couple. There's a passage of text carved in the

chest here, but it doesn't make much sense. What do you think this — "

"Down!" Jack's cry was nearly drowned out by a high-pitched whine. The soil around them erupted into geysers of dust and stone. A second explosion pelted Daniel and Sam with debris as they scrabbled desperately for cover behind the sphinx.

"O'Neill! Two o'clock from your position," Teal'c's voice rang out, underscored by a withering stream of fire from his staff weapon. Daniel glimpsed several figures dodging through the gullies back toward the Stargate.

Jack bounded down from the knoll where he was nicely exposed and dropped to one knee, firing burst after burst at their attackers. "How many?"

"Three definite contacts, there may be more," Teal'c called back.

Another round of fire drove the attackers into hiding. The resulting pause gave a brief opportunity to scope the terrain. Sam spat out a mouthful of grit, her weapon aiming in an arc over Daniel's head as he searched frantically in the loose earth for the precious camera, blown from his hand during the first attack. She turned, staring past the hindquarters of the sphinx and squeezed off a few rounds as movement caught her eye.

"Got it!" Daniel grabbed the camera, thankfully still working. He switched it off and shoved it into a pocket.

"Sir, we've got possibly two contacts in the rear."

Jack switched his weapon's selector to single rounds and sent two shots down-slope at a head that rapidly vanished into cover. Daniel scrambled up behind Jack and Teal'c, pistol drawn.

"Damn it, we're sitting ducks up here. Daniel, did you get anything off that statue?"

"The only inscriptions on it were four lines of text, and some of them have been damaged. I'm hoping what's left will indicate where to find the 'gate address. I just have to piece it all together."

"Do we need to stay here?"

"No, I've got it all on disc, but the address could be concealed here. We may have to come back."

"Okay. We're too exposed up here. There's scrub cover in that gully; two hundred meters down, fifty left," Jack directed, waving his binoculars at a small patch of growth in one of the shallow creek-beds below.

"Got it, sir," Sam called softly, covering their six.

"I see it," Daniel echoed.

"Teal'c, you've got the best range. Lay down some covering fire, then we'll bring you in. Daniel, behind me, then Carter. *Go.*"

Teal'c rose up and unleashed a rain of staff-fire at the figures below who were beginning to advance once more. Sam sent two rounds out over the hostile position in the rear and then they were up and running, bodies bent low as possible, past Teal'c and down the hill.

They skidded and dodged, following Jack's mad dash to safety. It seemed like the longest distance they had ever run, but suddenly they were there, sliding feet first down an embankment and under the thorny bushes. Sam scrambled around and lay flat in the dirt, mirroring Jack's position a meter away, head barely above ground level. Daniel skidded past them and thumped into the earth, covering the opposite direction.

"Ready, sir," Sam panted.

Jack thumbed his radio. "Teal'c. Go on three."

Upslope, Teal'c acknowledged by unleashing another storm of fire.

"...three!"

Jack and Sam rose and sprayed the area with bullets as Teal'c turned and sprinted down to them. Moments later, he was with them in a settling cloud of dust.

"I believe there are five enemy, O'Neill: three in the gullies between ourselves and the Stargate and two coming in from the right behind the sphinx. They are using Goa'uld weaponry."

"Jaffa?" Jack searched intently through the dim light for any sign of movement.

Teal'c considered for a moment. "I do not believe so. I saw no armor and their pattern of attack was not one a squad of Jaffa would employ."

"You think maybe they're Goa'uld, stranded here by the Trial?" Sam asked.

"I do, Major Carter, which means they will be particularly desperate to overcome us before our time here expires."

"To take us as hosts," Daniel said flatly.

"Indeed. We must be vigilant." Teal'c unholstered his zat and handed it to Daniel who accepted it with a nod, tucking the Beretta back in its holster.

"What I want to know is why so many got stuck on this one planet," Jack said. "I'm really hoping it's not because the 'gate won't dial out at all."

"Maybe they came through in a group and just missed the deadline." Sam shifted a little to clear her field of view.

"Or they couldn't find the address," Daniel offered, the text from the sphinx lurking tantalizingly in his mind.

"Well, they're between us and the 'gate, and our ammo is limited." Jack peered through his binoculars. "There's a stand of trees about a klick north of here. We make it there, then try to circle east; come up on the Stargate from the south. The more we keep moving, the harder it will be for them. If we get split up, RV point will be the gully with the dead Goa'uld. Daniel, can you work on the translation on the run?"

"Yes," Daniel replied wryly, making a mental note to add that skill to his CV.

"Okay. Carter, take point."

"Sir."

Sam slid down the embankment, then turned and crawled through the shrubs up the opposite bank to settle next to Daniel. Ahead and slightly to the left, they could see the dark stand of trees, spindly and sparsely foliaged but offering better cover than they presently had. The problem would be getting across nearly a kilometer of open, broken ground. Bright though the two moons were their light left deep shadows, offering cover but making the terrain particularly treacherous.

She exchanged a nod with Daniel and led the way; keeping as low as possible. One hundred meters out, she found the first of a series of dry creek-beds, this time heading north-east. By following them as far as possible, then ducking up, over and down into the next, she led the team across the open ground until safety was only two dozen meters away.

But, Daniel realized, safety was an illusory thing at best and as they headed into that final run, a nerve-jangling shriek filled the air, scant precursor to some kind of sonic blast that hit the ground, sending dirt and rocks flying everywhere. He dodged and ran full tilt after Sam, stumbling in the uncertain light while Jack and Teal'c sprayed return fire over their shoulders, more for effect than accuracy.

"*Incoming.* Go, go, go!" Jack's bellow was lost under the shriek of another blast. He cut left into the cloud of debris, Teal'c a pace behind.

Sam gained the tree line and plunged through, zigzagging a path around crooked branches, never slowing until two large bushes came into view. She slid feet first under one; Daniel followed suit into the other. Together they aimed past Jack and Teal'c, and delivered a barrage of covering fire until the two had angled to the right and slipped into concealment a short distance away.

Noise and gun smoke eventually cleared, revealing nothing but settling dust. Daniel stifled a cough. Sweat trickled down his temple, carving a sticky trail through the grime on his face. Movement near the tree line revealed their hunters, advancing stealthily toward them.

Sam opened the radio link and breathed, "Two contacts, one o'clock, my position."

She counted to five then let rip a burst of rounds, tearing leaves and limbs from the trees. A heartbeat later, Daniel triggered the zat, spitting blue fire in a steady stream, then they were up and off, crouching, running deeper into the forest, fire from Jack and Teal'c covering their retreat.

On it went, in an ever wearying pattern—cover, fire, run, cover, fire, retreat, retreat—through sharp-leaved scrub that caught and tore at clothing and skin, stumbling in the shadows over uneven ground littered with rocks and dead branches. The moons arced higher in their journey but the heat of the past day barely dissipated: a stifling warmth that sucked the moisture from their mouths and left a salty coating of dried sweat and dust on their skin.

Three and a half hours of this. Sam shook her head, eyes constantly searching for hostiles.

The team took cover in a depression surrounded by bushes, each facing a different direction, harsh breathing the only sound in the still air. They had taken no fire for the past forty-five minutes and had been moving steadily north-northeast. The trees were thinning out now, the forest reduced to disconnected clumps of vegetation. Time to change direction, before they were driven too far away from the Stargate. At least their kit was giving them ample camouflage this time, the desert camo BDUs blending in nicely with the terrain and at times even making it difficult to see each other.

"Sit-rep," the colonel said quietly.

"No more than five hostiles, sir."

"I am unfamiliar with the explosive weapon they carry, but it appears they possess only two of them. The others are armed with zats and at least one ribbon device." Teal'c bore grazes along one bare arm from being thrown off his feet by one such concussive blast. "O'Neill," he twisted around, indicating a sparsely vegetated area to the east. "If we take this direction, we will be able to angle around past the Stargate and come up in the rear from the south."

"Yeah," Colonel O'Neill nodded. "Whichever way we go I'm thinking they're going to hit us hard at the 'gate." He looked over each of them. "How's everyone doing?"

"I am fine." Teal'c did look fine, too; dusty and sweaty, but raring to go.

"I'm good sir," Sam said, attention not wavering from her watch over the terrain, but she could feel the weariness in her body. They were all starting to run a bit ragged after more than three days on the go—snatched sleep and infrequent meals were sapping their reserves.

Dragging his gaze away from the inscription he'd copied, Daniel glanced sideways and shrugged. "Tired. Hungry. Really need to pee."

Sam grimaced in empathy. They needed to shake the Goa'uld properly, get well ahead, retrieve their supplies, find the clues and get the hell out of here. "How are you doing with the translation?"

"I've translated the symbols and aligned them into sentences. It looks like it's a riddle."

"Goa'uld write riddles?"

"Apparently." Daniel fished out a packet of coffee candy and handed them out; even Teal'c took one.

Sam drew a deep breath and rose as the colonel took point, leading his team down a dry gulch that angled away from the forest. For nearly another hour they continued on through the thinning scrub, stopping only for water, powerbars and carefully guarded personal breaks. The moons were reaching their zenith, still shining brightly despite a few clouds gathering in the sky. There was little movement to be seen apart from a few small animals darting through the undergrowth after insects, and one big fat ground bird that had nearly been shot, zatted and roasted with a staff blast before reflexes prevailed and it had waddled off on its own business.

Of their pursuers there was no sighting, a fact that served only to make everyone more guarded. Changing direction once again, their southerly path led the team past clumps of cactus-like vegetation—some towering meters high and graced with vicious-looking thorns.

Squinting in the uncertain light, Sam found the memory of the dead host's body returning to her, bringing with it un-needed thoughts of the terrors the woman must have suffered while possessed by the parasite. Questions about Jolinar—unasked and unwanted—rose from Sam's subconscious, but she shoved them away, back in the box where they belonged. She glanced at Daniel, wondering if the encounter with the Goa'uld had revived memories of his wife, but his face was unreadable in the shadows. She looked away, her eyes scouring the landscape for any threat, and tried to ignore the tiredness in her legs and the weight of the pack pulling at the muscles in her back.

An odd buzz in the air gave only a second's warning, then Daniel stiffened as something wrapped around his legs with lightning speed. His feet were jerked out from under him, and with a choked cry, he was hauled away over the stony ground.

GATE FOUR Cont'd

"Nice Shootin' Tex"

"Daniel!" He barely heard Sam's shout, overlaid by a volley from Teal'c's staff weapon, as he was yanked away at frightening speed. He scrabbled desperately at the ground, hands and nails tearing in futile attempts to slow his pace. Whatever was wound around his legs bit sharply into his skin through the BDUs. His pack and vest were torn from his body, his boonie dragging from his neck like a choking anchor.

One of the thorny cacti appeared in his bouncing vision. He wrapped his arms over his face and threw his weight to one side, barely missing the deadly spikes, and yet his flight never slowed as his body slalomed over the ground, his breath battered out of his lungs.

And then, just as suddenly as it began, it was over. He slid to a halt. The agonizing pull on his legs faded, but still they were bound and hurting. Dazed and choking on a mouth filled with dirt, Daniel was barely aware of the figure that loomed over him until he focused on crazed, glowing eyes staring out of an emaciated face that descended rapidly toward him.

"Nghaah!" Panicked, Daniel flung his arms over his head once more and desperately tried to roll away from the Goa'uld, but his bound and battered body could do little more than curl in a defensive clench.

A single, echoing shot rang out from somewhere behind him. The Goa'uld seemed to pause above him, a red splodge of blood welling in the center of its host's forehead. The mouth opened—then vanished entirely in a flash of fire from Teal'c's staff. An MP5 roared again, this time on full auto-fire, riddling the faceless corpse with bullets until it finally collapsed into a grotesque heap.

Feet skidded in the dirt next to Daniel's head and a hand clamped onto his elbow.

"No!" Daniel jerked and wrenched himself away.

"Daniel—Daniel, it's me. You're okay, we got him." Jack's face swam in Daniel's vision. Blinking to clear his dust-filled eyes he rubbed his face, and found to his surprise that his glasses were still in place. He pulled them off, squinted at the body and grimaced. Teal'c's blast had obliterated the head Jack had drilled with his own single shot.

"You're okay, Daniel. The guy's Swiss cheese." Jack looked briefly at the body. "Grilled Swiss cheese, actually. You're okay, buddy."

"That's a matter of opinion," Daniel grunted. He sat up with Jack's help, scratched hands picking ineffectively at the thin metal cord wrapped three times around his legs, from upper thigh to calf. It was tautly embedded in his BDUs and cutting into his skin through the tough material.

"Get this off me."

Jack traced the end of the cord to a six-point barb, buried in the side pocket of Daniel's right pant leg. The razor points on the barb had shredded through the tape recorder in the pocket, but even that had not been enough to completely stop it from cutting into his skin.

"Damn." Jack winced. He pulled out his battered multi tool and tried to angle in properly to cut the head from the cable, but the line was too tight and Daniel was having trouble holding still.

"Will you quit wriggling?"

"Jack, get it off." Daniel kept pulling at the line, hating the feeling of being bound even more than the sharp pain.

"I will if you'll quit wriggling. Why's this thing so tight?"

Finally, the wire cutter slipped around the cord and he sliced through it. The second it was freed, the end shot out of Jack's hand, whipped away from Daniel's legs so fast the momentum spun him face down into the dirt, and retracted out of sight with a hum like a thousand angry bees.

"Gahh!" Daniel half-shouted, half-sobbed, as the metal scored a bloody trail around his legs. He buried his face in his clenched fists and muttered, "Jack, please don't help anymore."

"Sorry, Daniel."

"The area is secure, O'Neill." Teal'c towered over them. "However, we should not remain here. The sound of our weapons will draw the Goa'uld tracking us. Are you alright, Daniel Jackson?"

"No." Daniel coughed out. "Feels like my legs have been filleted." Gingerly, he rolled over, his boonie spilling its load of dirt down his neck. "What the hell was that thing?"

"The way it retracted, I'd say some kind of spring-loaded crossbow." Sam knelt next to him, first aid kit in one hand. She surveyed the thin lines of blood seeping through Daniel's pants. "It might be easier to do this if you stand up, Daniel."

"Sure. No problem."

Daniel lay sprawled in the dirt looking up at them, trying to convince his muscles to get with the program.

"Um...."

Jack got to his feet, left hand clenched tight over a bloody cut from the retracting line and together with Teal'c, slowly pulled Daniel upright.

"Oh." A dozen different aches made themselves known all down his back, arms and legs, while blood pounded in his ears in its rush to leave his thumping head. Dizzy, Daniel leaned into Teal'c's broad shoulders and closed his eyes.

A misplaced breeze had his eyes open a minute later, finding to his chagrin that Sam had his pants down around his knees and in the covered light of her flashlight was gently pulling the material away from the bloody welts circling his legs.

"Ouch. Well, it's messy, but I don't think it's cut too deep into the muscle, Daniel." She patted the bloody trail with sterile wipes. "The bleeding has slowed or stopped already in a lot of places. The worst is a long cut across the back of your left thigh. We'll have to keep an eye on that." She slathered on antibiotic cream and covered it with bandages. The rest she smeared liberally with the cream and sealed with spray-on bandage. "That's the best I can do at the moment, Daniel. We should get moving soon, before you stiffen up."

"Thanks, Sam." Carefully, Daniel straightened up from Teal'c's support and retrieved his pants from her helping hands. His back felt like it had taken a pounding from a lunatic masseur. Sam presented two painkillers and he swallowed them gratefully.

"Y'know, Daniel, it's a good thing you never do this up," Jack commented as he walked back to them, Daniel's retrieved vest and pack in hand. "You might have broken your back being dragged with this still on."

Daniel grimaced at Jack and took the heavy pack from him.

"Carter, you got any more of that cream?"

"Yes, sir." She swiftly cleaned and dressed the cut on Jack's hand.

"Okay. Let's move out. Stay sharp." Jack took the lead and picked up their former heading. Teal'c took possession of Daniel's pack and ushered him and Sam ahead. With a grateful nod, Daniel pulled on his vest and limped after Sam.

They passed a short metal brace anchored in the ground behind a group of bushes, the severed cable dangling from the winch that had so rapidly dragged Daniel away. Giving it no more than a cursory look, the team pressed on through the sparse vegetation, keeping well clear of the lethal-looking cacti. Their formation was tighter now and they moved on, wary and silent.

Daniel doggedly pushed on, ignoring the ache of his back and legs as Jack kept them going at a steady clip for another hour, until calling a rest-break in the concealment of a shallow wash. Jack took guard duty himself while Sam broke out their first meal since leaving the relative safety of water-world. Teal'c helped Daniel ease himself to the ground to sit gingerly on his wadded-up jacket. His legs were shaking, the lacerated skin and muscles burning an angry complaint at the constant exertion. His back prickled and ached, and he was not surprised when Teal'c knelt in concern at his side.

"Daniel Jackson, I believe your back has sustained some injury. If you will permit me, I will attempt to assess the damage."

Daniel managed a tired half-smile in acknowledgment. "Feels like I was attacked by a cheese grater." He pulled his t-shirt out from under his belt and sagged forward a little as Teal'c gently drew the shirt up.

"How does it look?" he asked, head bowed, eyes three-quarters shut under the brim of his boonie.

"Most painful," Teal'c replied. "You have sustained a number of bruises and grazes. I believe Doctor Fraiser's medicine would be beneficial."

Sam crouched next to them and surveyed the damage. She grimaced and dug out a tube of analgesic cream from her pack, handed it over and returned to the meals—gulping her own quickly so she could relieve Jack.

Daniel sat, half lulled to sleep as Teal'c's gentle warm hands massaged the cream into his abused back. When he finished, Teal'c carefully pulled Daniel's t-shirt down and left the tube by his side to tend the rest of the damage in privacy.

"Mmmh, thanks Teal'c." He picked up the MRE Sam had left him and, eating slowly, his mind began to click into gear once more, the problem of the riddle on the sphinx demanding to be solved. Almost imperceptibly at first, a light rain began to drift down around them.

"Um, guys…?"

"Yes, Daniel?"

"It's raining."

"Get out."

Daniel stared at Jack through narrowed eyes. "We're sitting in a creek bed."

"Yes, we are. A dry creek bed."

"Meaning, where there's a creek bed there is at, at least

occasionally, water," Sam filled in.

"Judging by the number and depth of dry watercourses here, there may be some substantial flooding occurring on a regular basis," Teal'c added.

"Could have happened centuries ago, T."

"Or weeks ago," Daniel needled. "Flash-flooding can happen even when it's rained a hundred kilometers away."

"Here's me without my rod," Jack conceded. He made a face at Daniel, warning duly noted.

Patchy clouds scudding quickly over the two moons dropped the landscape into a dull gloom, broken by frequent bursts of light whenever the moons were revealed. Daniel nodded to Jack and returned to the riddle.

"Okay, so the lines on the sphinx read;
'By this shall I consume,
By this shall I enter,
By this shall emptiness be filled,
By this will life be given'.
I'm thinking they all refer to the mouth, so the clues should be hidden somewhere in the vicinity of the mouth of the sphinx?" Daniel looked up at Jack and Teal'c, hoping his guesswork was not so wild.

Jack pulled a rueful shrug and got to his feet. "Sounds plausible to me, Daniel, and if that doesn't work, maybe a little C4 will shake things loose."

"Oh, right. Good idea." Daniel grimaced, not missing the slight smile on Teal'c's face as he also rose.

Despite the rain, the heat had not lessened and it created an unpleasant sauna effect. The hot, humid air made breathing more difficult and steamed his glasses up so much Daniel finally pulled them off and stowed them in his jacket pocket. He dragged out a spare t-shirt to provide his back with a little extra protection, before donning vest and pack once more. The weight rested sorely on the bruises, but he did his best to ignore the pain and fell into place as the team headed out again.

Little more than half an hour later, they were huddled behind the last of the covering vegetation. Before them stretched a vast, dried mud-flat, possibly a remnant of a lakebed, its surface deeply cracked as the moisture had evaporated. In the distance was the Stargate, sitting on its pedestal; suspiciously alone. But it was where they needed to be and a sprint across open ground was the only way to get there. The patchy light would have to be cover enough.

Fifteen minutes Jack held them crouched there, relentlessly scanning the terrain between their final hiding place and the Stargate. Nothing moved through the light drifts of rain. The Goa'uld, if they were lying in wait for them, were well hidden and seemingly patient now.

Finally, Teal'c led the way out onto the cracked earth, keeping as low as possible, his camouflage BDUs blending him into the barren, gray terrain. The parched ground quickly crumbled under their feet. What had looked to be hard, baked clay was revealed to be only a thin crust that shattered under every step. The further they progressed, the softer the underlying soil became. Mixed with the rain and compounded by their weight, it soon turned to a viscous, cloying mud that stuck thickly to their boots, making each step a battle against suction that threatened to mire them forever.

"Son of a bitch!"

Jack glanced back, weighing the risks of retracing their path and trying a different route. It wasn't worth it—they were almost to the halfway point; to go back and maybe spend hours finding a way around could cost them their chance to get off this wretched planet.

"Keep going," he panted, lurching sideways as his intended step was thwarted by the mud's grip. He pulled his leg out with an effort. This little predicament was going to cost them a lot of energy, to say nothing of leaving them exposed and unable to move quickly.

Time dragged by with irritating slowness, the only sounds

around them the constant squelch and suck of mud and grunts of effort from the four. Jack found old memories surfacing too. "Reminds me of a time in Germany."

"You engaged in battle in such conditions as these, O'Neill?" Teal'c leant over and gave Daniel a supporting shove forward.

"Of a kind." Jack's next step threatened to remove his boot completely. He backed up and tried a different angle. "Kawalsky, Feretti and I were coming back to base after a three-day leave — a little worse for wear. It was dark, we got lost, ended up in some farmer's turnip field."

He shifted his grip on his weapon and reached back to grab Carter's arm, hauling her through the mud. Behind them, Daniel's silence indicated he was spending all his energy on just placing one foot in front of the other.

"It was raining, real cats and dogs stuff. The field was freshly ploughed. We got so turned around we spent what seemed like hours wandering in circles, falling down. We were mud from head to foot." Jack alternated his gaze between searching for their elusive enemy and making sure his team kept close to him.

Teal'c kept a hold on Daniel's arm, alternately steadying and supporting him. Daniel's face was set, grim and stubborn.

"Eventually, the farmer's daughter came out to see what all the racket was, and there's Feretti sitting in the gloop, singing at the top of his voice. Nice lady. Hosed us down, dried us out and drove us to the base. Got us there five minutes before our leave expired." Jack smiled at the memory of the girl's enthusiastic farewell kisses.

They were edging nearer and nearer to the end of the mud-pan and gradually the footing became a little firmer. Everyone was heavily coated with muck from knees to feet, weighing them down with every step.

Their luck held; there was no sign of their pursuers as the four finally stepped onto firm soil, three hundred meters away from the Stargate. They were all breathing and sweating hard, and Daniel looked to be staying on his feet by will-power alone.

"We must be even more cautious now, O'Neill." Teal'c scraped caked mud off the blunt end of his staff weapon. "The Goa'uld will not let us leave this place easily." He passed his canteen to Carter who swallowed gratefully.

"That's what I'm afraid of." Jack offered some water to Daniel. "Teal'c, you and Carter head up to the sphinx, see if Daniel's theory about the riddle pans out."

"Jack, I should go…." Daniel straightened slowly from the bent-over position he had slumped into.

"Teal'c can read the lingo and I don't want you walking any further than you have to."

"Well, guys, look for a symbol depicting a mouth. It'll probably be an elongated oval, kind of like a…." His hands gestured ineffectively.

"Like a depiction of a mouth, Daniel Jackson?" Teal'c quirked an eyebrow at him.

"Yeah…."

Jack grinned and turned to the other two. "We'll get the gear standing by and be ready to cover you. If you do find the address and stuff, try not to look like you've found it, okay?"

"No jumping up and down, yelling Eureka. Got it, sir," Carter said, chiseling mud off her boots with her knife.

"Get out of here." Jack waved them away.

With the last box piled at the side of the Stargate, Daniel hunkered down with Jack in the cover of the steps, keeping an eye on Sam and Teal'c's now-tiny figures, toiling toward the sphinx in the distance. The rain had eased and drifted away. The air was a little cooler now, but they were both sweaty and sticky with dust and mud. Daniel found his gaze straying to the spot where the body of the dead woman lay, a flutter of cloth her only marker. Face impassive, he turned his head, searching for the Goa'uld still tracking them, yet time and again he found himself drawn back to the bleak patch of earth where she had died.

Next to him, Jack shifted restlessly. Daniel glanced over, saw Jack's eyebrows rise in silent query. Daniel looked away, trying to marshal the emotions churning inside him. After slow minutes of silence, he finally gave them voice. "That could be Sha're, one day."

"Yeah," Jack acknowledged quietly.

No false platitudes, for which Daniel felt deeply grateful. Jack stayed quiet, letting Daniel feel his way through the tangled thoughts of his wife.

"She's getting further and further away from me. The harder I search, the less trace of her I find. I thought when Apophis was taken by Sokar—whether he's alive or not—we would be able to track Amonet more easily, but she and Klorel seem to have vanished. We ask for information about them on every planet we visit, so do the other teams, but...." He sighed and squinted into the shadows. "It's very limited. There are so many planets where they could be. I won't find her this way. I need to be nearer, move among the Goa'uld, infiltrate their societies, get closer to the System Lords somehow."

Jack kept his attention fixed on the landscape around them, but Daniel's words had him stirring uneasily. "I'll have a word with Hammond when we get back, see if we can't get the Tok'ra to sniff around some of the Goa'uld lairs."

A fleeting smile graced Daniel's face. "I think the Tok'ra have enough to cope with without looking for two lost Abydonians, but I'm sure Jacob would try."

"But nothing. The Tok'ra have agreed to help us, so help they will." Jack watched through the binoculars as Teal'c and Sam disappeared behind the sphinx.

"Jack, it's going to take more than a few people keeping an eye out for them. At that pace it could take decades before we stumble upon the right planet or the right contact. I feel—I need—to be doing more."

"You want to leave the team?" Jack asked bluntly.

"No. Yes. No. I don't know." Daniel rubbed his leg in frustration. "Maybe a leave of absence. I'm not sure."

"And do what? Go out there on your own, no backup, no support, no friendly faces?"

"Well, maybe I wouldn't have to. I could raise a bounty; get someone like Aris Boch to do the looking."

"I get the impression Boch doesn't come cheap, Daniel."

Daniel pulled a face and nodded. "It's worth a try, Jack."

"Hey, I'm not knocking the idea. Extend your reach, use all resources possible. But if that idea doesn't pan out, then what?"

Daniel was silent for a long time. There were other ideas lurking in his mind, plans that were drastic, dangerous, frightening even. Plans that Jack certainly would not approve of.

"I don't know, Jack. I'll think of something," he finally hedged. "I miss them." The whispered words slipped out unintentionally, were caught and born away by the breeze.

Jack reached out, briefly touching the back of Daniel's head. In silent, watchful companionship they waited for the other half of their team to return.

Teal'c stood guard as Major Carter crouched by the sphinx's hindquarters, carefully making her way around the statue, searching every inch of the carved stone for any sign of a symbol depicting a mouth as Daniel had described. After completing two circuits, she shook her head in frustration.

"I don't get it, Teal'c. There's nothing here. I hate to say it, but I think Daniel's got this one wrong."

He arched an eyebrow at her in surprise. "Perhaps a deliberate obfuscation has occurred."

She sighed. "Of course they'd try to conceal it. The Goa'uld trapped here wouldn't want anyone else getting out ahead of them. So, if you were a Goa'uld where would you put the keys to the 'gate?"

Teal'c considered for a moment. "Near the heart of that which guards my secrets."

Major Carter moved around to the front of the sphinx, and quickly felt all over the statue's chest, searching for any patch of the stone that looked to have been disturbed. "Nope. Not there."

Teal'c studied the proud face of the sphinx. "Was there not a secret passage discovered on the back of the head of the Great Sphinx of Egypt, Major Carter?"

"Uh, wrong person to ask, Teal'c. But, it's worth a look."

Standing, she reached up to feel around the statue's head, down its nape, between the shoulder blades. "Here, there's a patch of stone rougher than the rest."

She traced the edge of the patch, and they could just make out a faint remnant of the mouth symbol that someone had painstakingly scratched away. A firm push caused the stone to retract and in its place a small panel of glasslike substance was revealed. Major Carter tapped the panel with the butt of her knife. "Now what?"

"Perhaps a trigger is required to activate this device."

"The riddle?"

"It is likely." Teal'c traded places with the major and leaned over the statue. Clearly, he recited the passages of the riddle in the lilting Goa'uld dialect. There was a brief pause, then the panel glowed with a string of symbols.

"Oh, that's just creepy." She quickly copied the symbols on the panel, which lay in the exact place where, on a human, a symbiote would enter the body of its host.

"Indeed," Teal'c echoed her sentiment.

"We've got a 'gate address. I'm presuming the other symbols are the password?" She held her notebook out for Teal'c's inspection.

"*Sabes*—'glowing'. It would seem so, Major Carter."

Teal'c thumbed his radio and swiftly shared both address and password with O'Neill. Major Carter tucked the notebook into her vest and primed her weapon. Trading a glance with Teal'c, she indicated her readiness.

"I think we're done here."

Alert and tense, they started back to the Stargate at a fast walk, a shared sense of unease growing in both of them until they were loping across the broken ground in a steady jog. Constant scouting of every gully and wash they crossed revealed no sign of the stranded Goa'uld, and Teal'c found himself more and more on edge. Clouds still sailed across the sky, throwing shadows into weird shapes; soon every bush was the illusion of someone lying in wait. Attack was imminent; he could feel it as sure as the blood pumping through his veins. Major Carter appeared to feel it too, anticipation speaking in her every movement.

When the attack finally came, he faced it with a surge of relief. That strange screaming weapon lanced at them from the right, missing by scant inches. In a wordless, synchronized maneuver, they threw themselves into the slight cover of a clump of rocks, return fire spitting from their weapons and drowning out a warning bellow from O'Neill over the radio. Movement to the rear brought Teal'c spinning around, his staff-blasts sideswiping then cutting down the figure racing toward them.

Major Carter kept firing at the Goa'uld wielding the odd weapon, her lip curled in frustration as he came closer and closer, bullets spanging off what they now saw was a personal shield. She broke off, conservation of ammunition more important than a show of force.

The Goa'uld apparently saw this as an admission of defeat and leaped up onto a boulder to stare down at them, his haughty expression not diminished by the rags he wore.

"Bow down to your God, slave and accept the gift of eternal life that is our blessing!" he yelled in a cracking falsetto.

"Give me strength." Major Carter slipped a grenade from her vest, primed it and muttered softly, "Fire in the hole."

Teal'c tensed, body poised to move.

She flung the grenade up and over, the action a blur against a sudden shaft of moonlight, and flattened down as the explosion showered them with dirt and rocks. Teal'c popped up, knife arcing through the air to strike the Goa'uld who, knocked off his perch by the blast, was still rolling on the ground. The knife impaled the ribbon device on his hand and the shield dropped. Teal'c finished him off with an efficient burst of fire.

Then they were up and running. Major Carter paused only to retrieve the knife and they headed flat-out for the Stargate. Coming closer they could see Daniel Jackson and O'Neill crouched by the DHD, weapons drawn to cover their approach. And someone else, advancing stealthily in the shadows of the broken ground.

"O'Neill, seven o'clock!" was all Teal'c could shout before the Goa'uld leapt out of cover and onto the colonel.

Jack went down under the wild force of the attack, his head impacting the DHD pedestal with stunning force. Daniel let out an inarticulate yell and lunged at the Goa'uld. They grappled over Jack's body. Punching, grasping for any kind of leverage, Daniel dragged the man off Jack. Still too close to his prone friend to risk firing, he clubbed the Goa'uld's head with his zat—to little effect. An elbow in the chest threw Daniel backward to land painfully in the dust, but immediately he scrambled back up to snatch at the Goa'uld's tattered robes, desperately pulling him away from Jack.

Jack collected himself with a disoriented shake of his head and saw the Goa'uld looming up before him. Instinct took over. He pulled his heels up and solidly booted the man in the gut, sending him flying back to land in a tangle on top of Daniel. Jack threw himself after the Goa'uld, grabbed one leg and hauled him off his friend, who squirmed and rolled away in the opposite direction, hands scrabbling in the dust for his zat.

It was like trying to land a marlin with his bare hands. The Goa'uld heaved and kicked in Jack's grasp, free leg and arms flailing wildly as Jack tried to bring his weapon to bear without letting go. In his peripheral vision he saw Daniel come to his knees, zat primed and aimed but unwilling to fire while Jack was attached to the Goa'uld.

"On three," Jack croaked, yanking hard on the Goa'uld and laying him flat again.

"One," Daniel panted. "Two."

There was an inhuman shriek from the Goa'uld, mingled with another — human — cry of agony as a fountain of blood and torn tissue erupted from the host's neck. The parasite propelled itself through the air in a macabre glitter of death, straight toward Daniel's shocked face. With reflexes that made Jack proud, Daniel fired the zat and threw himself to one side, the weapon spitting shot after shot of blue light. Jack had to dive for cover himself under zat fire arcing in sheets through the air as Daniel wildly scuttled away.

An angry squeal signaled a hit. The Goa'uld thumped to the ground right next to Daniel's leg. He rolled further back, then crawled painfully to his knees, aimed the zat and obliterated the creature from existence.

Panting for breath, Daniel looked at Jack, somewhat astonished they were both unharmed.

"Nice shootin', Tex." Jack clambered to his feet, stepped over the now-dead host and offered a hand to haul Daniel to his feet, feeling his own reaction mirrored by the tremors in Daniel's hand.

"O'Neill!" Teal'c's hail over the radio was echoed by his real voice, he and Carter only two hundred meters away now.

"We're good, T. Let's get the hell off this rock. Carter, dial us up." While she moved to the DHD, Jack started a slow three-sixty, wearily ready for the next attack.

The Stargate surged to life as the team came together. With little breath left for conversation, everyone grabbed the supply boxes and began heaving them through the wormhole until, without warning, the box holding their sleeping bags and tents exploded, sending them ducking to the ground under a cloud of feathers.

Carter unleashed a round of bullets as Jack heaved the box he was still holding through the Stargate. *"Daniel, go!"*

A slurp in the event horizon told him Daniel was safely through. Cautiously, they backed up to the Stargate. Teal'c sent several blasts in the direction of a suspect shadow as Carter bent to get a better grip on the final box, only to have it torn from her hands by a shot from that shrieking weapon. The lid sprang open and scattered the contents down the steps of the platform.

"Dammit, no!" She made an abortive move after the precious comm unit as it rolled, smoking and charred, into the dirt.

"Carter, forget it!" Jack clamped a hand on her arm and shoved her into the wormhole.

The Goa'uld showed herself, breaking from cover and desperately running toward them, and Teal'c took her down with a well-placed staff-shot. Still anticipating attack, he and Jack stepped backward into the wormhole and let the Stargate whisk them away to safety.

Before the ripples of their passage had settled on the surface of the event horizon, a dusty, slight figure emerged from concealment at the platform's base and slipped silently into the wormhole.

The Stargate snapped off, leaving a cloud of dust and gun smoke to drift slowly away.

GATE FIVE

Obscurer of the Way

Warm, loamy scents wrapped around Daniel's senses as he stepped out of the wormhole. Dizzyingly rich smells from a hundred different exotic flowers went right up his nose. He sneezed magnificently and nudged the boxes to one side out of the path of the next traveler. Zat still firmly in hand, he cast around for signs of any threat, but saw only luscious jungle crowded around the Stargate platform.

Sam stormed out of the Stargate, finger still on the trigger of her MP5, anger and frustration clear on her face. She stopped next to Daniel and yanked the cap off her head, slapping it against her leg and releasing a cloud of dust.

"Sam?"

"We lost our toolbox, Daniel. The comm unit...." She broke off as Teal'c and Jack emerged from the Stargate.

"Everyone alright?" Jack asked. He slowed but kept walking, moving down the eight steps and onto the thick grass surrounding the Stargate. Teal'c followed him, already looking intently at their new situation.

"Yes, sir." Sam picked up the MRE box and moved to the steps.

"Yeah, I—oh. Hello...." Daniel looked back at the Stargate as the wormhole disengaged, surprised beyond words to see a young man emerge seconds before it vanished. Daniel took two steps backwards, turned and jumped off the side of the platform, staggering as his injured legs gave under him.

The man made no move toward them and continued to stand next to the Stargate. Heedless of the four weapons pointing at him, he gazed around, drinking in the sight of this new planet with obvious delight.

Quietly, the team spread out, weapons trained on the intruder. Teal'c planted himself in front of Daniel, knowing his injured legs would hamper a speedy retreat.

"He's a Goa'uld, sir," muttered Sam.

Jack's response was to bring his gun up and steady the sight squarely on the man's forehead. Finally seeming to notice their presence, the man looked down at them, his young face still smiling. His clothes were mismatched and ragged, hanging loosely over his bony frame.

"He doesn't seem threatening," Daniel said, shuffling a couple of steps to see around Teal'c. Teal'c merely moved in front of him again and adjusted his aim.

"One hundred and forty seven years We have been trapped on that benighted world," the Goa'uld whispered in awe. "We are free… *free*." He beamed at SG-1, willing them to share his happiness.

Jack gently brushed his finger against the MP5's trigger. "We won't let you take one of us as a host, so I suggest you walk away from here right now."

The Goa'uld turned, his limp red hair catching in the breeze, and looked at Jack. "There is no need. We are well in Our host. The curse was a lie. A lie." He looked down at his body, patting it appreciatively.

"We shall return home. Yes. Yes, to Our own world where…." He broke off his monologue with a sudden grimace. "What is this?"

His hands clutched his chest and he doubled over with a keening moan of pain.

"No! It cannot be so. We are—We are immortal." He shuddered and fell to his knees. Gripped by bone-jarring spasms, he looked up at the four people before him and reached out plaintively to them.

"Help Us…."

The team stared back at him, mesmerized with horror as his skin appeared to dissolve before their eyes. Gaping red patches opened on his face, hands and chest; the skin melted away into huge open wounds, exposing the muscles, veins and bones beneath.

"Back away. *Now*," Teal'c said. He grabbed Daniel's arm and shepherded him away from the writhing man on the platform.

"This is what the nanocytes do?" Daniel stared at the man in dismay. "He left the planet after his deadline passed. Oh, jeez."

"You think he'll explode?" Sam asked, walking backward, unable to tear her eyes from the gruesome sight. The man was disintegrating. The pained, forlorn keening followed them as they left the Goa'uld and his host to their deaths.

Jack muttered something unintelligible under his breath, changed direction and walked several paces back towards the Stargate.

"Jack?" Daniel called after him.

Jack halted, brought his gun up and let off a single, well-aimed shot. The man jerked slightly then toppled to one side into the spreading pool of his body fluids. The echo of his last cry seemed to hang heavily in the warm air.

Somberly, the team moved away from the clearing, stopping only to test the DHD. With thirteen and a half hours until moonset, Jack led them onto a wide path. It sloped gradually downhill and within moments, the Stargate and the body of the unfortunate Goa'uld were lost to view. Keeping pace with Daniel's slightly slower limp, they walked in silence for ten minutes. As the track behind disappeared around another bend, Jack halted. Ahead, the path wound away into the trees; everything was peaceful, green and bursting with life. The ground bore no trace of human footprints, but the thick foliage could be hiding any number or kind of nasty surprises.

With the echo of the Goa'uld's death screams ringing in his ears, he turned to his teammates. "Ten minute break. We'll find a better position for a full meal later. How is everyone doing for water?" His own canteens were less than a quarter full.

"Running low, sir." Carter broke out a stash of powerbars and passed them around.

"Me too," Daniel added as he took a measured sip. His eyes met Jack's over the raised canteen, a glance of concern Jack accepted and returned with a brisk nod. Neither of them wanted to talk about what they had just witnessed, or the implications for their own survival.

SG-1 applied themselves to replenishing their energy, warily watching the surrounding forest. After ten minutes of undisturbed peace, Jack found himself much more at ease, the gruesome scene at the Stargate fading rapidly. Teal'c paced a few meters down the path, head cocked, listening intently.

"I believe I hear running water, O'Neill." Teal'c pointed off to where the track vanished into the trees. "Some distance away, but it could be a substantial creek or river."

"Then that's our first target. We'll fill the canteens then get looking for the address out of here." Jack looked at Carter and Daniel, saw the weariness on their faces that mirrored his own. "And hopefully, we'll have time for some kind of rest. Lead on, Teal'c."

They pushed their way through dense ferns, shaded from a warm sun by the towering canopy of enormous trees, the trunks of some more than twenty feet in diameter. Above their heads, dozens of different species of birds twittered, sang and shrieked in a raucous musical cacophony. Bright flashes of feathered bodies could be glimpsed now and then before being swallowed by the foliage.

"This place is amazing," Carter said, bending by a small plant with dark, furry leaves. She added both leaves and stem to her rapidly growing collection. "We have to work out some way of charting these planets and bring a team back. We could be walking through a whole pharmacy of undiscovered medicines here."

"Be nice if we could figure out a way off these planets first," Jack grumbled from the rear. His boot slid off a lichen-covered rock and he staggered back a couple of paces. He scowled at it and trudged tiredly after his team, their pale-colored uniforms standing out starkly against the greenery.

"T, you got any idea where you're going?"

"Toward the river, O'Neill, as we have already discussed." Teal'c's voice floated back.

"Well, I know *that*. Never mind." Jack glared at his feet, his head aching from the crack on the DHD a world away. There was an odd ringing in his ears and he was feeling generally out of sorts. *Put it down to job stress*, he thought. *One minute stuck in the mud, the next we're in Jurassic Park.* A clump of bright green flowers hung from a vine at the side of the path, the scent of its rich nectar wrapping around his nose and making his mouth water. Suddenly assailed by a childhood memory of laughing with his best friend as they stole the neighbor's honeysuckle flowers and slurped the nectar from them, he plucked the clump and without another thought sucked the nectar from the large cup-shaped blossoms one by one, leaving a trail of discarded petals in his wake.

The river finally came into view, a stretch of clear water running swiftly over a bed of shiny, round, green stones. Its soft burbling called to them, alluring after the hot dust of the previous planet. Jack stood on the bank and gradually zoned out, almost hypnotized by the sparkling water.

"Oooh, bath," Daniel moaned, and walked straight into the water. The pebbles twisted under his feet, threatening to dump him ass over teakettle before Carter reached out and hauled him back onto the mossy bank.

"What are you eating?" she demanded, staring at Daniel's cheeks, which were puffed out like a hamster on a binge.

"Nofing." Daniel shrugged her off and gave Jack an impish wink over her head, shoving in the last of the squishy red fruit he had plucked from a tree.

"If that's chocolate, Jackson, you're dead."

"Is not," Daniel replied loftily. "It tastes like a strawberry flavored banana. Best thing I've eaten in days—weeks, even. And I'm going to eat more. Lots more. Hey, gerroff! Get your own." He smacked Carter's grabby hands and danced away from her to snatch another fruit from a tree, pitched it at her and dodged away again to raid his own special tree-of-treats.

Carter caught the fruit one-handed—deftly—professionally—messily. It exploded on impact, showering her with blue, honey-scented pulp.

"Daniel!"

He laughed at her, eyes twinkling over a red-smeared mouth, and ambled off along the river in search of more fruit. The ache of his legs and back seemed forgotten in the heady scents of the forest around them.

Carter tried to shake the sticky pulp from her hands but merely smeared it further. She stared at the mess, and stuck her fingers in her mouth. "Mmm, yum. More, want more!" She cleaned the rest off her hands, then scooped up the pulp clinging to her t-shirt and vest and went in search of more.

Jack watched Daniel and Carter rummaging through the trees like a pair of demented fruit bats and shook his head. *Kids. Can't take 'em anywhere these days.* A warning bell was clanging in his mind, but it was far away and it stuttered and died as he caught sight of Teal'c: on his knees, enthusiastically digging into the dark soil with his knife.

"T? What'cha doing?"

"I am foraging, O'Neill. Foraging for supplemental food-stuffs that will keep our bodies nourished and our minds alert, so that we may excel in the challenges our quest presents us."

"Ah...."

Teal'c sat back on his heels, grabbed a protruding root with both hands and heaved. A black, oddly glistening tuber came free in a shower of soil. *"Kenatak,"* he exclaimed happily. He snapped the root in two and took a huge bite of the inner flesh, heedless of the stench rising from it.

"Holy *crap*." Jack backed away as fast as he could, stomach rebelling at an odor like week-old fish left to rot in the sun.

"Will you not join me, O'Neill? This is a feast fit for war-riors."

"Uh, yeah, thanks but no. God, *no*. I'm watching my weight." Jack fled into the water, thoughts of fish suddenly crowding his mind.

Headache forgotten, he stared into the swiftly flowing river, his attention immediately captured by flashes of silver darting past him. Wading in knee-deep, Jack saw they were fish; sleek silvery-red bodies, letting the current take them downstream.

"Mmm."

Visions of grilled fish crusted with almonds and swamped in lemon filled his head, so vivid he could almost taste it. The fish were moving too fast here; what he needed was a calmer pool where they would leap onto his line. Downstream.

"T. C'mon, let's follow the river, see if we can't catch us some supper."

Jack splashed out of the water, gave Teal'c's pile of stinky roots a wide berth, and walked off along the riverbank. The aroma wafting from behind told him Teal'c was following. They caught up to Daniel and Carter, liberally smeared with the remains of a fruit fight and giggling like children, their packs and pockets bulging with plundered fruit.

The narrow track alongside the river took them through the jungle for almost a kilometer. Here and there shafts of sunlight broke through the canopy in dazzling brilliance. Several times their approach startled small animals out of hiding, an angrily squawking, four-legged creature covered in bright green fur the most surprising. It scuttled away and was quickly camouflaged in the greenery.

After forty minutes of walking, the bank became rockier and the ground began to slope downward. From ahead came a muffled roaring and the scent of water in the air was much more noticeable. Forced away from the river by increasingly huge boulders, the four slowed as the track switched in and around rocks and tree roots, becoming steep and slippery as the moist soil gave under their boots. Fine mists of water vapor drifted through the trees, gradually becoming denser as they descended into a gorge cut through the underlying rock by millions of years of the river's passage.

Rounding a bend in the trail Carter stopped abruptly, the men piling up behind her. Awestruck, they stood on a mossy ledge, captivated by the waterfall that fell in a glittering rain from the river above to a deep green pool a hundred feet below. Curtains of mist brushed past them, seeping into their clothing and causing muddy rivulets to run down their necks and arms. All around them screeches and calls of unseen birds and animals rose up to near deafening volume. Thick foliage clung to every possible part of the rock; trees and shrubs glistened with spray. Rich, earthy scents assaulted them from all directions.

It was Paradise. Whether it contained any serpents was yet to be seen.

"Wow."

"Well said, Carter."

"No, really. This is... wow."

"A most gratifyingly impressive sight."

"That's what I meant. Wow."

"You know what I see?" Daniel coughed, vapor catching in his lungs. "A bath."

"Oooh." Carter stared at the inviting green water.

"With a running shower."

"Last one in is a stinky Goa'uld." She turned on her heel and raced off down the path, Daniel limping only seconds behind. Teal'c grinned broadly at Jack and loped off.

Jack gaped after them, a dozen protests sticking in his throat. He shook himself. The haze in the air made him feel as if he were underwater. Helplessly, he looked around at the deserted trail and with a surrendering sigh he plucked another spray of bell-shaped flowers from an overhanging branch.

"Kids," he muttered fondly, and ambled after them, sucking the nectar as he went.

Daniel passed Sam in their breakneck run down the path by simply crashing through the undergrowth, leaping, skidding and tripping his way until he emerged onto a wide, grassy bank stretched along one side of the pool. He shoved his boonie off his head and relaxed his shoulders, letting his pack and vest slide to the ground.

Oh, he felt so dirty. His skin itched and crawled with grit. Sweat left stinging trails down his bruised back. He couldn't tear his eyes from the green water, enticing him in with a promise to soothe his aching muscles and tired feet, to wash away all his cares as easily as the grime clinging to him. He stripped off his t-shirts in a flash, glasses tangling and thrown aside with them. Pants fell to booted feet. He struggled with the bootlaces, his fingers somehow clumsy and uncoordinated. The obstinate boots wouldn't come off and he tipped over, landing on his butt and rolling around until, with a mighty heave, they came away. He flung them aside with an inarticulate yell, pants, bandages and shorts followed, and then he was up and sprinting into the pond.

The clear, cold water snatched at his legs, tripping him and sending him plunging headfirst into the green depths. Daniel pulled himself down and down with strong sweeps of his arms, eyes wide and mouth open in a delighted grin. The water caressed him, its gentle grip leeching away all the pain and anxiety of the past couple of days. Finally, he coasted to a stop and hung suspended, looking down at shoals of little fish darting along the weedy bottom. Gently, the little air left in his lungs brought him up to the surface. He rolled onto his back and sucked in breaths of the sweet, rich air.

Sam splashed past in a mad flail of pale arms and legs, headed for the far side of the pool. Daniel raised his head a little and spied Teal'c cruising through the water with massive breaststrokes, submarining underneath for meters at a time.

Jack was wandering along the water's edge, half dressed and following his team with a slight frown.

"Jack! Get in here. It's wonderful."

Daniel's words were lost in the deep pounding of the waterfall striking the rocky pile at the base of the drop. Another curtain of spray obscured Jack and Daniel turned away, distracted by Sam hurling clumps of weed at Teal'c's head. Teal'c retaliated with a huge wave of water, leaving her laughing and sputtering. Daniel grinned and swam quietly up behind them.

Ducking under, he grabbed at Sam's legs and yanked her down, then surged off to seek shelter behind Teal'c before she could counterattack. Teal'c looked so good with a wide smile on his face, green pondweed curling around one ear. Still grinning, Daniel got a huge splash in the face. He choked and swallowed, then launched himself at Teal'c's hands, slipping and sliding as they batted and splashed and tumbled over each other. Sam joined in, alternately swatting at Daniel and trying to help him dunk Teal'c. More often than not, Sam and Daniel went under or found Teal'c's big hands heaving them away to crash down in fountains of water. They surfaced again and again, gasping and laughing and charging back until a coordinated attack finally brought the big man down and the water closed over his shiny head.

Victory, however sweet, came at a price, and their high fives and whoops of triumph turned to outraged yells as Teal'c surfaced and dunked them both.

Daniel popped back up and shook the water from his eyes. He tipped onto his back and floated. Water muffled the sounds around him and he drifted, now and then catching a vague recollection of something important, only for it to dissolve and float out of his grasp again.

How long he remained in limbo this way, he didn't know and didn't care. A bump against his foot made him finally straighten up. Jack lay sprawled on the rocks by the waterfall, sunning himself like a leopard, all loose, lethal grace in his limbs. He cracked open one eyelid and smiled down at Daniel, waggling his toes in the water.

"Hey, Danny."

"Hey, Jack."

Daniel pulled himself out of the water and draped himself facedown next to Jack.

"We should get moving," Jack said, apparently not able to

move a muscle himself.

"Mm hmm." Daniel tried to stay awake but his eyes were already shut, sound around him receding into a long, dark tunnel of blissful sleep.

An incessant, low chorus of insect calls eventually brought Daniel back to consciousness. Content in the warm sun, he sighed deeply and turned his head on his forearms. On a large boulder next to him, Jack lay sprawled likewise on his front, his brown eyes gazing sleepily at Daniel. A stone's throw away, Sam and Teal'c were chatting quietly, their bodies now dry.

"I feel so much better," Daniel yawned hugely.

"Hey, c'mon. I'm hungry."

"Perhaps you would care to sample one of the delicious roots I found, O'Neill. Daniel Jackson has already tried one on our walk through the jungle." Teal'c rose gracefully to his feet and extended an assisting hand to Sam.

"*Daniel* will eat anything you give him—this is a proven fact, Teal'c—so don't get too excited." Jack scrunched his face up at Daniel in disgust.

"Well, the smell of them reminded me of the stew Sha're's Aunt Tatti used to make," Daniel smiled. He stooped and filled his canteens with the sweet water, the others following suit.

"And you enjoyed it?" Sam grimaced. They dressed slowly and sloppily, leaving belts and holsters undone, jackets trailing from pack ties.

"Jeez, no—Uncle Tus used to hide in our house every time she made it. The stench of it floated over half the town."

Teal'c gave Daniel a look of wounded indignation and pushed past Sam, taking the lead along a narrow trail that led away from the waterfall.

Nuts and fruit hung in abundance from the trees they passed. All four snagged handfuls and ate as they walked. Jack declined the fruit and happily stuffed himself with soft, round nuts, leaving a trail of peeled coverings in his wake. Gradually, the roar and mist of the waterfall receded and the jungle seemed to swallow them completely, wrapping them in a noisy green blanket of foliage. Overhead, birds trumpeted their calls and little yellow-furred creatures that could well be primates shrieked at the human invasion and pelted the four with leaves and sticks.

They walked for quite a while, conversation and consumption of wild food gradually petering out, and the serenity they had all basked in at the waterfall faded away, replaced by an unsettling feeling that something was amiss.

Gradually Jack's pace slowed. He watched the others pull ahead of him with a frown. This wasn't right. They were missing something.

"Hey." His voice sounded muffled and was lost in the squawk of a fat orange bird overhead.

"Hey!"

Carter, Daniel and Teal'c stopped and turned to look at him.

"Something's wrong," Jack said vaguely, struggling to voice the uneasiness inside him.

"What?" Daniel asked.

"Well, if I knew I'd say, wouldn't I?" Jack snapped back.

"Did you leave something back at the pool, sir?" Carter asked. She was still clutching a half eaten fruit in one hand.

"No, don't think so." Jack glanced down. Kit, boots, pack, weapons. Surprisingly, the fingers curled around the trigger of his MP5 were white with the pressure of his grip. Shivers of warning crawled up his spine.

"We need to find a… thing." He glared at the others, who were gaping at him unhelpfully.

"A thing… a thing to do… a thing so we can… *leave.*"

The crawl up his spine turned into a cold shock that swept his skin from crown to toes.

"The 'gate address! The password. *We need to find them.* Crap—the time! How long have we got left?" He peeled his hand off his gun and clawed at his watch. Three hours, twenty-seven minutes to go. They'd wasted hours wandering the forest and playing in the water. The realization hit him like a physical blow. "What the hell is wrong with us?"

The others wandered closer and he saw the confusion on their faces. Saw them suddenly get it and saw them come back to themselves.

"How could we forget?" Daniel muttered, aghast. "We could have been trapped here forever. Oh, no—like the Goa'uld."

"There is something unnatural at work here, O'Neill." Teal'c had his staff half-lowered, as if expecting an attack at any moment.

"It must be the valley—or the water, even," Carter said. "Everything seems clearer here." She tossed the fruit and wiped her hands.

"Okay, the further from the water, the better we are. And we're heading who knows where." Jack looked about, trying to retrieve some sense of direction.

"Up. We go up out of this valley entirely, get a fix on our position." He stared at the others, still trying to shrug off their enforced forgetfulness. For even Teal'c to be as badly affected as the rest of them—it was unnatural.

"Move!"

They leapt away from him like startled sheep, sprinting along the path they were already on, then turning into another that inclined through the trees roughly in the direction of the Stargate's little plateau, Jack nipping at their heels and chivvying them along.

It took nearly half an hour of clawing along faint animal trails weaving up through the jungle before they broke out into a small clearing on the rim of the valley. The muted rumble of the waterfall drifted from far below. The sun lay low over the treetops on the far side of the river gorge.

Teal'c pulled his binoculars out of his pack and planted them against one eye, turning slowly to survey the jungle. "There." He pointed out the direction of the Stargate, sun glinting off the chevrons through the surrounding trees, some three hundred meters away. "Perhaps the information we require will be somewhere visible and out of range of the influences that impaired us near the river."

"I hope so." Jack stood nearby, legs braced against the adrenalin-fuelled reaction from the run up the slope. He looked carefully at Teal'c, following the look of consternation on his face, to the hand pressed to the Jaffa's belly. "Junior acting up?"

"It begins to revive now. It has been similarly affected by this unnatural lassitude."

"The Goa'uld must have installed some kind of neural transmitter here to confuse whoever comes through. It must dull the higher cognitive skills and stimulate the pleasure seeking zones of the brain," Carter said, likewise subdued.

Jack glanced at Daniel, who was staring out over the forest canopy, rubbing tiredly at his eyes. He took Daniel's lead and looked down. The treetops stretched on in an endless sea of green.

"Hey, I think there's something shining down there."

The others turned to follow Carter's pointing finger. Far down in the valley, a glint of refracted light sparkled up at them. Down on the valley floor but well back from the river, it was approachable from where they stood if they went straight down through the trees.

"I can see no other likely place for that which we seek," Teal'c said quietly.

Jack sighed; going down meant climbing back up again. "Let's get this done, then. Stay close, all of you." Taking point, he led the way into the trees.

Descending through the tangle of growth was as laborious as toiling up had been. Exposed tree roots caught at their feet and thorny bushes with leaves that stuck like Velcro to hands and clothes snagged them at every step.

When the slope finally leveled out, the underbrush thinned too, leaving the team standing on mossy ground amid the widely spaced tree trunks. Twilight was full upon them, making it difficult to see in the gloom. Daniel switched on his flashlight and flicked the beam through the trees. After turning a one hundred and eighty degree arc the light caught something that gleamed back a fiery orange.

"Watch yourselves," Jack ordered quietly, bringing up his gun and thumbing off the safety. Carter and Teal'c followed suit, spreading out to flank Daniel as he lit the way to their goal.

Fifty meters through the trees they came into a clearing. The forest pulled back to reveal an unexpected sight: a couple of dozen large glass globes suspended by invisible means in mid-air. Each gleamed in a different color—red, orange, green, yellow—all shades of the spectrum were brought to life as three more flashlights joined Daniel's.

"There's something inside this one." Jack nudged a sphere with the tip of his gun barrel. It rolled on its unseen axis but retained its place. From deep within the globe, a vaguely familiar symbol glowed a faint blue.

"Yeah." Daniel moved from one to the next, peering intently into each globe. "They look like the symbols representing some of the Goa'uld." He stared at a bright pink depiction of a sun disk resting between a pair of cow horns. "This—this is the sign of Hathor." He flicked the flashlight away and kept moving underneath the globes.

"These are the same symbols Dad showed us when he came looking for Seth," Carter said. "Are they all System Lords, do you think?"

"I am familiar with many of these signs," Teal'c commented. "However, some are unknown to me."

"Geb, Bastet, Thoth, Isis, Tefnut, Anubis." Daniel counted off the names as he circled around under the globes. "And here's Ra." He paused on the far side of the clearing. "Well, they all seem to be from the Ancient Egyptian pantheon. There are no other cultures represented here. That has to be significant."

"Didn't Jacob say there were thousands of Goa'uld but only

a handful of System Lords?" Jack wandered around the boundary of the globes, looking for the strings that had to be holding them up.

"Dozens of System Lords."

"So we've got more balls than System Lords... globes, than System Lords."

"I believe both statements to be correct, O'Neill." Teal'c gave Jack the eyebrow equivalent of a high five and marched off to do a perimeter check.

Carter bit back a grin and tried to get a better look inside a globe.

Daniel continued his examination, now sketching a map of each globe's position and the name it bore.

"So... what? Quick game of soccer?" Jack needled as he passed.

"No, I wouldn't recommend it."

Jack checked his watch again—two hours, seven minutes left. Darkness had fallen heavily on the jungle, hushing the wildlife at least. He stalked around the clearing, the time counting down loudly in his head. Opposite from where they had entered, a path led out through the trees. He prowled down it and twenty meters along came to a junction with another, wider path that looked more than familiar. To the right, the path angled up toward the Stargate, to the left it headed down to the river. He closed his eyes and mentally kicked himself for his lapse. They had walked right past this place and now were scrambling to catch up before they were locked out of the Stargate network for good.

As O'Neill jogged back into the clearing, Teal'c completed his perimeter check and joined Major Carter in dragging fallen branches away from an old stone pillar, their flashlights illuminating a scrawl of carved glyphs down one side.

"'Those who are our enemies, those who are our allies — know them by their names and know the might of your God, Ra'," Teal'c translated, eyebrows rising as he pondered the meaning of such a declaration.

"And what is that supposed to mean?" O'Neill asked.

"We pick the names of Ra's allies, or enemies, and get the 'gate address in return?" Major Carter surmised.

"That is a possibility, Major Carter."

"Well, which is it? Allies or enemies?" O'Neill bounced on his heels, impatience rising.

"It could be either," Daniel Jackson said, his face bathed in a faint, green glow from the globe above him.

"Well, pick one!" O'Neill demanded.

"Enemies?"

"Teal'c?"

"Knowing the enemies of the System Lord with whom one seeks service would be beneficial," Teal'c conceded.

"Enemies it is. Time's a'wasting, so can we get on with it, please?"

Daniel looked expectantly at them. "And we do that by, um…." He looked at the globe above him.

"You know, they remind me of those electrostatic ball things that were all the rage in the Seventies," O'Neill offered. Teal'c failed to comprehend the helpfulness of such a statement.

Daniel too stared blankly until Major Carter nudged him and said, "Try touching it."

Gingerly, Daniel reached up and placed his fingertips on the glass above him. "It's warm."

The golden glow inside brightened briefly, then quickly died away.

"Try your whole hand." Major Carter suggested.

Teal'c watched while Daniel Jackson pressed his palm to the globe. Gentle light seeped past Daniel's hand as the glow bathed his face. After a moment he gradually withdrew but the light promptly died once more. He turned to the others, expression uncertain.

"Perhaps one is required to speak the name of the Goa'uld depicted within, as with the password that unlocks the DHD," Teal'c said.

"Good idea, Teal'c." Daniel reached up once more and as the glow brightened, he said clearly as he could, "Ra."

From the ground under the center of the globes a beam of light, the same gold color as that coming from Daniel's globe, shot up through the covering of leaves and grass to illuminate the tree canopy overhead.

O'Neill danced away, weapon not quite coming up to firing position. "Hello!"

Daniel cocked his head, pleased with the first sign of success. "So who else do we try?"

"Okay." O'Neill remarked. "Teal'c, you've got the best working knowledge of the Goa'uld—who do you choose?"

Teal'c looked at the list Daniel Jackson handed to him, and considered the names of potential Goa'uld enemies of Ra. "This one." He pointed at the list. "This, this and this were all well-known foes of Ra."

"Well, let's see." Daniel looked up and located the globe bearing the first name. "I guess Apophis would be a good place to start."

"Quite," Teal'c murmured.

Daniel slapped his hand on the globe and clearly proclaimed, "Apophis."

Disappointingly, the globe refused to light up.

"You're sure he was an actual enemy of Ra's?" asked Major Carter.

"I am certain. Their battle to each overcome the other had raged for millennia, and is said to have begun when Apophis was a servant to Ra, in the time before Ra left the Tau'ri homeworld."

Brow creased in thought, Daniel Jackson stared at Teal'c. "Ra was almost completely immersed in the mythology of Ancient Egypt—he lived it. Of course! The rebellion against Ra on Earth happened well before the Greeks moved into Egypt and many of the gods' names were Hellenized." He turned and slapped the globe once more.

"Apep!"

The clearing filled with a deep red light as the globe lit up. Impressed, Teal'c followed Daniel Jackson around the circle naming enemies of Ra known to still be active up until a few years ago. Sokar, Heru Ur, Nefertum, and Anhur lit up, bathing the team in a mix of deep reds, orange and purples.

"What about Anubis, Teal'c? Jacob didn't have him listed among the major System Lords."

"I have heard only old tales concerning Anubis, Daniel Jackson. He was once a mortal enemy of many of the System Lords, but he was defeated a long time ago. His name remains only in tales told to children."

"Okay, well, we can consign Anubis, or Anpu, as MIA along with Het-Her and Set. What about Sekhmet? Earth legends told of her as Ra's hand, she was his wrath against his enemies."

"Tales are still told of the fall of Sekhmet. She allied herself with Apophis against Ra."

"Really? So we can put her on the enemies list?"

"Sekhmet was put to death in a manner so protracted and painful that the stories still circulate—two thousand years later. I believe she cannot be counted in this endeavor."

"Ah."

Teal'c allowed a small smile as Daniel Jackson reluctantly forbore asking further questions and consulted the list once more.

"Okay, well, that just leaves um, this one." Daniel walked slowly over to a darkened globe near the center, which Teal'c felt he had been deliberately avoiding.

He peered over Daniel Jackson's shoulder at the symbol in the globe. How could he not know the emblem of she who had been his master's queen, the one who had sat and held the power of life and death over him as surely as had Apophis? He curled his lip in disdain and reached past Daniel to slap the globe into life.

"Amonet." His deep growl echoed around the clearing, picking up an answering mutter from O'Neill's direction.

Daniel Jackson cleared his throat. "Well. I think we're done, then." He stepped back and they eyed the beautiful light display dubiously. "Nothing's happening."

The globes glowed cheerily in the dark for another two minutes then winked out together, plunging the clearing into darkness.

"Oh." Daniel clicked on his light and looked at the others. "Guess that was the wrong choice, then."

"Perhaps the allies of Ra are the ones requiring illumination, Daniel Jackson," Teal'c said.

Daniel consulted his list once again. "Well, there are certainly enough of them here. Who would you choose, Teal'c?"

Teal'c moved around the circle, considering carefully before placing his hand on one globe.

"Bastet."

The globe lit up and a corresponding beam of pale green rose up from the ground. Encouraged, they moved on to the next. "Khonsu."

"He was originally regarded as the offspring of Amon Ra and Mat," Daniel said, staring up into a sky-blue glow.

"Seshet."

"Goddess of scribes and history. I've always been a bit fond of her myself."

"She was known to be one of the more tolerant Goa'uld," Teal'c said, somewhat surprised as childhood tales of the 'gods' resurfaced in his memory, as vivid now as they had been nearly one hundred years ago when he had first heard them, sitting at his mother's feet listening to her nightly tales.

"What about Sia? He supposedly was a son of Ra."

"Sia disappeared many years ago during a dispute over territory with Apophis."

"Next one is Thoth. He was consort of Seshet, so I guess they'd be on the same side?"

"That name is unfamiliar to me, Daniel Jackson."

Daniel frowned as the inner light in Thoth's globe refused to come on. "Oh, of course. Djehuti!"

Djehuti's sphere lit up bathing Daniel's enchanted face in an eerie orange. They continued on, picking out likely allies of Ra. Major Carter slowly paced the circle, searching for the hidden power source of the globes floating above them. Further out, O'Neill prowled in the darkness, constantly on watch.

With Anher, Tefnut, and Wadjet added to the lit globes, Daniel and Teal'c paused.

"Oh, and there's Mat; Jacob said she was a favored consort of Ra's." Another purplish glow joined the spectrum. Daniel paused and called to O'Neill on the opposite side of the clearing. "Jack, remember the helmets Ra's guards wore aboard his ship?"

"Yeahhh— big bird things?"

"Falcons, yes. Horus guards. Horus was the son of Isis whose consort was Osiris, enemy of Seth, who was an enemy of Ra. So I'm thinking even though they may not be around any more, Ra might still have counted them as allies. Therefore— Jack, fourth one over this way." Daniel Jackson beckoned O'Neill toward him and said "Auset."

"Who?"

"Auset is Isis, so," Daniel made flapping motions at him from the other side of the circle until O'Neill smacked the globe and growled out something that sounded more like 'Ozzie' but sufficed to activate the globe.

"And that leaves Osiris." Daniel held his breath, reached above his head and said, "Asar." A warm orange, the color of a rising sun, flooded over him. The final beam of light rose up from the ground and mixed with the others.

The spotlights seemed to come alive, bending to join together in one dazzling multi-hued column of light that soared above their heads. It hung suspended in the warm, night air for a few minutes then slowly shrank back down. As it reached the ground there was a grinding of stone over stone as the base of each spotlight was covered with a stenciled glyph, each one bearing a different symbol or Stargate coordinate. In the darkness above their heads the beams of light projected seven glyphs and two words in Goa'uld script.

Three loud whoops drowned out Teal'c's murmur of satisfaction, and the team scrambled to record the address symbols and words before they vanished.

"Got it! Password means 'Slicer of Souls'. Nice." Daniel Jackson knelt on the ground and looked up at the others, his fingers tracing the slowly fading light from the point of origin.

"Nice work, guys," Major Carter said.

Teal'c inclined his head. "It is gratifying to be able to use one's knowledge of the Goa'uld for a beneficial purpose."

Daniel got to his feet. "Remind me to ask you about Sekhmet when we get home, Teal'c."

"I shall indeed, Daniel Jackson."

"Pack it up kids, we have got to *go*," O'Neill called to them.

Somewhat reluctantly, Teal'c followed his teammates as they picked up their packs and left the clearing, the gently fading light bidding them a silent farewell.

An insect chirped high in the trees above them, a sweet sad sound. There was a moment's silence, then as if a switch had been flipped, a deafening chorus rose throughout the jungle as thousands of the creatures began calling out to each other. Sam winced at the noise. Effectively silenced, SG-1 pushed on up the slope, finally emerging into the Stargate clearing with just ten minutes remaining.

"Get the gear, Carter, Teal'c." The colonel strode rapidly through the grass.

"Sir, shouldn't we do something about the, uh, remains?" Sam indicated the Stargate platform. She felt recharged and actually looking forward to the next planet on their agenda.

"I don't think there's much left to do anything with, Carter. He looks a bit flat to me."

Sam walked up the steps to the body and realized with rising dismay that all that was left of the unfortunate host and his Goa'uld were his tattered robes. Flesh, muscle, even bone had dissolved into a large, smelly puddle, dripping over the far side of the platform.

"Oh, erk." She turned away and moved to help uncover their gear, only to find the way barred by an outlandish little person standing not six inches in front of her.

"Whoa! Where the heck did you come from?" She backtracked, feet slipping in the puddle, and leaped over the side into the midst of the men. The four of them stood in varying degrees of astonishment, weapons slowly coming to bear.

"Carter?" The colonel's tone was almost accusing, as if she had conjured it out of thin air.

"Beats me, sir. I turned around and there it was."

The creature stared down at them from the platform, intense interest clear on its decidedly ugly face. It stood no more than four feet high, stumpy arms clasped over a very wide, very fat belly. Its broad head was distorted by grotesque teeth and enormous ears. Huge feet splayed out at right angles to each other. It wore no clothing over its scaly brown skin and its belly hung so low it was impossible to determine gender, not that anyone would want to try.

"That is a very unattractive individual," Teal'c announced, political correctness way out the window.

"Got that right," The colonel muttered, sidling around a few steps for a better line of fire. Sam looked at Daniel, expecting him to kick off his peaceful explorer shtick, but he was still gaping at the intruder.

"Uh, can we help you?" she tentatively asked.

Deep green eyes looked down at her, seemed to examine her inside and out before answering. "Much time has passed since one took up the challenge of the Trial of Moons. I had to see with my own eyes those brave souls come to test themselves."

The little being stumped to the edge of the platform and stared intently at them. "You belong to the same tribe and journey together, yes?" Its rasping voice seemed oddly soothing.

Sam shared a glance with the colonel, considering just how much intel he wanted to give out, but Daniel got in ahead of them. "Yes, in fact maybe you can help us. We didn't embark on this Trial willingly, we were lured into it. If you can help us find a way home, we'd be very grateful."

A gap-toothed grin opened up in the leathery face. "You are amusing, young one. That is nice." Its attention shifted to the pile of gear they had begun to uncover. "You may only take with you that which you can carry. Was that not explained to you?"

"No one else was present when we began the Trial," Teal'c rumbled, frowning deeply.

"Can you tell us who you are, how you got here?" Sam chipped in. "Do you live on this planet?"

"I am Bes, Keeper of the Barque. I wished only to meet you and bid you good fortune in your journey. We shall meet again, if you survive the Trial." With that, the little person made a flicking gesture at the pile of supply boxes and they, along with it, disappeared silently into thin air.

"No! Dammit." The colonel made an abortive leap toward the already missing gear. "Son of a *bitch*. Well, that's just great. Did it take everything?"

Teal'c bent and rummaged underneath the heap of fern branches that had covered their supplies and retrieved two remaining metal boxes.

"We are left with our ammunition and survival gear, O'Neill."

The colonel pulled off his cap and raked his fingers through his hair. "Well, it could be worse but I hope we don't end up in Antarctica next."

Just the thought of that bone-numbing cold sent shivers up Sam's spine. Bad enough being unprotected but if someone were injured....

"Tell me we've still got the first aid kits."

"Yes sir, and I've got the supplies we took from the Jaffa."

"And we've all got our vests and packs," the colonel finished. They carried many of the smaller items vital to survival with them.

Sam shifted the weight of her pack on her shoulders and looked at the others as the reality of their situation sank home once again. Down along the river all she had thought of was eating, running, playing, sleeping. Nothing had intruded on the desire to enjoy. Not the fact they were stuck far from home, nor the loss—oh, dammit—the loss of the comm unit. She'd been so sure it would have worked. No, they'd just eaten everything in reach, drunk untreated water, swum…. Well, at least they were all comfortable enough with each other not to be embarrassed over that. But barriers had been let down, and who knew what the price would be.

Now, they had lost most of their support gear. They were left with what they were carrying—and each other. Sam smiled as she followed the others to the DHD. They were fed, rested and ready to go. Most importantly, they were still together and as long as they stayed together, they'd be alright. Baring any further interventions from weird, wrinkly little aliens. Speaking of….

"Sir? That person, Bes? He wasn't a Goa'uld."

The colonel cocked an eyebrow at her. "Daniel, Teal'c, you know this Bes guy?"

Teal'c shook his head but Daniel nodded, the frown that had started on his face five minutes ago slowly deepening.

"Hold that thought, Daniel. Let's get going."

Daniel moved to the DHD, dialed up the next planet's address and spoke the Goa'uld phrase, *"Tent Baiu"*.

The wormhole burst into life, connecting them with the galaxy once again. The time spent in this jungle felt like a dream now, images of water and sun, colored fire and trees seemed to shift and blend in Sam's mind, leaving her with an ethereal, confusing mess.

She took one last look at the beautiful jungle, then bent and picked up one handle of the ammo box. Teal'c took the other and they followed Daniel and Colonel O'Neill into the blue ripples of the Stargate.

GATE SIX

Opener of Hearts

The wormhole disengaged and left SG-1 standing on a platform surrounded by acres of tall, rustling reeds. Salt-laden currents of air brushed softly by them, bending them in an elegant dance. Hidden beneath the grasses, water burbled steadily, heading toward the sparkling blue sea a short distance off to the left.

"Teal'c, check the time. Carter—DHD." Jack slipped on his shades as he did a quick three-sixty and saw nothing more threatening than plants and birds. "Daniel, this Bes character—what do you know?"

"Well, Bes is from the Egyptian pantheon. Old, very old. Much loved by families and women in particular. The, uh, ugly appearance was thought to attract evil spirits away from the people, thus protecting them. I can't imagine what function he served for Ra." Daniel slipped the clip-ons over his glasses and stared past Jack at the sea.

"We have six hours, fifty minutes, O'Neill."

The dying chevrons on the Stargate announced another failed attempt to dial home.

"Right, let's see what gear we've got left and then get moving. And this time—let's all try to keep our wits about us, okay? We've got enough food for two more days—half rations." Jack knelt in front of the two remaining supply boxes, opened them and started dividing up what was left.

"Two zats, six blocks of C4, five clips of 9mm, six magazines for the MP5s, six grenades, two climbing ropes, one harness, flares, stove, lightsticks, candles, water filtration bags, purification tablets, fishing kit, flints and steel, mirrors, ponchos and a hell of a lot of hot-sauce we can always throw at someone. We'll divvy up the ammo and the smaller items, carry them in the packs, put the nonessentials in the rope bags, and dump the boxes." Jack divided the lot between them and it was crammed into already heavy packs. The empty metal boxes were dragged into the reeds and hidden.

Teal'c, using binoculars, spied what seemed to be a cluster of buildings some way further inland along the hidden estuary. Following the direction indicated, Jack led the team out at a fast pace.

"Carter, you sure Bes wasn't a Goa'uld?"

"Definitely, sir. Which leads to an interesting question: why would such an, uh, odd-looking creature be given the position of Keeper of the Barque? The Goa'uld we've come across all seem to prefer being surrounded by attractive people, hosts or not." She leapt over a small clump of wildflowers, easily keeping the double-timed pace.

"Ra was known to be most eclectic in his tastes," Teal'c commented, loping along in the rear. "Perhaps Bes served a function on the Barque of Heaven that outweighed Ra's displeasure at his physical appearance."

"And whatever the Barque actually is, it must be fairly isolated," Daniel offered, jogging next to Jack. "If Bes truly is the Keeper of the Barque and he knew Ra was dead, surely he'd have no interest in maintaining the Trial?" He stumbled a little, but recovered and kept pace.

"All of which brings us back to whatever the Barque really is. Ship, city, planet—could be anything," Jack said.

"Might even be an entire solar system, sir," Carter said. "Isolated and still waiting for Ra to come home."

"Well, I just hope it wasn't the Ha'tak ship we saw him on, because that's floating around Abydos in a few million pieces."

"I surmise the appearance of Bes indicates the Barque does indeed still exist and that there is a place of culmination for this Trial," Teal'c added.

Jack veered to one side as Daniel seemed to swerve around

a non-existent obstacle and slow, then pick up speed again. Jack glanced at him but Daniel waved him on. Moments later, Jack flung a clenched fist in the air and skidded to a halt. He dropped to one knee, listening intently. The endless rustling of the reeds surrounded them, joined by an uneven wheezing from Daniel. Then, floating in from a distance, came the sound Jack had caught—bells, a number of them tolling happily, fading in and out as the breeze scattered the chimes across the estuary.

Jack motioned them forward at a cautious crouch. Fifty meters along, the reeds bent away to the left, following the water course and thinning out to finally reveal a wide stream running through fields covered in lush, green crops. On the far side of the stream he could see clusters of houses dotted along the bank, looking rustic and welcoming, if you ignored the tall stone obelisk rising up behind them. The golden Eye of Ra seemed to wink at him from its peak.

"Oh, swell." Jack pulled out his binoculars and focused on the village. Sure enough, the tolling bells were calling the occupants from their daily routine and dozens of people were heading for the temple.

"Daniel, you think this is because of us or just a regular call to prayer?" Jack kept counting heads through the binoculars for a minute before realizing Daniel had not answered. "Daniel?"

He looked at his friend and a chill of foreboding swept over him. Daniel was slumped on the ground as if his legs had given out on him, hands splayed out to keep his balance. The face that turned toward Jack was frighteningly pale.

"Don't feel too good, Jack," Daniel croaked. His arms buckled and only Teal'c's quick movement prevented him falling face-first to the ground.

"What the…?" Jack kept one eye on the people in the village as Carter leaned over Daniel, now collapsed in Teal'c's arms.

"Daniel, what's wrong? Daniel! Can you hear me?"

Anxiously she glanced up at Jack. "Sir, he's not responding and he's really cold."

"Allergy? Something he ate in that damned jungle, I'll bet." Jack scuttled around to get a better look. Cupping his jaw with one hand, Jack brought Daniel's face up and nearly let go again as a flash of heat swept up his neck and face, leaving his skin red and unnaturally hot.

"Jeez! What the hell is this?"

"Pulse is jumping all over the place."

"Daniel Jackson's breathing is quite shallow and rapid." Teal'c gently lowered Daniel to his side, while keeping a sharp eye on the people in the distance.

"Carter, get the epinephrine," Jack clipped out. He unfastened Daniel's pack and pulled it away. "Daniel? Focus on me for a minute. Were you bitten by something?"

Jack patted Daniel's cheeks, trying to get those hugely dilated pupils to focus. The flush was leaving his face now, his complexion going even paler than before.

"No bugs," he mumbled. "'kaara… thun… Ab… dos."

He shivered, a deep, full shudder from the core of his being. Teal'c's big arms curled around him and pulled him back against his warm body as Jack wrapped an emergency blanket over him.

Confused and more than a little alarmed, Jack looked at Teal'c. Barring being shot, nishta'ed or sarcophagus-addicted by off-world princesses with a crush, Daniel had the constitution of a horse. For him to go down so quickly was… unnatural. Still, who was to say what kind of hinky alien grass seeds were blowing around, just waiting to set up a reaction with sensitive human systems?

"Carter! Where's that shot?" Jack glanced around at Carter, expecting to see her ferreting through the first aid kit. Instead, she was on her knees, kit forgotten at her side as she weaved unsteadily, her face a distinct greenish hue. "Carter?"

Jack eased Daniel's head back to rest against Teal'c's chest. "Hold him," he said unnecessarily, and made a grab for the major before she fell into the puddle she was industriously expelling from her stomach.

"Whoa! Teal'c, you got any idea what's going on here?"

"I do not, O'Neill," Teal'c replied briefly.

Jack tried to look supportive and in-no-way-nauseous himself while Carter continued to retch at full volume.

"Carter, I know you're probably feeling bad, but keep it down will ya? The noise, that is."

"'essir," Sam groaned as another stomach-ripping spasm hit. She heaved and hurled and dangled like a rag doll in her CO's grip until she was empty of everything but frothy bubbles of stomach acid.

"No way is this natural. There has to be something around here triggering this. T, you got any ideas?" Jack administered the injection to Daniel. Rubbing Daniel's thigh, he tore his eyes away from his teammate's ashen face to stare at Teal'c. Was that sweat beading the big guy's upper lip? Teal'c rarely broke a sweat even in the hottest of places. "Teal'c?"

Seeming to return from some inner contemplation, he slowly looked up at Jack. "O'Neill. I believe we should seek the help of the villagers to assist Daniel Jackson and Major Carter. Quickly, before... before I am unable to be of use to you."

"You're kidding! Teal'c! You don't *get* sick."

Teal'c looked distinctly uncomfortable. "It is true I have not succumbed to illness since receiving my prim'ta. However, it now lies unmoving in its womb and I begin to feel most... odd."

Jack blanched. He stared disbelievingly at Teal'c, then his gaze shifted to Daniel, shuddering in the big guy's arms, then to Carter—huddled in a miserable ball on the ground. He placed a hand on her forehead, puzzled as to why she was not suffering the same temperature swings as Daniel. He detached his water bottle and gave it to her, keeping a loose hand on her vest in case she toppled over again.

"Jack."

Daniel's hoarse rasp pulled him back. "Hey. How're you doing?"

Another hot flush swept over Daniel's face, leaving him gasping and shoving the foil blanket aside.

"This," he flapped a limp hand at himself, "is… same thing… got on Abydos. Reaction to… Skandy Thorn." He panted harshly for a minute, the effort of talking draining him rapidly. "Shouldn't be happening… here… immune now."

"It has to be something the Goa'uld have done then. The test for this planet — I don't know." Jack grabbed the first aid kit and found the antihistamines Fraiser insisted they take with them. He popped two out and dropped them into Daniel's hand.

"Take these, too."

He turned to Carter and picked up the ignored canteen. "Carter. Here, take a sip. Keep drinking if you can."

She groaned as she straightened a little and accepted just enough water to wet her tongue.

"I'm sorry, sir. Must have eaten too much fruit or something. Haven't been this sick… ergh, since deployment."

"Not your doing, Carter. I'll bet my wings there's something else at work here."

He settled Carter on the ground, unclipped her MP5 and handed it to Teal'c. "I'm going to check out that village. Stay here, shoot anyone who isn't me."

"Be careful, O'Neill."

"I will. Keep your head down and look after them."

Jack managed a grim nod and turned away. Keeping low, he jogged to the end of the reeds, crouched and peered through the binoculars. The villagers had all vanished, presumably into the temple. Still bent low, he took off along the river bank and through the fields at a run. Coming to a shallow ford, he splashed across the silty riverbed, up the opposite bank and thumped down behind the cover of a stack of greenish hay.

Still no people in sight, but the sound of many voices chanting in unison drifted from the temple. Jack rose and scuttled to the side of the nearest house. Doors and windows stood open to the warm air and he peeked cautiously through one of the windows. Inside was a normal dwelling—beds, hearth, chairs, table, clothing on pegs, even flowers on the table. No Jaffa armor or weapons to be seen.

Jack turned and jogged around the back of the houses, stopping to check out two more before inching his way along the side wall of the temple. It was an open structure, with the wall surrounding the obelisk. The chanting was still in full swing, and sounded like the happy tones of a Sunday church service, rather than the militaristic intonations of soldiers affirming their readiness to die for their god that he had expected. He found the entrance unguarded and risked a glimpse inside. The villagers were facing away from him, grouped around a statue of Ra on the altar set before the obelisk. There were plenty of women and kids, the men were dressed in farmer's clothes and no-one seemed to be carrying weapons.

Slightly more at ease, Jack pulled back and made a recon of the village, hoping he'd find the next address for the Stargate left somewhere obvious, but naturally there was no such luck. Back where he had arrived, he sorted his options. He had less than five hours to get his team cured and off this planet, or at least away from whatever was affecting them. Much as it grated on him, he knew he couldn't do this alone. Jack rose and headed back to the others.

Things had not improved during his absence. Daniel had his eyes open at least, but Carter was still hunched over her cramping stomach, and Teal'c was definitely not well. Jack rummaged in Daniel and Carter's packs, pulled out their first aid kits, then sealed and stashed the packs under cover of the nearby reeds, placing a couple of stones as markers.

"On your feet, kids. We're going into the village, see if there's a way to reverse this."

He tucked the first aid kits into his pack and hauled on Carter's vest until she was more or less vertical. Keeping one hand on her, he grasped Daniel's arm and heaved. With Teal'c pushing from behind they managed to lever Daniel to his feet. For a moment the four of them stood, hands gripping onto each other, swaying like a group of elderly attempting a day trip.

"Okay. Let's do this nice and slow and steady. Whoa!"

Jack tightened his grip on Daniel as he wavered back into Teal'c, and Teal'c — big, solid, unmovable Teal'c — staggered, unbalanced and becoming grayer by the second.

"Daniel, come here to me. Teal'c, can you help Carter?"

"I can, O'Neill."

The threadiness of Teal'c's voice gave Jack the chills. He pulled Daniel from Teal'c's grasp, bracing himself as Daniel leaned into him. He kept a steadying hold on Carter until Teal'c held her firmly, got his arm around Daniel and started them toward the village.

It was only around eight hundred meters, not far on a good day. This was definitely not a good day. Their pace was slow at best, with intermittent stops to adjust holds or encourage Carter or Daniel to keep moving; it was an agonizing shuffle toward natives Jack couldn't feel one hundred percent certain of, and as they inched toward the village he alternated between worrying about his team and mentally checking within himself for the first signs of illness.

Eventually they reached the first of the houses. Walking — staggering — down the well-tended grassy main street, they soon had an audience of silent, passive-looking people leaving the temple, who stopped and stared at the team as they passed.

"Creepy," Daniel's voice panted in Jack's ear.

Jack could not see under the brim of Daniel's boonie, but he could feel the heat radiating off his friend's body. "I'll say. How're you doing?"

"Weird. It's like I have… symptoms, but not the cause. Like… a memory of being ill."

Jack raised his eyebrows at that but held off further questions as they came to a group of robed men and women, standing silently like everyone else, at the entrance to the little temple. He creaked to a halt and pulled Daniel a little more upright. These had to be priests; all wore Ra's symbol on their brows. None were armed, but Jack's hand was on the MP5's trigger regardless.

"Hi there." He smiled and tried to look harmless and invulnerable at the same time.

"Well-come and the blessings of our mighty Lord Ra upon you, worthy supplicants." The eldest of the group, a wizened old coot in striped satin robes, stepped forward and bowed gravely.

"Er, thanks." Jack gave a silent sigh of relief that the Stargate translator function seemed to be still with them. He gripped Daniel tighter as he began to sag. "My friends aren't feeling too well. I don't suppose you have a doctor here? A healer—physician—witch doctor—anything?"

Blank stares in pleasant faces were his only answer.

"Fine. Maybe you can just direct us to the address for the next Trial planet and we'll be on our way." He hoisted Daniel upright again, eliciting a mewling moan of protest. Behind them, Carter and Teal'c were braced side by side. Jack wasn't altogether sure who was holding whom.

"Your companions have been visited by the Eater of Foulness," said Stripey Robes. "Such often happens to those who visit us. We have prepared a place of rest for you. When you have healed your fellow supplicants, you may make your offering and receive the means to continue your travels."

"When *I've* healed…? I'm not a doctor. I don't know what's wrong with them and I don't know how to heal them," Jack protested. "And who's this Eater guy?" Was that ugly little Lilliputian responsible for this?

"Ah, you wish your companions to perish so that you may prove to Ra that you alone are worthy?" Stripey nodded amiably, as if people let their friends die at his feet all the time.

"No!"

Jack was appalled and his trigger finger tightened automatically. Daniel shifted in his grip, taking more of his own weight.

His boonie tilted as his head rose a fraction. "Please. Noble priest," he said between labored breaths. "Please help these weary travelers before you. Surely the great Lord Ra will look kindly upon you for your generosity."

Stripey puffed up a little and beamed happily at them. "Come, come and rest while your companion defeats the Eater." He scuttled off and vanished into the wooden house closest to the temple.

Jack glanced at Carter, hanging limply now in Teal'c's wavering grip. No way they were even going to make it back to the Stargate in this condition. He dragged Daniel into motion and walked past the ranks of hushed people into the house.

A surprisingly bright and airy room greeted them, one main space with a couple of doorways at the back, large windows on every side. The wooden walls were painted a cheery yellow and bundles of dried plants hung from the rafters, giving off a pleasant, homey smell. The floor was liberally piled with thick mattresses and cushions. Jack steered Daniel to one and lowered him down, not at all liking the way Daniel just lay where he landed.

Carter curled up nearby, looking very pasty and three-quarters asleep. She didn't even stir when Teal'c's pack hit the ground with a thud and he slumped onto the cushion nearby.

"Hey, wait!" Jack called to Stripey who was already on his way out the door. "Please, I need help here."

The priest stopped and looked back at Jack. "As you carried the Eater here with you, so you carry the knowledge to defeat it." The man's eyes seemed to focus on something over Jack's shoulder for a moment then returned to Jack. "All you require is within your reach." He bowed and left the house.

Jack glared after the man. At least the door remained open—they could leave whenever they wanted. He turned to stare at his team.

Oh yeah, be up and at 'em any minute now.

Carter was groaning and making retching noises again. Jack grabbed a pottery bowl from a window-sill, dumped the fruit out of it and placed it strategically by her head. He grimaced as his strong, feisty, dependable second-in-command dragged her face over the bowl and resumed gagging and moaning.

Jack backed away, his own stomach giving a sympathetic flip. He froze—suddenly convinced he was about to succumb as well. But then the sensation passed. He felt fine; better than he had even a day ago. He turned to Daniel and was somewhat relieved to see the flush had gone from his face. Crouching on the cushions, Jack prodded Daniel's shoulder.

"Daniel? You awake?"

Blue eyes peered up at him, unfocused and confused. Daniel seemed to be going paler by the second. Shivers wracked his body once again.

"What can I do, Daniel? Tell me how to help you."

Daniel closed his eyes and shook his head. "Can't. No cure. Just rest…." His eyelids slid shut then flickered open again. "Not real," he whispered.

Not real? Seems pretty real to me, buddy.

Jack repositioned the emergency blanket over Daniel's body, then shucked his jacket and added that too. Sighing, he turned to look at Teal'c and shock rippled through him at the sight; the Jaffa was gray-faced, covered in purple rash spots that seemed to be growing before his eyes.

"Teal'c?"

"O'Neill. I regret to inform you that I will be unable to complete the mission. I believe I am dying," Teal'c said matter-of-factly. Then his eyes rolled up in his head and he toppled backwards.

"Jeez!" Jack leapt to catch him but only managed to crash to the ground under Teal'c's weight. It took all his strength to roll Teal'c over into the recovery position, where he lay unconscious, his breathing shallow.

Jack sat on the plump cushions, surrounded by the ruin of his team. For one brief moment he allowed despair to creep past his defenses.

He tended his teammates for over an hour, to no avail. An anti-nausea shot in Carter's butt did nothing to stem the painful dry heaves. Daniel's body swung between violent hot flashes and bone-shaking cold seizures. Nothing in their first aid kits made a difference. Teal'c recovered from his faint but remained in agony from the lurid purple rash and muscle-twisting cramps in every part of his body. All Jack could do was cover his skin in antibiotic cream and try to massage out the crippling cramps. The few times Teal'c became lucid, he moaned and muttered about dying and kept asking Jack to return his body to Chulak for a proper warrior's funeral.

"Will you quit it already?" Jack finally snapped after the third such piteous request. "You're not dying."

"I believe I am, O'Neill," Teal'c gasped out in the best Greta Garbo style. "This illness is said to be deadly if contracted after adolescence by one who does not carry a symbiote."

"You mean it's a kid's disease?" Jack looked up from massaging Teal'c's right thigh.

"It is. I suffered it in my childhood, however not as severely as now. Please give my staff weapon to Rya'c."

"Oh, shut *up*, T. You're not dying." Jack looked over at Daniel who was once again sweating and tossing fitfully. "Daniel said something about Abydos, some kind of reaction he got to a plant. Not real. Teal'c, I don't think any of this is real. It has to be part of the Trial. And Stripey said I had what I needed to cure it."

Jack got up and moved away from the groaning Jaffa, eyes searching every inch of the room, from the scattered contents of the first aid kits to the flowers hanging from the roof.

"Why am I not sick? God knows we ate everything that wasn't nailed down on Jurassic World. If it came from there, why am I okay?"

He pulled Carter's blanket over her hunched shoulders and kept prowling the room. He sniffed the dried flowers and briefly considered using them, but rejected the thought quickly. There was too much risk of poisoning his people further. Crossing to the window, Jack looked out at a peaceful twilight scene.

Water birds swooped and soared over the estuary in the early evening light. Racks of fish lay drying in the open air. In the distance he could hear the shouts of children at play. Fishing nets hung over small white dinghies turned upside down on the riverbank, and further out where the estuary emptied into the sea a group of sail boats were heading home. He shook his head, idly plucking bell-shaped flowers from a creeper by the open window, and wondered about a Goa'uld who disposed of lives so casually and yet let these people thrive here. Had Ra forgotten them?

He stared down at the flowers, turning his mind back to the problem at hand.

And froze.

He looked, really looked at the flowers: brilliant green, bell-shaped flowers. The exact kind he had munched on for hours on tree-world. Had the others tried them?

Jack practically leapt on Carter, rolling her face-up and smacking her cheek until she focused on him. "Carter! Carter, wake up, dammit."

"Go 'way." She batted weakly at him.

Jack grabbed her jaw and shook her until she got both eyes open. "Major—look at me. Did you eat any of these flowers on the last planet? Major!" He shook her again and held the flowers three inches from her nose.

She frowned and focused with difficulty. Thought for a while, then managed to say, "No, sir." Satisfied she had answered correctly, her eyes slid shut again.

Jack let her go and sat back on his heels, thinking furiously. Was that it? There was nothing else in sight that might be a cure and at least he knew they caused no harm. He stripped handfuls of the flowers into his forage cap, then sat by Carter, methodically squeezing the nectar out of each one into an MRE spoon. When he had a full spoon's worth, he knelt over the major and shook her awake again.

"Major, I want you to swallow this."

Carter's eyes flinched shut.

"C'mon, Major. That's an order, Carter. Open wide."

From the look on her face she wasn't thinking nice thoughts about him, but he pinched her nose shut and when she gasped for air, he stuck the spoon in and smeared nectar all over her tongue. He clamped a hand over her mouth and watched with no little trepidation as she swallowed.

For a moment he thought it wasn't working, then her tensed muscles relaxed and she blinked at him, surprise and relief sweeping across her face. Warily, he removed his hand and sat back.

She sucked in a deep breath, then another. A disbelieving smile tweaked her mouth.

"Carter?"

"Sir, it worked. Oh, boy. Thank you." She sighed and sank back into the cushion. "It's gone."

"Rest easy, Major." Jack gathered up his bundle of flowers and headed for the boys. Teal'c was moaning piteously and was quite a sight now—covered with purple pustules—but Jack knelt instead at Daniel's side, concerned more for the archaeologist. The wild swings in body temperature could only be tolerated by his system for so long before his organs suffered permanent damage. Daniel lay curled on his side, glassy eyes fixed on nothing, breathing in slow, short, tortured gasps.

Jack quickly prepared another dose of nectar, then pulled Daniel up into his arms.

"Wakey wakey, Daniel. This'll fix you up."

He pried Daniel's jaw open and smeared the nectar on his tongue. As he automatically swallowed, Jack rubbed his throat, helping the nectar on its way.

"That's it." Jack anxiously watched for any change in Daniel's condition. "Heads up, Teal'c, you're next."

Teal'c, lying flat on his back staring bleakly at the ceiling, merely rolled his head to look at Jack. "It is too late for me, O'Neill."

"Oh, for crying out loud, you are *not* dying, Teal'c. Look at Carter—she's better already. You'll be fine in no time. Hey, have you heard of this 'Eater' that Stripey mentioned?"

"I have not. Major Carter!" Teal'c blinked at her in surprise as she carefully crawled over to him. "Are you well?"

"Apart from feeling like every muscle in my stomach has the tensile strength of Jell-O, yeah, Teal'c, I'm feeling much better. You're looking colorful." She flopped next to Teal'c and surveyed the lurid rash.

"He's got the Jaffa version of chickenpox," Jack said, trying not to smile. Now he knew his team was not in mortal danger, he could allow himself a moment to smile at one big bad Jaffa, moaning like a kid and covered in spectacular spots. He pressed a thermometer strip to Daniel's forehead and saw with relief that there was a marked improvement. Daniel wriggled a bit and opened his eyes.

"Hey."

"Hello."

"How do you feel?"

"Light. What's going on?"

Jack quirked his eyebrows at the 'light' but skipped over it. "Oh, you know; another day, another brush with death. Same old."

"Oh. Sam okay?"

"She's fine now. Teal'c will be too in a minute."

Daniel grunted, his color starting to return as he began to warm up and relax. Jack settled him back onto the cushions and went to gather more flowers.

Teal'c proved a more recalcitrant patient and Jack had to practically order him to open his mouth to get the nectar in. When he finally did, Jack grabbed his jaw to stop him closing it again.

"Here comes the airplane!"

Teal'c proved he could do that thing with his eyebrows even while lying down and Carter scuttled off to sit with Daniel and hide her giggles.

A mere thirty minutes later, in the flickering light of candles dotted around the now darkened room, Jack was having a hard time believing any of them had been ill, let alone scaring him into thinking they were dying. Replenished with electrolyte and vitamin-packed drinks, his team were on their feet and getting ready to go.

"I just don't think it was real, sir," Carter insisted.

"Believe me, Carter, you were hurling like a world champion. That kid in *The Exorcist* had nothing on you." Jack was adamant.

"The symptoms were real enough, sir, but I think this 'Eater of Foulness' just mimics a disease that each person has already suffered. It must be something engineered by the Goa'uld, possibly even in the fruit we ate."

"The last time I was really ill was on Abydos," Daniel added thoughtfully. "I was collecting thorn bushes for the mastages with Skaara and one of them scratched me. Apparently it was quite rare to have such a severe reaction, but I had the same symptoms as I had today."

"Must have been scary," Jack grimaced, picturing Sha're trying to care for Daniel with no modern medicines.

"Sha're did an amazing job, but she bawled Skaara out for days after I recovered."

Carter nodded as parts of the puzzle started to make sense. "It must mimic the last major illness a person has had. Mine was salmonella poisoning from dinner in an army unit's mess in the Middle East. Teal'c, yours was a childhood illness?"

"It was, Major Carter," Teal'c acknowledged, trying to regain his dignity but unable to stop scratching the healing rash on his body. "I believe we should leave this place, before we are afflicted once more."

With that he turned and marched out of the hut, his grinning teammates right behind him.

"We have to find that guy in the striped muumuu. He said something about making an offering to get the next address," Jack told them.

"An offering? That doesn't sound good." Daniel frowned.

They looked around the temple and, sure enough, surrounded by a circle of burning torches, an alabaster altar stood before the gold-capped obelisk, ready and waiting to receive offerings to the sun god. The silent populace had vanished, but the cluster of priests remained and bustled over to greet them. Stripey gave them a gap-toothed smile and clapped his hands delightedly.

"Well accomplished, good travelers. The Eater has been defeated. Now, come, come, make your offering to Ra and be on with your journey." He turned and pushed through the priests, headed for the open-air altar.

"Oh, just a moment there, Mister, er, Priest." Jack strode after the man. "What kind of offering are we talking about?"

Stripey stopped short, causing Jack to dodge to one side. "Ra demands an offering from the soul of each supplicant," he said, as if surprised they did not already know this.

"And how exactly does one go about that?" Jack loomed over the shorter man, making a show of patting his weapon.

"By sharing that which is most precious to each supplicant. A memory that will prove he is of good character and worthy of service to our Lord Ra."

"That's it? A memory?"

"Yes. Come, come." The priest trotted off again toward the altar.

Jack looked at Daniel. "You buying this?"

"Well, there aren't any bowls," Daniel contemplated.

"What?"

"No bowls for sacrificial blood to drain into, not that *human* sacrifice was ever a feature of the worship of Ra, so yeah, it's possible they just want to test our character."

Jack shook his head and looked at Teal'c and Carter.

"Our version of good character may be completely different to theirs, sir," Carter offered.

"If we speak from the heart we shall be judged truly," Teal'c rumbled. "The Goa'uld prize fidelity and honesty in their slaves most highly. After all, a servant who cherishes duplicity or treachery would not be trusted within a System Lord's court."

"Oh, don't get me started on the Goa'uld's sense of honor," Jack growled. "Okay, let's get this done. We only have an hour and fifty-eight minutes till ship-out time."

They moved up to the altar and the priests fanned out in a circle around them. The waning moon, a cheery yellow disc, gleamed directly onto the obelisk, limning it in golden fire. An expectant silence settled around the four travelers as they stood before the altar.

Jack slid a sidelong glance at the others. He knew he should go first, fearless leader and all, but opening himself up in front of total strangers? "Guess 'Mary Jane behind the hay-shed' wouldn't cut it?" he mused.

The silence dragged into throat-clearing, foot-shuffling minutes. Finally, Carter looked at him and he nodded at her to go ahead.

She looked over at the priests, then pointedly faced her teammates. "Well, I guess my most precious memory is of my mother. She was a teacher and she used to show me all kinds of amazing science projects. She gave me a love for knowledge and understanding the unknown that I still have today and I treasure her memory for that." She dropped her head, face reddening. Daniel squeezed her shoulder.

"Thank you, Carter." Jack realized he'd never heard her speak of her mother before. He glanced at the priests and saw them nodding in approval. Well, they were on the right track, at least.

Jack tilted his head at Daniel and Teal'c to see if they wanted to go next. Teal'c was frowning and Daniel stared back at Jack, looking wide-eyed and defenseless.

"Okay. Me next." Jack turned his back to the intruding priests and centered his focus on his team.

"I…," his voice faded. *Just do it, already.* He looked at his team. He'd fought and bled side by side with them, argued with them — for them, died and explored the stars with them. Not many people had seen what they had seen. The glib story he'd been about to deliver faded on his lips and somehow the truth slipped out.

"My… whole life changed the day my boy was born. I've never felt so scared, so proud, so weak or as strong as that first moment when he left his mother's body and lay in my hands. Everything I'd ever been, whatever I had planned to be, nothing mattered anymore. My whole life belonged to him and—I know nothing will surpass that moment."

Jack looked down at his boots, away from the understanding faces in front of him. He'd never spoken to them of Charlie before, except that one night, lost on another planet with a shaggy-haired archaeologist. He probably never would again.

Eventually, he looked up at the carefully schooled expressions facing him. Daniel cast a furtive glance at Teal'c, then plunged in. "My most precious memory, surprisingly there are a lot to choose from but the one I call on most, is of my wife, my Sha're. Um, it was just an ordinary night in our home, in our bed. Sha're was never one to be short of words. She was always talking, singing, laughing, even shouting. But that night, she spoke to me in silence. She said everything in her heart and never uttered a word. And what she told me was that I was loved. Deeply, utterly, forever." He sucked in a long breath. "That is my most precious memory."

Jack gave him a slight nod. Even though the four of them were standing apart, he could feel a bond weaving between them and he'd defy any snake-head to try and break it.

That just left the big guy.

Jack, Carter and Daniel all tuned out the muttering of the priests behind them and turned to Teal'c, who seemed to end his internal conversation and drew himself up to stand stiffly at attention. Quietly, he began to speak.

"I hold most dear to me the memory of those I love. I have lived many years and have been blessed with the gift of a child… five times."

Teal'c's voice died away as the faces of his friends filled with astonishment. Gently, he forged on.

"Five times my chosen mates gave me a child: Nanith, first born and filled with laughter; Tak'arek, strong and quick of mind; little, sweet Shonni, with her mother's eyes; Maa'ti, always with a tale to tell. And Rya'c, who grows tall and strong and free. Four are lost to me, but all fill my heart with joy, every day."

Dear God. Four.... Jack closed his eyes in empathy. *How do you do it? Every day...?* He opened his eyes and looked—really looked—at Teal'c and saw a glimpse of the inner strength of the man. For a moment, Jack was glad they had fallen into this trap of Ra's.

They made their way back to the Stargate at a fast walk, in moonlight, in silence. The priests had been quite impressed with the offerings and had grandly presented them with a copper tablet bearing the address and password to the next world.

How magnanimous of them. Jack scowled darkly at the reeds along the path. *We open a vein for them and all we get is a two-bit platter.* He shook his head, frankly awed by the fortitude of the people around him. There was a lot of touching going on too, quick darts of the hand from one to another, reassuring steadying pats, bumps of shoulders from walking too close. Nice.

They retrieved Daniel and Carter's packs, bolted a quick, cold meal and moved on. This world and all its weirdness had taken a lot out of each of them. Carter was moving slightly hunched over and Daniel was looking tired and washed out. Teal'c was quiet, but not in a closed-off way. Jack pushed away his own weariness and promised himself a night out with Teal'c when they got home.

Following the reeds along the estuary, Jack was dragged from his musings by a glimpse of something in the tall stalks. He slowed, thinking at first it was a frog. He peered closer and found himself staring at the incomparable face of Bes. The little guy blinked solemnly back at him. Jack opened his mouth but the words got stuck as Bes blew him an exaggerated kiss and vanished. Jack jerked upright and scuttled after the others.

SG-1 moved on through the warm night, surrounded by the croaking of frogs and the far-off splash of fish in the river. Wrapped in their own thoughts, they were all a little surprised when the Stargate loomed before them, gleaming majestically in the moonlight.

Daniel punched in the address and gave the Goa'uld words for 'Strident of Voice'; *"Aaa Kheru."*

In the cool reflected light of the wormhole, the four looked at each other. Carter beamed at Daniel who passed on a smile to Teal'c. Teal'c quirked his lips and inclined his head toward Jack. Jack broke out his cheesiest smile, gave them all a lop-sided grin and ushered them to the Stargate.

"Hi ho, hi ho!"

"Oh, please, you're not going to sing, are you?"

"And what's wrong with my singing?"

"Nothing a good coach couldn't fix, sir."

"There are legends of a planet where those who cannot sing in tune are highly revered."

"Hey! I'll have you know...."

GATE SEVEN

Roaring Voice

"**I** have a wonderful singing voice." Jack declared as the wormhole spat them out into a cold dampness that wrapped around their bodies like a shroud. They edged closer together on the Stargate platform, itself no more than a narrow shelf of rock. Clouds of mist hung listlessly in the air, blurring definitions of land and sky into one vast, dreary morass. Glaring directly into their eyes, a swollen sun sat just above where the horizon should have been. Its angry red light merged with the mist in the atmosphere and seemed to reach out to them with malevolent intent. Even as they watched it sank lower into the mist's embrace, only minutes from setting.

"Spooky," Daniel muttered.

Jack nodded. The chill, red-tinged fog lent the impression they were standing on a film set, waiting for Count Dracula to enter, stage right. The light that did get through was diffuse, making it difficult to discern objects and distance. Reflected blue shimmers from the wormhole behind them added momentarily to the eeriness before the Stargate shut down. Jack cleared his throat, feeling as if his ears were clogged.

"You know the drill." The words echoed oddly in his head.

The team spread out, Carter to try the DHD and Daniel to check their time limit. Teal'c strode onto the slick rock surrounding the platform. Jack twisted around to look through the Stargate at a sheer wall of clammy rock that rose up until it was lost in the fog.

Secure in the rear, at least.

Daniel straightened up from the moon-clock. He pulled his boonie firmly onto his head and zipped his jacket against the pervading cold. "Seven hours, forty minutes, Jack." He scowled at the eerie light. "This place gives me the willies."

"The willies?" Jack grinned briefly. "Well, stick close and don't wander off. Let's hope we don't have to travel too far in this muck."

"Yeah." Daniel stepped through the ring and stood next to Jack, hands shoved deeply into his pockets. He peered morosely into the mist.

"Daniel?"

"This is the seventh planet we've gated to in, well, I've lost track of how many days. There are still six more before we reach the end of the Trial and whatever is waiting for us there. How much longer do you think we can keep this up, Jack?"

"As long as it takes. *Whatever* it takes."

"Till we run out of food and ammunition, get too injured or exhausted to leave in time?"

"Then we find food, we find other weapons. We're not going to let some stinky *dead* snake get the better of us."

Daniel slid a skeptical glance at Jack.

"Are we?" Jack demanded.

"No. No, of course not." Daniel said the words but the optimism Jack was looking for seemed to be as faint as the fading light.

"As long as we stick together, we'll get through this, Daniel." Jack clapped him on the shoulder and drew him down the five steps to the DHD.

"No go, sir," Carter looked up, the odd light making her look pale and delicate.

"Right. We've only got until 0517 before the door shuts, so let's get moving."

Jack turned and stopped dead in his tracks as Teal'c appeared out of the gloom, the rubicund gleam of his skin from the setting sun giving him an almost demonic aura. The image was not helped by trails of mist curling around his head.

"I have found the next Stargate address and password, O'Neill."

Jack blinked at him in surprise. "Just like that?"

"A row of posts define the boundary of this shelf of rock. Each bears an address glyph and the words of the password."

"They're just sitting there? No hocus pocus or funny walks to get them?"

"They are in plain sight." Teal'c spun on his heel and walked into the mist.

Not even a Fish Slapping Dance? Jack and the others trailed after Teal'c.

Sure enough, not fifteen meters from the Stargate they came across a small stone post, the top of which bore a carved symbol of Crux. It seemed to be glowing faintly, perhaps an effect of the sunset reflecting through the fog. To the right they could barely make out the shape of another. A scant meter beyond the first post, the moisture-slick rock ended abruptly and the fog was sucked over the edge as it flowed toward what seemed certain to be a very long drop.

"There has to be a catch," Carter said. "Why leave them so visible when we've had to search or fight for the others?"

"Well, I'm not about to look a gift-post in the mouth. Daniel, T, go get 'em." He paused, a niggling thought resurfacing. "Carter, do you have the C4 detonators in your pack?"

Daniel trailed after Teal'c, writing down the seven glyphs and the symbols of the password from the eight posts. Teal'c was in no mood to talk and stood silent guard as they moved around the border of what turned out to be a small, half-oval shaped shelf of rock. Once, Daniel glanced up at Teal'c and saw not the friend and trusted teammate he relied upon so much, but a stranger whose cold, expressionless face was bathed in the sun's dying light. A shiver of unease shot through Daniel and he quickly looked away. For a brief moment he felt an angry, evil presence pressing down on him, suffocating him. His breath caught in his throat and his mind blanked out all thought. His hands shook and his skin crawled all over, standing his hair on end. The next moment the sensation was gone.

He forced himself to look up again and this time it was just Teal'c standing there, alert, capable Teal'c.

"Got them, Teal'c." Daniel's voice sounded subdued in his own ears. He coughed the cloying mist from his throat and managed an uncertain smile. "Let's go back to the others."

Teal'c glanced at him, inscrutable and remote. He inclined his head and Daniel followed him through the red mist to where Jack was kneeling on the ground, his open pack before him. Sam stood over him, her body tense, gun gripped tightly. Teal'c seemed ill at ease here too. Daniel had a sudden desire to be gone from this planet—now.

Teal'c frowned at Jack and moved to face the setting sun. "We should leave this place, O'Neill."

"We will, T, we will. Keep your hair on." Jack sat back on his heels and surveyed the gear that he had dragged out of his pack. "I don't get it. I *know* I put the detonators in here. Carter, give me your pack."

Sam stifled an exasperated sigh and handed the pack over. She too turned her back on Jack and looked out into the fog. "Wow. Look at this."

Daniel joined her standing near Teal'c, Jack a step behind. Spread out in panoramic glory before them, the sun was sinking rapidly into the horizon's embrace. Its color shifted into an even deeper, angrier claret. Fiery shafts of light streaked up, reaching out over half the sky. It took only a couple of minutes for the last half of the burning sun to completely disappear. As the final crescent vanished, the reflected streaks of color likewise died, as if a plug had been pulled. The cliff and surrounding rock were plunged into a sudden, sinister darkness.

"Well. That was...."

"Abrupt."

"Amazing."

"Most unsettling."

Their voices seemed somehow muffled by both the darkness and the fog which began to lap thickly at their feet. Guided by two flashlights they returned to their packs. Jack pawed through Sam's, searching vainly for the detonators. He cursed under his breath and grabbed Daniel's.

"Jack, I don't have them. Why do you want them anyway?"

"They have to be somewhere. There was nothing left behind, I checked." Jack shoved the pack back at Daniel and eyed Teal'c, weighing his chances.

"I do not have detonators in my pack or on my person, O'Neill. You will cease this fruitless endeavor and allow us to take our leave. Now."

Jack opened his mouth but Daniel caught Sam's eye. Together they grabbed their belongings and began to gear up.

As Daniel hefted Sam's pack for her to clip on, he looked up at the wall of rock behind the Stargate. Astonished, he watched as a sea of fog flowed down the cliff face. Within seconds, it hit ground level and spread out. It engulfed the Stargate and surged forward to completely cover the four of them. Like a wave, it swept on to pour off the edge of the shelf, an unending tide of cold dankness. He fumbled the pack into place, barely able to see what he was doing. The fog caught in his throat and he coughed, vainly trying to clear it. His head seemed wrapped in cotton wool all of a sudden and his breathing sounded loud in his ears. He coughed again, bending over from the force of it, and nearly leapt out of his skin when a hand grabbed his arm and shook him.

"What? Jeez, Jack. Don't sneak up on me like that."

Jack leaned in close, getting right in Daniel's face. He seemed to be trying to say something but no sound left his lips.

"Jack, what's wrong with your voice?"

Jack stopped trying to talk and stared hard at Daniel. What the hell was wrong with him? First he didn't hear him yelling in his ear and now he seemed to have lost his voice. Daniel tried to speak again, concern creasing his brow, but Jack couldn't hear him.

"Carter, Teal'c, something's wrong with Daniel."

Now there was a statement guaranteed to get a response and yet, they didn't acknowledge him, just proceeded to gear up, their faces turned away from their teammates. A horrible suspicion crept over Jack. He looked back at Daniel who seemed to be talking once more. Jack reached out and lightly wrapped one hand around Daniel's throat.

Surprise stilled Daniel's mouth. Jack glared at him and signaled to keep talking. Eyebrows wriggling, Daniel mouthed a few more words, something along the lines of *'What do you think you're doing?'*

Jack could feel the vibrations inside Daniel's throat as he spoke, but no sound reached his ears. Likewise, Daniel could not seem to hear him. Jack slid his hand around the back of Daniel's neck, drew him close and practically screamed in his ear, *"Can you hear me?"*

Daniel jerked in his grip and turned to stare at him. He nodded, fingers measuring a tiny amount. He spoke again, hands gesturing at his ears, then grabbed Jack's head and brought his lips to his ear. Faintly, as if through a long tunnel, Daniel's voice reached his ear, inflection indicating he was yelling at full volume.

"I can't hear you. Something's wrong, Jack."

Jack looked over at Carter and Teal'c, both standing staring off into the mist like they were waiting for a bus.

"Hey!" He whacked Teal'c's shoulder for good measure and was rewarded with a flinch of surprise the like of which he'd never seen from the big guy before. Teal'c turned affronted eyes on him, mouth open and forming silent words. Jack did his pantomime routine once more, while Daniel tried to communicate with Carter with much flapping of hands. Teal'c nodded his understanding and indicated the thick fog flowing around them, evidently considering it the cause of the problem. Before Jack could wrap his head around the idea, Carter suddenly grabbed Daniel, bawled something at him and took to her heels, disappearing in the fog within seconds.

Daniel waved frantically at Jack and Teal'c, and took off

after Carter. Jack nearly smacked into them a few meters away by the DHD. Carter turned to stare at them, eyes wide and gesturing madly at the DHD.

The collective penny dropped with quite a thud. The DHD would only activate the Stargate with a *spoken* password.

"Well, crap." Jack's words echoed hollowly in his head.

Daniel pulled out his notebook and dialed the address from the boundary posts. As the last chevron lit up dully on the Stargate, he lowered his face almost onto the center crystal and screamed the password, his neck muscles bunching and cording with the strain.

The Stargate stayed inactive, useless to them.

Looking more than a little desperate, Daniel motioned for the others to join him. He dialed once again, showed them the phonetic spelling of the password in his notebook and the four of them yelled as loudly as they could. The result was a mere whisper in their ears.

The chevrons winked out again. The fog wrapped the Stargate in an obscuring shroud and curled clammily around SG-1 as they slumped, trepidation chilling them as surely as the fog.

Three hours. Three hours, twenty seven minutes, forty five seconds to be precise. Jack flipped shut the cover of his chrono with a snap he couldn't hear. Three hours Carter had been at it and they were still no closer to getting the Stargate open. He glanced at her for the hundredth time as she sat cross-legged on the ground, the guts of the DHD scattered around her, desperately trying to cobble something together that would amplify their voices enough to activate the Stargate.

He packed away his shaving kit and looked at the rest of his team, sitting close by. The fog swirled thickly, leaving them barely visible in the light of a three-quarter moon. Teal'c was sunk deep in kel'no'reem. He had conferred with Carter on notepads about the nature of the crystals within the DHD and pointed out those most likely to be of use to her, then he had planted himself on the cold rock and zoned out.

Jack felt the Jaffa's disapproval radiating through the fog at him.

Yeah, I'm carrying the ball on this one, big guy.

In retrospect, it was obvious something would hinder their departure, with the information they needed just sitting there in plain sight. Turning out their gear in a mad search for the detonators had been crazy. He'd been so sure it was vital to find them, and yet, for the life of him he didn't know why. Now... they were stuck here on a rock in the fog of doom and he didn't know what had possessed him.

Teal'c wanted away from here. Should have listened. Should listen more to him generally. The man has three lifetimes' worth of experience.

Jack shifted uncomfortably on the pack underneath him. He stared at Teal'c: so controlled, so intelligent, so alien. Little acknowledged demons rose up in the silence to taunt him. His own military life seemed insignificant compared to Teal'c's. Some days—not many, but some—he had the distinct impression Teal'c was only tolerating his command. That Teal'c would one day reject an order he didn't agree with and leave them. The thought of losing the strength and wisdom, and yeah, friendship he relied on left an even colder chill in his gut.

Need to tell him... what? How much we value him, how much I need him.

The image of him attempting a heart to heart with Teal'c filled his mind and quickly resolved into the two of them staring speechless at each other for hours.

Hockey! Take the man to a game. That'll do it.

Plan of action settled, Jack turned his attention to Daniel, who was hunched over their last remaining camp-stove, heating up coffee for them one cup at a time. Lost in his own thoughts and wrapped in a thermal blanket, he seemed more like the Daniel Jack had dragged back from Abydos—lost and out of his depth—than the self-assured explorer he was now rapidly turning into.

'Are you going to leave the team?'

'No. Yes. No. I—don't know.'

Condensed fog dripped off his cap and into one ear, sending shivers all over. There had been a lot left unspoken in that conversation. Daniel *was* getting further from Sha're and Skaara.

Little wonder he's getting frustrated. If it were my family out there....

Daniel looked up and reached over, offering Jack a steaming cup of coffee. He took it gratefully, the heat leeching through the metal into his numb fingers. Jack settled back, thoughts about his team still bouncing around his skull.

The incessant chill of the fog crept steadily through Daniel's clothing. The lightweight desert camos seemed to absorb the heavy moisture in the air. His two shirts and jacket were slowly losing the fight to keep his body warm, despite the thermal blanket. Water managed to find a path down his neck no matter how tightly he pulled his collar close. His butt was numb and the lacerations on his back and legs ached with a dull, annoying throb. The mist smelled strange, too.

Aggravated, Daniel got up once more and paced slowly around the small perimeter of illumination cast by the flashlight Sam was using. He tucked his fingers under his armpits and stepped over Jack's legs. He kept moving, feeling the boundaries of this new prison encircle and slowly collapse in on him. The urge to break free and just run taunted him, despite a sure and quick death being the only thing that lay beyond the precipice, hidden beneath the fog.

Feeling adrift in the gray morass that churned all around them, he forced himself to remember the warmth of Abydos—the memory of sun on his skin and wide blue skies stretching to far horizons. He sighed and felt his nerves settle.

Sam's on the right path. We'll get out of here. We'll get home....

And then there would be decisions to be made, decisions

that had been fermenting for some months. He shied away from thinking too much about what his future held. It felt as if he was betraying his commitment to Jack, Sam, Teal'c, and the general too, but change must come and it was something that he would have to face soon enough.

We've explored so many worlds already and still no sign of them. One day the SGC's goals will be so focused on weapons and war there'll no longer be an opportunity to search for them.

He stopped pacing, stood in the swirling mist and stared at his three teammates, his three friends.

One day my path will take me away from you. I don't want that, but I know I'll do it. As long as it takes, as far as I have to go... I will keep looking for them.

A stab of pain seared his heart at the thought of leaving them, of forgoing the security of one family to search for the lost shreds of another, of being out there alone amongst the Goa'uld — but that course had been charted in his fate two and a half years earlier and there was no denying it. That Jack or Sam or Teal'c could be hurt or, heaven forbid, killed when he wasn't there to help them....

He shivered and walked on.

The meditative peace of kel'no'reem faded as Teal'c returned to the conscious world. Silence hung close about him, thick and cloying. Denied the comforting chatter of his comrades, he was left with only the stirrings of his hated symbiote and in the unnatural silence, he could almost hear its evil radiating up from its womb.

Teal'c shook himself and forced his mind to more constructive thoughts as Daniel Jackson emerged from the moonlit mist like a troubled wraith. Hands shoved deeply into pockets and head bent, he walked a circle around his team and the DHD, vanishing and reappearing in the darkness. Teal'c looked over at O'Neill, who was stretched out asleep, one hand curled possessively around his gun. Further away, Major

Carter worked determinedly to ensure their exit from this benighted place. He found their presence comforting in a way he had rarely encountered from comrades in his many years. His trust in these three people had developed so quickly, to such a degree, that when faced with the choice of revealing the existence of his lost babes or using another, less meaningful memory to place at the testing altar, he had known deep in his soul that the memories of his children would be treasured and held safely by his friends. The mere mention of their names, so long unspoken, seemed to bring them closer to his heart now.

Daniel Jackson emerged from the fog once more and stopped by Major Carter's side. That none of the three had pressed Teal'c for details of the children and their loss endeared them to him even more.

A particularly thick drift of fog passed between him and the others, suddenly obscuring them and leaving Teal'c isolated. He frowned. A chill that had nothing to do with the fog ran over his skin. He felt… a presence, one so old and imbued with ill-intent that for a moment he froze, unable to defend himself or his team from the evil that he was certain would consume them all.

As swiftly as it had come, the sensation passed and he sprang to his feet, weapon primed. He swung in a circle to meet this new foe and found nothing but swirling mist. Unsettled, he looked closely but could discern no threat. A faint puff of wind stirred the mist once more and revealed the dim outlines of the others.

Teal'c straightened up and moved closer to his friends. He took up sentry position between O'Neill and the DHD and glared out into the fog.

Four and a half hours she'd been at this and still nothing. Sam looked at the pile of crystals, tools and supplies at her feet; every nonessential component she could haul out of the DHD and scavenge from the equipment they carried had been examined, tinkered with, tried and failed to produce a jury-rigged amplifier that would carry their voices with sufficient volume into the DHD and trigger the voice-activated device that would engage the Stargate.

Seized with a sudden fit of pique she hurled a stone away into the shadows. It bounced once then disappeared, not even giving the satisfaction of a decent clatter.

The silence was driving her batty.

You'll never know what you'll miss until it's gone.

Was she really so dependent on sound to keep her grounded? She focused on the memory of the jungle noise from the rainforest planet: the chaotic blend of bird and animal calls, the wind in the trees, the rush of water hurtling onto rocks at the base of the waterfall. So beautiful. Now, all there was were her own thoughts and the pulse of blood in her temples. She missed hearing her teammates' voices; even when sniping at each other it was noise, companionship. Comfort.

She looked over at them again, something that seemed to be developing into a nervous habit, checking they were still here, that she wasn't alone in this dark, dank place. Teal'c had returned to sentry-duty, a barely visible shadow. The colonel had finally given up staring at them all and stretched out for a nap. She envied him that ability to drop off to sleep, whatever the surroundings. Daniel sat nearest her, his restless pacing abandoned. He had followed the colonel's lead and shaved. Now he was still, the notebook he had been writing in lying forgotten in his lap. He was staring at the scraps of moss on the rocks in front of him, his only movement the fingers restlessly rubbing his injured leg.

They're all so trusting that I'll get them out of here. Nothing we have is sufficient to transmit a voice at the volume we need.

It hadn't taken much effort to deduce the fog, or some element—natural or Goa'uld designed—in it, was causing the sound dampening effect. The way it had swept down from the cliffs the moment the sun's rays had vanished suggested it could be a common phenomenon on this planet—one Ra had exploited for his little game. Or it was just another of the dirty tricks set up by Ra for the Trial. If one were lucky enough to arrive during daylight there was presumably no problem dialing straight out. Be caught here after dark and here you stayed.

With a lab full of equipment and enough time, Sam knew she would be able to isolate the cause of the sound dampening and find a truly ingenious way to engage the audio pickup, but here and now…. Despair threatened to swamp her but she angrily pushed it away. *Focus, dammit. You need to come at it from a different direction.*

Her eyes fixed on Daniel — always the foil she needed to kick up new ideas. She crawled over to him and grabbed his arm, making him startle out of wherever his thoughts had taken him. He looked cold and miserable, with moisture dripping off his boonie and soaking into his collar. Sam grabbed his notebook, flipping past what looked like Ra's family tree and a sketch of Bes to a fresh page. She pulled his pen from his hand and scribbled quickly across the damp paper.

'Nothing is working. The crystals, the radio — I even tried using the black filaments in the DHD — nothing will transmit enough volume.'

Daniel frowned over her words for a while, then wrote, *'Could you reverse the audio pickup thingy in the DHD?'*

'Tried that — no go.'

'Head-butt DHD?'

She let out a breath of laughter.

'Don't tempt me!'

She sighed and clawed a strand of damp hair off her neck. Her gaze drifted to the now cold stove by Daniel's pack. *Heat disperses fog.* But one small stove would not be enough to drive back the fog. She looked around them. Even before the mist had descended, she had seen nothing but rock and moss on the shelf they were confined to. Certainly nothing combustible.

Daniel nudged her, silently querying the frown on her face.

She took up his pen again. *'If we could generate enough heat we might be able to burn the fog away from the DHD.'*

Nodding, Daniel thought for a moment then crawled over to the colonel and shook him awake. Sam followed and Teal'c joined them as Colonel O'Neill read her words in the notebook Daniel showed him. The colonel pursed his lips in thought, then dragged his pack up and pulled out three blocks of C4. Looking up at Teal'c he motioned for him to retrieve his own supply of the explosive, then rose to his feet and headed toward the DHD, leaving Sam and Daniel staring at each other in trepidation.

Sam had an inkling of what the colonel intended. She climbed to her feet and with Daniel, walked to the DHD. The colonel and Teal'c were already laying the blocks of C4 in a tight circle. She gathered up her scattered equipment and shoved it into her pack and out of the way. Standing next to Daniel, they watched the colonel show Teal'c how to strip the Mylar covering off the blocks to reveal the explosive within. With the blocks set in position, Colonel O'Neill stepped back, clearly thinking his plan through. He looked at Daniel, still wrapped in his space blanket, and smiled, then pulled his own folded poncho from his tac vest and indicated to Sam and Teal'c to do likewise.

Shaking out the poncho, the colonel pantomimed his plan: they would set fire to the C4 around the DHD, and using the ponchos and blanket to trap the resulting heat in the circle, burn off the fog and dial out. Sam nodded, impressed with the simplicity of the plan. It might just work. Daniel shrugged, willing to give anything a try. They returned to their gear and stowed what they had been using, dropping the packs and their weapons within easy reach.

The colonel positioned them around the DHD with ponchos and blanket spread wide over their shoulders. Pausing for a moment, he then went to Daniel's pack, rummaged for a bit and came back with a bag of disposable face masks. He passed them out, making sure they each had one secured over nose and mouth. Sam knew how toxic the smoke from burning C4 could be.

With everything set, Colonel O'Neill produced a lighter and began to ignite the blocks. Sam saw Daniel flinch a little and gave him a thumbs-up reassurance that there was no real danger of an explosion—as long as no-one tried to stamp out the fire. Once all the blocks were burning the colonel joined them outside the ring and raised his poncho.

Like four enormous butterflies they made sweeping, scooping motions with their arms, producing enough draft with the material to stir the rising heat upward and around the DHD. Face averted from the fumes, Sam caught a vivid image of her teammates illuminated in the fires' glow: their bodies and faces burnished a stark red against the darkness behind. It was a strange, ethereal moment—one that would stand out in a career full of other-worldly exploits.

Slowly, the fog began to thin until Sam realized she could see the others' features quite clearly. She caught the colonel's gaze and he nodded.

He opened his mouth and seemed to bellow, "Can you hear me?"

It was much softer than his usual loudness, but she *could* hear him. "Yes! Colonel, it's working!" she yelled.

"Flap harder!" he hollered back. "Daniel, get that password ready."

Daniel nodded and dropped the space blanket. Notebook in hand he stepped up to the DHD and dialed the address for the next planet. He hesitated, and with an indication from the colonel, slapped the activation crystal and shouted the password, *"Uaau!"*

Time paused for one awful, suspenseful moment.

The Stargate blossomed into life with a silent surge of light. It powered forward then backward through the ring, stirring the fog into mad swirls and leaving a clear hole both fore and aft as the event horizon settled into peaceful ripples.

The colonel let out a whoop Sam could actually hear.

Grabbing up her pack, poncho and weapon, she ran to the Stargate, the others hard on her heels, leaving the C4 to burn itself out. Inches away from the event horizon she paused, until her teammates flanked her on each side. With a quick glance to ensure they were all together, they stepped as one into the wormhole and were swept away.

GATE EIGHT

Bringer of Darkness

Sam instantly regretted sucking in that first instinctive breath on exiting the wormhole; air that felt like liquid nitrogen filled her throat, freezing her tongue and making her teeth ache.

"Mmph!"

She clamped her mouth shut, but that just made her nose ache too. Cold—sub-zero, shrink-your-eyeballs kind of cold—hit her all over. And it was dark. Very dark. All too aware the glow of the wormhole made them a target easily seen for some distance, she brought her weapon up. The others slurped through the event horizon beside her and immediately set up a chorus of complaints.

"Man, this is colder than a polar bear's ass."

"Oh boy, this is too much." Daniel's hands were already back under his armpits. "Can't we go home now?"

Even Teal'c looked daunted by the cold, but he braced himself and glanced enquiringly at Sam. "May I ask why you are smiling, Major Carter?"

"I can hear you all again. I can hear me!"

"Nice to hear your dulcet tones too, Carter."

The wormhole whisked away to nothingness and left them standing in utter darkness.

"Whoops."

"Nuts." The colonel switched on his MP5's light. "Daniel, the flashlights are in your pack."

"Uh, no they're not. I've got a pen light somewhere." Daniel's slightly darker outline could just be seen bending over.

The colonel snapped open the cover of his chrono and the

phosphorescent dial shone out like a tiny moon. "Yes, they are. I put them there."

"I know, but I took them out to make room for one of the first aid kits because Sam ended up with two of them."

"Carter?"

"Um, I don't think I've got them, sir," she replied, also turning on her gun's light.

"Well, how about we all just stand here in the dark and whistle then?" the colonel said acidly.

"I believe I have them, O'Neill." Teal'c fished around in the duffle he carried and finally produced four flashlights.

Daniel found his small, powerful pen light, switched it on and pointed it outward to find — trees.

"That's a lot of trees." Sam peered past the glare at the forest of slim, straight trunks surrounding them in all directions.

Daniel shone the beam on bare earth then up into stark, empty branches. Three more beams joined his to illuminate the ghostly limbs.

"Everything's dead."

"They could have been like this for hundreds of years," Sam said, her face wreathed in moisture condensing from her breath.

"They probably died of the cold, like I'm about to," the colonel snapped. "Can we skip the nature tour and get on with it please?" He shook out his poncho and began refolding it.

Teal'c straightened up from the moon-clock. "Eight hours, twenty-seven minutes."

Sam tipped her face up and drank in the beautiful sight of a clear black sky studded with millions of bright stars. Out there in space not too far away blazed a nebula in green and gold glory.

"No moon in sight."

"None of the indicators are lit yet, Major Carter."

"Daniel, go dial home."

Daniel walked cautiously over to the DHD. This time there was no platform for the Stargate to rest on, merely a patch of ground. Nothing grew around either machine. There was a morbid quiet to this place, unsettling after the enforced silence of their last stop-over. Sam watched him stand for a moment, working out how to dial up without removing his hands from under his arms.

"Anyone else feel a bit… off-balance?" Daniel asked.

"Could be an inner ear thing from fog-world." Colonel O'Neill stuck a finger in his ear and gave it a good poke. "Place reminded me of all those old British black and white movies."

"I think it's more likely this planet's gravity is lighter than what we're used to, sir," said Sam. "Actually, it's surprising we don't come across more planets with higher or lower gravity than the Earth norm."

Teal'c grunted derisively. "The Goa'uld dislike the sensation of low gravity. It makes them irritable."

The colonel let out a hoot. "Goa'uld are *born* irritable. How can you tell the difference?"

Teal'c's face twitched in a slight smirk. "Higher gravity sends them to sleep. They therefore choose planets that have gravity similar to that of Earth."

"Interesting," mused Sam, adding the information to her list of potential weapons to use against their enemy. She watched Daniel punch in the address for Earth, one hand still tucked under the opposite arm and his right hand fisted inside his jacket sleeve. He was shivering already.

As expected, the Stargate failed to open.

"Right, before we do anything, I suggest we put on as many clothes as possible, or hypothermia's going to be a problem real soon."

They followed the colonel's lead and pulled out all the spare clothing they had from their packs, which, considering they had kitted out for a three day mission and most of their gear was lost, was precious little. Teal'c frowned as Daniel pulled on a long-sleeve t-shirt and contemplated the remains of his only other spare: a shredded souvenir of the earlier Goa'uld attack. Teal'c leaned over, pulled the shirt out of Daniel's hand, and replaced it with his own long-sleeve tee.

"You will be much warmer wearing this, Daniel Jackson."

"Teal'c, no, you need it."

"I do not. My symbiote will sustain my body temperature at acceptable levels. I know you are bothered by the cold."

"Yeah, remind me again why you live in Colorado Springs, Daniel?" the colonel asked.

Sam smiled in the darkness. One of the recent betting pools at the SGC had been about how many layers of clothing Doctor Jackson could arrive on base in and still be able to move.

"I'm conducting an anthropological study into the effect of severe cold upon the higher reasoning function of males in the mature populace."

Colonel O'Neill's grin soured and he glared at Daniel. "Here, Teal'c, you'll need this at least." He leaned over and yanked his woolly beanie down over the bald head.

Teal'c's eyebrows disappeared into the hat, perhaps seeking out the promised warmth.

"Thank you, O'Neill."

Everyone pulled on extra socks, tees and shirts. Daniel tied his bandana on, well down over his ears, and pulled his boonie on top. His thick work gloves and space blanket completed the ensemble. He was still hunched over against the cold. Sam knew how he felt. She zipped and buttoned her jacket and snugged the collar up around her neck, but the silk lining lay cold against her throat. She pulled a compass from her pack; the small thermometer she had attached to it bore the bad news.

"Minus seven degrees."

"Great. Now I really feel cold," stuttered Daniel.

"The compass is jerking all over the place." She looked at the little red needle which flitted randomly back and forth. "Must be some interesting magnetic forces at work here."

"Which rules out splitting up to search for whatever it is

we're supposed to find here," the colonel sighed. "Alright, line search then."

He plucked a lightstick from the remaining survival gear, bent and shook it and placed it on top of the DHD. It shone like a beacon in the encompassing dark.

"Daniel, you'll be the anchor, twenty paces out. Teal'c, twenty paces out from Daniel, then Carter, then me. Keep the lights on either side of you in view at all times and radios on. If anyone loses sight of a light, stop immediately and hail us. We'll go clockwise, walking pace." He handed out a lightstick to each of them and tucked one in his vest pocket. "Keep these on you for backup. Good to go?"

They nodded and murmured acknowledgements, faces eerie in the puffs of condensing breath drifting over the green glow of the lightstick.

"Let's do it."

Colonel O'Neill took the lead, measuring twenty careful paces away from the DHD into the silent, dead forest. There he stopped, looking back to ensure a clear line of sight to the green beacon on the DHD. He nodded to Daniel and left him behind with a brief touch on the arm. Twenty paces further on, Teal'c took up position and the three of them glanced anxiously back to Daniel, his flashlight and pale uniform making him seem like a specter hovering among the trees.

The colonel clapped Teal'c on the shoulder as he and Sam left, then did the same to her as he headed out alone on the final twenty paces—small touches that kept him connected with his team. Sam could see his light clearly, Teal'c's a paler glow. Daniel was completely swallowed up by the inky night.

"Everyone got a sighting on their next-in-line?"

"Five by five, Colonel."

"Acknowledged, O'Neill."

"Yeah," Daniel puffed, sounding as if he were jogging on the spot. "Need to move. Now!"

"Okay. Clockwise, that's facing twelve o'clock away from the 'gate. Daniel, remember to walk slowly, we've all got more ground to cover. Okay… by the right… go."

Slowly they paced through the darkness, following their flashlight beams in a circle around the Stargate. It was not easy; their progress hampered by the need to search around for anything other than a tree while keeping the light of the next person in line in clear view and not banging into or tripping over the close-packed trunks.

A bundle of white sticks caught Sam's eye and she crouched next to them. "Think I have something," she managed over the chattering of her teeth.

"Everyone hold," ordered the colonel.

"Oh, it's a body. Skeleton, actually. Whoever it was, they've been here a long time."

She gently picked over the bones, but found nothing of use. She grimaced and stood back. This was a very lonely place to die. A sudden, creeping sensation of something standing right behind her made her swing around, sending the flashlight's beam darting madly over stark tree limbs. Her lungs and brain seemed to seize up. For just a fraction of a second she was consumed by the certainty that evil was all around her—and then it was gone again. There were only shadows and trees, stars and the distant lights of her team. She shook her head and pulled herself together.

"Nothing of use here, sir. Ready to continue."

"Okay. Forward ho."

For over an hour they searched the forest, the cold leeching into their bones, numbing feet and fingers, noses and cheeks. The silence of the place was just as chilling.

"The lack of animal life is disturbing," Teal'c said quietly over the radio.

"Not even any insects." Sam cast another look up through skeletal branches at the glorious night sky. "That we can see," she clarified. "Life on Earth has been found in the most inhospitable places. Could be there are animals in hibernation, insects under the ground waiting for the sun to return." She sighed. "These planets are amazing. I wish we had the time to study them properly, or at least find a way to break what's controlling the Stargates and come back some day."

"Never say never, Carter."

"Ah, guys? I think we're back where we started."

Sam peered through the darkness in Daniel's direction but he remained invisible to her.

"Damn. Nothing nearby even remotely snaky." Colonel O'Neill changed direction and headed toward her. They collected Teal'c and returned to Daniel.

"Well, at least we seem secure here; we've made enough noise and light to wake up a platoon of Jaffa." The darkness pressed closer around their lights and Jack could see the effect the cold was having on them all, Teal'c included.

"Daniel, break out the stove. We could do with something hot. You've all got your thermal blankets? I'm going to get a fire going." Jack moved a little way into the forest seeking fallen timber.

Daniel shared a puzzled look with Carter, but they trailed after their fearless leader who already had an inquisitive Teal'c on his heels. "You're not going to use C4 again, are you?" Daniel asked with trepidation. "You've been itching to blow something up for days now. I'm just hoping it's not us…" He trailed off as Jack found a likely log, isolated from any others, and shot a glare back at him.

Jack picked up a handful of twigs and planted them in a hollow half-way along the tree's length. He pulled out his ancient lighter and set fire to the wood. Within minutes the dried-out tree was well ablaze and the four were clustered around it, well upwind of the smoke, like cats seeking the warmest spot in the house.

Two cups of hot soup later, Jack sighed and repositioned his feet by the glowing tree. The flames had subsided into cheery red coals and they were all feeling much more alive.

"Nice fire, Jack." Daniel was huddled as close as he could

get to the warmth, trying to judge if his boots were smoking too much.

"Which reminds me, where did you pick up the idea to use C4 like that, Colonel?"

"On a little trip to Central America a few years back, Carter." Jack and Teal'c sat with their backs to the fire on opposite sides of the log, keeping watch, quietly discussing how they would find the next address and password in this consuming darkness.

"It doesn't get that cold in Central America does it, sir?"

"Nope. It wasn't cold. Just needed to start a fire." Jack shelved that particular memory and looked up into the jeweled sky. The stars had wheeled on in their journey, the nebula was higher in the sky and impossibly, more beautiful. He tilted back further. The light gravity made him feel tenuously connected to the earth, as if it would take only one push to float upward and soar amongst the stars.

"On nights like this, one often gets the impression that others are looking down at you, as you look up at them," said Teal'c softly, likewise gazing into the heavens.

"I read a quote once," Carter said. "'What we have learned is like a handful of earth; what we have yet to learn is like the whole world'."

Daniel dropped his head back and let his eyes roam the sparkling velvet sky. "There's so much to explore. Even knowing there is life beyond Earth now, I still wonder what kind of people are out there; what they're like, what their histories are, if they'd like us."

"If they'll shoot us before they eat us."

"Nice one, Jack." Daniel threw his soup packet at him.

"Hey, call me Mr. Practical. And I do believe our moon is on the rise."

He pointed to a brightening in the sky behind the Stargate, as an orange glow suddenly defined the horizon. It rose majestically, taking just five minutes to become a full spherical shape, easily four times the size of one of Earth's full moons.

Its color was not the expected gentle white, but rather a violent, angry orange.

"It's on fire."

"Holy buckets."

They came to their feet, craning for a better view between the trees.

"Actually, I think it's volcanic." Carter dragged out her binoculars. "Oh, wow, is it ever volcanic. The entire surface is covered in eruptions and lava flows."

The closeness of the erupting moon brought an eerie amber light to the dead forest.

"At least we might be able to see further now." Jack abandoned a half-assed plan to set a stretch of the forest on fire and took the binoculars from Carter. Suitably impressed, he held them out for Teal'c. When they were not taken, he looked around. Teal'c was facing into the darkness, body tense, hand clenched on his staff weapon.

"T? What is it?"

"I caught a glimmer of light, some distance away."

"Here." Jack handed him the binoculars.

Teal'c pressed his right eye to the glasses and stared intently. His night vision had always been better than Jack's.

"There is something reflecting the moon's light. I am unable to gauge the distance in this darkness, however."

"Alright, well, it's better than nothing. Pack it up. We'll leave the lightsticks as markers."

Reluctantly, they extinguished the fire and followed Teal'c away into the cold night, their warmed skin quickly chilling. As they went, they left a trail of lightsticks, their green glow marking the way back to the safety of the Stargate.

What loomed out of the blackness was unexpected. In place of stone—monumental or otherwise—SG-1 found a dome-shaped structure, entirely made of a clear, crystalline material.

Daniel tapped the surface experimentally as the others prowled warily around it. A faint harmonic chime reverberated along the wall. The whole thing gleamed, reflecting the violent light emanating from the moon. "Looks like a mineral of some kind."

"Looks like a gazebo to me," Jack decided. "And if anybody starts singing *'Sixteen Going On Seventeen'*, so help me.... There's only one way in."

"This does not resemble any Goa'uld architecture I have previously encountered." Teal'c lapped Jack on another circuit around the structure.

Daniel's silver-shrouded figure followed him, looking instead at the detail of the construction. "There's no decoration, no name to indicate ownership. I can barely even see any joins in the surface. I don't think the Goa'uld made this. Ra probably just appropriated it, like everything else the Goa'uld use."

"Is there anything to show that Ra did use it?" Sam asked, joining them as they stopped before the single narrow doorway.

Four flashlight beams danced inside, illuminating a pedestal in the center of an otherwise empty room. Upon it stood a golden statue, three feet tall, in human form with a sharp-beaked bird's head. One outstretched arm supported a star, one foot rested on an Eye of Ra symbol. Apart from the statue and pedestal, the structure was empty, the orange light casting eerie reflections through the crystal walls.

"I'd say that's a yes, Carter." Jack stepped forward but was stopped by Teal'c's arm across his chest.

"O'Neill, perhaps we should reduce the illumination we use in this place." Teal'c indicated the outer walls of the 'gazebo', now brightly reflecting their flashlights, a sure announcement of their presence. Three beams clicked off and they followed Jack and his light into the chamber.

"Daniel." Jack motioned him forward, switching off his own light as Daniel turned his on and circled the pedestal.

"Well, this is different." Daniel stared up at the statue. "The ibis was used to represent Thoth, or Djehuti, and he's standing on the Eye, which would indicate a close association with Ra."

"Do we know this guy?" Jack asked Teal'c, who frowned and shook his head.

"He was one of the oldest creation gods, god of the moon, creator of everything, the original Scribe." Daniel's eyes shone with anticipation. He discarded the thermal blanket and pulled out his camera. He knelt and focused on the writing carved into the pedestal. "In early times he was sometimes known as Seshat—goddess of libraries—before the mythology split into two separate identities and genders."

"Librarians have a god?" Jack's lips twitched.

"Well, libraries actually. More specifically writing, time, knowledge, that kind of thing."

Jack shook his head and wandered out the door for a quick recce.

"Anyway, the writing here talks about the Books of Djehuti. Djehuti—the Goa'uld, that is—seems to have been something like Ra's personal historian: 'The Voice of Ra'." He traced the raised script with his fingers as he read.

"There's something else here." Daniel backtracked around the pedestal. "Ah, got it. It says, 'By proclaiming these words, will the supplicant show his', I think it's 'readiness, to hold the Books of Djehuti and will reveal', something like that, 'all that is hidden in the stars, see the sun and moon in their true form, perceive the birds of the air and the beasts of the land, behold the true face of the god and receive the keys to the Trial of Moons'." An excited thrill ran through him at the thought of what they could be about to discover. He straightened and looked up at the others as Jack returned.

"I think we just say the phrase here and we get not only the next address but the Books of Djehuti as well. This is incredible! The Books of Thoth were said to contain the secrets of the gods themselves. Think of the knowledge we can gain of Ra's history."

"Why would Ra give out information like that?" Sam

frowned.

"Well, presumably he'd want people, if they succeed in the Trial, to have a comprehensive knowledge of his accomplishments when they take up his service. If they don't succeed then the knowledge dies with them."

"I am uncomfortable with this situation, Daniel Jackson. I do not believe we have all the information we require."

"Well, take a look yourself, Teal'c. That's all there is."

"Sounds way too easy to me, Daniel." Jack peered at the characters engraved on the pedestal.

"What form do these Books take?" Sam asked.

"It doesn't say." Daniel stepped back as the three others inspected the statue and pedestal. He shivered—cold again—and bit back a sigh of frustration that his teammates couldn't share the excitement he felt. Even an edited history of Ra would be invaluable to the understanding of the System Lords.

"How about I just say the phrase and we find out?"

"Not so fast there, Daniel." Jack didn't even glance back at him. "Teal'c, you got any idea what these 'Books' are?"

"I doubt they would take the form of your paper books, O'Neill. Most likely they would be in some kind of data storage unit. Perhaps it is merely a holographic display."

"Well, we won't know unless we activate it," Daniel persisted.

Sam looked at him, an odd expression on her face. "We do need to be as prepared as we can, though, Daniel. You of all people should realize the danger of using unknown technology; Machello's readers looked harmless enough. Have a little care for yourself."

"I do, I…." he trailed off, stung by her words.

"Can we find a way to see what these Book things look like before we activate them?" Jack frowned at Sam.

"Yes, sir."

Twenty minutes of Teal'c and Sam poking and prodding at the pedestal got them nowhere, while Daniel, wrapped once more in his blanket, scowled at them.

"There is no way to access the inner compartments of the pedestal, O'Neill, if indeed there are any."

"Great. *Now* can I activate it?" Daniel asked, trying only a little to temper his impatience.

Before Jack could answer, Sam jumped in with both boots. "Well, why should it be *you* who activates it?"

"Because you and Jack don't read Goa'uld script. Teal'c's not an archaeologist. I am. What's the problem?"

"The problem is it could be dangerous. If it is Goa'uld technology of some kind then I think Teal'c should be the one to deal with it, so we don't have to deal with you losing your mind again." Sam's eyes widened and she clamped her lips shut in a useless attempt to take back the words as her brain registered what she had said.

"Carter!" Jack barked at her, anger and astonishment in his voice.

Daniel blinked at her, offense and betrayal spearing through him.

"Daniel, I'm sorry. I didn't mean it to come out that way."

"No, I'm sorry, Sam, if my apparent instability was inconvenient to you." He folded his arms and frowned at the crystal floor.

"That's not... I'm just concerned. I have this feeling... I don't know where it's coming from. Maybe it's Jolinar, I'm...."

"Oh, yes. Here we go." Daniel's head came up, irritation flaring up to replace the hurt.

"What's that supposed to mean?"

"It means you keep coming up with these odd little bits of information from Jolinar, but they're really nothing special are they? Nothing that Teal'c doesn't already know. Why don't you try for something a bit more meaningful for once?"

He could see Teal'c shifting uneasily behind her and Jack was getting ready to shut them down. Daniel knew his words were hitting way too close to something she had been skirting around for months, but she wasn't yet ready to admit it.

"Like what?" Sam bristled.

"Oh, I don't know. How about something simple? Like where my wife is?" He bit the words out, voice brittle and contained, a store of anguish bottled behind carefully constructed walls.

"How could I *possibly*... I don't...." He saw her remember, even as he spelled it out for her.

"In the brig, Jolinar said she knew where Sha're was. Why can't you remember, why can't you tell me, when it means my whole *life?*" His voice caught and he had to look away.

"I *don't* know, Daniel. God, if I did... I'm...." *Afraid*. The word hung unspoken in the chill air between them.

"Enough." Jack's voice was harsh. "Carter, head out and do a recce will you?"

"Sir."

She spun and walked out into the darkness.

Teal'c stood uncomfortably in the strained silence that settled over the three men.

"Sorry." Daniel Jackson heaved out a big sigh. "Tired. Cold."

The colonel patted him on the arm. "Let's just get this done, shall we?"

"O'Neill, I believe Major Carter is correct," Teal'c said, softly, insistently.

O'Neill tightened his grip on Daniel, quelling another outburst. "How so, T?"

"This Trial was designed to be undertaken primarily by Goa'uld or Jaffa. Whatever these Books are, they could prove harmful to someone not carrying a symbiote." Teal'c caught a glimpse of the look on Daniel's face—mutinous to say the least.

"Noted. But, on the other hand they could be designed to harm someone *with* a symbiote. It may be prudent to safeguard our only asset in that regard. Nothing about this setup has been easy. Daniel can do it—but let's be on our toes for anything hinky. Okay?"

Teal'c acceded to the request but it did not sit well. Prepared for the worst, he took position near Daniel Jackson as he stepped up to the pedestal.

For a moment, Daniel re-read the inscriptions, then looked up and spoke the words meaning 'Mistress of the Night'. *"Nebt Usha."*

The star, held in the statue of Djehuti's hand, unfolded like a flower and brightened as a violet crystal rose up from inside it. It angled around, tracking the direction the phrase had come from, until it faced Daniel square-on. The color and an accompanying whine deepened, then seemed to pulse and a tiny object flew out, directly toward Daniel Jackson.

Teal'c reacted with instincts honed by decades of training. One large step and he crashed into Daniel's left side, pitching him into O'Neill. As the two of them staggered, Teal'c felt a sharp pain in his side, just behind the hip bone. Unbalanced, he slammed painfully to his knees.

"Ooof." O'Neill staggered with an armful of archaeologist. He set Daniel on his feet and they both turned to yell at Teal'c.

"What the hell was that for?" Daniel got in first.

"My apologies, Daniel Jackson." Teal'c replied. He felt odd, his self-possession compromised. His legs would not obey his desire to rise. "I feared for your safety. I hope I did not injure you."

"I'm alright," Daniel frowned, rubbing his left side.

"Teal'c, you okay?" O'Neill extended a hand to help Teal'c to his feet. "T?"

"You're bleeding." Daniel knelt by Teal'c and reached out tentatively to the stream of blood already flowing from under his jacket.

"Carter, get in here," O'Neill yelled, a split-second before she hurried through the doorway, already alerted by the commotion. "First aid kit."

Teal'c closed his eyes and shuddered. A strange sensation was sweeping over him, from scalp to the soles of his feet. It was as if he had been cut adrift. He could barely feel his teammates' hands as they tended his wound. And he could not feel the symbiote—at all.

"You may have been correct, O'Neill," he whispered.

"Y'know, it does say 'Colonel' on my office door for a reason." The colonel found himself with an armload of Jaffa this time as Teal'c slowly sagged forward. "Get a bandage on that wound. Daniel, did you see what hit him?"

"No, I just got a brief glimpse of something small and purple." Daniel Jackson's voice was filled with annoyance and concern.

They eased Teal'c to the ground and he lay quietly, trying to assess the sensations he was feeling as he listened to his teammates inspect the tiny hole in his skin. It bled profusely, but whatever the projectile was, it was deeply embedded and out of sight. After several minutes of applied pressure, the bleeding slowed. Major Carter swathed it in antiseptic and a field dressing as Teal'c began to stir.

Chill waves swept through his body, followed by an unaccustomed surge of nausea. He looked up at his teammates anxiously hovering over him. His strength returned, slowly but not completely. There was something else, a presence or undefined otherness, just out of perception. He even glanced over his shoulder to check another person had not joined them.

"Well?" O'Neill demanded testily.

Teal'c concentrated inwardly and then—he knew. "I believe the Books of Djehuti have been implanted within me." He was filled with wonder as hints of the knowledge contained in the projectile made themselves known.

Voiceless passages whispered in his brain.

"I have words, *'Maa Nefert Ra'.* 'Beholder of the Beauty of Ra'. It is the password to unlock the Stargate. Also, yes, the address for the next planet."

"Okay, that's a good thing," O'Neill conceded. "Any side

effects?"

Teal'c frowned. Searching past the whispers in his mind, he reached out for that other familiar presence. It was barely there. He pulled his shirt free and dipped a hand into his pouch. The symbiote moved against his fingers, sluggishly, as if drugged.

"I believe my symbiote has been neutralized in some way."

Daniel gave a snort of exasperation. "I'm not going to say I told you so."

"Can you move, Teal'c?" Major Carter asked.

"I can."

He fumbled around, seeking and not finding the strength to rise. Finally it took his three teammates to shove and haul him to his feet.

"Daniel, you got everything you might need from here?" O'Neill asked.

"Yes, I've made copies of the inscriptions."

"Right, fall back to the 'gate. Carter, take point. Daniel, give me a hand here."

Teal'c leaned heavily on O'Neill and Daniel Jackson as they assisted him though the forest, following Major Carter along the trail of markers back to the Stargate. The moon sat directly above their heads now, hanging so close Teal'c fought the instinct to duck. Its infernal light cast the dead forest into a demonic display of grotesque shapes and shadows so dark the eye skittered over them, unwilling to look too closely. He grimaced and forced his weakened legs to move more quickly.

In contrast to the fires raging above them, the cold was even more intense, stealing into their muscles and bones, sapping their life's warmth. Major Carter maintained a slow jog, keeping to the pace of the men behind her, Teal'c's staff clutched in one gloved hand. The line of green markers loomed out of the dark, leading back to the dead coals of their fire. She paused there, but the colonel jerked his head, indicating to keep moving, no breath left to spare for words.

Finally the Stargate rose out of the gloom, a welcome friend in this alien place with its chevrons gleaming in the flickering moonlight. They staggered to a halt and propped Teal'c against the DHD. He braced himself, relieved to find he could stand unaided.

"Teal'c, how are you doing?" Major Carter asked as his helpers caught their breath, wheezing and puffing like two old men.

"My strength returns somewhat, Major Carter."

"These Books, are you picking anything else up from them yet?" asked O'Neill.

"Vague impressions only." Teal'c placed a hand over his pouch, satisfying himself the symbiote was still there. "There is great knowledge within them, of that I am sure."

"There were a number of legends, stories, about the Books of Thoth," Daniel wheezed. He began to walk slowly around the DHD, rubbing a cramp that threatened his left leg. "The holder was supposedly given the power to raise their Ka—see their souls. Although, how the Goa'uld have interpreted that is anyone's guess," he added wistfully.

O'Neill sidled up to Teal'c. "What possessed you to shove him out of the way like that?"

Teal'c straightened and glanced at Daniel Jackson before answering quietly. "I fear one day such harm will befall Daniel Jackson that I will be unable to protect him, and my failure in my duty to him will be complete." He lowered his eyes from O'Neill's gaze, troubled but unrepentant.

"Can't argue with that. Well, I can, but it can wait for somewhere warmer." O'Neill opened his mouth to give the order, but another voice overrode him.

"You have progressed well in your Trial. I am pleased for you."

They whirled around to find ugly little Bes standing inside the ring of the Stargate. He blinked at them and smiled. The orange glow from the moon made him look particularly alien.

"You again," O'Neill groaned. "If you're planning on stealing any more of our gear, think again."

"I wish only to see you are well. I look forward to greeting you at your journey's end. It has been too long since I talked to another." Bes's big eyes peered intently at each of them.

"You bear the Books of Djehuti?" he asked Teal'c.

"I do," Teal'c growled. This creature disturbed him beyond rational thought, leaving him torn between wanting to cleave him in two and bow down in reverence.

"Bes, can you at least tell us what will happen to us when we complete the Trial?" Daniel stepped forward, trying to still the shivers wracking his body.

"You will be welcomed to the Barque of Heaven."

"Which is… a boat? A ship, space-ship, a city, a planet, what?"

"It is as its name describes, young one." Bes gazed almost benevolently at Daniel, the only person not pointing a weapon at him. "Its pleasures shall be your reward."

"That really doesn't tell us much."

"Soon. Soon. Be well."

With a gap-toothed grin, Bes vanished as soundlessly as he had appeared.

"Perfect end to the perfect day. That guy gives me the creeps." O'Neill motioned to the DHD. "Teal'c, get us out of here."

Under Teal'c's guidance, the Stargate sprang to life, the blue glow from the wormhole making the dead forest look even more forsaken.

"At least this time the wormhole won't seem cold." O'Neill ushered Teal'c ahead of him.

Pausing in front of the wormhole, Major Carter caught Daniel Jackson's arm. "Daniel, what I said—it was thoughtless and I was wrong. I'm sorry."

Daniel managed a tired half-smile. "I know, Sam. It's okay."

"And, what you asked—I will try."

He nodded and led her through the wormhole. Teal'c traded an approving glance with O'Neill, relieved his teammates would not let a difference of opinion fester into bitterness. He pushed his shaky legs into motion and left the cold darkness behind.

GATE NINE

Knife of the Shining One

You got a feel for wormhole travel the more you used the Stargate network. Regardless of how many times Sam insisted that time did not exist within the wormhole and therefore any illusion of the passage of time during the journey from one Stargate to the next was just that—an illusion, the sensory perception imprinted upon Daniel's deconstructed neurons was that this particular journey felt like it was taking a lot longer than usual.

Daniel's body reassembled in the blink of an eye as he emerged through the event horizon, lungs automatically sucking in air the instant he had fully re-formed, eyes opening to see flagstones zooming up toward him. Well-honed reflexes barely had his arms up before he slammed into the ground and tumbled awkwardly over and over; hands, elbows, ribs and knees battering the hard surface. Pain stabbed through his side, sharp and vicious, leaving a shocked tingle in its wake. He finally stopped rolling and lay stunned, gasping in strained breaths, trying to regain his equilibrium.

A chorus of yelps, grunts and curses surrounded him as the rest of the team was spat from the vortex like so much discarded garbage. Daniel finally looked up. Ignoring another warning twinge along his side, he reached out to Sam and pulled away her cap, thrown across her face by the hard landing.

"Sam? You okay?"

"Ow. Yeah. But, ow."

"That felt like a really long trip this time." He coughed slightly as they dragged each other to their feet.

"Are *you* alright, Daniel? You look a little pale."

"Just a bit winded. Why did we get thrown out of the 'gate like that?"

Duly diverted, Sam glanced at the Stargate, the wormhole already disengaged. "I'm not sure. Usually exit speed is equal to entry speed. Perhaps there was some kind of astronomic interference along the route." She pulled a face at the thought of the possibilities.

Jack staggered to his feet and rubbed his butt. "Interference my ass. That was a really long trip down the pike. Same thing happened when I visited with the Asgard."

Sam rolled her eyes at Daniel and avoided another round of Jack's griping by turning to join Teal'c. "Holy Hannah on a bicycle."

Jack and Daniel blinked at each other in bemusement, then turned to see what was so exciting.

"Well, I'll be...."

They stood at what seemed to be the center of the largest, most exotically stocked armory any potentate could have ever imagined. Stretching out of sight in all directions were mounds of crates; boxes big, small and enormous, barrels and containers of all sizes and shapes, some stacked under open-sided shelters, others piled neatly in the open. To one side of the Stargate a row of Tel'taks sat shining brightly in the sun. Beyond, partly obscured by yet more mounds of stores, four Al-kesh bombers crouched temptingly amid a virtual squadron of Death Gliders.

Like a set of dazed marionettes, SG-1 turned slowly in a circle, trying to take in the riches surrounding them. Behind the Stargate, small mountains of semi-refined naquada gleamed in the sunlight.

"'Great shall be the holdings of our Lord God Ra. The wealth of his land and the might of his arm shall cause all to tremble before him'," Teal'c uttered the words quietly. "We stand in Ra's storehouse, resting place for that which he plundered from the worlds under his rule."

Slowly, almost reverently, they began to spread out through

the incredible array of goods.

"Zat'nik'tels, staff weapons, explosives…. Enough lies here to supply his army for years." Teal'c shook his head in wonder. A stack of round blue barrels caught his eye. Cracking the seal on one, he pulled out a fistful of glittering green powder. "*Nezanat* powder, from the planet Punt. Tempered in a furnace at one thousand degrees for five hundred days, it forms the material that is used as the core framework when building the great Ha'tak vessels."

"Really?" Sam was by his side in a flash, unable to resist bagging a sample. "Is it only found on the one planet, Teal'c?"

"Indeed it is. A most rare and valuable resource."

"Valuable? How valuable?" Jack changed course and headed over for a look.

"This one handful would purchase the entire state of Colorado, O'Neill."

Jack whistled, suitably impressed and glanced at Carter. "Gonna need a bigger bag." He kept turning in circles, adding up the amount of ordnance around them. "Hey, how come this place hasn't been looted by the other System Lords? I'll bet Apophis would have loved to have got his hands on this."

"The locations of Ra's home planet and most prized territories were always deeply concealed. It is possible that only a few of his trusted underlings knew of this planet's location. If they were with him when he perished, that knowledge died with them."

Jack popped open a crate and stared at the collection of weapons within. "The JCS would wet themselves over this stuff."

They kept wandering through the aisles of the dead Goa'uld's private repository, Teal'c pointing out items of particular interest. Huge hexagonal crystal barrels filled with fluorescent green liquid stretched for dozens of meters down one row. "Liquid naquada, probably from the refineries on Zephron."

Daniel turned to look at the glittering mounds of naquada

behind them. "Naquada from Abydos?" he asked quietly.

"No doubt, Daniel Jackson. Rarely was better quality found."

Daniel stared at the piled results of the Abydonian slave labor, visions quickly assaulting him of his wife, brother, family and friends, and all who had suffered in the hellish mines. After a moment he felt a tug on his arm and let Sam pull him away to trail after Jack and Teal'c. He drifted along, reading the stenciled descriptions of the goods within each stack and absently rubbing the receding ache in his side. All were weapons, power sources, minerals or spare parts for ships. Nothing held any knowledge or information. Nothing that he held as valuable.

A faint muttering intruded on his thoughts. Believing it was Jack, Daniel looked around and found the others were a fair way in front of him. The voice was coming from his right.

Holding his body perfectly still, he drew his Beretta, reached up with his left hand to click the call button on his radio three times, then pushed the earpiece into his ear.

"Daniel? You got trouble?" Jack's voice came softly to him.

Daniel clicked once for yes.

"Visual?"

Two clicks for no.

"Audio then. How many?"

One click.

"Hold position. Be there in ten."

Daniel froze, thankful for the camouflage his BDUs gave against a dusty pile of wooden crates beside him. The voice seemed to drone on in a steady, solitary monologue.

A long ten seconds later, Jack materialized by his feet, lying flat in the dirt, weapon primed and ready. He tugged Daniel's pant leg and Daniel sank slowly down to join him. Sam and Teal'c appeared a moment later on the far side of his stack of crates, having circled around from the rear.

Daniel pointed out the direction the voice was coming from.

It rose and fell as the fitful wind carried it past them. Jack hand-signaled Teal'c to take point. Silently, the big man crept along the alleyways twisting through the stacks of supplies. Jack followed, then Daniel with Sam bringing up the rear.

A couple of wrong turns and a lot of muscle-wrenching sneaking around brought them to the side of a metal pavilion. Bright curtains flapped as the wind turned in their direction, bringing a strained voice to their ears.

"That's English!" Daniel whispered hoarsely, brow creased in confusion.

"*...characteristics, and target vulnerability are treated in limited detail required by the mission planner...*"

"That's not English." Jack shot to his feet as if popped out of a box. "That's the Joint Munitions Effectiveness Manual—Special Operations."

Teal'c and Daniel gaped at him, but Sam's face brightened as she recognized the voice. "That's Lieutenant Simmons!"

"What?" Daniel exchanged another baffled look with Teal'c and scrambled after Sam and Jack.

The four piled into the pavilion. Pushing past the billowing curtains, they found themselves in the midst of rack upon rack of control panels and equipment—the operations hub of the supply dump. The voice continued to chatter on, reciting rules and regulations from some hidden source.

"I believe Major Carter is correct. That is the voice of Lieutenant Simmons," Teal'c said as he raked each bank of equipment, searching for the comm unit.

"Graham? How could he possibly know we're here?" Daniel asked, feeling more than a little out of step.

"Find it! Damn it, where's it coming from?" As Jack reached a pile of wooden chests that had fallen onto a bench from an overhead shelf, the voice—it was Simmons, of all the unexpected people—cut off, leaving only a faint hiss of an open, very long-distance channel.

"Oh, come *on!* Don't give up now."

The four of them stared at each other, nerves jangling at the phantom contact with home.

"Simmons!" Jack's frustrated bellow echoed mockingly in the desolate silence around them.

"Good morning, Galaxy!"

The words blasted out behind Jack, sending them all diving through the clutter on the bench.

"That's Lou!" Daniel said, not believing his own words as he pawed over panels of flickering lights.

"Damn right it is, he loved that movie."

"...respond if you are receiving. SGC calling SG-one niner, please respond."

"Ferretti, where the hell are you?"

"Here!" Teal'c stood a couple of feet down the bench from Jack, wiping layers of dust off a cover that bore the symbols denoting a long-range telecommunications device, the floating ball used by the Goa'uld. He triggered the release. The hatch slid back and the already active sphere rose into the air to hover a few feet above their heads.

"Aaaannnd... Radio SGC welcomes you to hour 47 of 'Where's SG-1'. To start things off we have a special message from the gang in the canteen...."

Major Ferretti's voice reached out to them all, loud and clear now it was free of the compartment. Slightly distorted but still the sweetest thing any of them could have hoped to see that day, Lou's face filled the ball, looking from immeasurably far away to a point somewhere over their heads.

"How on earth did they get that working?" Sam croaked in wonder.

"C'mon Colonel, give us a sign here. Or I'll sing. I swear, I'll sing!"

"Oh, no, don't let him sing," Jack laughed. "T, where're the controls to this thing?"

"Here, O'Neill." Teal'c located the transmission controls and opened up a two-way channel.

"She'll be comin' round the mountain...."

"SG-one niner calling SGC. Do you read? Over," Jack

yelled out over Ferretti's off-key tenor.

"...when she... Colonel!"

"SG-one niner calling SGC. Acknowledge."

"Colonel?"

"Ferretti!"

"Colonel O'Neill?"

"Hey Lou, how're you doing?"

"Son of a...! This is Stargate Command, we read you loud and clear, SG-one niner, over. Simmons, go get the general. Now!"

In the tele-ball, Lou's face turned and stared at the four dirty, lost members of SG-1, seeing them now for the first time. *"Well, I'll be a monkey's uncle. It worked! Are you all okay, sir? We've been calling on this thing for days, ever since General Carter brought it in. It's good to see you all — Daniel, Teal'c, Sam."*

Ferretti looked at each of them, a huge grin on his face. In the background they could hear a buzz of excited voices. Realizing they could all speak at once, the team let loose a torrent of delighted shouts.

"It's good to see you, Lou."

"A pleasure indeed to make contact with you, Major Ferretti."

"Lou, I never thought you'd find us, but it's great to see you."

"Yeah, what's with the *singing*, Ferretti?"

"Bit of a time filler, sir. It's 0400 here. We've been broadcasting non-stop in the hopes you'd hear us when you gated to that planet." Ferretti looked away, then back and started to rise out of his chair. *"The generals are here. I'll see you guys soon."*

A grin and one of those achingly familiar winks, and he slid out of view to be replaced by General Hammond, looking unruffled by the early wake-up call and wearing the biggest of smiles.

"Well, well. SG-1. It's good to see you. All of you. Is everyone alright?"

The team clustered a little closer together—Jack, Sam and Teal'c unconsciously straightening up. Daniel reached out and wrapped a hand around Sam's elbow, needing a little contact to ground him in reality. Two minutes ago they had been lost and far from home and now they were talking to the general as if he were in the next room.

"We're fine, sir. A little dirty and banged up here and there but we're just fine. How the hell did you find us?" Jack looked up at the general's face inside the ball, a grin resurfacing. "Sir."

"When you failed to check in on P3R-779 and our attempts to establish a wormhole also failed we contacted the Tok'ra." Hammond leaned back and another welcome face joined him.

"Sam, Jack, boys. Nice to see you all safe."

"Dad." Sam grinned at her father. Daniel gave her arm a squeeze as Jacob took up the story.

"We found the team that was supposed to join up with you. They'd all been drugged and disabled, except Miseanu. We caught her attempting to flee Vorash. Questioning revealed her symbiote, Remeda, had been forcibly removed and replaced with one called Tel'es—a Goa'uld mercenary. All he gave us was that he was aiming to collect the bounty on your heads, and that you were to be delivered to P3R-779. Seems it was the intent of whoever set the bounty to lure you into this Trial of Ra's."

"Did you discover the identity of the one behind this bounty, Jacob Carter?" asked Teal'c.

"We never did find out which System Lord was behind it. The best we got out of him was that whoever hired him wanted each of you to suffer greatly. He then chewed his way out of Miseanu, attacked two of my people and was killed."

Jack grimaced at the image. "How did you know the TV would be on here?"

Jacob yielded the speaker to Hammond.

"There we got lucky. Turns out a Tok'ra operative actually undertook the Trial two hundred and seventy years ago

in order to infiltrate Ra's inner circle. She succeeded. Her reports provided a lot of information about the Trial, including a planet that served as one of Ra's hidden store houses, and that there was an active telecommunication device on it. We've been broadcasting non-stop in the hope you would hear us." Hammond paused to smile at them again.

"Half the base and all the on-world teams have taken a turn. We've been plotting your progress with each attempt you made to dial home, but in case we miscalculated we've kept the communicator live the whole time."

"You mean you could tell every time we dialed home, sir?" Sam asked.

"The chevrons lit up but no wormhole formed, Major. Once we knew what had happened, we backtracked all the misdials. There were a lot during the first day of your mission, so we were never completely sure which planet you were on. The Tok'ra kindly sent a ship to P3R-779 to see if you were still there."

Jack suddenly flinched as realization hit him. He turned to stare at his team. "We didn't dial out here and we didn't check the time limit."

Corresponding shock and surprise settled on all three faces.

"Carter, Daniel. *Go!*"

His two fastest runners turned and sprinted out of the pavilion.

"Keep your ears on," Jack yelled after them.

"Colonel?"

"Sir, we have a limited amount of time on each planet. Basically we have to gate out before moonset or we don't get to leave at all."

"Yes, Colonel, the Tok'ra intelligence suggested as much."

"It's still daylight here, sir. We should be okay, but still. I slipped up. Didn't check the time or the DHD when we arrived. This place, it's… Tinker Base a thousand times over. You wouldn't believe the ordnance that's lying around here."

"Really? What kinds of ordnance, Colonel?"

"Oh, you know, refined naquada, zats, staff weapons, and a fleet of those Al-kesh bombers."

"A fleet...?"

Jack grinned as Hammond blinked, not quite concealing the surge of lust on his face. "All ours for the picking, sir."

"Colonel!" Carter's voice blasted through the earpieces, making him and Teal'c both jump.

"Ow. I read you *really* clearly, Major."

"Sir, we've only got thirteen minutes until moonset."

"What?" Jack twisted around, half expecting night to have fallen in the last few minutes. It hadn't; daylight still burned brightly outside the pavilion.

"How is this possible, Major Carter?" Teal'c strode outside to glare upward. Searching the blue sky, they finally saw a thin quarter moon sliding toward the horizon, previously hidden from them by the row of parked Al-kesh ships.

"Damn. I knew this place would be too good to be true." Jack was at his side, glaring at the certain sealing of their fate. Of all the planets they had passed through, only one had offered up the hidden addresses with ease. "How the hell are we going to find the next address in all of this?"

"Jack, I've got it." Daniel's disbelief sounded in their ears. "The—the address and the password, they're carved into the side of the DHD."

"Say again?" This day was just full of surprises.

"I have the address and password for the next planet," Daniel said, slowly and patiently.

Jack stared in bewilderment at Teal'c, noting the slight sheen of sweat on his brow. "Why would they leave it out in the open like that?"

"Perhaps the test of this planet is whether or not to let the temptation of all that is here sway us into staying and thus fail to complete the Trial."

"Colonel O'Neill!" Hammond's voice brought them back into the pavilion.

"Sir. Sorry, sir. We've only got, oh, twelve minutes left before we have to bug out, sir."

"You won't have to, Jack," Jacob spoke up. *"The coordinates of the planet you're now on were the only ones the Tok'ra operative included in her briefing notes. We dispatched Martouf and a team in a Tel'tak three days ago. They should be with you soon and we'll have you all home in no time."*

"Marty's on the way? Sweet."

Teal'c stepped closer behind Jack and addressed the hovering ball. "We are unable to leave any of the Trial planets by ship, General Carter. We have all been implanted with nanocytes that will result in certain death should we stray too far from the Stargate."

"Yeah. Certain, painful, very messy, very melty death," Jack shuddered at the memory.

"We've got that covered, Colonel," Hammond said. *"Our labs have been working on a counter-agent to the nanocytes, based in fact, on your experiences on Argos."*

"Oy. I mean, that's good news sir."

"You'll be able to ship out with Martouf and be home in time for Groundhog Day."

"Not that I would ever doubt a scientist's word but are they sure, sir? We've seen what these things can do, kinda like what happened when they opened the Ark in *Raiders*."

Hammond grimaced but shook his head determinedly. *"We'll get those things out of you. You don't need to complete the Trial, Colonel."*

Daniel and Carter skidded into the pavilion in time to hear the general's last sentence. Jack flashed his team a big smile.

"Looks like we're going home, kids."

He turned back to Hammond's beaming face. "And you can get these Books of the Grateful Dead out of Teal'c, right? It's put a real damper on Junior and I'm starting to miss the little guy."

"I'm sorry, Colonel. The Books of what?" Hammond frowned at them and Jacob leaned in close to the viewer.

"The Books of Djehuti," Jack said very clearly. "They're implanted in Teal'c, neutralized most of the good stuff from Junior." He really didn't like the way Jacob and the general exchanged glances.

"I'm on it, Jack. Give me two." Jacob disappeared from their view. In the background of the communications center a chatter of voices and commands could be heard.

"Don't worry, son," Hammond said to Teal'c. *"We'll get you fixed up."*

"I would be most appreciative, General Hammond. I believe the side-effects may become quite disturbing."

Behind Hammond, Ferretti leaned into view and handed the general a note. He sent the missing team a wink and a grin before stepping out of view.

"Good news, Colonel. Martouf and his crew have your planet in sight. They'll be with you shortly."

"Always happy to see the Tok'ra, sir." Jack sighed inwardly, feeling some of the burden of the last few days begin to slide away. He glanced at his team. Teal'c was still managing to look invincible despite the dirt and lines of strain around his eyes. Carter had her head down, hiding a smile that had appeared at the mention of Martouf. She stood at parade rest, easy yet ready to go. Daniel, a step behind Carter, seemed a little out of breath from the run to the Stargate, but his eyes were bright and he was busily searching the equipment banks around them on his never-ending quest for more information.

Jack often felt proud of his oddball team, but sometimes, like this very moment, they gave him a real warm fuzzy feeling. Not that he'd ever tell them that....

"Uh, George? We may have a problem here." Jacob returned, face now grim with bad news. *"We're reviewing Linbal's debriefing records but she does clearly state that the Books of Djehuti can only be removed when the bearer has reached the Barque of Heaven. The bearer gets to choose one element of the Books that will become his own, then all others are removed and he is restored to health. Any attempt to*

prematurely remove them will, well, you wouldn't survive it, Teal'c. I'm sorry."

Jack lowered his head so his glare didn't melt the viewer. That burden slid right on back to its old place once more.

"Then I shall continue the Trial alone, General Carter, General Hammond."

"Like hell!" Jack snapped.

"What? No!" Carter joined in, anguish in her voice where there had been happiness only moments ago.

"Teal'c, you can't go on without us," Daniel moved over to the Jaffa's side; his voice soft, persuasive. "What if you get too ill to dial out in time? You'll be stranded somewhere we'll never be able to find you."

"Perhaps, but I will find great comfort in knowing my teammates shall be safe."

Jack exchanged a look with Hammond, who gave him a faint nod. This was a field decision and he had the right to sort it out. "Okay. Carter, Daniel—"

"Jack, don't. Don't say what you're about to say," Daniel cut him off. He moved around Teal'c to stand directly in front of Jack. "Just, hear me out. What if Teal'c gets too ill to move on his own? You can't carry him yourself. You need us."

"Daniel…."

"Sir, with due respect, Daniel is right. What if you get hurt too?"

"Or you need to translate a dialect that Teal'c doesn't know?"

"Or solve some kind of scientific puzzle that's out of your field of expertise?"

"Safety in numbers, Jack."

"We've come this far together, sir."

"Don't break up the team, Jack." Daniel stared intently at Jack.

Jack glanced at Teal'c, saw his feelings mirrored in the big guy's face. He opened his mouth only to have Daniel cut him off once more.

"Besides, I'm not staying behind." Daniel planted his legs and folded his arms across his chest, stubbornness radiating from every pore.

There was a moment of strained silence as Jack scowled at Daniel's defiant face. Jack turned to Carter, standing there as straight and still as a cadet. His eyes raked her from top to toe, her reluctance to stay behind clear. Time to rein this in. Daniel he would take argument from; hell, half the time he expected Daniel to take exception to his orders, but he knew Carter would follow an order and at least they would be safe. On the other hand, a team at half-strength was vulnerable—and secretly he'd always believed that the four of them together could handle anything the universe could throw at them. He didn't want to leave them behind any more than they wanted to stay.

He opened his mouth, but got no further as Daniel, naturally, interrupted, his voice soft yet steely with intent.

"Jack, Teal'c. We know you want us out of this, as much as Sam and I want you both safe. But how would we feel if you don't come back and we find out that something we could have done might have saved you? Even an extra pair of hands could make all the difference." Daniel gazed at Jack, a force of will behind those eyes. "Don't do that to us. Please."

"Damn it, Daniel. This is not a democracy."

"No, it's not Jack. It's a team. Don't break it up."

Daniel's watch beeped in the tense silence. "Five minutes until lock out."

"Alright! If you'd let a guy get a word in edgewise. We go on and we stay together." He spun away from their relieved faces and looked up at the tele-ball.

"Generals, it looks like we're going on. Pass on our thanks to the personnel. We'll meet you on the other side."

"Understood, Colonel. We'll keep tracking your dial-ins and try to find the location of this Barque of Heaven."

"Yes, sir. We'll do four dial-ins each planet—one for each of us."

"Take care, SG-1. We'll see you all soon." Hammond's face clearly showed his regret that the anticipated rescue was now a lost cause.

Jack stepped back, snapped off a salute and ushered his team toward the door. Teal'c bowed his head to both generals and headed out of the pavilion. Daniel gave them a nod and half a wave then turned away. Carter took a step toward the viewer.

"I'm sorry sir, we'd stay if we could. Dad, I...."

"It's okay, Sam. Go. Be safe." Jacob's wavering image smiled down from the ball.

She tore herself away and ran out of the pavilion, Jack hard on her heels. Without another word they turned and sprinted for the Stargate.

The run back to the Stargate seemed to take forever. Jack pounded along behind Daniel, anger churning over the missed chance of rescue. Damn the Goa'uld — even when they weren't in sight they were still messing with his team.

"Two minutes," Daniel gasped out, focusing on his watch with difficulty.

Teal'c, in the lead, dodged through the stacks of crates, the others following at breakneck speed. They skidded around sharp corners and pelted down the wider aisles, until, with surprising suddenness the Stargate stood before them.

Daniel aimed for the DHD and slid to an abrupt halt that left him half bent over the console. Notebook open in his left hand, his right hand began to slap down the glyphs before he had even straightened. He mashed down the red crystal and shouted, *"Ankh em Fentu."*

"Go, Teal'c, go!" Jack grabbed Daniel's arm and tugged him into the wormhole, bellowing over their shoulders for Carter to get through.

Sam was a scant two feet behind Daniel and the colonel. As their boots were swallowed in the rippling blue, she heard a thunderous sound from the sky overhead. A supersonic boom—the kind made by a ship entering planetary atmosphere. A brief glance up showed an artificial orange light sweep over the sky.

She closed her eyes and let the cool embrace of the Stargate sweep her away. She did not have the courage to look back again.

GATE TEN

Boundless In Courage

Rain pounded her face and body. Sam halted behind the men on a water-slicked slab of rock which was patchily covered in sand. Gusting wind buffeted hard drops of rain in sweeping curtains, blending with the surf that crashed onto the wide beach in front of them.

She stood with the others in the battering elements, trying to reconcile what had just happened. One minute they were talking to Hammond as if it were just another mission report and now—now, they were as far from home as ever, that fleeting moment of safety just an intangible and surreal memory.

The colonel shook his head and turned his face into the wind and rain. He looked down at the Tacs in his hands, instinctively grabbed on the run to the Stargate. He stowed them in his BDU pockets and looked around.

Teal'c was searching for the moon-clock but Sam stared back through the Stargate, trying to keep hold of that connection to the SGC and family, now severed and scattered upon the winds. She shook herself and kicked her brain back into gear. Cold rain slid down her neck, making her shiver. She looked for Daniel, found him standing where the platform disappeared under encroaching sands, still breathing hard from their short run. He glanced over briefly, his face streaked with water underneath his sodden boonie.

Daniel gestured at the sand by his feet and yelled into the wind. "Jack, I don't think we're alone here."

What he pointed to was a pile of oval shells, crustaceans of some kind, cracked apart and empty of their contents. He knelt and carefully extracted a wedge-shaped sliver of stone from the mound. Holding it up, he ran a finger down its chipped and worn edges.

"It's a tool, fashioned for a specific purpose."

The colonel nodded and peered past Daniel along the beach. Unbroken coastline stretched away in both directions until lost in the obscuring rain. Inshore, scrubby, weather-hardened bushes formed a dense barrier. The land was flat with only a hint of faraway cliffs, glimpsed through shifting sheets of rain.

"Any idea if it's Goa'uld?"

"It could be, someone stranded here with no sophisticated technology perhaps, or it could just be a native life-form. People have been using tools like these for hundreds of thousands of years." Daniel shrugged and slipped the stone into a pocket.

"We have only seven hours, fourteen minutes here, O'Neill," Teal'c called over the thunderous crash of surf.

Sam hunched a little in her already soaked uniform, water cascading off the bill of her cap. "Sir, I saw what could have been a planetary shield come on just before I went through the Stargate. Martouf may not have been able to land. Do you think the SGC will find us again?"

"Carter, I'm sure they will. They managed to track us down once, they'll do it again."

"Yes, sir."

"Why don't you dial home, let them know we're all here safely."

"Sir."

Sam walked over to the DHD where sand lay in drifts at its base and dialed up Earth's address; once, twice, four times the chevrons lit up and sent a message across space that four lost travelers were alive and well.

They headed out along the beach, direction unknown, as this world's sun remained hidden behind thick gray clouds. Compacted by the rain, the sand was easy enough to walk on. The thick weave of their uniforms kept in precious body heat and ponchos kept off a certain amount of rain. After ten minutes of drenching, the rain slowly eased to a scattered drizzle. The wind continued its gusty howl, catching in caps and ponchos with tiresome regularity until Sam and the colonel dug out their little-used boonies and yanked them on securely. Daniel had the string on his boonie done up so tightly, she wondered it wasn't strangling him. Teal'c blithely ignored the drips running off his scalp and down his neck.

"You know," she said, "I've been thinking about that bounty the Goa'uld have offered for our capture. Aris Boch was going to hand us over to Sokar who, if Dad's information was right, would have delivered us to P3R-779, expecting to claim the bounty as Miseanu was going to. Why send us there? Why not parade us in front of the System Lords, make an example out of us?"

"Are you suggesting that it was one specific Goa'uld who wanted us captured, rather than the System Lords in general, Major Carter?" Teal'c asked.

"Well, I'm sure a number of Goa'uld want us caught, Apophis for one. But he's been dead—we presume—for months now and yet we've only heard about this bounty recently. It can't be something he initiated and it doesn't seem feasible that the System Lords would want us sent somewhere so isolated and unknown."

"So, what…? How many folks in Goa'uld-town would have known about Ra's little setup here?" Colonel O'Neill asked.

"Not many. Maybe someone close to Ra?" Daniel mused.

"That might be more likely," Sam said.

"Okay, then who are we talking about?" The colonel shook his boonie out and resettled it on his head.

"Ra was known for keeping apart from the other System Lords," Teal'c said. "His eminence within their hierarchy was paramount and he did not engage in their power plays. His favor was much sought after but seldom granted."

"So that would certainly limit the options. What about a

wife? Did Ra have another consort after Hathor?" Daniel asked.

Teal'c was silent for a time. "The few times I was at Ra's court when Apophis was granted an audience, Ra had no-one at his side other than child attendants. The only likely consort I have heard of is Mat. She was once favored by Ra, but has not been spoken of for many years. His son, Sia, fell from his grace centuries ago."

"So, bottom line, we have no idea who set the bounty, but we could be looking at only one Goa'uld, instead of a whole group of them."

"Uh, yeah, I guess so, sir." Sam shrugged and moved ahead of the team.

Daniel, walking a few steps ahead of Jack, shortened his stride a little to accommodate the persistent ache in his left side. He didn't think it was anything more than another bruise, added to a collection that was becoming less easy to ignore. Hardly surprising. Some ninety-six hours out from the SGC now—running, sometimes literally, on catnaps and infrequent meals—they were all feeling the tiredness in muscles and bones. He looked out at the stormy sea and just kept plodding on.

"Daniel?" Jack came up beside him and gestured at the frayed rips in Daniel's pants. "How's the leg?"

Daniel tore his eyes off the pounding surf and looked over at Jack. "Oh, it's healing, I guess. A bit stiff and sore, but okay."

"Good. How are you holding up otherwise? That run back to the 'gate seemed a bit hard on you."

"No, no. Actually, I landed pretty hard when we came through, think I bruised a rib or something. I'm okay." Daniel's eyes held Jack's gaze for a moment, then flickered away.

"You'd tell me if it were anything worse?"

"Of course. You know I would. How are you doing, Jack?"

"My feet hurt. And don't get me started on the knees, the back, the neck…" Jack grimaced and turned to the others. "Carter, Teal'c, how're you both holding up?"

"Doing okay, sir," Sam replied, not glancing away from her position on point. "Knife wound is healing up and the rest, well, nothing a few hours in a Jacuzzi wouldn't fix."

"Amen to that, Major. Teal'c?"

The hesitation before Teal'c replied spoke volumes more than his actual words. "I am becoming aware of the consequences of carrying the Books of Djehuti, O'Neill."

"How so?"

"My symbiote is less active than usual. I do not feel I am in optimal condition. It is—most disturbing."

"About *how* less optimal condition are we talking?"

"Approximately eighty percent of my usual strength." Teal'c frowned and looked away.

"Ah. Well, I wouldn't sweat it just yet, T. Even fifty percent of you would equal a hundred percent of anyone else."

Teal'c crooked an eyebrow at the compliment.

"Teal'c, are you getting anything from the Books?" Daniel asked as they splashed through a mini lake of rain and sea-water.

Hesitating again, Teal'c reluctantly admitted, "I have found myself thinking of words and picturing writing of a kind I have never encountered before."

"Any idea what these words mean?" Jack prodded.

"No."

"Ah. Well, you let us know how that goes, won't you?"

It took a few moments for Jack and Sam to realize they were the only ones moving. Daniel and Teal'c had stopped, Teal'c staring at the sky while Daniel stared at him, astonishment quickly turning to indignation.

"It's not Goa'uld script? Or *anything* we've come across before? Not even the pictograms the Abydonians used centuries ago or the Furlings' script from Ernest's planet?"

"I do not believe so, Daniel Jackson."

"You know what this is. Don't you?" Disappointment filled Daniel as he realized exactly what the Books of Djehuti held. "Teal'c? How... I... I'm right, aren't I?"

"Right about what?" Sam asked as she and Jack walked back to them.

"The Books of Djehuti are revealing a language that I am unfamiliar with, one somehow connected to Ra and yet it is not the dialect of the Goa'uld."

Daniel backed away a few steps, frustration rising. "An entirely new language—*that's* what you wanted to protect me from?" He turned and stalked off along the beach.

"Daniel Jackson, I did not know this would be the result of my actions," Teal'c began.

Daniel wheeled about and strode back to him. "You should have trusted me."

"I will, of course, place any skill I gain at your disposal, Daniel Jackson."

Seeing the regret in his friend's eyes, Daniel gathered himself and deflated. "Of course you would, Teal'c. I'm sorry, I just... I'm so tired I'm not thinking straight." He gestured aimlessly and turned away, embarrassed at his outburst. He shrugged his pack into a more comfortable position and walked on past Jack and Sam.

He looked up at the gloomy gray clouds scudding by overhead, a tired grimace on his lips—and then the world tore apart with a searing flash of light and shriek of sound and he was falling into a maelstrom of stinging wet sand and blackness.

It was the rain that brought him awake again, cold rain pelting onto his unprotected face. Dark—had night fallen? He blinked, squinted, saw nothing.

Oh, no.

Blind. That old, insidious fear leapt out of the dark, strangling reason with primal fear.

Can't see.

He fumbled a wet and gritty hand to his face, but felt no injury. Glasses were gone. Was he lying down? Vertigo seized him and spun him in dizzying loops.

Clenching his teeth, he forced himself to calm. Big, slow gasps of air gave space for reason to return. He was lying on his belly, the weight of his pack pressing his chest into the sand. There had been a flash of light... oh no. A Goa'uld shock grenade? He lay still, listening with all his might. No voices or footsteps nearby. No sign the others were awake. Just wind, rain, and surf disintegrating on the shore.

Eventually he couldn't bear the silence any more.

"Jack?"

He rolled over on his side, new aches making themselves known.

"Teal'c?"

He pushed himself to sit up, his pack making him list to one side. He put out a steadying hand and found his fingers curling around familiar thin, metal frames, so welcome yet so useless now.

"Sam?"

He fumbled in his BDU pockets and pulled out the pen light. He switched it on and squinted for all he was worth to see even a glimmer of light. Nothing. He shook it, turned the switch on and off until he'd lost track of the clicks. Maybe it was broken. Maybe he really was blind. Maybe not.

Daniel sat on the wet sand, isolated in darkness and silence, surrounded by the roar of nature, resigned to waiting for the light to return.

Sam became aware of the world once more but it seemed to have been turned on end. Her hips and legs were immobile, wrapped in something strong, yet her head and arms dangled free. Everything was dark, confused. Slowly her brain sorted itself out and — oh boy. She was hanging upside down, draped over the bony and... furry shoulder of something that jolted the breath out of her with every lumbering step.

She strained to listen for signs of the others, in pursuit or captive also, but there was nothing beyond the howl of wind-driven rain, harsh breathing and the thump of very big feet.

Too disadvantaged to do anything while blind, Sam hung limply, playing possum until fortune favored her once more.

Consciousness returned to him in a sudden jolt. He lay face up; pack gone, wet darkness pressing down on him. He opened his eyes and found only more darkness, vision stolen by a Goa'uld shock weapon.

Confident his sight would return in due time, he sat up, groping to either side but found no-one near. Sound seemed to echo oddly around him. He felt, somehow, that barriers stood close by. He reached out and knocked his knuckles against damp earth. Kneeling, he ran his hand up until he could reach no more, then down to the ground. It felt rough though free of protrusions. He moved to one side, all too quickly coming to a right-angle. The same rough earth followed on to another corner, then another. Four sides: each no more than seven feet long. A pit, a prison, a trap. Within the earth.

Teal'c lifted his face to the rain pouring onto him and stood, feet sloshing in puddles. He stretched and strained, but could not reach beyond the flat slippery walls.

The first faint sense of lighter darkness gradually gave way to a stronger gray haze. Impatiently blinking, Daniel squinted and strained his eyes, desperate for some sign of the others. He fumbled out a tissue to clean the muck from his glasses but smeared as the lenses were, they hindered more than helped. He tucked them away safely and rose to his knees.

Still on the beach.

He caught a flash of white out of the corner of his eye. Blinking furiously, he jerked around but couldn't make out anything tangible. He froze for over a minute, heart pounding, fingers clenching in the wet sand beneath him. Nothing moved. Finally, he relaxed a little and peered around.

The rain was easing again, shapes becoming clearer. No sign of Goa'uld, Jaffa, anyone. Weird. Nothing moved other than water; slipping out of the sky, sliding up the beach, crashing down in thunderous waves.

He turned in circles again, desperation starting to kick in. *There.*

Half hidden by a pile of sand, a still form lay—arms and legs out flung. BDUs made it nearly impossible to discern the features, but Daniel knew who it was.

"Jack!"

Daniel scrambled over the churned-up sand, tripping and falling into holes, brain inanely remarking how well the camouflage of their uniforms actually worked. He dropped to his knees by Jack's side and shed the wretched pack from his shoulders. "Jack?"

His eyesight was still blurred, the rain running into his eyes not helping. He stared at Jack, who lay with his face turned away. So still, so utterly… unmoving. Daniel felt time seize and slow around him. He wanted to reach out, touch Jack, believe the warm pulse of life was beating in his friend's veins, but—*no—don't touch—because if you do then it will be real.*

"Jack." His voice was a strangled whisper, his heart a thudding monster. *"Please…."*

Jack's chest did not move. Nothing moved. Even the wind and rain seemed to pause between one moment and the next.

"No."

There were a hundred things he should do, but he was frozen, as dead inside as….

"JACK!" Fear lent his voice a thready strength.

And Jack sighed, shifted and woke.

Time clicked back on, rain resumed falling, and Daniel began to breathe. Giddy unreality whooshed from his lungs and he leant over Jack. "Jack, it's Daniel. You okay?"

"Whoa, what happened?"

"Goa'uld shock grenade, I think. I can't see Sam and Teal'c anywhere."

"I can't see at all."

"You must have been closer to the blast. I've been awake for awhile."

"Hostiles?"

"No, there's no-one. We're still on the beach."

"Damn. Help me up."

Daniel pulled Jack up to sit next to him.

"Are you injured, Daniel?"

"No. I'm... good. I thought...."

"What?"

"Nothing."

"How long have we been out?"

"Oh. Uh oh. Two hours, ten minutes since we gated in."

"Two *hours?* Damn. Gives us five hours to find the others and get out."

"Yeah."

Jack slumped and leant his shoulder against Daniel's, his weight a solid and comforting presence.

Within ten minutes Jack's vision had returned and they were prowling the beach, finding disturbing evidence of their attackers.

"That's not human," stated Daniel, staring at the imprint in the sand: ten inches long, six inches wide, four round toes over a central pad.

"May not be an animal either, only two prints per track."

"Jack, there's another set over here." Daniel was five meters away, circling a patch of trampled sand. "And," he bent and pulled a number of dirty, wet objects from the sand, "Sam's pack and guns and knife."

"Damn. Think it's an Unas?"

Daniel frowned, thinking back to the two creatures they had previously met. "No. They had long claws on their feet.

I don't think they were retractable, either."

They followed the two sets of tracks up the beach to the fore dunes. As short, spiky clumps of grass began to poke through the sand, the tracks diverged, one heading inland, the other paralleling the shore. Here, they also found Teal'c's staff weapon and pack, the clips broken by some considerable force. Of Teal'c and Sam, there was no sign.

Jack hunkered down in the straggly grass and considered their options. "Whatever these things are, I think they've got Carter and Teal'c."

"That's a pretty big creature, to be able to carry Teal'c off." Daniel stood facing out to sea. The rain had eased again and there looked to be a break in the weather. Further back along the beach, the Stargate glistened in a random shaft of sunlight.

"Big, stinky monster," Jack agreed.

"Big, stinky monster that can use Goa'uld technology, so therefore probably intelligent." They had found two of the expired grenades in the sand.

"Which makes them more or less dangerous?"

Daniel considered that and shrugged; no easy answer there.

"One of these tracks is much deeper than the other," Jack pointed out. "My bet is that one's got Teal'c. We have less than five hours to trail them, rescue Carter and Teal'c, find the password and address and get out of this sandpit." He looked at Daniel and saw the man he was now, far removed from the sneezy dweeb who had horned in on their first mission.

"We'll split up," Jack decided. He pushed himself to his feet and Daniel turned away from the sea. "You follow the tracks along the shore, Daniel. That's probably the one with Carter. You may have to carry her back if she's incapacitated."

"Well, I hope you don't have to carry Teal'c back."

"Hey, you and my knees both. Teal'c's got the greater

chance of being mobile though. Now, Teal'c's taught us both a fair bit about tracking. Take it easy, but don't go too slow. Keep your earpiece in, Carter and Teal'c will try to contact us if they're able and if you have any problems, you call me. Okay?"

"You're sure about this?" Daniel took the extra zat that Jack dug out of Teal'c's pack and one of the purloined Tacs.

"I don't like splitting up, Daniel, but we're two hours behind them already. They may turn out to be fifteen minutes away. They could be hours away. We might rescue one of them and then what? Go and leave the other one here or all stay and fight off stinky monsters? Separating is the best option we've got."

Daniel nodded slowly. "Wonder why they didn't take us?"

"Maybe 'cos you smell bad? Or… we… smell bad."

"And Teal'c smells so sweet," Daniel grinned.

"Oh, you betcha." Jack stashed their teammate's packs in a shallow scoop of dune. "I'm not even going to comment on what Carter smells like."

"No, not if you value your health."

Jack stood, settled his pack and picked up the staff weapon. "Ten minute check-ins. Be careful."

Daniel bobbed his head, returning the sentiment. "You too."

For over an hour Daniel jogged along the fore dunes, tracking the widely spaced footprints of whatever had taken Sam. For the most part it had made no attempt to hide its path, but Daniel had lost the trail three times, backtracking with increasing anxiety until picking it up once more. The bruising on his left side, from being thrown out of the Stargate on the previous world, was a dull, annoying throb that joined the chorus of complaints from his legs and abraded back. Still, he pushed on doggedly, breathing around the pain, trying not to limp as the healing gash in his thigh stretched and pulled with every step. His whole body ached with tired-ness, but it was unimportant—he had to find Sam, or was it Teal'c?—and bring them safely back to the Stargate.

A patch of loose sand gave under his feet and he fell and slid on his rump down a dune. The temptation to lie there, close his eyes and sleep for a moment was agonizing. Daniel groaned and rolled over, got his feet under him and clawed his way back to the top. At least it was a moment's respite from the battering wind coming off the ocean. He crawled up to the crest of the dune and sat to indulge in a precious sip of water. The canteen was less than half-full now, something else to worry about. Daniel creaked to his feet and pushed on, following the big footprints that were slowly being filled by sand.

Ten minutes later he found proof that Jack's assumptions were right. A small black box lay in the sand behind one of the footprints. An SGC-issue radio. Relieved, he sank to the ground and activated his own radio.

"Jack, do you read?"

"Go ahead, Daniel." Jack's voice came back to him, muf-fled by the background howl of the wind.

"I found a radio, one of ours."

"Is it damaged?"

"No. It may have just fallen loose."

"Good work, Daniel. Keep going."

"Okay. Out."

On he went, feet sliding in the unstable dunes, his skin leeched dry by the salt-laden wind. Thirty-five minutes on, the trail suddenly angled inland, through small, sparse scrub toward a stand of tough-looking trees, all leaning defen-sively away from the wind.

"Jack? I'm heading inland now, looks like it's gone towards the trees."

"Acknowledged, Daniel. Remember you'll be more visible in greenery. Stay low, scope it out before you move."

"Okay. How are you doing?"

"I'm in the trees already. Rain's coming down. Check-in again in ten."

"Roger that."

Jack chuckled down the airwaves. *"You coming over all military, Doctor Jackson?"*

"Been hanging around you too long," Daniel admitted. "Bye."

Keeping as low as possible, Daniel moved toward the trees, leaving the beach to stretch endlessly on behind him.

It was raining again. Runoff poured in over each side of his prison, sending rivulets of mud splashing into the pit. Teal'c failed to suppress a shiver that crawled over his entire body. Unable now to sit down as the water steadily rose around his legs, he ended another fruitless attempt to raise the team on the radio and leaned against one wall. He was trapped, simply and efficiently. He shivered again. His symbiote stirred weakly, unable to stop the slow drop in his body temperature.

"Lahntil." The word slipped out, its meaning unknown and no help to him here.

This enforced impairment and imprisonment filled him with anger. Teal'c eyed a patch on the rim of one wall not being eroded by sluicing water. He focused, mind and body concentrated, willing strength into chilled muscles. Bending his knees he sprang, legs powering him up the side of the muddy wall, hands outstretched and grasping, clawing for a grip in the soft earth. His fingers sank in and held; his feet slipped and scrabbled for purchase.

So close—mere inches from the top. Teal'c grimaced with the effort. Oh, so carefully, he slid his left hand up, aiming for a chunk of rock only slightly higher. His fingers brushed it, then with nature's cruel irony the soil supporting his right hand gave way and he fell back in a muddy torrent.

"Grrhh!" On his knees in freezing water, Teal'c let frustration take hold momentarily.

Denied the reassurance that the other three were even still alive, he could do nothing but wait. Eventually whoever had placed him in this predicament would return, perhaps presenting an opportunity for escape and then he would be able to go to the assistance of his teammates.

Sam peered through barely open eyelids as the person—creature—stopped moving. Beyond its furry rump she spotted a clearing in the dense trees. It huffed and muttered to itself, in gentle, almost musical cadences. Surreptitiously, she tensed and prepared to slide off its shoulder and make a run for freedom.

There was a clang from somewhere behind her that sounded definitely metallic. Jerking up, she grabbed for purchase on the creature's shoulder as its huge hands clutched painfully around her waist, and found herself flying through the air. Then she was falling. She came away with two handfuls of fur and managed to deliver a stinging kick to its chest before landing hard inside a barred cage.

Sam surged up instantly, only to be smacked down by a furry paw. The lid of the cage banged down and she was trapped.

"No! Dammit, I'm not your enemy."

The creature stepped back and she got her first real look at it—nearly three meters tall, solid muscle covered by glossy brown fur. Big brown eyes looked back at her. Its head was decorated in a wreath of twisted vines.

"Please. Do you understand me?"

It turned away, unheeding. Picking up a coiled rope, it pulled and her cage creaked up to dangle from the overhanging branches, high off the ground.

"Whoa, hey! Will you listen to me? I'm not here to hurt you."

Well, that much is painfully obvious.

"We're peaceful explorers," she added lamely to the creature's back as it shuffled out of sight. "Nuts."

Soft mist continued to drizzle down on Teal'c's head, the rain not stopping completely. The water pouring in over the edge of his pit was not abating, however. It cascaded in little muddy waterfalls, bringing the level now up to his thighs. The cold was seeping into his very bones and the expected counteraction from his symbiote was not forthcoming; it seemed to be merely creating enough energy to warm itself.

Teal'c pushed aside his physical discomfort and refocused on his connection to the Books of Djehuti. He had unlocked a store of knowledge in this unknown language. The initial confused chatter in his mind had subsided and with a little experimenting, Teal'c found if he thought of a word or sentence it immediately translated into a beautiful melodious dialect. With each word came an intricate and complex script, the written version of the language.

Using his considerable powers of concentration, Teal'c pictured the writings on the walls in Ernest Littlefield's fortress, but none bore any resemblance to the elegant script remembered so clearly. Despite his dire situation, Teal'c smiled in wonder and desperately wished to share and discuss his discoveries with Daniel Jackson. Was this what his young friend felt as he explored the intricacies of a new-found language? It was exhilarating, liberating.

And he had denied Daniel Jackson this joy.

The smile left Teal'c's face as he acknowledged that he had, by seeking to avert physical harm, caused a deeper wounding of his friend.

Jack moved steadily through the trees, weapon ready, eyes darting from the occasionally still-visible footprint to the gloomy shadows around him. The rain, which seemed to sweep over him in broken showers every twenty minutes, was once again pouring down. Water cascaded off the brim of his hat and down the back of his neck.

He cranked up the pace, painfully aware of every second ticking by. Nearly five hours gone now, a little less than two and a half remained before they were locked out for good.

"Jack?" Daniel's voice crackled in his ear. *"Come in,*

Jack."

"Read you, Daniel. Go ahead."

"I've found Sam. She's alive and okay, I think."

Jack took cover under a bush. "Any sign of what grabbed her?"

"No. There's nothing in sight. She's in a cage, Jack, hanging from the trees in a clearing."

"Could be using her as bait, Daniel. Be careful. Can she see you?"

"No, I'm under cover. She's doing something—I think she's trying to break out."

"See if you can get close enough to talk to her. Find out where and what took her. Stay under as much cover as you can and watch your back."

"Okay."

Jack slipped out of his own cover and pushed on.

Several minutes later, Daniel whispered, *"I'm as close as I can get. I'll try and get her attention."*

The slim path Jack had been following bent around one of the densely foliaged trees. He slowed and edged along, to find himself staring into a clearing some six meters wide. Set dead center, a large square hole gaped blackly. Runoff from the never-ending rain ran in channels from every direction, following a natural depression in the clearing to pour with alarming volume into the hole.

And Jack just knew what he would find at the bottom.

Daniel crept as near to the cage as he dared. Still no sign of whatever it was that had kidnapped Sam. He picked up a stone and carefully sighted on her. She had her back to him, concentrating on doing something to her prison. Gently he lobbed the stone. It fell through the widely spaced bars and hit her back.

For a moment he thought she had not felt it, then her head slowly turned in his direction. Her eyes widened as she saw him. Careful not to move too much, she waggled her fingers at him.

Daniel waved back, then silently mouthed, *"Okay?"*

Sam nodded and gave him a thumbs-up.

"How many?"

She held up one finger.

"Where?" He mimicked a walking motion with his fingers.

She pointed to a gap in the trees, ninety degrees from Daniel's position.

He nodded, then tried to get a better look at the cage and the rope holding it. He fished out his knife and held it up.

Sam shook her head and held up her own pocket knife. She pointed to the blade then indicated the cage bars.

Daniel nodded in understanding. Metal cage—no cutting through it then. Keeping a careful watch on the undergrowth around him, he crawled closer. The rope, a dirty twisted thing, was secured to a rusted pole out in the clearing. Gingerly, he crawled over to it, hoping to cut through it quickly.

He touched the rope and all hope of a fast rescue evaporated. It was a cable, made of fine strands of wire, strong and utterly unbreakable. Daniel looked up at Sam and gestured helplessly.

"Metal," he whispered.

Sam grimaced, her face closing over in thought. Daniel sidled back into the trees and called Jack.

"Jack? I've got a problem."

"Seems to be the day for them, Danny." Jack crouched next to the pit, staring down. Well, at least he'd found Teal'c and he was unharmed. He might be standing chest-deep in water, twelve feet down, but he was alive. "I found Teal'c."

"You did? Is he alright?"

"For the moment."

"Oh. Uh, Sam's in a metal cage, which is secured by a metal cable. I can't cut her free."

Jack looked at Teal'c, staring bleakly up at him. "Back in a flash, T." Returning to the cover of the trees, he unhitched his pack and rummaged through it.

"Daniel? Get out the Tac. Set it to cover you while you free Carter. You're going to have to use the zat to fry the lock. Gun's too noisy and the ricochet might hit one of you."

"Jack—the cable will conduct the charge. It'll hit Sam."

"Can't be helped, Daniel." He pulled out a length of climbing rope and his own Tac. "You need to get her out of there, ASAP."

"Jeez." Daniel's voice clearly carried his revulsion at the thought of hurting Sam. *"Remind me to pack some of those flash things next mission."*

"Will do. It's only temporary, Daniel. Get it done and get moving."

"Yeah."

Daniel clicked off and Jack swiftly got on with his own rescue attempt. He secured one end of the rope to the base of a tree and clipped a karabiner to his belt. He looped the rope around his waist, through the karabiner and leaving the pack hidden in the trees, dashed back out into the clearing. He set the Tac to cover the area behind him. Moving back to the pit, he found Teal'c patiently waiting for him. The water was lapping ever higher and had to be uncomfortable to stand in.

"How're you doing, Teal'c?"

"I am… quite cold, O'Neill,"

"I'll bet." Jack read that as 'near frozen'. "Daniel's found Carter. She's up a tree. He'll have her loose in no time. Any idea what these things are?"

"None. I awoke here. There was no-one else in sight. My radio is damaged and I was unable to contact you."

"Damn things never hold up like they should."

Jack swiftly settled the rope, and using himself as belay point, flung the remainder down to Teal'c. He backed up and braced himself, feet none too secure in the channels gouged by the runoff flowing into the pit.

"All set, Teal'c. C'mon up."

The rope jerked and Jack found himself skidding as the slick sides of the pit gave no purchase for Teal'c to take some of his weight on the climb. Jack let the anchor rope support him and hauled with all his might, the rope slowly sliding up and through the karabiner.

A lot of grunting and effort finally produced Teal'c's mud-covered hands, groping at the rim.

"Nearly there, big guy," Jack ground out.

Teal'c replied but his words were lost as automated fire lanced out from the Tac. Startled, Teal'c slid back several inches, dragging Jack off-balance. He barely managed to lock the rope off before his feet slid out from under him and he was pulled to his knees. The Tac fired again. Jack craned his head and caught a flash of something big, brown and furry. It bellowed: pain, fear, anger? Thankfully it came no closer, the Tac doing its job for the moment.

Jack lost all the air in his lungs as Teal'c slid again. Torn between bringing his gun up and trying to keep the rope from dissecting him, he braced his knees, pulled with all his might and slowly toppled sideways and backwards.

"Gahhhh!"

Something low in his back speared pain up and down his spine. Those few extra inches helped though and Teal'c got one elbow up and over the rim, relieving a fair amount of the strain.

Teal'c looked up over his prone body and Jack followed his gaze. In the corner of his eye he saw the creature—huge and bleeding from numerous Tac hits. It held a rock in its hand and with unerring accuracy, pitched it at the Tac. The weapon shorted out and rolled away.

"O'Neill, two o'clock. Now!"

Jack, breath whistling in gasps with his body still being pulled in two directions, ratcheted the MP5's safety, pointed it over his shoulder and hauled on the trigger. Bullets sprayed in an uneven arc and he kept the trigger depressed until a wounded bellow indicated a hit. There was a great deal of shuffling and crashing, but he couldn't turn his head enough to see.

"It is injured, O'Neill, and retreating into the trees."

Teal'c heaved, forearms bulging as he pulled his entire weight up from the pit. His boots sent cascades of mud back into the water below. Slowly, he wriggled out and finally lay, soaked, chilled and exhausted next to Jack. He glanced over and met Jack's gaze, eyebrows rising at the sight of him: lying still, legs bent under him, covered in spent shell casings and his face grimacing with pain.

"What has happened, O'Neill?"

"Back's gone out—dunno—doesn't matter. We have to get out of here."

"Indeed. The creature has gone but it is wounded and may be even more dangerous." Teal'c rolled to his feet and untangled the rope.

Jack experimented getting his legs straightened, found they still worked and put out a hand. Teal'c hauled him gently to his feet.

"Thanks. Oh, damn." He grimaced. "What's with the pit, anyway?"

"I am unsure. Perhaps a method of keeping its prey fresh until consumed."

"Nice. Jaffa stew." Jack staggered over to his pack, dug out a handful of painkillers and anti-inflammatory pills he usually kept in case his knee blew out on a mission. He washed them down rather desperately. He could walk, but it was going to be a new kind of hell getting back to the Stargate.

Teal'c reloaded the pack and slung it over his shoulder. He handed the staff weapon to Jack to use as a walking stick. "My thanks, O'Neill, for coming after me."

"Any time, Teal'c, any time."

They headed back into the trees as fast as they were able; one race over and another begun.

Daniel waggled the zat at Sam as he crept out of the sheltering trees. She got it immediately and grimaced, reflexively pulling her feet in to her body. There was nowhere to escape contact with the metal of the cage; it was too small for her even to crouch on her feet. At least the charge would have to travel a bit before hitting her. Daniel looked up, exaggeratedly mouthing *"One."*

"Two."

She braced and he fired before the three-count. The arc of blue fire hit the point where the cable was locked off to the pole. Sparks spat out and, seemingly amplified instead of dispersed, the stream of energy danced away up the cable and over the bars of the cage and into Sam. She jerked as the current went through her and slumped awkwardly into one corner.

Daniel kicked viciously at the lock and it broke apart. Freed, the cable whipped away. His hand snatched it in blurred reflex. The cage and its contents, far heavier than they appeared, sagged toward the ground. He clung on, obstinacy kicking in, and became the cage's counterweight. Sam floated gently to the ground as he rose up to the tree canopy. He dangled for a moment, hand slipping on the wet surface, then sure she was safely on the ground, he let go. The force of the fall drove him to his knees and he rolled, pack pushing painfully into his bruised side.

Gasping, Daniel scrambled to his feet and fumbled at the cage. He released the lid and felt for her pulse. Strong. Alive. No breath left to waste, he hauled her out and dragged her backwards into the bushes.

Sam was unconscious, but he found no other injuries needing attention. Quiet as he had tried to be, the creature was bound to come now. Daniel crept into the clearing, disabled and retrieved the Tac and returned to Sam. He propped her up and with a lot of heaving and staggering, got her onto his shoulder. He teetered for balance, then he was off, back along the path he had come.

Slim as she was, Sam weighed a ton on his tired shoulders. Daniel was more than happy to set her down when she began to stir.

"Hey, Sam. How's the head?"

"Still there. Ugh. Nice shot."

"Sorry about that. It was Jack's idea, you can blame him."

"I'll make a point of it."

"We should get going, if you're up to it."

"Lead the way."

He pulled her up and they continued on at a fast walk.

"How long do we have left, Daniel?"

"Two hours and twenty-six minutes. Sam, we have no idea where the next address is."

"What about the colonel and Teal'c?"

Daniel gave her a quick run-down on events since the blast on the beach. "I'm due for another check-in." He keyed his radio, "Jack? Come in, Jack."

"Read you, Daniel." Jack's voice floated out of the speaker on a cloud of static.

"I've got Sam out. We're heading back to the beach. Should be there in about an hour and a half."

"Good job, Daniel." Even through the static, Jack's voice sounded strained. *"Teal'c's fine, we're heading back too."*

"Any idea where we'll find the address?"

"Nope, not a one."

"We must have missed something at the Stargate. Jack, there has to be something pointing to it."

"Roger that. Meet you there. O'Neill out."

Sam and Daniel traded worried glances. "He didn't sound too good, did he?" she asked.

"No. C'mon, let's pick up the pace a bit."

As they jogged along, Daniel voiced another worry. "Sam, did you see what took you?"

"Yeah, it was bipedal. Big, lots of muscle, brown fur all over," she said as she paced at Daniel's side. "It wore a circle of flowers and vines on its head. Which surprised me. It was delicate, carefully made."

Daniel glanced at her. "They're intelligent. The cage, the

pit Jack found Teal'c in, using Goa'uld weapons — it all points to sentience."

"Do you think they're natives to this world?"

"Possibly. Or they were relocated here by Ra. Their actions definitely seem to be part of a test of some kind."

"They could have easily killed us at the beach." Sam ducked under low branches as the path narrowed through the dense trees.

"So, perhaps the reason for taking you and Teal'c captive was to see if you could free yourselves or if Jack and I could rescue you."

"Another test."

"Exactly."

"So, the reward for passing the test…?"

"Might be the password and address for the Stargate," Daniel finished. "I just hope we're not running away from them."

The rain returned to pummel them when they were still a couple of kilometers from the Stargate. Trying to maintain the pace he had originally set was increasingly difficult for Daniel and he gratefully followed Sam as she took the lead along the dunes. Head bent against the lashing rain, he focused on her boot-heels and pounded obstinately on. He felt like he was drowning in fatigue, his body one big ache and there was an odd, dull pain starting up in his left shoulder.

Thoughts of his big, comfortable, warm bed at home tantalized him. Distracted, he collided with Sam as she slowed. "Sorry."

"I think it might be easier going along the waterline now, Daniel." Sam put out a hand to steady him. "I caught a glimpse of the Stargate up ahead. Not long now."

He nodded, breathless, and slid down the small sand dune after her. The sand along the tide-line was harder packed and made for easier running, but each step jarred his body. He angled into Sam's slipstream and staggered on.

Daniel was drifting in a dazed fog of exhaustion when they finally reached the Stargate platform.

"Daniel!" Sam's hand on his arm pulled him off-course and his feet caught in the softer sand. He tripped and plopped down on his knees. "We're here. Let me take this." She unfastened the pack from his vest which he had stubbornly refused to give up earlier. She pressed a canteen into his hand and dropped into the sand beside him. "No sign of the others yet."

Daniel turned to sit on the wet sand, then flopped back, letting the rain pour onto his overheated face. Eyes closed, he fumbled the radio on. "Jack, Teal'c? We're at the 'gate."

After a long pause, Jack's voice came through, scratchy and faint. "Read you, Daniel. We're about fifteen minutes out. Get looking for that address."

Daniel groaned and rolled upright, too cold and tired to expound theories over the radio. "Okay."

He looked blearily at Sam, wishing the weather would permit the use of his glasses.

"The platform?" she asked.

He nodded. "It's the only structure we've seen." He pulled out the small collapsible shovel and a trowel from his pack and they got to work scraping the sand away from the weathered stone.

Nearly twenty minutes later, Jack and Teal'c emerged out of the obscuring rain. They had retrieved the two packs and weapons, stashed further down the beach.

"You two okay?" Jack called as he limped up the sand, Teal'c hovering behind.

"We're fine, Jack. What happened to you?" Daniel gave up the fruitless search and sat down.

"Oh, nothing a week with my chiropractor won't cure. I take it there's no address?"

"Nothing here, sir." Sam indicated the cleared flagstones surrounding the Stargate.

Jack closed his eyes against the stinging rain. So much time wasted, running around dunes and trees and now here they were, back where they started, less than twenty-five minutes before lock-out and no nearer to getting off-planet. Weariness crept through his entire body, his back a steady misery.

"Um, guys? We've got company."

Daniel's cautious announcement sent the other three whirling around, weapons lifting. Jack tossed Carter's zat to her and trained his MP5 on the huge brown shape materializing out of the rain.

"Jack, don't. Don't fire." Daniel pushed himself to his feet and began to walk toward the creature.

"Daniel, these things attacked us. Get back here."

"Jack, they're intelligent. I think what they did wasn't an attack as such, more a test of our own resourcefulness."

"Daniel…."

Arms outstretched peaceably, Daniel advanced slowly on the huge being. "Hello. We're, ah, supplicants undergoing the Trial of Moons. Can you understand me?" He repeated the sentence in Goa'uld.

The enormous brown eyes fixed on Daniel. Studying him? Understanding? Sizing him up for its dinner plate? It began to move forward, taking deliberate, long steps toward him.

"Alright, that's enough." Jack moved to the right, clearing his aim on that massive chest. "Heads up!" He fixed the target in his sight, only to lose it as Daniel planted himself in front of his gun.

"Jack, *don't*. I think it can help us."

Pain-fuelled frustration snapped Jack's patience. "We are running out of time!"

"I *know!*" Daniel yelled back at him.

Their big furry visitor was still advancing. Carter and Teal'c slowly backed up, keeping it covered with their weapons.

"Sir, I have a shot."

"Please." Daniel tried to stare Jack down.

"One of these days, Daniel. Not every big ugly monster wants to make friends, you know."

"I know," Daniel repeated, this time much more softly.

"Hold fire."

Soft whuffling sounds came from the creature. It looked intently at Daniel, then each of them in turn, hooting steadily.

"Sister." Teal'c spoke up suddenly, surprising even himself. Everyone turned to stare at him.

"What?"

"What?"

Teal'c indicated the creature. "I... can understand it. The language it uses—in my mind, it translates into English. Also into Goa'uld." Teal'c's eyebrows were hanging off the clouds. He uttered an experimental hoot and the being hooted back in a long excited ramble.

"Well, I'll be." Jack shook his head but his weapon remained fixed on target.

"It must be the Books of Djehuti, remember?" Daniel stumbled over to Teal'c. "'Perceive the birds of the air, the beasts of the land.' It's translating for you." Longing washed over his face. "What is it saying?"

Teal'c gripped his staff weapon a little tighter. "It, she, says she is called Yerryk. She and her sister were chosen to respond when the Stargate activated and to test those who came. She is pleased that we succeeded in returning to the Stargate within the allotted time."

"Sweet. Ask her how we get out of here," Jack growled.

Teal'c hooted and chuffed back at Yerryk. The others stared at him; this was not something they saw every day.

"Yerryk asks of her sister, the one who tested you and me, O'Neill." Teal'c's gaze flickered to Jack, then back to their guest.

"Tell her we haven't seen sis since we left the pit," Jack ordered, voice unwavering.

Teal'c considered him for a moment, then delivered the message.

Daniel glanced sidelong at Jack. "Jack? What did you do?"

Jack ignored him and concentrated on their furry friend.

"Yerryk says we have earned the right to pass on to the next world. The password is *'Aken Tau-k Ha Kheru'*. It means 'Raging of voice'. She will dial the coordinates herself." Teal'c hooted a few words of thanks and bowed solemnly.

"Great. Good job, T. We're outta here."

Jack turned and marched back to the DHD. Nineteen minutes to go. Good enough. Carter, Teal'c and Daniel closed up behind him, watching expectantly as Yerryk dialed up the Stargate. Teal'c leaned over the DHD and called out the password. The wormhole surged into life, vaporizing the rain and leaving a stinging smell of ozone in the air.

"Carter, on point. Go," Jack snapped out.

She moved off and disappeared into the watery circle. Daniel followed close behind.

"Teal'c?"

"I am coming, O'Neill."

Jack lingered, unwilling to leave anyone behind with these... people. Teal'c paused by the event horizon and looked back at Yerryk. He uttered a long stream of hoots and whistles to the creature. It — she — blinked thoughtfully at them, then seemed to sigh in resignation.

Teal'c bowed gravely and with Jack at his side, stepped into the Stargate.

GATE ELEVEN

Reveler of Heat

It was like stepping into an oven. Dry heat surrounded them; pricking at their eyes, scorching down throats, setting their clothes steaming. Sam ducked her head against the fierce glare from a sun newly risen and fumbled in her vest pocket for her sunglasses.

"Ugh...."

"At least it's not raining, Carter." The colonel pulled his boonie off and struggled out of the clinging poncho.

"I get the feeling it hasn't rained here in quite a while," Daniel said. He moved carefully down three crumbling stone steps onto the sun-baked clay pan.

Desolation stretched away in every direction. No vegetation had found purchase in the hardened ground. The land was flat to the horizon and already reflecting a shimmering heat haze. The only break in the bleakness was a cluster of strange sandstone formations grouped all around the Stargate. They sat low, no more than three feet high, and with the highest part facing into the prevailing winds they resembled a group of seals; mute sentinels protecting the Stargate and any who would arrive through it. Sam followed Daniel and knelt by one. Beneath the loose surface dust lay ancient fossilized shells—remnants of a long-lost sea.

"We have eleven hours, fifteen minutes here, O'Neill." Teal'c jumped down from the platform, his uniform shedding flakes of drying mud.

"Something tells me we're going to want to be out of here quicker than that." Colonel O'Neill grimaced and walked rather delicately down the steps. "Twenty minute break, then we'll get going again." He leant against one of the sand seals and slid down to the ground. "So, Teal'c, what did you say to that thing back there?"

Teal'c arched an eyebrow at him. "I advised Yerryk that her sister may need assistance and apologized for any harm we caused her. That our actions were driven by ignorance and not ill-will."

"Right." The colonel tilted his head and caught Sam staring at him. "What? It was attacking us. I shot at it," he said defensively.

"Didn't say a thing, sir." She exchanged a glance with Daniel. Despite being knocked out, kidnapped and caged, she felt no animosity toward the big, furry creatures. If anything, she wished they had had more time to talk to them.

They all stared out into the emptiness surrounding them. Sand and sky seemed to meld into wavering brown curtains of heat. Far off, almost indistinguishable in the haze, Sam glimpsed a more solid shape. She dug a pair of binoculars out of her pack and focused on the object, eyes aching from the glare.

"Sir, I think there are ruins or something, maybe two kilometers, over that way."

"Let's see," Daniel murmured, taking the binoculars from her. "Looks like a structure. Not much left though."

"It's a starting point at least. Carter, dial home. How is everyone situated for water?"

"Daniel and I filled up at a stream on our way back to the last 'gate, sir. We're running out of purifiers though. The bulk of our supplies were in the boxes we lost."

"You may have mine, Major Carter," Teal'c offered. "I do not usually require them."

"Considering Junior's on strike, Teal'c, I think it might be wise to use them now," the colonel said.

Teal'c grimaced but dropped a tablet into his canteen before passing over the rest to Sam.

With the all-too short break over, they began the weary

trudge to the ruins. For a while they walked in silence, too tired for idle chat. Wet jackets were shed and their clothes dried, making them stiff and uncomfortable.

"I've been thinking." Sam finally spoke over the thud of their boots.

"Again?"

"About Aris Boch," she glanced at the colonel and went on. "He knew who we were, obviously. He knew about the bounty, about Teal'c rejecting Apophis. He knew your reputation as a, well…."

"Pain in the *mikta*."

"Thank you, Teal'c."

"My pleasure, Major Carter."

"He knew I'd hosted Jolinar and had knowledge from her, however useful that might be. But what he knew about Daniel was minimal, and in one case wrong."

"Spit it out, Carter," the colonel grunted.

Sam caught the pained lines in his face and glanced away. "Boch thought Daniel was a medical doctor. He had no clue what an archaeologist was. Also, he didn't seem to know anything more about you, Daniel, other than you opened our Stargate."

"What else should he have known, Sam?" Daniel asked warily.

"Well, how about a little thing like helping raise the rebellion on Abydos and killing Ra, two events that completely destabilized the status quo among the System Lords?"

"Oh, that."

"Yeah, that," she grinned at him.

"Well, Jack was there too," Daniel pointed out. "He should get half the blame."

"Hey, I only tried to blow up the ship. You were the one who showed the Abydonians the true face of their 'gods'. If anyone deserves a big price on his head, it's you, *Doctor* Jackson."

"My point precisely, sir. Why isn't Daniel wanted for that as well, instead of just opening up the Stargate? It doesn't make sense."

"News of the rebellion on Abydos and the death of Ra took some time to filter out to the System Lords," Teal'c offered. "Apophis learned of it only weeks before he journeyed to Earth looking for hosts. He was most eager to visit worlds previously under the domain of Ra. To do so earlier would have brought down considerable retribution from Ra."

"I guess their intel isn't as good as they make out, then. Or they do know about Daniel and Boch lied, for some reason." Sam frowned. Either way, it didn't really make sense.

"Well, not wanting to sound selfish, but I'm kind of glad they don't know," Daniel said.

"As are we all, Daniel Jackson." Teal'c strode on ahead of him, leading the way to the structure which was slowly growing closer.

Daniel paced next to Sam as they walked, questions he had long wanted to ask bubbling to the surface once again. She looked at him and he lost his nerve. It was such a touchy subject with her and after their blow-up in the crystal gazebo....

"What's up?" She glanced over again, eyes lost in the shadow of her boonie.

Do it already.

"Sam, what...." He sighed. "I hope you don't think I'm prying, but I need to know. What was it like, with Jolinar... having a, a Tok'ra inside you?" He trailed off as her expression shut down. "I'm sorry, I know you don't like to talk about it, but... I need to know."

"*Need* to? Why?"

"I just need as much information as I can find, in case... in the future... if we can't find Sha're and Skaara. I need to know what options I have."

"Daniel, the Tok'ra don't know where they are. Dad's gone through all the latest intel. There's been no sightings of them."

"I'm grateful to him, of course. But that's not really why I'm asking." Daniel glanced behind them, ensuring Jack was well out of earshot. "What was it like?"

Her head jerked up and she gaped at him. "You don't mean you're considering becoming...."

"The Goa'uld live very long lives, Sam," he said quietly, eyes fixed on his boots. "Very long. I'm only human."

"Oh, Daniel." She looked away from him and stared at the endless stretch of desert around them. "No, you can't."

"I won't give up on them. If it takes forever." His soft determined words were swept up by the breeze and scattered like a promise across the sky.

Eyes fixed on the horizon, she reached out and rubbed his arm. After a long, silent pause, she quietly began to talk.

By the time they reached the structure they were all sweating heavily, even Teal'c. Packs were dumped on the ground with relief and they spread out to investigate. What remained of the building were three stone archways, six meters high and two meters thick, standing in a line some ten meters apart. Around them, the remnants of earth walls were marked by crumbled sand and stumps of stone pillars.

"This is old," Daniel ran his hand over the carved stone of the first archway. "Very, very old. There's mention of Ra here. It might have been an outpost or trading station originally."

Sam passed through the doorway and handed him a tube of sun-block. "Nice place to be stationed."

"Thank you. Yeah, I'll bet Ra's least favored lackeys got sent out here."

The second archway bore another set of faded carvings; none seemed more recent than a millennium ago.

"Found a well," Jack called out. He stood by the remains of a low circular wall, gingerly trying to peer in without bending his back.

Teal'c knelt by the edge and dropped a stone into the darkness. It clattered down, ending in a thud that echoed back to them. He traded a glance with Jack and they moved on to the third archway, forlornly guarding the entrance to the vast emptiness beyond. Here, clearer engravings drew Daniel's attention.

"Found something."

He traced the writing—Goa'uld script this time rather than the pictograms on the outer archways. Teal'c came to stand behind him, reading over his shoulder.

"Here we go. 'Light of Ra...' and so on, 'defeat the invaders and earn the keys to unlock the Gate of the God'." His eyes flicked rapidly over the heavily carved stone, eventually coming to rest on stylized rays emanating from a depiction of Ra standing, arms outstretched, ram's head glaring down at them from the lintel of the arch.

"Interesting. He's used a human form this time instead of the Eye symbol." He traced the path of the sun rays down the left side of the doorway and found a small glyph. "*Kheperi*, one of the old names for Ra. It means 'infant sun of morning'. I wonder... dawn? Beginning, perhaps?" Daniel extended a finger and pushed firmly on the glyph.

A gentle hum filled the silent air and he stepped back as a large stone slid aside. A metal arm came out and from it unfolded a large, glasslike panel.

"This is different," Jack commented as they crowded round to look.

"It is a training device," Teal'c said. "Used for battle simulations in three dimensional holographic projections."

"Oh, wonder what kind of power it's running on?" Sam crouched down to examine the underside of the panel.

"Never mind, Carter. Let's just do this and get going." Jack turned to Daniel. "We run the sim, win the battle and get what we need, right?"

"Yes," Daniel nodded. "That seems to be the general idea."

"Fire it up, T." Jack planted his feet and settled into a more comfortable stance.

Teal'c activated the panel and miniature fortifications, troops, weapons, armed vehicles and air ships popped into holographic life, ready to be dispatched into battle.

"Our objective is to capture this installation intact." Teal'c pointed out a dome, high on a hill overlooking a plain criss-crossed by rivers. "Enemy numbers and arms will only be revealed as the battle progresses."

"Okay, Master Jaffa, take us through our ordnance."

Teal'c, Jack and Sam settled around the board, ready to battle for their lives. Daniel wandered back to the first archway and its inscriptions, and left them to play.

Over two hours later, they were still at it. Calm calls for tactical support or coordinates for weapons fire drifted along on the hot breezes that had picked up as the sun rose higher. Nothing else stirred in the emptiness surrounding the ruins.

Daniel had wandered back through the first two doorways, recording the structures and their inscriptions and making sure they were indeed alone this time. Had any other supplicant been trapped here, he decided, it would be very unlikely they had survived long in this unforgiving heat.

After retrieving the packs and handing out water and crackers where needed, he settled in the archway's shade and with no trouble at all, fell asleep.

Daniel jolted awake some time later as a whoop of triumph rose up from the battle sim. He straightened slowly from where he had been curled on the ground, every muscle protesting. His skin itched and crawled with dried sweat, salt and sand which was finding its way into tender areas. His toes in particular seemed to attract stray grains, no matter how many times he emptied out his boots and changed socks to a less dirty pair. The ache in his left shoulder had not lessened with rest, if anything it seemed sharper. He shook his head, puzzled over an injury he couldn't remember receiving, but put it down to being dragged off by his ankles — how many planets ago? He pulled his canteen out and sacrificed a dribble of water to moisten his bandana, then tied it over his head and reset the boonie on top.

Staring up at the lintel of the archway, Daniel blinked as he realized there was a carved face peering down at him. Ugly and misshapen, it looked just like the being who had twice visited them during the Trial—Bes. Big, round stone eyes contemplated him, and then one slowly closed, deliberately winking at him. As Daniel's mouth dropped open, the face broadened into a wide grin then vanished completely.

"Okay. Right. Okey dokey." He crawled away from the wall and stood. Determinedly not looking at the smooth stone behind him, he circled the archway and rejoined his team.

"How's it going?" Daniel walked over to the players and regarded the battlefield. It was a mess; downed ships, decimated troops and smoking fires were littered everywhere.

"We are near to victory, Daniel Jackson," Teal'c told him, a hint of a smile tweaking his mouth.

"Whoa, fifth columnists, ten o'clock from the advance patrol," Sam blurted out.

"Bring up F troop, Carter. Teal'c, get an air strike in there, coordinates 21.12.03 by 11.32.18." Jack was in full command of his little war and quite enjoying himself.

"I'll just...." Daniel backed away carefully as little explosions blossomed in the chaos.

He stepped over the crumbled wall and walked through the third archway for a more detailed exploration than his first security checks had allowed. There was around three meters of mud brick wall still attached to either side of the arch, topped on the left side by weighty capstones. On the right side of the arch the capstones and a substantial chunk of wall had fallen and lay in a tumble of stones at the base. The area behind the arch appeared to have once been a courtyard, fenced in by low, crumbling brick walls around three sides. Here and there, paving stones showed through the baked earth, and the stumps of three pillars stood alone at the far end. Beyond the wall, the bleak landscape stretched unbroken until the sky leant down to swallow it.

The earth here had the same seared quality to it as the rest. Daniel squatted by the fallen piece of wall, examining the fine clay bricks. There seemed to be a lot of water erosion on the top and broken sides, evidence of powerful and plentiful rain that had dissolved the earth, only to be hardened once again in the sun.

He scratched off a piece of brick, then bent closer as a shape at odds with the angular blocks caught his eye. It was rounded, caked in a layer of thick clay. Pulling out his knife, Daniel gently chipped away the soil to reveal—the sole of a shoe. More precisely, a shoe with its owner's leg and foot bones still attached.

He grimaced and sat back on his heels. The leg bones disappeared under the fallen section of wall. Considering the angle, Daniel decided whoever it was had been either standing or sitting by the right side of the arch when the wall, possibly weakened by heavy rain, had crashed down.

The victim long dead and posing no threat, Daniel decided not to interrupt the three-D version of Gettysburg. He stepped around the debris and found contours in the baked mud eerily resembling a head and partial torso.

He frowned, turning to consider the archway. "What were you doing here?"

The muffled voices of his team from beyond the wall were his only reply.

"Were you resting before you left? No, not if it was raining hard enough to bring the wall down."

"Daniel?"

"Just talking to, er, myself, Jack."

"We're nearly done here."

"Okay."

He looked closely at the archway. There was a small square opening just above his head in the stone casing on the right side. Tentatively, he reached up and brushed his fingers inside the hole. The three sides and top of the tiny space were smooth and blank, but the bottom was hollowed out—into the all too familiar shape of Ra's Eye. He pulled back and looked at the stone on the left of the arch. This was unbroken. Peering closely, he could just see an outline of a matching cavity, now tightly filled with a cube of stone.

He stepped back and considered. One cavity filled. One open. Dead body by the open cavity.

"Uh oh."

Daniel fetched his pack and pulled out his tools. He brushed away what loose soil there was covering the body, revealing the outline of a head, shoulder and torso down to the lower ribs and the right arm stretched outwards from the body, all covered in a hard layer of clay. It was all too easy to imagine the unfortunate person desperately trying to claw their way free.

"Hooah! Score one for the Air Force!" Jack's exultant voice broke through Daniel's ruminations.

He got up and walked through the archway to see Sam doing a one-sided high five with Teal'c. The game board was still, a frozen image of carnage. Jack beamed, the smile lighting the tired lines of his face.

"Good guys won, Daniel."

"Congratulations. Did you get the keys?"

On cue, the board went dark and retracted into the archway. There was a click of stone on metal and the arm slid out again, bearing a tray with two indentations in the shape of an Eye of Ra. One was filled with a glittering diamond cut into the Eye shape. The other was empty. Jack picked up the diamond and the tray retracted into the wall, the stone cover settling back into place.

Jack frowned. "Shouldn't there be two?"

"The instructions did say keys—plural—didn't they, Daniel?" asked Sam. She looked worn too and pulled her boonie off to shake out her sweaty hair.

Daniel crossed his arms over his chest and stared at the diamond in Jack's hand. "I think you'd better come see this." He turned and walked through the archway. Baffled, the others followed.

Succinctly, Daniel pointed out the two apertures in the arch, both now open, and then the remains under the fallen wall. "I think this is the last person to have attempted the Trial. They played the simulation, won, brought the keys here. Inserted the left one, went to insert the other and the wall fell on him, or her."

Jack held the diamond up to the reopened hole. "It fits."

"Logically therefore, this person was holding the other key when they were struck down." Teal'c knelt by the body's outline.

"Yes." Daniel winced as he saw Sam and Jack's previous elation evaporate.

"It could be anywhere." Sam hunkered down in the shade of the doorway.

Jack stared at Daniel. "You mean we have to sift through who knows how much dirt in…" he checked the countdown on his chrono, "a little under six hours? In this heat?" He flung his arms out in exasperation.

"We're dead," Sam whispered.

Daniel crouched next to her. "Sam. Don't worry. This is what *I* do. We'll find it."

Going for the most obvious target first, Daniel set to work excavating the body's right arm. He fitted together his collapsible shovel and changed the head for a small pick. Gently but firmly, he peppered the clay with blows hard enough to penetrate the surface without damaging what lay buried. The ground gave way reluctantly, clumping in rock-like lumps. It took a full half-hour to break enough of the surface away so that he could begin troweling off looser soil beneath. The body was buried under nearly eighteen inches of clay and soil. Relief filled him when he did reach the limb; it was mummified, robbed of its moisture by the dry subsoil.

Daniel pulled on a face mask and shifted around on his knees, carefully following the arm up to the hand. With the trowel's point he scraped away enough dirt to reveal what was probably a male's arm, bereft of clothing. The hand was clenched shut.

"Looks like he's holding something," Daniel said. He looked up in surprise as a shadow passed over him. Sam and Teal'c had fashioned an awning out of their four rain ponchos; knotted together and strung on cord from the wall to two packs at the other end.

"Oh, good idea. Thanks."

"Can you see what he's holding?" Sam crawled under the shelter and peered at the exposed limb.

"Not yet. Uh, don't get too close, Sam. Bodies can be full of nasty surprises sometimes."

"Right." She pulled back and watched Daniel's deft movements uncover more of the buried hand.

"How's Jack?" he asked quietly.

"He took the first sleep break."

"Oh. That bad?" Daniel darted a glance at Jack, asleep sitting up in the shade of the arch. "And Teal'c?"

"That wound is still bleeding. Infection's bound to set in soon and he won't be able to fight it." She sighed tiredly.

"How are you holding up, Sam?"

"I'm fine. Although, I keep having visions of really huge bath tubs, swimming pools, lakes, margaritas…. So I'm probably starting to lose it, actually." She quirked a smile.

"Sounds perfectly normal to me. Here we go. Um, you might want to look away for a minute."

Sam's eyes widened as she saw Daniel place his hands on the corpse's dried fingers. She didn't look away, but was unable to repress a flinch at the cracking of bone and dried flesh. Daniel extracted a small object and held it up for inspection.

"I don't think that's the key."

"No, it's not." He stared at the oval shape; its blue metallic covering glinted in the bright light. "Teal'c? Can you have a look at this?"

Teal'c appeared at the edge of the shelter and crouched, taking the object from Daniel. "It is a personal recorder. Such things are quite common amongst the Goa'uld. They are used either to store personal mementoes or to send messages."

He tapped the tiny controls and a small holographic face appeared in the air above the recorder. Off kilter and blurry, it was the man whose body now lay at their feet, his pale and blood-stained face looking out at them. No sound emerged from the device but he appeared to be speaking. Teal'c snapped the recorder off as the dying man's head drooped.

"Even if he was a Goa'uld, it's a sad way to die," Sam said quietly. "I hope the host didn't feel anything."

Without quite knowing why, Daniel took the recorder back and stashed it in his pocket.

"We're going to have to tear this site apart. If the key was in his other hand it'll be under the wall. If it was thrown from his right hand it could be anywhere in a ten meter radius."

"He might have put it in a pocket." Sam eyed the heap of rubble with an air of despair.

"Yes, he could have. Sam, can you use the shovel head to clear around his hand? Teal'c, we'll have to get through this clay and move the bricks." Daniel looked at the collapsible pick, nowhere near adequate to the task. "Wish we still had my tool box."

"Perhaps another method would be more efficient." Teal'c got up and disappeared around the wall. Moment's later he was back, bearing his staff weapon and a determined gleam in his eye.

"Oh. Right! Excavation by staff weapon. Why didn't I think of that?"

Daniel and Sam scrambled out of the way. After some discussion about points of impact and vector levels, Teal'c dropped to one knee, sighted carefully and gently pressed the trigger. The bolt of plasma ripped across the top of the debris. It sent a cloud of dust and dirt chunks flying up into the air and brought one sleeping colonel rolling to his knees, weapon aimed and primed even before his vision had cleared.

"Whoa, hold fire, Colonel!"

"What the hell was that?" Jack sagged back onto his heels.

"Sorry, Jack. Teal'c's just helping excavate the body."

"With a staff weapon?"

"Well, not... well, yes."

"And I was having such a good dream too — donuts, Mary Steenburgen...."

"Go back to sleep, Jack."

"No, I'm good now. Where do you want me?"

"Can you sift through the soil as Sam digs it out?"

"You got it."

They settled in to a hushed, almost frantic pace of work. Sam used the shovel-head to dig through the dry earth in the most likely direction she could project, while Jack sifted her spoils with a leaf trowel. Daniel directed Teal'c in a few more well-placed shots that broke through most of the baked clay and dislodged the top layer of bricks.

Together they attacked the wall. Bricks were tossed into an ever-increasing pile, but it was hard work and taxed their already depleted strength. Daniel found himself favoring his left hand as the ache in his shoulder increased and he had to crawl about on his knees in deference to his healing back and leg. The dull throb in his side was not worthy of notice.

"Daniel Jackson, I have uncovered clothing," Teal'c stepped back from the tattered rags revealed in the hole he had cleared.

Daniel peered up at him, squinting despite his sunglasses. A faint shock ran up his nape at the sight of Teal'c: dusty face streaked with sweat and lungs heaving from labor, which under normal conditions he would have done one-handed. Junior's peculiar talents were now noticeably absent. There was nothing they could do, words of concern would only make Teal'c feel self-conscious.

Removal of the cloth revealed a leg. Encouraged, they wielded pick and trowel, hauled on half-buried bricks with cramp-curled hands, until nearly two hours after Teal'c had fired the first shot in the excavation, the body lay completely exposed. No pockets were found in the clothes. No Eye of Ra lay conveniently by the remains' side.

"We'll have to turn it over." Daniel wiped sweat out of his eyes with the back of his glove and removed the face mask. "Fifteen minute break first," Jack called from where he sat, surrounded by carefully sifted hills of Carter's spoil.

They dropped to the ground around him and shared the last of their food.

"Moon's up." Sam pointed to a near-full white satellite, well into a low arc across the sky.

"Water's getting low." Another obstacle to their survival here. If they didn't find the key, they would all be dead within a day. "Better hope the next planet is more hospitable," Jack said. "We're going to be foraging from now on."

The sky remained a deep, dark blue, unmarred by even the merest hint of a cloud. Jack closed his eyes, visibly battling a headache. In the silence, their remaining time seemed to tick loudly by.

"Carter, you should take a break."

She shook her head, more to wake up than signal refusal. "I'm good, sir. I had some sleep on the last planet."

He cracked open an eye at her. "You were unconscious."

"Same thing, sir. Besides, I was faking it while Daniel carried me," she grinned.

"Hey!" Daniel cried, feigning outrage. "You just liked being the damsel in distress for a change."

Daniel refastened his canteen to his belt, the water warm and metallic in his mouth. Not wanting to expend further energy getting up, he crawled back to the body. He exchanged his thick work gloves for rubber ones and repositioned the white mask over his mouth and nose. Bending close to the ground, he cleared the soil around the body with sweeping strokes of the trowel, his left hand sifting each freed pile of dirt.

Teal'c joined him and accepted the gloves and mask Daniel offered. When they had cleared six inches under the body's left side, Daniel nodded and they set aside their tools. They placed their hands under the withered torso and heaved. With a gruesome cracking of dried flesh, they pushed the body up and over as far as the stiffened right arm would allow.

"Hold it up."

Daniel attacked the dirt-encrusted clothes with trowel and brush, knocking away clods of earth. The left arm had been broken and crushed under the body. There was nothing in the hand. The clothes on the body were simple pants and a thin, sleeveless shirt, two pockets in each. None contained the key.

"Oh, please. It has to be here, somewhere." He groped through the dirt where the body had lain, heartbeat picking up each time an object came under his hand, but three stones, a flask top, a button and some kind of decoration or brooch were all he found.

Jack and Sam stopped in their own search as Daniel sank into the dirt, overheated and close to despair. If the key had been dropped and washed away in the rains they would likely never find it, certainly not in time to save their lives.

Teal'c, still holding the corpse on its side, indicated a slip of fabric, coarser in weave than the body's clothes, barely showing in the hardened mud. "Daniel Jackson, there is something buried in the ground, above the head."

Daniel leapt on it like a desperate gopher. He found a strap, and the strap was attached to a carry bag. He yanked it free and sat back in the dirt. Teal'c respectfully lowered the body back to its resting place.

The bag, half rotted, fell to pieces in Daniel's hands. Tools, water flasks and a broken comb scattered to the ground as he sorted quickly through each mud-covered item.

"Yes!" An odd but familiar shaped lump stuck to the side of a flask caught Daniel's eye. He attacked it with a brush and from the cloud of dust emerged a dull twinkle of red; a carved Eye of Ra. "We've got it!" he coughed hoarsely.

Teal'c smiled and settled himself next to the diggings. Sam groaned with relief and flopped backwards into the dirt.

"I am turning in my trowel." Jack dusted it off and stashed it in Daniel's pack. "Nice job, Daniel, all of you. Let's get this over with and then we'll head back to the 'gate. I'd like us all to have some proper rest before we go through."

"I do feel the need for kel'no'reem," Teal'c admitted. "However, should we not rebury this one?"

"Seriously T, I don't think any of us have the energy to spare."

"Just push the dirt back over, Teal'c." Daniel crawled back to his pack and pulled out a small leather roll holding his fine-work tools. "The wind will do the rest in no time."

He selected a slim dental pick and carefully cleaned the crusted muck from the Eye. Barely finding enough spit to clear away the last trace of dirt, he held up a beautiful carved ruby. He shoved the tool roll into his pants' pocket and presented the ruby to Jack.

"Try it."

Jack took it gingerly and tossed it and the diamond to Sam. She groaned and rolled to her feet. The rest of them followed suit with a chorus of grunts and complaints, and staggered to the wall. Once out of the awning's shade, the heat and glare hit with renewed ferocity.

Sam fitted the diamond into the aperture on the left-hand side of the archway. A panel of stone closed over it with barely a noise. She reached out and dropped the ruby into the slot on the right. It too was pulled inside the archway. There was a tense few moments of silence, then a holographic display appeared in the shade of the doorway; seven address glyphs and a phrase in Goa'uld script.

Daniel quickly jotted them down, double-checking that he had the phrase *'Teb her kehaat'* correct, then compared it with what the others had memorized. He made three copies and handed them out.

Drained, they stood for a couple of anti-climactic minutes; exhaustion gnawed at them now the urgency was gone.

"C'mon." Jack clapped Daniel on the shoulder and frowned

at the resulting wince.

"Teal'c, I'd like to re-dress that wound when we get back to the Stargate," Sam said.

"I would appreciate that, Major Carter."

The awning was dismantled and the body given a scant reburial. Within ten minutes they had shouldered packs and were walking back through the ruined temple.

It was a slow hike back to the Stargate. As they plodded along, Teal'c found his attention diverted inwards as the silence of the desert wrapped close around him. The half-thought words and impressions that had been irritating his sub-conscious for two planets now rose up in his mind, clamoring for attention. Satisfied the team was not currently at risk, he let the images crowd his thoughts.

Tumbling, entangled, they flooded together nonsensically; released from the confines of the Books, words and sounds merged and separated in rivers of confused meaning. Teal'c brought his powers of meditation to bear, and with a mental snap that sent a shiver down his spine, the streams separated, slowed and gave up their meanings.

The words, if that was the correct term, paraded past his inner eye in the delicate, flowing script. As each word came to him, so did its meaning and its pronunciation in a melodic dialect, coupled with its equivalent meaning in Goa'uld.

For some time Teal'c lost himself in the joy of discovery as more and more of the language made itself known to him. With a little mental practice, he found the control needed to marshal the information, ascertaining where it was storing itself in his mind and how to stop and start it up again. With the confusing babble tamed, Teal'c finally rose out of his light meditative state and looked around, surprised to see the Stargate looming distinctly before them.

He glanced over at Daniel Jackson, tramping along, eyes half shut and walking on auto-pilot. Having denied the man who loved languages the discovery granted by the Books, Teal'c felt constrained to share.

"Daniel Jackson."

"Hmm? What?" Daniel roused himself and looked up at Teal'c.

"The Books of Djehuti are unfolding their language to me and I am beginning to comprehend it."

Daniel stumbled to a halt. "Really?"

"Not the language of the creatures on the last planet?" Major Carter drifted to a stop and pulled her canteen free, the sloshing of the water within a reminder that their supplies were running low.

"It is not, Major Carter. This is quite different. While I was able to understand Yerryk's speech, I had no insight into her species' written language. I believe that ability was included in the Books merely to allow access to the Stargate. Now however, I am… learning both the written and spoken elements of this new language."

"Show me," Daniel nearly demanded. He pulled his notebook from its plastic baggie in his BDU pocket, and thrust it and a worn pencil at Teal'c.

Teal'c considered carefully, then wrote a short passage in the flowing script.

"I've never seen this before." Daniel peered intently at the words. "And you can pronounce it?"

"I can. It reads, *'Dal cho'thlin pas weh-ah'*. It means," he paused as the Goa'uld words came readily to mind and he translated those into English. "Bright wings bear the morning light."

"Write down the translation for me," Daniel pushed the notebook back to Teal'c, unable to tear his eyes from the beautiful writing.

Teal'c complied and they walked on in silence as Daniel studied the script.

Eventually he said, "I don't get it. Why would Ra give people attempting to enter his service access to a language that isn't Goa'uld?"

"This I do not know, Daniel Jackson."

"I always thought the Goa'uld were pretty xenophobic when it came to other species or races," O'Neill said. "All the Goa'uld and Jaffa we've come across have used the same basic language, haven't they?"

"You are correct, O'Neill," Teal'c said, trying not to sound surprised at their leader's perception. "A central language has been imposed for millennia as a means of better controlling conquered planets."

Daniel nodded, sounding the new words quietly to himself. "Except for isolated communities like Abydos, who evolved their own dialect and even that shares the same root language as basic Goa'uld. This—this is really odd, Teal'c."

"Indeed it is."

The sun, in its higher arc, was chasing the moon toward the horizon when they arrived at the Stargate. Daniel stopped a few paces away, his eye caught by a pile of stone slabs next to one of the seal formations. It wasn't a natural formation and the crust coating the rocks heralded what could be a hidden life-saver.

"Guys, I think I've found water." He dropped his pack and knelt.

Removing the topmost slab released a puff of steam, redolent with minerals, rising from a dark cavity.

"A thermal water course." Teal'c stooped beside him and shone his flashlight into the hole. Less than a foot down, clear water glinted with bubbles lazily rising to the surface.

"It's hot, but it should be drinkable," said Daniel. "If we pool what water we have left, we can refill the rest of the canteens."

A dark stripe of shade along one side of the platform offered a slim place to rest. Lining up six canteens to cool, Daniel sighed in relief. Despite the sleep he had snatched earlier, his head was thumping with exhaustion and his eyes felt rough and gritty.

"Shouldn't we push on, sir? Get out of this heat at least?" Sam rested her back against the warm stone and fanned her face with her boonie.

"We've got... two hours, seventeen minutes left." Jack

dropped his pack and sat in the shade of the Stargate's ring. "We're slowing down too much. Who knows what's waiting next. Now we have extra water, we can take the time to rest a little. Carter, you and Teal'c get your heads down. Daniel, I'll trade you off in an hour."

"Yes, sir." Sam slid down, head resting on her pack and was asleep in minutes. Teal'c folded himself into the welcome peace of meditation and was lost to the outside world.

Daniel stretched out in the shade. He drifted into a tenuous, half-dream state full of shifting images. Goa'uld and hairy monsters chased first him, then each other, through deserts where it rained all the time. He reached out for his friends, but they ran past him and disappeared into the dense trees now growing in the desert. He called to them, ran after them, but it was dark and he was alone, the wind and rain tearing at him, pulling him down into hot, wet sand that choked him, swallowed him up until there was no air left to breathe....

He jerked up, shocked awake, heart thundering in his ears. Daniel fumbled his canteen free and sucked down the bitter water, aware of Jack sitting above him in the meager shade. He looked at his watch. Thirty minutes left. Quite sure he didn't want to go back to sleep, he climbed onto the platform and shooed Jack away to rest.

Silence settled around them, constricting in its intensity. The occasional snore from Sam or huff of breath from Jack were the only sound.

Daniel dug his digital camera out of his pack and studied the readouts. The memory card, the fourth he had used on this mission, was almost to capacity. He pulled it out and tucked it with its predecessors in a small plastic container, stashed safely in the side pocket of his BDUs. Almost as an afterthought, he fished out the dead man's recorder and set to cleaning away the encrusted muck with his dental pick, glancing up every minute or so to ensure they remained alone. With infinite care, he unearthed a tiny speaker on the device. He stared at it for quite some time before activating the recording. The dying man's face hovered in the hot air, his voice reached out from beyond his dusty grave, harsh and hollow in Daniel's ears.

'Sidhe, beloved. I speak to you from where I shall now never leave. Misfortune has struck me down and my Trial is at an end. I engaged this Trial with all my confidence, certain its reward would bring all that I hoped to bestow upon you, give you the richness in life your devotion and love has given me through the long years of our bond.

'Never did I regret undertaking this glorious Trial, but with my dying breath shall I regret not being by your side every day of the life you will live without me.'

The dying man broke off, consumed by a coughing fit. Daniel stared at the projection, eyes prickling in the dry heat. Was this man not the Goa'uld they had thought him to be?

The coughing finally ended. Gasping, the man wiped away bloody spittle—and his eyes flashed a dim, unnatural golden light.

Goa'uld then.

'Remember your Bacis, my love, as you walk the fields of our home. I shall, as ever, walk by your side. Think of me only as absent and waiting for you until we are joined once more in the life beyond.'

Bacis choked again, weakening coughs that petered away. The picture wobbled as his hand dropped to the ground. He shuddered, then stilled as the light left his eyes.

Daniel was about to turn the display off when Bacis' eyes dragged half-open. A few whispered words stuttered from his lips in a language Daniel had never heard before. Then, with a sigh of exhaling air, the host, too, passed away.

Daniel sat, disturbed to say the least, as the shade moved away from him, until it was time to rouse his teammates and forge once more into the unknown.

GATE TWELVE

Within the Cavern of Her Lord

That first breath of fresh, cool air was sweet nectar to Jack as he stepped out of the Stargate. His parched lips welcomed the moisture around them as bright afternoon sunlight shone down. He moved a few steps forward as his team slurped through behind him, weapon half-raised, his gaze darting around him, taking in a shale beach bordering an ocean, flowering bushes along the edge of the shore that would be ideal for camouflage and....

"We've got company!"

Jack thumbed the safety off his gun and took aim as armed Jaffa scurried out of the bushes' cover like so many rats. One, two dozen, more. He held fire and dove off the Stargate platform after Teal'c, Daniel and Carter likewise hurled themselves over the far side.

"We're too low on ammo to make much of a fight of it," he said, nevertheless aiming at the leaders in the group running toward them.

"Another phalanx approaches from the rear," Teal'c said urgently. "We are without means of retreat."

"What do you think, is this part of the Trial?"

"I am uncertain, O'Neill. We have encountered Jaffa before, however these seem much more aggressive."

Odds were decidedly against them.

"Carter, Daniel, hold your fire. Let's see if they're willing to talk," Jack yelled over the stone platform.

The troops were nearly upon them. Jack lowered his gun, fighting the basic instinct to start shooting and take as many of the enemy with him as possible. Horus-helmeted soldiers spread out around them: their expressionless metal faces filled

Jack with foreboding. Several marched straight up to SG-1 and with no more preamble than pointing weapons in their faces, proceeded to strip away every weapon the four carried.

"Hey, watch it, pal." Jack leant back reflexively when one came at him with a knife and attempted to cut away his side-arm, holster and all.

The soldier responded with a stinging backhand. Beside Jack, Teal'c moved to intercept and was pounced upon by three Jaffa who wrestled him to the ground. Within seconds, Jack was overpowered, his arms yanked behind his back and he was forced to his knees. Bitterly, he glared at their inhuman masks and regretted not taking the slim chance they'd had to fight.

Sounds of a scuffle rose up from the other side of the platform. Jack and Teal'c both craned to see Carter grappling with two Jaffa who had Daniel pinned, struggling furiously, to the ground. It took three more to pull her off and hold her down long enough to remove her weapons, vest and pack, and bind her arms. Daniel, Jack and Teal'c were also swiftly stripped of their gear, then a metal-shod boot in the back sent both Teal'c and Jack to the ground.

"I think we may have a problem here," Jack muttered into the shale which pressed painfully against his face. The boot between his shoulder blades kept him down, while rough hands hauled his arms back and bound them tightly together—from elbow to wrist. He couldn't help the small moan that escaped him as fire zinged along his spine.

"Jaffa! Hear me." Teal'c reared his shoulders up off the stony beach, struggling against the two soldiers holding him down. "Know that your god, Ra, is no more. His death is freely acknowledged among the System Lords. Your devotion to him is admirable, but futile."

One soldier separated from the pack and walked toward them. At his gesture, Teal'c and Jack were hauled to their feet. The man's falcon-shaped helmet retracted with a metallic slither, revealing a handsome, dark face of indeterminate age, a gold tattoo of a disc nestled in a half-circle etched into his forehead. He studied them closely and smiled.

"We do not serve Lord Ra, Master Jaffa," he said simply. "Come."

With that, he turned and led the way over the shale. Teal'c and Jack were prodded into motion and joined by Carter, still giving the Jaffa attitude, and Daniel, whose bleeding nose and unfocused eyes gave reason for her defiance.

"Daniel barely got two words out and they belted him with a staff," she growled, glaring at a Jaffa who was crowding too closely.

"'M'okay," Daniel murmured. He tilted his head back, sniffed, then leant forward and spat out the blood running down the back of his throat.

Jack pushed through the Jaffa in front of him and addressed their leader. "Uh, you should know we didn't embark on this Trial of Ra's by choice. We're just looking for a way home. You let us go, we'll be happy to get out of your hair."

The first prime, never breaking his rapid stride, turned his head and gave what Jack could only think of as a feral smile, then the helmet folded around the man's head like a metallic flower and all hopes for conversation were lost.

They were prodded along the shingle in silence, following the curve of the shore around a small headland. As the Stargate was lost to their view, another vista opened up before them; mile after mile of coastline stretched straight on until it vanished in the far distance, bordered on one side by towering sandstone cliffs and on the other, the sea—blue, calm and enticing. Flocks of gulls wheeled and dove for fish along the shoreline. Beautiful though it was, SG-1's attention was captivated by the throngs of people moving about, on the beach and up into the cliffs looming over them. It seemed they had stepped into a village, albeit a semi-permanent one.

Brightly decorated tents lined the strip of grass between the shale and the first rise of the cliffs. Open fishing boats were hauled onto the beach where clusters of folk were sorting through baskets of fresh-caught fish. Women bustled amongst the tents, cooking over fires, washing clothes or children. In fact, children of all ages roamed the camp, playing or help-ing to untangle nets. Almost to a person, as SG-1 was escorted through the camp and onto the wide path leading up the cliff-face, everyone stopped what they were doing and stared at them.

"This is—unexpected," Jack muttered.

"It's not a permanent camp," said Daniel, squinting and gri-macing in the bright sun.

"Do you get the feeling we were expected?" Carter asked.

"Yeah," Jack grunted, trying to find a less painful posture as the path inclined steeply. "Keep on your toes, everyone."

"Did you see the Akhet symbol on the first prime's tattoo?" Daniel said quietly. "It's the same symbol that was on Mat's globe, back in the rainforest."

Jack nodded and filed the information away. They were led up and up, walking in single file as the path narrowed until it gave out into the opening of a large cavern stretching back into the cliff, its furthest recesses lost in shadow. No civilians were here, only Jaffa, closely ranked in pairs along the walls and standing rigidly at attention.

They were pushed inside, away from the comforting day-light and swiftly immersed in shadows and flickering orange light from scores of fire-sconces set around the perimeter and dotted randomly across the cave's rocky floor.

Teal'c subtly flexed his muscles, testing the bonds on his arms. Jack tried the same but there was no give in the ropes and the way their elbows were pulled back so tightly meant there was precious little movement left to him. The Jaffa arranged around them retracted their helmets and seemed poised expectantly. There were at least forty guards in the chamber, all armed and alert—leaving little hope for a suc-cessful escape attempt. And should they manage to escape the Jaffa, how in hell were they going to get off this planet?

A stir of movement at the back of the cavern announced

the entrance of a number of people from what had to be an adjoining cave. With balletic synchronicity, every Jaffa, with the exception of the first prime and four guarding the prisoners, dropped to their knees in deep obeisance.

Gentle blue-white light advanced toward them, held aloft in deep bowls by two lines of women, all clad in diaphanous white dresses. Walking placidly, proudly in their midst was another woman, her elegant bearing clearly indicating this was someone of importance. The team shifted restlessly and exchanged uncertain glances.

The lines of women approached and then moved to either side around the captives, ringing them and bathing them in their gentle light. The lone woman glided to a halt in front of them and SG-1 stared at her in surprise. She was sheathed in a luminous blue gown that gleamed in the light and left nothing of the slender body beneath hidden. The low-cut neckline was crowned with a wide collar of multiple strands of lapis and carnelian beads. Her rather ordinary face was rendered quite extraordinary by eyes as black as a starless night, dramatically highlighted by dark kohl-lines. A solid gold Akhet symbol crowned her straight, black hair.

Without comment, she walked up to each of the four and carefully studied their faces. First Teal'c, then Jack, Daniel and Carter; Jack she paid particular attention to, Daniel she barely glanced at. Finished with the major, the woman prowled back to Jack and for the first time her expressionless features changed, slowly twisting into a look of such deep hatred that Jack actually pulled back in surprise.

"Er, hi there," he began gamely. "As I've tried to explain to your boy over there, we're just travelers who… awk!" He broke off as the woman knocked his boonie off, grabbed a handful of hair and gave it such a vicious yank that her hand came away with a clump torn out by the roots. She spun on her heel and seemed to be battling to regain her poise.

"What the hell was that for?"

"Jack, shush," Daniel whispered urgently.

"What shush? She ripped out my hair!" Indignation only made him louder.

"It's a sign of contempt, deep contempt."

"Pulling my hair?"

"Yes, like spitting in a person's face. If she were of Semitic origin she would have hit you with her shoe."

"Why?"

"I don't know! Be quiet, she's mad enough," Daniel hissed as quietly as he could.

The Goa'uld, still with her back to them, gestured imperiously at her first prime. He came to attention with a clang of armor.

"Silence! Be blessed, for you stand in the glorious presence of our Goddess, The Lady Mat."

"Wasn't she...?" Jack trailed off.

"Wife of Ra," Teal'c supplied somberly.

"Oh boy." Carter shifted uneasily. "I don't think this is part of the Trial."

Mat turned around, black eyes now blazing with inhuman light. She drifted back to Jack, her voice the unmistakable double-tone of the Goa'uld.

"O'Neill." She drew the syllables out as if savoring a delicacy.

Jack's eyebrows rose in feigned ignorance. "I'm sorry? The name's Merrin, actually."

Mat smiled, not at all convincingly. She lifted her hand, displaying for the first time the delicate gold finger caps and central jewel of the Goa'uld's favorite lethal weapon. She stroked his neck and face and he tried not to shy away from that cold touch. Still smiling she clamped her palm to his forehead and unleashed a nightmare upon him.

Pain engulfed every nerve in Jack's body. His vision went, hearing distorted into a confusing Doppler of sound, his center of gravity did loop-the-loops and his stomach tried to crawl up into his throat. His head felt like it had been in the oven way too long and could someone take it out please, before it exploded and left a nasty stain?

Cold washed down his torso, his legs buckled and delivered him to the floor. Thankfully the contact stopped but it was a century too late. He slumped on his knees, not coordinated enough even to fall over, while a mini-war erupted around him.

More Jaffa rushed into the room and moments later, his teammates were thrown to the ground beside him. Jack crumpled and flopped onto his back. How the hell had Daniel coped with this being done to him, *twice?*

Mat stared down at them; sprawled on the ground, held there by pain, pure force or primed weapons. Her face smoothed out to that earlier emotionless guise.

"Come."

She turned and walked through the circle of handmaidens and led the way into the darkness.

Daniel, together with Sam and Teal'c, was lined up against the rock of an intimate, well-lit chamber, arms still painfully bound. Each had a thick metal collar around their necks, attached chains holding them fast to the rock. Jack hung by his wrists from chains welded into the very rock of the cave roof, slowly coming out of his stupor, feet just scraping the floor. Daniel knew all too well how he must be feeling: brain slowly regaining its functions, thoughts scattered like sheep.

Jack put a little extra weight on his feet and looked around. "Well, isn't this all too medieval?"

"Sir, are you okay?" Sam managed to croak out.

"Peachy, Carter. Thanks for asking. You?"

"Hanging in, sir."

"Of course he is well, human. Do you think We would risk harming him permanently, when We have expended so much effort to bring him here?"

Mat stepped out of the darkness behind Jack and walked around him.

"Bring...?" Daniel echoed. "Then we were right. This

whole Trial, it was all a setup?" He sagged against the wall, trying unsuccessfully to ease his aching body and head. "Why?"

"Why would a powerful Goa'uld such as yourself go to such means to apprehend us?" Teal'c elaborated.

"You? You are merely a bonus. You shall be disposed of at Our pleasure. This one," Mat ran her hand seductively over Jack's stained t-shirt. "This one We wish to suffer greatly. We knew of Our Lord's Trial and set the bounty on your heads, knowing there would be one who would eventually accept Our terms and lure you to Tintara where you would have no choice but to face the Trial." She directed the glowing jewel of the ribbon-device over his chest, scorching a trail of heat over Jack's ribs and lungs, making him flinch and swear.

"We wished you to suffer greatly. It does not appear that you have. We are… displeased. However, We shall enjoy the long, long time We will have together."

"Believe me, sister, we have suffered," Jack grunted.

"Why?" Sam ground out, straining against the collar. She sounded very, very angry. "What the hell have we done to *you*? We'd never even heard of you until a few days ago."

"What did you do to Us?" Mat echoed. The heat from the jewel in her hand increased, focusing down into a pinpoint that burned through Jack's shirt and skin. He choked and tried to pull away.

"What—you—did!" She punctuated each word with a spear of fire into Jack's vulnerable torso. "You—killed—Our—*love*."

"Gahh!" Jack writhed in pain as the burns assaulted his chest, sides and back. His breath caught in his throat, and he tipped his head back, desperately trying to suck in some air.

"Ra!" Comprehension dawned and the word was out before Daniel could think twice.

Diverted, Mat whirled about and stalked toward him.

"Ra was still your, what? Consort? Husband?" he pressed.

Mat's hand flashed out and struck his face, metal finger-caps leaving four stinging impressions in his cheek.

"We are, and ever shall be, the soul-mate of Our beloved, the one who ruled over and commanded devotion from all of Our kindred and brought your kind out of its ignorant savage ways to the glory of servitude to Us."

"Ow." Daniel eased his aching head up and dragged in a deep breath. "Oh, yes, right. How can we not be grateful for that?"

"You arranged this whole setup just to take revenge on us for the death of Ra?" Sam stared hard at Mat. "Well, you've got it wrong. We didn't have anything to do with Ra dying." She flinched as Mat moved to her and threaded those cold fingers through her hair.

"Host of Jolinar of Malk-shur," the Goa'uld purred. "Do not try your pitiful deceits upon Us. We know what that traitor took from Lord Cronus and We will delight in watching him retrieve its location from your mind." Mat twisted a handful of Sam's hair and viciously yanked her head back. "And when your mind is empty of all thought — of all you ever knew — We shall barter your husk from Lord Cronus and fill it with one of Our children." A cold smile flickered across her face and she pressed her cheek against Sam's in a horrible parody of intimacy.

"Such a pretty vessel. You will be suitable to hold Our child for all eternity."

Mat released Sam with a little pat on the head and moved back to Jack. She considered the ribbon-device for a moment, then sent a controlled concussive blast at the dangling captive's body, smiling happily at the resulting groan as he rocked in his chains.

"Do not doubt the breadth of Our knowledge, Tau'ri. We know it was this one who journeyed to Abydos and destroyed our beloved on his great ship. This information came to us dearly, but any price would have been paid for the capture of this... assassin." She spat the word and sent a narrow blast of fire scorching along Jack's hip.

Jack twisted in the chains and gave a convincing yelp of

pain. Mat circled him, occasionally zapping his body to punctuate her narrative.

"We were far away, for such a long time. Ah, what wonders We found, riches only dreamed of by Our brethren: raw minerals to sustain our empire for millennia, such jewels, such delights. We returned in triumph, so eager to share Our fortune with Our beloved. But he had vanished. His court had awaited his arrival for months, his ship had not been seen anywhere. We finally traced it to Abydos. The headman of that pitiful mine told us they had delivered their tribute and Our beloved departed. Then they saw a great light in the sky and Our beloved came to them no more." '

Mat widened the focus on the hand-jewel and sent another concussive blast at Jack. The impact must have felt like being slammed into a brick wall. The groan seemed ninety percent genuine this time.

Daniel exchanged a glance with Teal'c. Kasuf had not mentioned a visit from Mat, but then, there had been a few more pressing matters they had been forced to deal with on their trip to Abydos the previous year.

"You would blame an explosion in space upon one man from a planet many light-years away?" Teal'c spoke up, as Jack now hung limply. "That is beyond reason, even for a Goa'uld."

Mat sashayed over to Teal'c, studying him with great interest.

"Teal'c. First prime to the idiot Apophis. How you shamed him by your betrayal. His standing amongst the System Lords was greatly harmed by your actions. We were most amused when his mate came to us, begging Our favor."

Daniel jerked his attention away from Jack and stared at the woman.

"I am pleased my stand for freedom has undone that tyrant's power," Teal'c snarled. "It shall not be long before Jaffa everywhere reject the Goa'uld for the false gods they are and end your reign completely."

Mat merely smiled as her fingers traced the bloody wound on Teal'c's side. She pressed hard, savoring the grunt of pain that escaped him. "Foolish. You may defy the weak-minded Apophis but when you are strung up in the System Lord's summit, suffering eternal torment, you will recant your traitorous words and every Jaffa under Goa'uld rule shall hear you."

"Should such come to pass, at least I shall die free." Teal'c glared down at her.

"Ah, but you will not die — ever." She jabbed her fingers into the wound, not caring that this time he swallowed the pain, and left him, blood running anew down his side.

Mat turned to Daniel and examined him curiously. He did likewise, studying with a sickened feeling in his gut the sheer dress, makeup, hair and crown — all lifted from the Ancient Egypt he adored; a living mockery of his former life.

The Goa'uld ran her hands over his chest, sliding them up under the torn and stained t-shirt, making him flinch back in disgust. "Such beautiful bodies, yet so easily damaged that you must take a healer with you on your little adventures."

So that's where Boch got that from.

Daniel caught Sam's eye and she gave a faint shake of her head. Not really caring what the Goa'uld thought she knew, he focused on what she had said to Teal'c. "So, you had dealings with Amonet. Don't suppose you know where she hides out these days?"

Mat's hands were running up and down his ribs, so lightly it tickled. He gamely resisted reacting and stared at her. "You believe We would tell you — Daniel Jackson — where Amonet resides in the husk that was your mate? Why would you wish to know that?" She looked up at him, batting her eyelashes teasingly. "Do you believe you can rescue her? How charming!"

Mat laughed and leaned against him until he was pushed against the cold stone wall, arms cramping painfully, every inch of the host's voluptuous body pressing into him.

"Do you hold the dream of returning her to your bed, of living your pathetically short lives together?" she murmured in his ear. "I fear, pretty boy, this will never happen, unless We aid you in your romantic quest." She rubbed her face against his, teeth nibbling his ear.

"Yes, this vessel is too beautiful to trade away. We shall keep you, honor you with one of Our children. And perhaps one day, when Amonet comes begging Our favor once more, we may include you as part of the bargain, and you can spend eternity bedding your mate. Is that not so much better than a few short years with your ignorant, un-bonded woman?"

She pulled her head back to gauge his reaction and seemed perplexed by Daniel's failure to appreciate her gift of bonding. He was quivering for certain, but her smile faded as she realized it was not with delight.

He could barely contain his anger. "You corrupt... *snake*." His voice was shaking as much as the rest of him. "A nanosecond of my wife's life could not compare to the whole of your miserable existence. I *will* get her back. I will kill Amonet if I have to cut her out myself, and I *will* kill *you*."

Mat shook her head sadly. "Stupid child, do you not realize there is nothing of your wife to retrieve? She has given all of her mind to her mistress. There is nothing left of her now but her pretty shell."

Daniel closed his eyes, cold denial seeping through him. "No. Lies. Everything you say is a lie. She's alive. I've spoken to her."

"All that the host knew now belongs to Amonet. How else did we gain the knowledge that O'Neill was the one on Abydos with the bomb that murdered Our beloved? Amonet came to us with this information to trade for safe passage after Apophis fell to Sokar. Your—wife—betrayed you and delivered O'Neill, all of you, to Us."

"No...."

"Fret not, sweet one. You shall see your mate again." Mat kissed him gently on the lips, leaving his mouth cold and feeling filled with venom.

Daniel opened his eyes, his stomach churning and stared past the lustrous black hair and shining crown, desperately trying to sort through Mat's taunts. Something was missing. He focused on Jack's hands, bound in their chains. It took a moment to realize that those strong, lethal hands that had been hanging limply were now slowly curling around the chains, preparing....

Daniel looked down into Mat's pampered face, saw the host's features distorted by the evil possessing her. *Sha're has to go through this, day after day....*

"Perhaps you're right. I would do anything to spend eternity with Sha're." A hollow chuckle escaped him. "But never on your terms."

Without warning, he jerked his head forward and butted her right between the eyes.

Stunned, Mat staggered back, within range of Jack's legs as he kicked out and wrapped them around her neck. He hauled up on the chains and with a lightning-quick squeeze and jerk, the woman fell to the floor. Unconscious or dead, it was hard to tell.

Chaos erupted. Jaffa surged forward from all directions, hammering Jack into submission.

In the ensuing melee Teal'c and Sam responded with kicks of their own, until Mat's first prime shouted some order into the room. He stalked up to Jack, now bloody and unmoving, then turned to Daniel.

"You dare strike a goddess?"

"No goddess of mine," Daniel spat.

Two swift steps brought the first prime to striking distance and he let fly a blow with two-hundred pounds of muscle behind it, straight into Daniel's stomach.

The pain was immediate and shockingly intense. Somewhere in his dimming mind, as his knees buckled and his throat was constricted by the metal collar, Daniel felt something deep in his belly shift and tear.

He sank into oblivion, and his one last thought was of his wife.

GATE TWELVE Cont'd

"To Go Forth by Mourning"

Sam sighed for the tenth time, and glared at the dripping rock walls of the small cave into which they had been dropped, literally. In the aftermath of the colonel's attack on the Goa'uld, the first prime, with his mistress' lifeless body in his arms, had ordered them released from their chains, dragged along dark, torch-lit passages and dropped into a black hole gaping in the floor of another chamber.

That terrifying push into nothingness still gave her shudders, the second of freefall still stretched out in her head as a plunge to the center of the world. It couldn't have been more than a three meter drop but it was enough. The brief glimpse she had of the tiny space with its slick walls, before the Jaffa's retreating torches left them in utter darkness, had told her how difficult escape was going to be.

She stilled and listened to the sounds from the others. The colonel breathed harshly, still in pain but coming up out of the sleep he had dropped into thirty minutes ago. Teal'c seemed at ease but the faint, distracted muttering he'd started as they settled in the dark was increasing. That in itself was alarming enough. The master of reticence, Teal'c *didn't* mumble to himself; when he wanted to say something, everyone heard it.

Daniel still lay in the recovery position she had rolled him into after his unconscious body had landed on top of Teal'c. His breathing was changing from slow and deep to shorter, faster gasps as he—hopefully—climbed toward consciousness. Sam ran her right hand through his hair, willing the comforting touch would bring him back to wakefulness. Her left hand was still wrapped around his wrist, not losing contact with that pounding pulse. He was hurt, that much she knew, but how badly was impossible to tell in this darkness.

"Silwanet."

"Teal'c?" she turned her head in his direction, ears straining. "You okay?"

"Major Carter." His voice was soft, distant. "How is Daniel Jackson?"

"I think he's starting to wake up. The colonel, too. What... what's going on with you?"

Teal'c's pause seemed to increase the isolation she was feeling.

"Teal'c!"

"Forgive me, Major Carter. I find myself distracted by the words of the Books of Djehuti. Their sounds and images are most engaging."

"Oh, boy. Can you control it?" A Teal'c without his faculties didn't bear thinking about.

"I can." Teal'c's voice was reasonably convincing.

To Sam's right, the colonel woke with a snort and a groan. "Gah! Son of a *bitch*." He shuffled around, his boots kicking her legs in the cramped space.

"How do you feel, sir?"

"Super, Carter. Fine and dandy. Fit as a fiddle. Oh, damn...."

"Sir?" She didn't let go of Daniel, but strained her eyes in the colonel's direction.

"Nothing major, Major."

She grinned briefly in the dark.

"A few bruises, killer headache. I swear, if that overdressed snake in the grass has burned off my chest hair, I'll kill her."

Sam could hear him shuffling around, searching out the extent of his injuries. "You already did that, Colonel."

"Sweet. What happened then?"

"The Jaffa got a little fractious. There wasn't much we could do, sir. They attacked you and that first prime guy hit Daniel, hard. Daniel passed out. I was afraid he'd choke to death before they unlocked us." She turned her head back in

Daniel's direction, fingers rhythmically stroking his short hair. "They dragged us through three tunnels and dropped us down a hole in the floor. We're in a pretty small cave." It was hard keeping the defeat out of her voice.

"So—Goa'uld dead, no guards about—I'd call that a result."

"Most likely Mat's people have removed her to her Ha'tak vessel where she will be resurrected in a sarcophagus." Teal'c's voice informed from the dark.

"Ha'tak?" Sam was surprised. Daniel had said the camp on the beach was temporary but there had been no time to work out how Mat had come to be here.

"Her presence here is not part of the Trial of Moons." Teal'c sounded distracted still, but certain of what he was saying. "If she is responsible for our being trapped in this situation, then she came to this planet to mete out her final revenge upon O'Neill. The Stargate here would be inoperable to her. Therefore she must have landed in a vessel of some size."

"There'll be a lot of Jaffa between us and the 'gate, if we can get out of here," the colonel remarked gloomily. "Daniel passed out from one hit to the stomach?"

"Well, it was a pretty vicious blow, sir," she replied, defensive for Daniel's sake.

"I'm not doubting that, Carter, but Daniel's a tough man, despite appearances."

"Didn't he fall hard when we were thrown out of the Stargate—way back on the planet with the ordnance? Maybe the Jaffa got the same spot he bruised then. I can feel some swelling on his left side."

"His shoulder was hurting a while back, too," said Jack.

"When? Which shoulder?" Sam straightened up, alarm bells ringing.

"Uh, last planet, I think. I thought it was just a bruise. Why?"

"Left or right shoulder, sir?"

"Left. What is it, Carter?"

"I don't know for certain, sir. The pain in his left shoulder could be a sign of referred pain—he may have internal injuries. I wish I could see him properly." As Sam spoke, Daniel shifted under her hand, waking slowly. "We have got to get out of here—now."

"I hear you, Major," The colonel sighed. "So, one team member with possible internal injuries, one with an open bleeding wound—the cause of which has kyboshed Junior. The way I feel, Ernest Littlefield could down me on the first attempt. At least you're still fighting fit, Carter."

"Daniel's waking up, sir." Sam leaned over Daniel, still monitoring his pulse. "Hey, Daniel. How are you feeling?"

"Umph… what happened?" Daniel rolled over onto his back, hand brushing hers as he reached to knead the pain in his side. "It's dark. It is dark, isn't it? It's not me?"

"It's not you. We're in a cave. They threw us down a hole, basically. Where do you hurt?"

"Oh. Um. Shoulder, stomach, head… what are you doing?"

She felt him twitch as she lifted his t-shirt and ran her fingers over his belly.

"At least your hands are warmer than Mat's. Oh, Sha're, love. What she did…."

Sam's fingers stilled. "Daniel? Are you in pain?"

"No. Well, yes, but that's not it. I've just realized what Sha're did." He subsided into silence. Under her hands his chest rose and fell with deep, controlled breaths.

"What did she do, Daniel?"

There was a shuffle from Teal'c's direction and she found a sopping bandana pushed at her, full of water soaked up from the walls.

"Thanks Teal'c."

She fumbled it at Daniel's face until he caught it and sucked on the moisture.

"Mmh, that's good." He sighed. "Mat said Amonet told her Jack killed Ra. That Sha're 'gave up' the information. But she didn't know about me, about Kasuf or the Abydonians rising up against Ra. It was just Jack. Which means...." Daniel paused for long moments. "Which means, Sha're kept our involvement from Amonet. She protected us. Amonet must have found some memory of the ship exploding in Sha're's mind, but she covered for me, for us. Oh, boy. To Amonet, I was just Sha're's husband, a doctor, harmless. She gave up just as much about Jack as would satisfy Amonet. Sorry, Jack...."

"Hey, she did exactly the right thing. She barely knew me, but she knew enough to pick the guy with the big guns and bad temper. That's a hell of a woman you're married to, Daniel."

Daniel choked out a sad laugh in the concealing darkness. "Yes, yes she is."

"On that note, may I suggest we blow this hole and bug out of here?"

"For all we know we've already missed the lockout on this planet, sir."

"But we don't know for sure, so all the more reason to hurry, Carter."

"Where do you suggest we go, sir?" Sam wiped the cloth over Daniel's face again, her hand squeezing his.

"Well, I may be hallucinating, but I think there's an opening just below roof level on the wall opposite me."

"Really?"

"There's a faint draft coming through and if you look out of the corner of your eye, there's a glow, like phosphorescence."

Sam clambered to her feet, trying not to step on Daniel. Her groping hands found the colonel and he turned her ninety degrees.

"There—twelve o'clock high."

It was faint, so faint it disappeared completely if she looked straight at it, but sidelong there was a definite blue glow, just outlining a hole in the wall, big enough for a person to crawl into.

"The entrance would be out of sight from where we were thrown in," Teal'c said, hands brushing Sam as he fumbled up the rock wall.

"I'm an idiot," Daniel muttered at their feet. He shuffled around; there was a rip of Velcro, a click and suddenly a dull beam of light illuminated their little prison, leaving them all squinting at each other. Daniel had the bandana over the lens but even dimmed, it was enough to see the tunnel entrance directly over Teal'c's head.

"Now he remembers," the colonel smiled down at Daniel. "Bus is leaving, kids."

"Wait, I just need to check Daniel out." Sam knelt by his side and took the little pen light from him.

"Sam, I'm okay. Just a little sore."

"Here?" She pressed gently over his spleen.

"Ow! Oh—feel sick."

"Left shoulder still hurt?"

"Yeah… why?"

"Daniel, I think you've suffered some damage to your spleen. This area seems a bit distended and certainly tender. We're going to have to be very careful to avoid it rupturing."

Daniel blinked up at her. "I keep getting hit in the same spot," he complained.

"I know. We'll have to avoid that in the future. Here." She pulled his glasses out of her pocket and handed them to him, then took his hand and gently pulled him up to sit. "We can't do too much about it but try not to over-exert yourself."

"While we're crawling through tunnels escaping a pack of angry Jaffa?"

Sam grinned at him. "We're SG-1, remember? Piece of cake."

"We ought to make that our motto." Daniel smiled tiredly. He made a flapping motion with his arms and she and Teal'c hauled him carefully to his feet.

"Mmmm, cake," the colonel Homered. He sent an approving nod at her over Daniel's shoulder. "Time to go."

Daniel sighed in relief as the team paused at yet another junction of two tunnels, both bearing near identical glyphs. A short time spent wandering undecided through the tunnels had put them back on the course of the Trial of Moons: a labyrinth of natural passages through the caves, intersections signposted by a choice of two or three glyphs Teal'c identified as being in the language of the Books of Djehuti. This was the fourth such set encountered since crawling from the mercifully short shaft leading out of their prison. Teal'c and Jack had carefully boosted Daniel up to Sam's grasp. Teal'c had declared his own attempt at entering the tunnel to be less than acceptable—hands slipping from a solid grip on the edge in a sudden flash of weakness that nearly dumped him on his backside like an old man.

Teal'c was now artfully ignoring the concerned glances coming his way.

"What do these two mean?" Daniel limped to Teal'c's side, studying the convoluted glyphs in the guarded beam of the pen light.

"This," Teal'c pointed to a crossed circle surrounded by three concentric ripple lines, "means 'To go forth by morning'. This one," he turned to the glyph on the right-hand tunnel, identical but for an added miniscule curlicue, "depicts the phrase 'To go forth by mourning', the definition being grief here rather than the start of day."

"You have *got* to teach me this," Daniel said wistfully. He sighed in frustration. Even fighting off pain, he couldn't switch off the constant nagging puzzlement over this language only Ra seemed to have used. Which, of course, was impossible, one person didn't create and use a language all of their own, not to this degree of complexity. Did they?

"Where to from here, T?" Jack asked.

"This way." Teal'c confidently led them down the left-hand tunnel.

Daniel followed Jack, walking on automatic pilot. The walls seemed to press in on him as he moved. *Always seem to end up in tunnels... catacombs....*

Suddenly and achingly vivid, Sha're's face floated before

him, smiling tentatively in flickering torch-light, sounding out long-unused words, following him half afraid as he gave voice to a story lost for centuries.

"He was the last of his kind."

"What?" Sam staggered off-balance as Daniel stopped mid-stride in front of her.

Daniel looked at her, his gaze sliding on to Jack as an idea began to form.

"Jack, you were there—in the catacombs beneath Nagada. The story on the walls; about Ra, the rebellion on Earth. 'He was the last of his kind'. It said so. I thought later it was an embellishment but now...."

"I remember, Daniel." Jack leaned against the cold rock, clearly glad of a moment's respite.

Daniel surged on, barely keeping ahead of the theories as they formed. "As far as we know, Ra was the first Goa'uld to come to Earth—ten thousand years ago. All that time, on and off Earth, he ruled over the rest of the Goa'uld—his forces were never beaten and yet no-one seems to have known anything about him, we've never even found a reference to his home planet. And he has a fully developed written and spoken language that has no resemblance to the Goa'uld language." He stopped for breath as his words began to run together.

"What if Ra wasn't a Goa'uld?"

Three astonished faces blinked back at him.

"Wait a minute, we saw a human body with glowy eyes," Jack finally managed. "That says Goa'uld to me."

"We know one parasitic race can inhabit humans, what's to disprove there wasn't another that could do the same thing?"

"Daniel...."

"What if the story on the wall was true—"

"No," Jack butted in again. "Just, no. Alright? I have a hard enough time with the fact that Junior's evil, upstart, cross-dressing cousins are running around wearing humans like a cheap suit. There are *no* others."

"But, the language—"

"Could have been devised as a means to communicate sensitive information that other Goa'uld were unable to interpret," Teal'c offered softly.

"Yes, but...." The look on Jack's face evaporated the rest of the sentence and Daniel found the spurt of energy his conjecture had produced was fading right along with it.

"Besides," Jack nodded to Teal'c to head off again. "Ra's parasitic ass is floating in a cloud of atoms in space and that's the end of it."

Sam darted a skeptical look at Daniel and followed Teal'c. Jack narrowed his eyes at her retreating back.

"What? I know what atoms are."

"Never said a word, sir."

Jack glowered exaggeratedly at her and ushered Daniel on. He shook his head and trudged after Sam, not quite sure if the muttering coming from Jack actually contained the word, *"magnets"*.

They had been on the move for twenty-five minutes, so far without sounds of pursuit, a situation that was not going to hold for much longer. They pushed on. Teal'c chose a tunnel that led them into a small cave, their single tiny light throwing eerie shadows from the rock formations hanging from the roof. There was more water here, running down calcified walls and dripping steadily off stalactites to join a little stream that trickled erratically across the cave floor. An earth-deep chill seeped through the air around them, sapping precious body heat and energy.

With their canteens confiscated along with the rest of their gear, they made do with sopping water up in a couple of bandanas and dribbling it into parched mouths. Thirst somewhat assuaged, they moved on silently. A bend and a careful crawl over slick boulders later, the rock around them opened up into an enormous cavern.

"Wow." Major Carter's voice echoed off a forest of stalactites and stalagmites, many of which shone a lustrous pearly color in the beam of the flashlight. "You could get a B-52 in here."

Small streams wandered out from other, unseen tunnels and joined into a decent-sized creek in the center. Their meager light was lost in the vastness but proved unnecessary as the blue phosphorescence found in earlier caves was here, spread thickly over the entire roof.

"Is it me, or is the roof moving?" O'Neill asked suspiciously.

"It is moving." Teal'c gazed at the glowing mass that shifted and shimmied over the roof. He walked after Major Carter as she moved out into the cave, peering intently upward.

"They're bats, or something like them. There must be thousands of them." O'Neill shuddered and turned his attention to the trickling water. "Let's take a minute and drink as much as we can."

They splashed into the central creek, each selecting an area that was flowing and deep enough to scoop water out with cupped hands. The water was sweet, numbingly cold, but tasting of earth and minerals and quite the most delicious Teal'c had tasted in a long time. He drank steadily while keeping watch for any sign of pursuit. Thirst slaked, he turned to look at Daniel Jackson, silently slumped on the rocks. He cast the pen light over his friend's pale, sweating face. "I believe we should go in this direction." He led off at a steady, but easy pace.

It took them nearly ten minutes to traverse the uneven floor of the cavern, O'Neill assisting Daniel Jackson, Major Carter guarding their rear. Un-erringly, Teal'c took the direction of the stream into another tunnel and there—finally—daylight beckoned. Quiet exclamations of relief followed him as the team splashed through the water.

Fresh sea air filled their lungs when they neared the opening. Satisfaction surged through Teal'c, almost immediately replaced by concern as he emerged onto a narrow shelf. He stopped. The stream flowed around his feet and plunged into a cascade that dropped down sheer cliffs to the beach below.

He flung out an arm to stop the others.

"Oh, for crying out loud." O'Neill peered over Teal'c's arm.

"I regret I have made an error, O'Neill."

"Swell. Can't be helped, Teal'c." O'Neill kept a steadying hand on the tunnel wall. "Let's see if we can get our bearings."

They leaned out as far as they dared. Below, the shale beach was empty. It curved away to their right and with a stretch they could just see the crown of the Stargate above a clump of trees. In front and to one side of the ring stood a sun temple, where a familiar-looking obelisk glinted in the late afternoon light. They both searched the blue sky but no moon was yet visible.

"I'm thinking the only way to head is for the 'gate," O'Neill said, "and hope we come across the address we need on the way." When Teal'c did not answer, he pulled back and clapped his friend on the arm. "You can do this, Teal'c."

"I believe I made an error in preventing Daniel Jackson from accepting the Books of Djehuti, O'Neill. I do not believe I am the best person to interpret the writing of Ra." Teal'c glanced past him to Daniel—resting against the rock wall with eyes closed, one hand pressed against his stomach—then turned away to stare bleakly out at the sea, unwilling to meet O'Neill's eyes.

"No, Teal'c, you did exactly the right thing. I think he's been carrying this injury for a while now, without realizing it. If he had to deal with this Book thing as well, we could have lost him already. Now, I know this isn't your field of expertise, but we're all here and we're gonna work through this, as a team. Okay?"

Teal'c finally looked at O'Neill, and saw the wisdom in him despite his fewer years. "You are a good leader, my friend."

"A leader's only as good as his troops," the colonel smiled tiredly. "And I have *the* best troops."

They gathered up Daniel Jackson and Major Carter and

retraced their path. Halfway across the cavern, sounds of voices and metallic boots echoed back to them.

"Sounds like we've missed the party. Let's pick up the pace." O'Neill urged them into a stumbling trot until they were back at the last junction and much closer to the searching Jaffa. "Run."

They dodged into the other passage, heading ever deeper into the cold, dim warren of tunnels and caves. The choice of directions came more and more frequently, a good sign surely that they were on the right course; but each time was a delay that brought their pursuers closer and did little to bolster Teal'c's confidence in his new-found abilities.

For all Teal'c's doubts, only twice did they end up in a dead-ended tunnel and were forced to retreat. Sounds of pursuit at times seemed only meters away, other times it was an indistinct mutter or gleam of light in the far distance.

SG-1 plunged on into the darkness, determination fighting bitterly against exhaustion and the steady count of time.

Sound echoed on all sides, bouncing off jagged stone walls and low hanging ceiling: ragged, gasping snatches of breath, water dripping endlessly onto the ancient rock floor, the far away ring of metal-clad boots.

Jack looked around, through the little clouds of his breath condensing in the still, frigid air. Maybe this niche in the tunnel walls would offer a few moments' respite. No movement showed in the passage they had just raced through. Ahead, another tunnel angled away into the darkness, offering at least somewhere else to run.

His team gathered near him, faces turned toward the tunnels and watchful for any trace of pursuit. Carter balanced on her left leg as she scanned the darkness, denying the ache in her right ankle, twisted on the treacherously slick rock. Teal'c faced the opposite direction, alert as ever, yet his utter weariness could be seen in his slumped shoulders and slowing movements, his skin an unhealthy grayish hue.

Daniel was leaning against the dank wall, the façade of stubbornness on his face slipping as surely as his body was sliding down the uneven rocks, his lungs now emitting what was little more than a distressed wheeze. His left fist was still firmly planted on the pain below his ribs.

Jack shifted slightly, vainly trying to ease the muscles knotted along his spine and the stabbing pain that had been his constant companion for what seemed like his entire life.

How the hell did we end up like this?

Movement flickered in the corner of his eye — Carter's hand coming up and signaling they were about to be discovered.

He sucked in a gasp of cold air, reached over and grabbed a fistful of Daniel's shirt, helping his teammate as they staggered off in Teal'c's wake — plunging on into the unknown.

Within seconds SG-1 had vanished into the darkness, the eternal rock showing no trace of their passing.

Huddled against the dripping walls in a space barely big enough for two, let alone four, heaving bodies, Jack placed a hand on Daniel's head and pulled him to his chest, muffling the pain-filled wheezes the cramped position was causing. Behind him, Carter and Teal'c pressed a little closer, then froze as footsteps clanged past them.

A ten-count after the steps had faded away, everyone relaxed. Teal'c and Carter stood up and cautiously checked the Jaffa really had gone. Jack let Daniel go and grimaced when he sank against the wall. "Gotta go, Danny."

"Wait…," Daniel panted. He fumbled in the thigh pocket of his BDUs and pulled out his roll of fine tools, forgotten since the last planet.

Jack opened his mouth for a ready-made smart remark but Daniel silenced him with an upraised finger. He pulled the roll open and pulled out two scalpels and a dental pick.

"They're not much as weapons go, but better than nothing?"

Jack took the slim tools. The blades and pick end were razor sharp. Keeping one himself, he handed the others to Carter and Teal'c.

"What else have you got in those pockets?"

"A rope ladder, my lunch box and of course, my invisibility cloak."

Jack smothered a snort and gently pulled Daniel to his feet.

"O'Neill." Teal'c loomed up beside him. "I have found another glyph."

"Only one?"

"Yes. There appears to be no choice this time."

"What does it translate as?" Daniel wobbled into Jack as he tried to see the glyph.

"It merely represents the words 'to ascend'."

"Ascend?" Jack echoed.

"Maybe there are stairs nearby," Carter panted.

"No… I think it means," Daniel caught Jack's eye, mutual understanding flashing between them. "Rings," they said together.

In moments, Carter and Teal'c were crawling over the ground, hands brushing away dirt and rocks. Jack held the light above them. He was the first to catch the dull metallic gleam of a ring transporter track.

"There—Carter, under your knee."

She scuttled backwards and swiftly they uncovered a small ring transporter circling the alcove they had sheltered in.

"Looks like the mini version."

Jack and Daniel were already standing inside the circle. It would be a tight fit for four. He flicked the light over the walls and found a ruby crystal activator.

"All aboard the elevator. Next stop, sporting goods."

"Perhaps we should go separately, O'Neill." Teal'c eyed the cramped space doubtfully.

"No, no splitting up. For all we know it's one ride per… whatever. Budge up, Daniel."

Jack looped an arm around Daniel's shoulders and pulled

him close. Carter stepped in and plastered herself against Daniel's back. Teal'c joined them, wrapping his arms around all three.

"And with one click of the ruby slippers...."

Jack pressed the crystal and yanked his hand back as the rings shot up around them. A beam of light from above blinded everyone and swept them up.

They emerged into warmth and light. Sam and Teal'c stepped back, wearily alert for guards or pursuit, but they were alone inside a bright, limestone-walled compound. Behind the transporter ring, fronted by an alabaster altar, the squat obelisk they had sighted from the cliffs rose up into a sky turning indigo with evening. The setting sun poured amber light through the archway entrance.

"Sir, we've got a moon," Sam announced quietly, pointing out a small, beautifully blue full-moon sixty degrees above the compound. Teal'c moved quietly to the opening in the wall.

The colonel grimaced as Daniel sagged against his shoulder, one hand clutching his t-shirt as a pained grunt escaped his lips.

"Daniel?"

"Okay...," Daniel panted, his whole body tensing. "Just give me a minute."

"All clear, Colonel," Sam whispered as Teal'c signaled from the archway.

Several controlled puffs for air brought Daniel's head up. He pulled back from the colonel and shakily looked around at their new surroundings. Sam noted, with a sinking heart, the pallor of his face and the smudges of exhaustion and pain under his eyes. Colonel O'Neill beckoned her with a jerk of his head and lowered Daniel to sit on the edge of the altar.

"Daniel, let me take a proper look at you. How do you feel?" She evaded his protesting gestures and lifted the hem of his tattered t-shirt. Under his ribs, his belly was badly bruised and distended. He hissed and pulled away.

"It's bearable, Sam." An unconvincing smile flickered over his face. "There's nothing we can do about it anyway, so...." He shrugged.

Sam sat down next to him on the altar, the brush of their arms all the comfort she could offer. She looked up at the colonel, his bruises and the burns on his torso plain to see now through his ripped t-shirt.

"You don't look too well either, sir."

"I'm fine, Carter." He evaded further questions and moved to mirror Teal'c's position at the entrance.

Sam sighed and relaxed a little beside Daniel, who was three-quarters asleep. Her ankle throbbed annoyingly; the rocks in the tunnels below had been a nightmare to walk on. She glanced up at the sky which was rapidly turning to a velvet black and dotted with a brilliant array of stars. She got a fix on the moon and in the silence of the twilight, tracked it until she was certain it was moving downward. Judging by its quick rate of descent, they had one hour at most before it would set.

After a short conversation with Teal'c, the colonel limped back to the altar.

"T thinks he has a handle on the glyph thing. There's another by the entrance. He thinks it points the way to the 'gate address, something to do with a mathematical code."

"I'll go help him, sir. Why don't you sit down for a while?" Sam was up and hobbling off before he could object.

Teal'c pointed out to her the complex strings of numbers—all in Goa'uld script—that made up the code he had found. It needed to be translated, decoded and then reassembled in correct order.

"This could take some time."

"Time we may not have to spare, Major Carter."

Sam took a deep breath, but before either of them could begin, there was a flash of light and suddenly the little being, Bes, was standing on top of the wall looking down at them. Sam swallowed a yelp of surprise and backed into Teal'c.

"The rules of the Trial of Moons have been broken," he said

solemnly. "You have been unfairly disadvantaged. I wish to assist you." He blinked at them and held out one hand, bearing a large plant leaf with markings scrawled over it.

Teal'c cautiously stretched out a hand and as his fingers brushed the leaf, Bes vanished with a loud popping sound, like air released into a vacuum. Sam and Teal'c both grabbed for the leaf as it fluttered to the ground. On it, written in what looked and smelt like thick treacle, were a Stargate address and what had to be the password they needed. They stared at each other, then turned and sprinted back to the altar.

"Oh for…. Now what?" The colonel creaked to his feet. "Will you keep it down?"

"O'Neill, we have the address and password to leave this planet."

"What? How?"

Sam opened her mouth, wondering exactly how to explain what had just happened.

"Never mind. Put it in the report. We're *so* out of here. Teal'c, take the rear." Colonel O'Neill indicated Daniel to Sam with a shift of his eyes, and headed to the archway.

Without making undue fuss, she shadowed Daniel's haltering, silent progress.

They sidled out into the open and turned left. Fortune was co-operating once more as their tattered BDUs camouflaged them against the sand-colored walls surrounding the sun temple. Jack led them around to the rear of the complex, where, through spiny coastal bushes, the arc of the Stargate could be seen silhouetted, less than a kilometer away.

He kept up a steady, smooth pace, every sense attentive for signs of pursuit. In the distance, shouts of the searching Jaffa reached them intermittently. Hopefully they would still be concentrating on the caves and leave him a clear run to get his team out of here. Mat's nasty little promises were floating through his mind. No way was he going to let her get her fangs into his people again. God knew what Cronus wanted with Carter, but it wouldn't be nice and Teal'c being kept in an unending cycle of torture and death was just beyond comprehension.

Not a chance in hell, snaky.

As for what Mat had threatened Daniel with…. Jack grimaced and made particular effort to be quiet. He'd put a bullet between Daniel's blue eyes before he'd see that particular threat come to pass.

The journey back to the Stargate was torturous. Sudden, indeterminate sounds forced them to freeze or scuttle into cover time and time again. Twice, patrols of Jaffa crashed through the brush nearby, headed in different directions. Neither discovered the fugitives. Each time the four resumed the slog to the Stargate their pace dropped off a little more.

Jack could feel the burn in his legs and back, a lingering memory of energy long since used.

Just a little further.

Carter was sticking close to Daniel, a steadying hand or touch on the back enough to keep him going.

When they did reach the Stargate, sliding down an embankment of sandy soil to the concealing shadows of the last of the scrub, they could only stare with suspicion at the empty platform. No guards awaited them, no figures lurked in the starlit night. It was too quiet: an obvious trap.

Jack peered out from the bush he was sprawled under and stared hard at the moon, now barely above the calm sea. He slid back a couple of feet and turned to his team.

"I think we can expect someone to show up here, but we've got no choice," he whispered. "Stick together—no heroics. Teal'c, get to the DHD and dial. Carter, Daniel, we'll take cover behind the DHD. As soon as the 'gate opens, we're through it. Got it?"

Carter and Teal'c nodded. Daniel squinted at Jack and said, "It sounds good in theory."

Jack nodded curtly. "Go."

Bent low, Teal'c launched out of cover like a jackrabbit and charged to the DHD. The other three had taken only two steps forward when a chillingly familiar chime filled the air and transport rings descended on a beam of light.

"Dammit, run!"

Six paces on and the rings shot up, revealing Mat and four burly Jaffa. Jack and Teal'c, in perfect tandem, launched themselves at the Jaffa who stepped in front of their goddess. Teal'c cold-cocked one with a mighty fist and grappled with another as Jack slammed into a third.

Carter and Daniel dodged a staff blast from the fourth guard. The major pushed Daniel toward the Stargate and, spinning around, lunged for the guard's staff weapon. She yanked the staff toward her, pulling the man off balance. As he staggered forward, her fist flashed out and met his throat. Blood spurted and he fell, one of Daniel's scalpels poking obscenely from his neck.

Jack was trading thumping blows with a man twice his mass. He managed to hook a leg around what felt like a metal-clad tree trunk and toppled the Jaffa to the ground. Huge fingers closed around his throat and he retaliated with a thumb in the eye. The man gargled in pain and he heard Carter yelling above him.

"Colonel, break off. Go right, go right!"

The grip loosened around his throat and he reeled away, catching a freeze-frame sequence of Carter as she leaped feet first onto the Jaffa, landing with a pained cry. One boot impacted the man's groin, the other the symbiote pouch and he was down for the count.

Jack rolled right over and surged to his feet. Nearby, Teal'c was having a knock-down smack fest with his opponent, driving the man back with every blow. Jack spun around further, tracking the Goa'uld — and found her stalking Daniel.

As Teal'c dispatched the last Jaffa, Carter and Jack moved in on the Goa'uld. The sudden cessation of fighting let Daniel's voice carry over to them.

"...so superior, so smug. You're nothing but a parasite, a

helpless leech."

Mat prowled toward him, hands clenching in rage. "Silence, slave. You know nothing of Us. We have ruled the stars since before your pitiful species could make fire. We shall continue on long after your miserable planet is dust."

"No, I don't think so. You're about to die, just like Ra. No-one is going to mourn you. But before you go, I'd like to set you straight on a couple of things. *I* helped kill Ra. You see, I was there with Jack in the pyramid and we both sent that bomb into Ra's ship while my wife and the Abydonians rose up and killed Ra's soldiers."

"Fabrications," Mat hissed. "We know the truth—ripped from your mate's empty shell by Amonet." Mat's hand ribbon began to glow as she raised her arm.

"Sha're lied to Amonet. She protected me and her people. Your—*mate*—died alone, deserted by even his child-slaves."

Mat howled a furious scream, flung out her arm and loosed a blast that Daniel barely ducked. In the same moment as Jack and Carter closed on her, Daniel pulled back his right arm, opened his clenched fist and let fly the object he held concealed. It hit her square between the eyes, with force enough to stagger her. Jack tackled her and with Carter's added weight, brought her down. A half-pace behind them, Teal'c reached down and snapped her neck.

Chest heaving for oxygen, Jack staggered to his feet. One foot rolled off the bright object Daniel had thrown. Carter picked it up.

"What on earth is that?" Jack asked.

Daniel straightened up gingerly. "A plumb-bob."

"A plumb-bob?"

"The archaeologist's friend." Daniel managed a grin which soon faded. "Jack, she has to die."

"Ding, dong. She is dead, Daniel. Again."

"Exactly. You know they'll revive her. She's a danger to Abydos. To Earth now, too."

"He has a point, sir." Carter turned toward the sound of Jaffa, rapidly approaching.

"Yeah. Teal'c, dial us up. Carter, give me a hand here."

Together they dragged Mat's body to lie face down, draped through the Stargate. Stepping back, they pulled Daniel out of range. Teal'c punched in the address, smacked the activation crystal and uttered the password in a hoarse shout.

"An hra!"

The Stargate churned to life, its brilliant watery glow suddenly lighting up the area as the body of their enemy disintegrated. Tensely they waited for it to settle. The backwash spiraled out then in, revealing nothing but sand and bushes around them.

The event horizon sloshed to stability. Teal'c joined his teammates and the four of them, drained beyond thought, lunged into the Stargate and were gone.

GATE THIRTEEN

Sharpener of Souls

They stumbled out of the Stargate and turned, expecting more of Mat's Jaffa to appear, until finally the wormhole disengaged and they were safe. A cold wind whipped around their bodies as they stood on yet another stone platform. It was night here, a dark unfriendly place of stony ground between two desolate mountain peaks, their tops lost in cloud far above.

Daniel staggered as the adrenalin from their long flight through the tunnels and the fight with Mat drained away. He had little left now; his legs shook and his head roared as blood pounded through his veins. He reached out, caught Jack's arm and barely managed to control his collapse to the ground.

"Daniel?" Jack grabbed at him. He knelt awkwardly, wincing with his own aches.

Daniel could manage barely more than a breathy groan. "Rest... need rest." He slumped on the cold stone, Jack hovering over him. Close by, Sam wavered on her feet, weight mostly on one leg, gamely attempting to stay vigilant and survey their new surroundings. Teal'c moved slowly to the rear of the Stargate and leant heavily against the ring to inspect the moon-clock.

"Here, lie down for a while. We're safe now." Jack eased Daniel down onto his right side. "At least Mat's goons aren't still on our tails. We should have time to rest here."

"We do not." Teal'c pushed away from the Stargate and sat with a thump on the stone steps. "The clock indicates the moon will set in two hours, thirty-seven minutes."

Daniel shivered and pushed himself upright. He looked at Jack's tired face, appearing even more drained in the uncertain light as clouds shrouded the bluish moon. They had no gear left, bar their boots, pants and ragged t-shirts. Everything else was lying in a cave on some distant planet they could never return to—not that they wanted to.

"What number planet are we up to?" he asked suddenly. "This is thirteen, isn't it?"

"Yes, this is the last one," Sam replied tiredly. "And I think that's where we have to go." She pointed down to the far end of the canyon where shadows rippled as the clouds raced across the moon, releasing flashes of brilliance to shine out like a celestial disco. One bright burst illuminated a forbidding structure; its black stone seemed to swallow the light wherever it touched.

"Nice," Jack muttered. "Well, at least we don't have to go looking for it. C'mon, let's get this over with."

Daniel gathered himself and wondered bleakly how he was going to get to his feet, let alone all the way down to the edifice. Every breath was cut short with a jolt of pain under his rib cage and a corresponding stab through his shoulder. The pounding headache and every other aching muscle added a synchronized background hum of misery. He closed his eyes for a moment, then looked up at his teammates—saw his weariness reflected in their faces.

"Guess misery really does love company," he muttered.

"Daniel?"

"Help me up, Jack."

Jack staggered with his weight and Teal'c lent a hand to get him wobbling on his feet, blood draining from his head in a dizzying flood. The canyon stretched away before them, cold and sinister, prickling his senses with a foreboding that set his nerves on edge. There was something bad here....

"Oh!" Sam's head jerked up and she peered intently out into the shadows.

"What?" Jack and Teal'c both tensed, hands twitching for long gone weapons.

"I've just remembered something. Actually, it's not my memory... it must be Jolinar's." She turned to stare at Daniel, her eyes huge in the moonlight. "I know why Mat seemed so familiar. I—Jolinar—saw her. It must have been over a year ago. Jolinar was working undercover in Cronus's court. He went to Mat's homeworld to do a deal, and... Amonet was there." She broke off as Daniel felt his gaze harden. She gulped and forced herself to continue.

"Amonet had traded information to Mat for a refuge. Oh, Daniel. I'm sorry. I did know where she was."

Distressed, she glanced away. Daniel sighed, and forced himself to stand straighter despite visions crowding his mind of Sha're surrounded by Goa'uld. And if he had known earlier where she was, what then? His tired brain couldn't settle on any kind of logic.

"It's okay, Sam." His soft voice brought her turning toward him. "We'll work it out."

"Okay, let's shelve this for the moment, shall we?" Jack nudged him gently and Daniel got one foot moving, then the next. As he came up to Sam, she reached out and clutched his arm. He caught her hand and squeezed back.

A hesitant smile flickered over her face and she pressed something cold into his palm.

"Don't want you to go unarmed."

He looked down at his plumb-bob, shining dully in the moonlight. Daniel nodded and they slowly trailed Jack and Teal'c away from the Stargate.

Sam fell in behind Daniel, but paused at the edge of the stone steps as a shimmer of white caught her eye and a chill of dread swept over her. She whipped her head around, but could see nothing amiss. She became aware of Daniel halting and turning to stare past her toward the Stargate.

"Do you feel that?" he whispered.

"Yes." Slowly she turned, peering through the shadows.

"I've felt it before—on the foggy planet."

Sam looked at him in surprise. "So did I, on planet eight, in the trees... and, oh, wow, way back on the water planet. It was the same feeling." Momentary relief that she was not imagining things gave way to a full case of the creeps at the thought of what *could* generate such feelings.

The shimmer caught her eye again. There, by the Stargate, it wavered, then resolved... into....

"Oh, boy," Sam uttered the words in the same instant as Daniel.

A ghostly skeletal figure emerged from the shadows. Thin and lithe, its enormous eye sockets seemed too dark, even hollow. It stood no taller than her and seemed to be solid one moment and as insubstantial as mist the next, as if it hovered between the worlds of the living and dead.

"*Go,*" she hissed at Daniel, unable to tear her gaze from the apparition. Whatever this—creature—spirit—was she knew instinctively there could be nothing good coming from it. She shivered.

Daniel needed no urging to get as far as possible from it. He certainly seemed to have no desire to talk to it. She took his right arm and hauled him along. Carefully, they backed away, off the stone and onto the rocky earth.

The creature flitted after them, but went no further than the stone paving around the Stargate. When they had retreated a short distance, Sam turned her head and hissed, "*Colonel, Teal'c.*"

Teal'c got to them first, looking beyond them for a new threat.

"There's a—um—something, actually, I'm not even sure, but it...." She trailed off, feeling foolish now that she'd been scared by that—thing.

The colonel stopped next to her and gave her a baffled look.

"It's evil," Daniel filled in firmly. "Evil, angry, and we need to get anywhere that's not near it."

"And we're sure our imaginations aren't playing with us, are we?"

"Yes, we are. I felt the same thing on the seventh planet and

Sam felt it too, a couple of times. Whatever it is, it's following us."

"A cold impression of ill-intent and dread; is this what you felt?" Teal'c asked.

"That's it exactly, Teal'c." Sam shuddered and looked over her shoulder again.

"I, too, experienced a similar feeling on the seventh planet, when we were isolated by the fog."

"What? Why didn't you say anything?" The colonel glared at him. "Why didn't anyone say anything?"

"Because whining about creepy feelings in the dark is just too much of a cliché, and we know how you feel about those. Can we go now?" Daniel tried not to lean too heavily on Sam and made little shooing motions at their leader, heroically resisting a glance back.

"Are you going to make it?" asked the colonel, eyeing him critically.

"I'm feeling much better now, thank you," Daniel lied through his teeth.

"Teal'c, you holding up okay?"

"I am fine." Teal'c's voice didn't waver but its threadiness had Sam shooting a covert look of concern at him.

Colonel O'Neill frowned and shrugged. "Carter?"

"Raring to go, sir."

The colonel didn't buy it for a second. He shook his head, turned and stalked off, muttering about trading his team in for bone-head Marines after all.

Teal'c overtook him with huge strides and led the way into the narrowing canyon. The colonel slowed to let Sam and Daniel hobble past, and then trudged along in the rear. Frequent glances over their shoulders revealed no pursuer.

The wind picked up as they walked. Steep, bare rock rose up on both sides, limiting their view of the clouds scudding over the moon. The chill in the wind cut through their ragged clothing and sent gooseflesh shivering over all of them.

Several feet ahead of Daniel and Sam, Teal'c let out a cry of pain and stumbled to one side. Crying out once more, he teetered off-balance and ended up with one hand on the ground, bracing his widely-spaced legs.

"Teal'c? What is it?" Colonel O'Neill jogged past them and headed for Teal'c.

"Come no further." Teal'c's voice was harsh and pained.

The colonel skidded to a halt and peered in the uncertain light. A meter in front of him the ground seemed to be littered with gleaming stones; from one canyon wall to the other, they stretched on toward the black temple. Two meters in, Teal'c was frozen in his awkward position, making no move to straighten up.

"Talk to me." Colonel O'Neill put out a hand to halt Sam and Daniel as they came abreast of him.

"These stones—they are as sharp as knives." Teal'c grunted in pain and shifted his hand so that only his fingertips were braced on the ground. There was a sheen of wetness on his palm. "They have cut through the soles of my boots with great ease."

"For crying out loud." The colonel tentatively touched his boot to the closest and they watched in horror as it sliced into the rigid sole as if it were made of cream-cheese. "Oh, swell. How the hell do we cross this?" He paced along the perimeter of the stone field to the rock wall, then turned and crossed to the opposite rock wall, twenty meters away. The glinting stones lay thick and unbroken by a path or any other means they could use to pass through them.

Sam edged out from under Daniel's arm and joined the colonel. She carefully picked a stone up and grimaced at the wickedly sharp edges.

"There has to be a way across. Teal'c, can you see any deviation in the stones? Any different shape or texture?"

"I cannot," Teal'c ground out, his voice filled with pain.

The colonel stalked back to them, unable to pick out anything clearly in the dim light. Sam looked at Daniel who was standing, left arm pressed tightly to his side, looking not at the ground, but at the temple, then back to the Stargate.

"The temple and the Stargate are in exact alignment. This might be significant...." He trailed a few steps to one side, lining up between the two structures. She followed his line of sight. The clouds obligingly parted company with the moon, allowing a shaft of bluish light to shine down on them.

"There! Do you see it?" she yelped, aborting the instinct to lunge forward. "A wide, flattish stone—Teal'c, it's just to your right."

"*Stepping-stones.* Miserable son of a fake god," the colonel cursed as Sam leaned as far as she could, just making out a path of stepping stones, set about a meter apart, winding erratically into the field of deadly flint.

Teal'c gingerly pulled himself upright and focused on the nearest step. He gathered himself, his usual steadiness notably lost. He tensed, then launched through the air. His left foot landed square on the step and he flailed wildly for balance as his momentum threatened to carry him over. Finally he put his right foot down safely.

"Thank you, Major Carter."

Daniel winced and sighed. "How do we get over this without falling and getting cut to ribbons?"

They watched Teal'c rip a strip off his t-shirt and bind his bleeding hand.

"What do we have we can use?" Sam asked.

The colonel shook his head and made a show of covering the exhaustion lining his face. "Precious little."

She pulled a face and pushed on with the obligatory follow-up. "What do we need?"

"A rope, a plank... beer would be nice." He scrubbed his face with his hands and then lowered them, staring at Daniel. "Give me your belt."

"What? Why?" Daniel frowned at him, hands going protectively to his waist.

"We need some way to steady each other. We tie our belts around our wrists and take each stone one at a time."

"Well, it won't help much if my pants fall down."

A snort of laughter escaped Sam before she could stop it.

"Carter. Belt. Now."

"Sir! Yes sir!" She pulled her belt off and handed it to the colonel, patting Daniel's rump as she passed. "That's the advantage of having hips."

"I have hips," protested Daniel as the colonel tied one end of the belt in a thick knot around his wrist, and the other around Sam's.

"Yeah, but you don't have any meat on them." He tied his belt to Daniel's left wrist and secured the other end to his own.

"Teal'c, we're coming out to you. We'll tie off, then get this show on the road, okay?"

"Understood."

Colonel O'Neill lined up closest to the first stepping stone. "By the right, and...."

He made the leap easily, turned and beckoned to Daniel. The stepping-stone wasn't large, but it would fit two people in a pinch. Sam held her breath as he leapt onto the stone. He teetered alarmingly for a moment until the colonel could steady him.

"Okay?"

"No, but keep going."

The colonel nodded and turned to Teal'c. "Here I come, big guy."

Teal'c opened his mouth to reply but ended up with an armful of the colonel instead. They balanced quickly, aided by the belt stretching back to Daniel. Teal'c tied his belt between the two of them and they watched anxiously as Sam sprang to join Daniel on his stepping-stone.

Teal'c jumped neatly to the next step. Daniel jumped to Colonel O'Neill, where they shuffled about until the colonel joined Teal'c once again and Sam was with Daniel. Then the process began all over again.

"Oof."

"Ow."

"Son of a…"

"Ow, Sam!"

"Sorry, Daniel."

"Please do not place your hand there, O'Neill."

"Carter, wipe the smirk off. There's nothing funny about sticking your hand in a Jaffa's…."

"Yes, sir. Whateveryousaysir."

Sam felt a exhaustion-fuelled sense of unreality threaten to swamp her as she poised on her stepping-stone and lined up the next jump. All around, the flint gleamed in the moonlight, looking deceptively benign. But, one false step and—she didn't want to think what the result would be. She tensed, and once again sprang into Daniel's embrace, trying to cushion the impact against him.

"Hi there. Come here often?" she breathed into his ear.

Daniel smiled faintly. His body felt too warm against hers and he was breathing heavily. The burst of adrenaline that had got him off the Stargate platform and moving was clearly exhausted.

"Oh, yeah. I hear the band is really good."

She chuckled and they clung together for a moment until their focus returned. They turned to face the next leap and found the colonel and Teal'c standing on bare earth, impatiently waiting for them.

"Oh, thank heavens." Sam urged Daniel on. Her heart seized as he stumbled on landing and would have been sliced to pieces if Teal'c and the colonel hadn't lunged and pulled him to safety.

She threw herself across the last obstacle and landed on shaking legs. "We did it," she gasped.

"*That's* my team!" Colonel O'Neill beamed proudly at them. He turned toward the temple.

"Aw, crap."

The temple stood, dark and sinister, not two hundred meters away, and in front of it lay a five meter wide trench, filled with oily-looking water. Like the flint, it stretched from one side of the rocky walls to the other.

The four stood for a moment, breathing hard. Mechanically, they undid the belts, reattached them and walked toward their next hurdle. A few feet from the moat they stopped, daunted by what should have been an easy task.

Jack straightened up, objective fixed in his mind. "Just do it. No thinking, no talking. Get in, swim, get out."

He turned to Daniel and pulled the glasses off his friend's pale face. He secured them in a pocket and steered him to the water's edge while Daniel was still mustering an objection.

"I'll go first, sir."

Carter sat on the edge of the trench and dipped her legs in the water. She gasped at the chill of it. It looked thick and sludgy and stank ferociously. Taking a deep breath, she slid in and pushed off, her face screwed up and held high to avoid contact with the muck. It wasn't far but getting out was more difficult than expected. She rolled onto the ground like a landed trout and turned to help the men.

Jack and Teal'c eased into the water with Daniel between them and slowly but surely towed him to the other side. They boosted him up and Carter caught him under the arms, helping him roll onto dry land, where he lay, breath catching in pain-filled gasps. As Teal'c and Jack slithered out and clambered to their feet, water sluicing off their bodies, Carter stiffened and pointed to the Stargate side of the moat.

"Sir, look. That's the thing we saw."

Jack's eyebrows rose at the ghostly figure staring back at them. A chill of deep, instinctive fear crawled over him and suddenly he felt as vulnerable as those first primitive humans must have felt, sheltering from the dark in a cave, hoping for the dawn's return.

"We're out of here."

He bent carefully to help Teal'c get Daniel up. Fear, controlled but insistent, chewed through his gut. They had taken an hour and twenty minutes to get this far, more than half their allotment. How were they going to complete the final task and get back to the Stargate before it locked them out? Daniel was in no condition to move quickly, the rest of them weren't much better off.

And even if—when—they did make it, Ra's Barque of Heaven would no doubt present some new hell for them to face.

Teal'c took most of Daniel's weight and they staggered after Carter as she limped to the temple entrance.

As they neared the building, the wind finally chased the clouds away and the moonlight gave them their first clear view. What had previously seemed to be black stone was now revealed to be a beautiful deep blue with flecks of gold and silver flashing in the moonlight. A central doorway of enormous proportions was flanked by two equally massive statues of Ra, each standing proudly, arms outstretched to welcome their visitors. The statues' faces seemed monstrous in the uncertain light, despite the copious gold decorations surrounding them.

"Still looks sheepish to me," Jack muttered as they passed through the open doorway.

Daniel pulled Teal'c off-course by leaning to run his hand over the sparkling blue stone. "Lapis! The whole thing is covered in lapis lazuli." He craned his head up, mouth falling open in awe until Teal'c pulled him inside. "The wealth he must have had to create a structure like this in such an isolated... oh. Wow."

Daniel trailed off as they all slowed, stunned by the beauty of the interior. In a courtyard, easily a hundred meters long, six rows of pillars stood in imposing majesty, each nearly thirty meters tall, slender and gleaming brilliantly in the moonlight. Painted in bright white, each was decorated with images of life along a river bank; water lapped at the bases, flowering papyrus floated in clumps, populated with clouds of butterflies, dragonflies and dozens of species of birds. These took flight, drawing the eye up to the crown of each pillar, which was carved and painted in the shape of palm trees, their fronds stirring in an imaginary breeze.

Jack's chrono beeped loudly in the stillness. "Damn. One hour, people. Let's move."

Teal'c flashed Jack a look of concern, clearly realizing that they were running out of time. They pulled Daniel forward, both limping and pushing the limits of their strength. Daniel's breath whistled distressingly in their ears. Carter paused at the bottom of a steep flight of steps.

"Go ahead, Carter. We're right behind you."

Teal'c faltered, and Jack took a firmer grip on Daniel's left arm, hooked a hand in his belt and helped them both up the steps. Daniel's face was ashen and bathed in sweat. Just as alarming, Teal'c was gray and perspiring. A cold feeling of doom tried to settle in Jack's gut, but he shoved it aside. They would do this, and he would get his team home—no way were they going to fail so close to the end.

The steps led out into a much smaller room, roofed and in near darkness. Daniel pulled the pen light from his pocket but the little light shorted and failed, damaged by the moat water. Carter fumbled with something in her pocket and produced a box of matches, wrapped in a baggie and only a little damp around the edges. On the third try a match flared to life and illuminated a number of pedestals circling the room.

She counted them quickly before the flame reached her fingers. "Twelve. Coincidence, do you think?"

"Nothing's been coincidental with this setup," Jack muttered. "Shine a light in the center, Carter."

Another match flared up and she followed him to a small sphinx crouched on the floor, a plaque held between its paws.

The light died again.

"Daniel, Teal'c, come take a look at this."

As Carter struck a third match and knelt next to the statue, Daniel slithered out of Teal'c's grasp and sagged into a crumpled heap on his knees. Teal'c knelt beside them with a heavy sigh.

The light went out again and Jack swore. Even their clothing was too wet to use as a torch.

"Can you read this?" She lit a new match and held it close.

"Uh, 's blurred. Can't see." Daniel fumbled in his BDU pockets for his glasses while Teal'c leaned over and began to read.

"'By the name of the heralds who guard the Gateway'..." Teal'c paused as Carter lit yet another match. "'Give voice to them and behold the majesty of your god, Ra'."

"Herald—that's what the passwords were called way back on the first planet, wasn't it?" Jack asked. He grimaced as pain tingled up his back.

"Yes," grunted Daniel from the floor.

Jack thought for a moment. His notebook was still secured in his jacket—on another planet. "Tell me someone still has their notebook."

"I do." Daniel weakly flapped a hand at Carter. "Sam, it's in my left side pocket."

She groped along his leg and found the notebook, neatly secured and sealed in plastic.

"Got it." She pushed the notebook into his hands and struck another match. Daniel flipped through the slightly damp pages to the first entry. As the light died again, he raised his head and spoke the first password they had found.

"Sahu."

To their left, they heard a click and a fizz and suddenly a flame sprang up in the darkness. On the pedestal closest to the stairway, a bowl containing some kind of oil now sported a flame flickering in its center.

"Good. Keep going," Jack urged.

Instead, Daniel let out a grunt of pain and slowly folded over. Carter caught him and cradled his head in her lap.

Bleakly, Jack bent and pulled the notebook from Daniel's lax hand. "Stay there, Teal'c." He patted Teal'c's shoulder and shuffled to the first pedestal. In the wavering light he could make out the passwords written in Daniel's flowing scrawl, and Jack gave silent thanks that Daniel had added the vowels in his transcriptions.

"*Semetu.*" His accent might be off but it got the job done. The second light popped into being.

"*Ashebu.*"

"*Sabes.*"

"*Tent Bayou.*"

The fifth flame refused to light.

"I believe it is pronounced 'Ba-ow', O'Neill," Teal'c said.

"Ah. *Tent Bay-ow.*" The flame lit. Squinting tiredly in the uncertain light, he continued on.

"*Ah Kheru.*"

"*Uaau.*" That one hurt his throat.

"*Maa Nefert Ra.*"

"*Ankh em Fentu.*"

"*Aken Tau-k Ha Kheru.*" He felt particularly pleased when that one lit up.

"*Teb her kehaat.*"

"*An Hra.*"

In the light of the twelfth flame Jack let out a huge sigh of relief as the combined fires brought to life a passage of Goa'uld script embossed in gold on the wall opposite the stairway.

"The thirteenth password." Carter sounded suitably impressed.

"Teal'c, you got this?"

Teal'c shoved himself up to stand on his obviously aching feet. "I do."

Jack's relief died aborning when Carter suddenly twisted around, searching the other walls, floor and ceiling. "Wait, there's no 'gate address."

"Did we miss something? Was there anything else on that statue?" Jack bent to examine the little sphinx. "There's nothing else here."

Teal'c peered over his shoulder and retranslated the passage. "There are no other instructions."

Jack glared at the thing. They were so close....

Daniel turned in Carter's lap, tugged on her pants and whispered something indistinct.

"Daniel? What did you say?" She bent over him to catch the faint words.

"Password. Say it—out loud."

She looked up and nearly bumped noses with Jack, his face an inch from hers. His eyes widened.

"Teal'c—say the password. *Now!*"

Teal'c turned to the center of the room and in a clear, deep voice announced, *"Khesef Hra Khemiu."*

Instantly, a deep grinding noise filled the room and the middle section of the back wall rose up to reveal another set of stairs rising up into the darkness.

"Yes!" Jack leaned on the sphinx and summoned a last dreg of energy. "C'mon, kids. We're nearly there."

Teal'c felt each second ticking down with more and more finality. O'Neill helped Major Carter pull Daniel up and between them they steered his unresisting body toward the stairway. Thirteen difficult and slow steps took them up into another, even smaller chamber. In each of the four corners stood an alabaster bowl, so fine they glowed with light from the flames already flickering inside them. In the center was a tall pillar, also made of alabaster, a golden Eye of Ra at its crown. Teal'c, the last to step inside the room, had barely moved through the doorway when the stone panel ground down, sealing them within the chamber.

There was a beat of silence. SG-1 halted, staring at the only other object in the room—a carved, wooden life-size statue of Ra. This one stood at the far end of the chamber, side-on to them, one hand outstretched to the now closed door, the other toward the back wall.

"Now what?" O'Neill demanded. "We've run out of passwords." He adjusted his grip on Daniel's waist.

Major Carter turned to look at them all, her eyes huge. "We don't have enough time to get back to the Stargate. We're stuck here."

Teal'c hobbled slowly around the statue, leaving a trail of bloody footprints behind him. "Major Carter is correct," he said softly. "We have failed."

"Lighten up, Teal'c," O'Neill snapped. "We're not finished yet. There has to be something... oh, tell me I'm seeing things?"

Teal'c followed his stare over Daniel Jackson's bowed head. Behind the alabaster bowl to their right a white shimmer began to coalesce. In a blink it was gone, then it was back again, gaining substance and resolving into a near skeletal figure. Its empty eyes seemed to track each one of the four and its mere presence filled the room with death and cold, cold malevolence. It raised one hand and, seemingly from nowhere, dropped a half-dozen objects to the floor: O'Neill's detonators, lost from his pack half-way through the Trial.

"Oh, no."

Major Carter and O'Neill both stumbled back, eliciting a moan from Daniel as he was dragged with them. He squinted blearily at the specter as it advanced toward them.

"That can't be real."

"It is indeed quite real, Daniel Jackson." Teal'c stepped closer to the apparition.

"Teal'c, get away from that thing."

Teal'c looked at O'Neill, then was drawn back to the specter. Now that he could see it clearly, he knew this creature for what it was. His skin shivered in horror but at the same time he was captivated by it. Evil, ancient as the beginning of time, emanated from it, filling the chamber with a stink of something long dead, yet still—somehow—living. This was no mindless entity. It exuded intelligence and a purpose that had kept its mortal body alive for millennia. Teal'c felt a thrill of recognition. The place where the Books of Djehuti resided opened inside him, as if to embrace that which they now faced.

"Can you not see?" he whispered, spellbound as it moved toward him.

"All we see is Casper's creepy cousin."

"You are wrong, O'Neill. *This* is Ra."

"I *beg* your pardon?"

"Rather, it is the spirit of Ra, the essence of the being who ruled as Ra."

"Is that you or these Books talking, T?"

"The knowledge does come from the Books. Remember—they give the bearer the power to see the true face of the gods."

"Well, swell. Ask it how we get out of here."

Teal'c blinked at him in surprise. "I cannot. It has passed beyond the mortal realm."

"Ka." Daniel Jackson suddenly spoke up.

"Car? What do you mean, Daniel?" Major Carter stared at him.

"Ka—K. A.—*Ka*, the shadow soul. It was said to live on after the death of the body." He shivered and panted for air. "We must have set it free when Ra died."

"Indeed."

"And now it's haunting us?" At his words, the specter turned toward them, paused, then in a white blur, flew through the air straight at O'Neill.

O'Neill dropped Daniel's arm and dodged sideways, but not fast enough. It passed right through him in a sickening distortion of time and gravity. He fell, uttering a choked moan as if his very soul had shriveled and frozen. In slow motion the specter tracked Daniel Jackson and absorbed right into him, then emerged and reformed as Daniel cried out and collapsed.

Major Carter stumbled away, terror and revulsion twisting her features. "Teal'c, there has to be something you can do!" She ducked, but the thing was on her in a flash. She yelped as the shimmering specter seemed to consume her and she sagged into a corner behind an alabaster bowl.

Teal'c lunged forward, his momentary paralysis broken and yelled to attract the spirit's attention away from his fallen comrades. It floated toward the statue, then hovered and seemed unsure what to do.

Teal'c sensed a wave of anger and vengeance spilling from the *Ka*, and a longing to—rejoin? Was that correct? But how could a spirit join that which was now dust?

"Teal'c." Daniel Jackson's soft whisper drew his attention to where his teammate lay huddled on the floor. "Oil… water… offerings. Return it," he trailed off as a fit of coughing consumed him, but one hand pointed toward the statue of Ra.

Teal'c nodded his understanding and desperately cast about him. The bowls were full of aromatic oil, but there was no water in sight.

The specter turned away from the statue and drifted toward O'Neill once more, malevolence radiating from its very core. In two steps, Teal'c was at one of the bowls. He scooped up two handfuls of the oil, turned and flung it over the statue. The *Ka* halted in its advance as if pulled by invisible hands. It turned and snarled soundlessly at Teal'c.

Teal'c flung out his arms. "I need water!" he roared in frustration.

In unison, from opposite corners, two worn voices replied, "T-shirt!"

Berating his short-sightedness, he pulled his still-wet shirt over his head and leaped to the statue. He twisted it tightly, carefully wringing a few drops of stagnant water onto the head of Ra's image.

The spirit suddenly pulsed with brilliant light. It opened its mouth and issued a soundless shriek that he felt in his bones. With a blur too fast to comprehend, it was sucked into the statue.

Within the sculpture, they could see the shade clearly, glowing hotly white and thrashing with fury. The statue began to rock from the force within. Teal'c staggered back, alarmed that the figure might topple and shatter. Would the spirit then be released once again? He turned, scooped more oil from the brazier and flung it over the statue. Carefully, he plucked the burning wick from the bowl. The enraged *Ka* writhed ferociously as Teal'c leaned forward and touched the flame to the oil-soaked wood.

It ignited with a surging whump of heat, sweeping up to engulf the entire sculpture in seconds. For a moment there was a sheath of flame, then with a soundless, agonized scream of fury and despair that seemed to echo from centuries long gone, the statue collapsed into a crumbling tower of ash. It sank in on itself and cascaded to the floor. The *Ka* within faded away until only a faint, lingering reverberation of its last cry remained. Silence settled around the four teammates.

"And it's good night from him."

O'Neill staggered to his feet, as Teal'c blinked at him in bemusement. "Master Teal'c, *Ghost Buster* extraordinaire! How we're gonna write this report up, I have no idea. Everyone alright?"

Before they could answer, his chronometer beeped — a few small sounds that effectively sealed their fate.

"We're stuck here," Major Carter whispered from her corner.

The four of them stared at each other. Teal'c opened his mouth, but there was nothing left to say.

The sound of deep grinding filled the air. They looked up to see all four walls slide out and down, disappearing completely to leave them standing under a roof held up by four corner pillars. Fresh air flooded in around them.

In the distance, the last crest of the moon could be seen framed by the Stargate, only minutes away from setting. In the opposite direction, the new dawn brightened the sky.

"Call me optimistic, but I think something's about to happen."

The sun inched up over the horizon and the first rays streaked across the land, funneled through the canyon to light upon the Eye of Ra on the central pillar.

"Look!" Teal'c pointed at the moon, almost set now. Its final gleam hit the Stargate and seemed to be magnified by the ring. A pale beam of light arced across the valley of flint and struck the other side of the Eye.

From under their feet, a powerful hum of energy began to build.

"Oh, jeez. No, no, no, no, no—rings! Jack, there are rings here," Daniel Jackson gasped out as the sunrise revealed what was on the floor, not two inches from his face.

O'Neill looked down, and was moving and yelling in the same moment that realization hit.

"Teal'c, Carter—get in the center—*now.*"

He grabbed for Daniel who was vainly trying to rise, snatched his arm and belt and heaved, sliding him into the now glowing circle of the ring transporter. Teal'c was already there, an arm flung out to Major Carter as she hurled herself toward them.

The hum built to that familiar chime of readiness. Major Carter dived and crashed into the circle, and Teal'c wrapped her in his arms as the rings rose around them.

Brilliant white light eclipsed the rising sun and setting moon. SG-1 held their breath and were swept up and away.

THE BARQUE OF HEAVEN

The rings descended, vanishing into the ground. Released from his frozen crouch over Daniel, Jack teetered off-balance and landed on his butt. Wildly, he glanced around. Carter blinked at him, tangled in Teal'c's arms on the soft grass.

"We're all here," Jack croaked. "Damn, we did it." He shook his head in disbelief, fingers still clutching at Daniel, who remained sprawled in the dirt.

Teal'c raised his head and managed a ghost of a smile. "We have succeeded."

"I'm not so sure." Carter rolled off Teal'c, rubbing her ankle with a groan. "This doesn't look like a space vessel."

They looked in confusion at their surroundings. Swathes of bright grass, reeds, a greenish-blue sky, and a warm sun beating down on them—not any kind of Goa'uld ship they'd seen before.

"Did we get it wrong?" Jack asked.

"I think not, O'Neill. Everything in the temple was engineered to direct us toward the ring transporter. We are where it was intended for us to be."

Jack considered Daniel's condition. His eyelids were fluttering shut, his breathing harsh and strained; he seemed unable to muster the strength to even raise his head.

"Then let's get the hell out of here. There has to be a Stargate around somewhere." Jack clambered painfully to his feet.

"Not necessarily, sir."

"Carter, if I say there is a Stargate, then there is one." He ignored the incredulity on her face at that piece of logic and pulled her to her feet.

"Ah, ow, damn it!" She hopped unsteadily on one foot.

"How bad?" He steadied then caught her as the ankle gave

way. "Bad enough. We'll get you and Daniel under cover of those reeds." Without waiting for a reply he hauled her toward the nearest stand of plants, while Teal'c attended to Daniel.

They quickly found a patch of flowering grasses inside the tall reeds. Jack lowered Carter to the ground and as fast as he could, limped back to help Teal'c with Daniel. Tiredly he considered their options, thinking through different plans to get them home as soon as possible. And get home they would—all of them; after everything they'd been through, well, there was no other option. One look at Daniel's condition was enough to make that imperative. Teal'c had not been able to rouse him beyond a semi-delirious mumbling.

"O'Neill," Teal'c conveyed a wealth of concern in one word.

"I know." Jack dropped to one knee and between them, they gently hauled Daniel up, trying not to hear the moans of distress they caused.

"Just over there, Daniel. We'll get you under cover and then we'll find a way out of here."

The short distance to the reeds was the longest and slowest they had ever walked. Gently, they lowered Daniel to lie in Carter's embrace, half sitting to help him breathe, his head resting on her shoulder. She wrapped her arms around him and held him tight.

Jack stepped back, body thrumming with the need to go, walk, run, and find the Stargate. "We'll be back as soon as we can, Carter."

"Yes, sir. We'll be here."

Teal'c regarded her solemnly then brushed his hand over Daniel's head, almost in benediction. "Be well, my friends." He pushed painfully to his feet and pulled his shirt back on. Jack led the way out onto open ground.

Sam shivered as the reeds closed behind Teal'c. Isolation smothered her and she felt cold, despite the warm sun beating down. She hugged Daniel close, the weight of his body familiar and welcome.

"You'll be alright, Daniel. Please, be alright," she whispered. He sighed and relaxed a little in her arms.

The rushes suddenly bent in a gust of wind. Unnerved, Sam glanced around, but the plants stood tall around them, limiting her field of view. They rustled again and in the same moment, the hair on her neck rose. She jerked her head around, a yelp escaping her lips as she found herself nose to nose with the grotesque face of Bes.

"Whoa... where did you come from?" Reflexively she gripped Daniel tighter, turning her body as much as she could to protect him. "What do you want?"

"Welcome, friend, to your reward. You have succeeded in your Trial!" Big soulful eyes blinked at her as Bes sat on his haunches. He flashed a huge, gap-toothed grin and clapped his hands in childlike glee.

"Riiiight. *Colonel. Teal'c!*" Daniel flinched at her yell. "Can you tell us how we get home, Bes?" she managed in a gentler tone.

"Many seasons I have waited for someone to complete the Trial. It has been so long since one came to me... although, the last one left only a little while ago...." He trailed off, visibly confused.

"Oh, boy. C'mon, c'mon, c'mon," Sam muttered, willing the others to return. Daniel gave a start and tilted his head to look at Bes.

"What's...?"

"Shh, it's okay. Go back to sleep," she said, despite her relief that he was waking up.

"Bes?"

"Yeah."

"You are very dirty," Bes chipped in, disapproval plain on his face.

Sam glared at him, offended. "Well, so would you be."

"You are both very pretty."

"I—what?"

"You smell unpleasant."

Daniel made a weird grunt and mumbled something like, "Told you so," into her chest.

"You know, we didn't come all this way to be insulted," she bridled. "*Col*... oh." She aborted the yell as Teal'c and the colonel burst through the reeds and skidded to a halt. "Found a friend, sir."

"I can see that," he panted.

"Do not attempt to harm our companions," Teal'c menaced Bes, looming over the stunted creature.

Bes gaped delightedly up at the new arrivals. "Your odor is most displeasing," he informed them brightly.

The colonel mugged at her, demanding an explanation and she shrugged. "Seems we missed the shower planet," she said, trying not to smile at the look of affront on Teal'c's face.

Bes jumped up and clapped his hands. "I shall cleanse you of your journey's remains," he announced.

Before she could flinch away, Bes reached out, a large white jewel attached to his palm by a spider-work of gold wires, and laid a gnarled hand on Sam's head. She froze as an intoxicating tingle swept over her, spreading from Bes's hand down to her feet. Stunned, she watched the grime on her skin vanish. The stains of dirt, sweat and pond slime on her shirt, pants and boots all faded and disappeared. In their place, flowers and twining leaves bloomed from nothing to adorn her clothing and hair. A rich, invigorating scent filled the air.

"Oh, my God. How…?"

Teal'c and the colonel stepped back, astonished, as the effect swept on from her to work on Daniel. The dirt and stains on his clothing faded, the rips in his pants reformed and were made whole, and right up to his hair he was covered in delicate flowering plants. His eyes flickered open, brow creasing in confusion.

Bes clapped happily and turned to Colonel O'Neill and Teal'c. Without any visible effort, he directed the effect at them and crowed with delight as they too were cleansed of the evidence of their trials and left wreathed in sweet-smelling flowers.

"Such a rectification! Now you are fit to be presented with your reward." Bes made to leave but Teal'c reached down and caught his arm.

"You must not go," he said quietly, forcefully.

Daniel suddenly stiffened and Sam tried to soothe him as he turned his face into her breast and gasped in pain.

"If you have the ability to alter our appearance in this manner, can you not also heal our friend's injuries?" Teal'c implored softly.

"You feel pain?" Bes blinked at him, surprise writ large on his face.

"*None* of us feel too good," the colonel broke in. "But, please, at least can you do something for Daniel? He needs a healer, medicine, something."

Bes turned back to stare at Daniel. "But he is presentable, now. Everyone is cleansed."

"He's hurt—inside," Sam said, one hand hovering over Daniel's abdomen.

Head cocked, Bes seemed to consider Daniel for a long time. "Can he not heal himself?" he finally asked.

"No, none of us can."

Again, a long nerve-wracking consideration, until finally he decided. "This is irregular. Supplicants heal themselves when gifted with their reward, but if you cannot, then I believe I am permitted to do this for you."

Bes squatted next to Sam and Daniel and laid a hand over Daniel's heart. For agonizing moments nothing happened, then a gentle white light swept from the jewel in his hand out over Daniel's entire body. Daniel's eyes fluttered open and he turned to stare at Bes's face, only inches from his own.

"So beautiful."

Sam barely heard Daniel's whisper, before the tingling, thrumming light penetrated her own body, leeching some of her multitude of aches and restoring her ankle to almost perfect condition. She gasped in relief and watched in awe as the light flowed on to both Teal'c and the colonel, visibly relieving their injuries. Within a minute they both stood straighter, pain obviously fading from their bodies. Teal'c lifted his shirt and examined his skin in wonder. The infection around the puncture wound had vanished, although the wound itself was still visible.

The light dimmed and receded down their bodies, returning to Daniel where it brightened for several moments over his prone frame. Finally it withdrew to Bes's jewel and disappeared completely. Bes touched Daniel's cheek in a gentle, loving gesture then pulled back and stood.

Astounded, the four members of SG-1 looked at themselves and each other, unable to believe the pain and exhaustion they had endured was so suddenly leaving them. Daniel sat up slowly, his hands touching his side in awe.

"Daniel, how do you feel?" Sam asked, watching him closely.

"Good, I think. There's just a bit of soreness, but I feel great." He smiled at her and she couldn't stop herself from grabbing him and hugging him for all she was worth.

"Thank you, thank you…." She reached out and caught Bes's hand. *"Thank you."*

Bes blinked happily at them as Sam insisted on lifting Daniel's flower-decked shirt and examining him closely.

"Sam, really, I feel a lot better. Most of the pain is gone."

"The bruising has certainly receded, Daniel." She palpated his side and abdomen carefully, Teal'c and the colonel peering down to check for themselves. "The swelling has gone down too. Does this hurt?" She pressed firmly on the remaining bruise under the ribcage on his left side.

Daniel dragged in a hiss of breath. "Yeah, still hurts. But nowhere near as bad as it was."

"Well, we have to leave something for Janet to do," she beamed at him, sure now that he would live to return home.

She looked up at the others and saw her relief reflected on their faces. "Teal'c, sir, how are you both doing?"

"Almost back to normal, Carter. Teal'c?"

"I regret there has been little improvement in my condition, O'Neill."

Bes peered intently up at Teal'c. "The Bearer of Djehuti's Books must make his choice before being restored."

"To what manner of choice do you refer?" Teal'c dropped to one knee next to Bes.

"You must choose between knowing the God's secret speech and holding the records of His deeds. Decide, and then I shall release you from their burden."

"I will be permitted to keep either the language of Ra or his historical records?"

"Yes. Which do you choose?"

Teal'c settled back on his heels and regarded his teammates. "Should I choose to know Ra's language it will no doubt be of great interest to our scholars." He inclined his head at Daniel. "However, we would then lose Ra's history, no doubt an invaluable account. Should I elect to keep the history, we will be unable to unlock its secrets if we cannot understand the language in which it is recorded." He stared thoughtfully at Daniel.

"Chicken and egg," the colonel muttered helpfully. "A language is not much use without anything to translate."

"Indeed. However, I have all faith that with time, Daniel Jackson will be able to translate the historical records."

Sam grinned at the modest flush of pleasure on Daniel's face.

"I choose the Histories of Ra," Teal'c announced.

"A meritorious choice!" Bes extended the hand bearing his jeweled device and placed it over the wound in Teal'c's side. There was a brief hum and a flash of light. Teal'c gave a surprised grunt as two small capsules were withdrawn from the wound and fell into Bes's palm. He picked one up and presented it with a flourish.

"The wisdom of the God. Use it with virtue in your service to Ra."

"That little thing?" The colonel squinted at the tiny oval shape.

"It is a record chip. It can interface with a number of Goa'uld-designed viewing instruments." Teal'c accepted the plastic container Daniel pulled from his pants' pocket and dropped the crystal in to rest with the cards from the now lost camera. He contemplated the container for a moment, then returned it to Daniel's keeping.

"How do you feel now, Teal'c?" asked Sam.

Teal'c quirked an eyebrow in pleased surprise. "My symbiote is becoming active once again. Thank you." He nodded to Bes.

"So." Colonel O'Neill stood back and rubbed his hands together. "We're all feeling a lot better now. Bes, do you think you can do something about these flowers?"

Bes cast a critical eye over the four of them. "No, I believe you are adequately adorned. Any more flowers would be ostentatious."

Bes led them, promising rewards most resplendent, along the banks of a wide river the team had been too preoccupied to really notice before. The odd little being's gait was slow and rambling, a pace which suited them now that the immediate need for assistance was allayed.

O'Neill dragged his attention away from the bucolic setting and fell in step with Teal'c. Shaking his head as Daniel Jackson's laughter drifted back to them, he caught Teal'c's eye and peered intently at him.

"Teal'c, you're *sure* you're okay?"

"I am, O'Neill." Teal'c smiled gently at him. "I am once again in full control of my faculties and in good health. I am pleased to see we are all no longer threatened by our injuries."

Once again, Teal'c found his gaze sliding toward Daniel Jackson, seeking reassurance that their youngest was indeed healthy. He smiled to himself as Major Carter surreptitiously touched Daniel, obviously seeking the same reassurance. For his part, Daniel Jackson strode along in Bes's wake, once again in full inquisitive explorer mode.

"But, Bes really, we don't need a reward for completing the Trial. We didn't intend to undertake it in the first place. We just want to go home." Daniel waved his arms in eloquent exasperation as Bes once again changed course, this time wading into the water through floating papyrus plants and disturbing a great flock of stilt-legged birds.

"It is my penance to provide the supplicants with their due reward," Bes said, his voice flat as if repeating a well-rehearsed line. He stretched out a hand and an enormous pelican dove from the air to land on his arm. It clacked its beak and received a mouthful of fish from Bes.

Teal'c frowned. There had been no fish moments earlier. Certainly the little man had no pockets. He felt a surge of wonder as he stared at Bes. In all his many years he had never encountered a sentient being so fantastic in appearance. However, he no longer felt alarmed by the little person, and surprisingly he was beginning to quite like Bes and his odd ways.

"Penance?" echoed Daniel Jackson. Bes did not respond to him and Daniel shared a frustrated glance with the others.

"It was our understanding that we would be taken to the Barque of Heaven upon completion of the Trial of Moons," Teal'c took up the conversation. "Can you tell us about this vessel? Does it possess a Stargate? How are we to board it and what may we expect when we arrive?"

"Yeah, how come there are no Jaffa waiting here to drag us off to Ra's headquarters?" O'Neill added.

Bes turned to him and grinned, now with a pelican on each arm and one on his head. "This *is* the Barque of Heaven, dear one."

Teal'c blinked in surprise and Bes's simple declaration was met with a storm of outcries.

"What? We thought it was a ship, a Ha'tak or something like that." Daniel waded through the water to him.

"Wait a minute. Those stella ben-ben things we found at the start of this said we'd earn a place at Ra's side on the Barque of Heaven." O'Neill splashed into the river, scaring the birds into flight. "So, what? We're stranded here in la-la land with *you?*"

Bes turned and ambled back to shore, oblivious of O'Neill's hostility. "It is a little whimsy of Ra's. He promises his servants the pleasures of Heaven, but it does not last for them. It never lasts...."

O'Neill churned back through the water, impatiently plucking a flower that seemed to be growing out of his ear. Teal'c watched, bemused, as it instantly re-grew.

"Sir, I don't think he knows Ra is dead," Carter said quietly.

"You're probably right, Major." O'Neill sighed. "Let's try and get some sense out of this munchkin.... Where the hell is he?"

They looked around, surprised to find Bes suddenly some distance away in the grass, standing among tables laden with food of all descriptions. Tempting scents drifted toward them.

"Is that *food?*" Daniel Jackson started for the tables, drawn like a marionette on a string. Teal'c was one pace behind him, floral adornments nodding in the breeze, stomach loudly proclaiming its readiness to be filled. Even his symbiote was flipping excitedly at the prospect of a meal by proxy.

Daniel paused, indecision swamping him as he gazed at the enormous selection of food on the tables.

"Do you think it's safe?" Sam asked, somehow having arrived first.

Jack flung his hands out. "Don't ask me, Carter. I stopped understanding anything about this place when we turned into walking flower arrangements."

Teal'c scooped up a large pastry. "This is quite similar to those Drey'auc cooked for me when I returned home from battle." He took a huge bite, savoring the flavors flooding his mouth.

The others were likewise enchanted with their food. It was some time before they slowed and looked up from their banquet. Bes was standing close by, a sad look now crinkling his features.

Picking up a pot of fragrant curry, Daniel moved over to him and knelt in front of the little man. "Bes, who are you? Why are you here?"

"I am Keeper of the Barque. I am the Welcomer. I am the Bearer of the Lord Ra's Burdens."

"Right. Well, obviously you don't know, but Ra is dead. It happened three and a half years ago, which probably doesn't mean anything to you, but it's been a while now. If Ra was keeping you here against your will, you're free now. You can leave."

Bes stared at him, head cocked. "Is the food to your liking?"

"Uh, yes, of course, it's fantastic. Did you understand me? Ra is dead."

"I provide the reward to the successful supplicants. So many fail. I sometimes watch them. It is nice to speak to people." He blinked sadly at Daniel for a moment, then his expression changed, slowly morphing into thoughtfulness. "Ra is more powerful than you imagine, dear ones. Death is beyond him."

Sam crouched next to Daniel and patted Bes's gnarled arm. "How long have you been here, Bes?"

"Our rebellion failed," he replied.

Sam and Daniel traded puzzles glances at the non sequitur. "What rebellion?"

"The First World was such a beautiful place. The people were very loving. But they were beaten down by Ra's rule. I could not bear to see them suffer." Large tears formed in those huge eyes and rolled down his cheeks. "I tried to help them to fight the injustice. I could not. Ra punished me and then he punished the people." Bes reached out and brushed Daniel's cheek as he had earlier. "Your people."

"Our people? You mean, you were on Earth?" Daniel asked quickly. "Uh, Midgard? Here?" He scratched the Stargate glyph of Earth's point of origin in the dirt.

"Yes. The place of my disgrace. Ten thousand of your world's years I have accepted Ra's punishment for my failure to your people."

"Oh, no." Daniel and Sam both uttered the words in shock. A low whistle from Jack echoed their feelings.

"You have been imprisoned here, for all that time?" Teal'c asked gently.

"It is my penance and my vengeance that condemned me here." Bes straightened a little, a defiant gleam in his eyes. "I was beautiful, treasured by my kind. But I moved amongst your people in my mortal form, and Ra caught me and bound me, forever denying me contact with my kindred. He collects those of beauty, surrounds himself with that which is pleasing to the eye, to hide from the ugliness within his soul. In the instant of my bondage, I used the power of his own devices to take this ugly form. I denied him the pleasure of looking upon me, so he confined me to this place, hidden from the searching gaze of my people. I am allowed to travel within the Trial planets, but no farther. Even that, I have not done for many years—until you came." He smiled up at them. "You were very entertaining."

Daniel settled himself carefully on the grass and searched for the right words.

"Firstly—you didn't fail, Bes. We know there was a rebellion on Earth ten thousand years ago, and during it, Ra was deposed and he fled. He never returned. The people of Egypt have been free of Goa'uld domination for all that time. *You succeeded,* and we thank you for what you did." He gazed intently at Bes, watching as his words sank in.

Bes stared back at him. "You are speaking the truth," he finally said.

"Yes, I am. Secondly—Ra *is* dead. We rediscovered the

Stargate on Earth and journeyed to Abydos. The people there also rose up against Ra and we," he reached up and caught Jack's arm where he stood behind him, "destroyed Ra's ship with him in it. He has no hold over you, or anyone else, anymore."

Bes slowly shook his head. "Ra is… unlike others of the Goa'uld race. His power transcends death."

Daniel nodded and shifted a little to ease the bruise that remained on his side. "What do you mean, Bes?"

Bes blinked solemnly at him, the sad vagueness of his voice suddenly gone. "For ten millennia, Ra remained in the same host. Such a close bond for so long a time can change the very nature of a being. Ra is unlike any other."

"Well, powerful or not, he *is* dead."

Bes was silent for a moment, then he sagged down next to Daniel. "Such was the power of Ra, he lives on after the death of the body. His soul, his essence of life is so strong, he was able to sacrifice a portion of it to entrap me and keep me bound to these planets of the Trial of Moons."

"Sacrifice…" Daniel trailed off, trying to imagine how someone could slice-and dice their own soul. It would seem the *Ka* really was a living soul, separate—or able to be separated—from the mortal body.

"Ra sealed part of his essence on the last planet of the Trial and it is this that will forever be my jailer." Bes looked at the four people around him. "You may have seen it, on your travels. It likes to bother the supplicants, but I keep it from causing real harm. It is a little game we play." A little twinkle sparked the big brown eyes. "I have the freedom of the other twelve planets, and of course this garden we sit in. It is freedom enough."

"Yes, we did see the spirit, several times. In fact, it came after us on the thirteenth planet," Daniel said carefully, noting the flash of alarm on Bes's face. "I think it recognized Jack and me as the ones who destroyed its physical body."

"I regret I was unable to assist you."

"That's alright, Bes. In fact, Teal'c managed to trap the *Ka* in a statue of Ra." He broke off as Bes jumped to his feet, bringing his wide, shocked eyes level with Daniel's.

"How could you achieve such a thing?"

"Uh, well, in Ancient Egyptian times oil and water were used as offerings to the *Ka* of the gods. I hoped that the practice was another that had its roots in Goa'uld interference with human mythology."

"As indeed it did," Teal'c rumbled gently. "The offerings bound the *Ka* into the statue—which I then burned to ash. It, and the spirit of Ra, is no more, my friend. You are *free*."

Daniel watched the emotions play across Bes's face as their words sank in; first disbelief, followed by hope, quickly replaced by anger which was chased away by delight. Bes straightened to his full, tiny, height and looked each of them intently in the eye.

Then he simply vanished into thin air.

"Hey! Come back here, you little…." Jack twisted around, vainly searching for him.

"Great, now what?" Sam flopped onto the grass and gazed at the sky.

"I believe I may partake in another meal," announced Teal'c, making a beeline for the desserts.

Daniel shrugged and followed him.

"You're all taking this very calmly," Jack groused, selecting a huge slice of pie.

"Bes will come back, Jack. He's probably just gone to check things out for himself."

"Meanwhile, we're still stuck here, looking like the Flower Pot People." He plucked the annoying flower out of his ear again.

"Oh, it's not so bad, sir," Sam said, biting into an enormous fruit. "Besides, I think it's growing on us." She grinned innocently at him.

"Very funny, Carter." Teal'c hid his own smirk as Jack snorted a laugh.

Daniel settled back on the lush grass, sated and at ease. They might be no closer to getting home, but the absence of danger was a significant improvement to their lot.

They stuffed themselves as much as was decent, and then some. Afterwards, they lay in the grass drowsing, minds adjusting to their new circumstances while their bodies caught up with the healing process. With no kind of threat here, they relaxed in the company of dozens of different birds and animals that went on about their business around them.

Jack sighed, rolled over and stared at Daniel. "How are you feeling, Daniel? Really?"

"I'm feeling good, Jack. *Really.*" Daniel tilted his head to look at Jack, not bothering to move from his prone position in the grass. "My side is fine, shoulder doesn't hurt, back and legs are okay. Although, I think I might have eaten too much."

"Resurrection Boy rides again." Jack shook his head in wonder.

"Daniel?" Carter flopped onto her stomach and regarded him sleepily. "What did you see, back in the reeds when Bes started to heal you? You said something like, 'so beautiful'."

Daniel frowned. "I did? I don't remember, Sam. I just had an impression of bright light and a sense of great possibilities. And flowers. Lots of flowers—that don't make me sneeze." He brushed back his floral bangs and let his eyelids slide shut, dozing until a sweet voice intruded.

"Hello."

Jolted awake, they dragged themselves into varying stages of alertness.

"Helloooo," Jack drawled. He rose to his feet, taking in the young man who had appeared in front of them.

"Oh." Carter's soft exclamation summed up his own thoughts. The man was exceptionally beautiful. Gleaming black hair fell over bare shoulders in gentle waves. The muscles of his torso, arms and legs were lightly defined and his skin gleamed golden and vibrant. A white kilt was his only clothing. His face was straight out of a Pre-Raphaelite painting.

"Bes?" Daniel got slowly to his feet.

"Hello, Daniel."

"It is you? Bes?"

"This is your true form," Teal'c stated softly.

"It is my mortal form, yes."

"Where did you go?" Carter pushed herself to her feet, unable to take her eyes off the man.

"I traveled to the place where the supplicants are sent to give their service to Ra, Samantha. No one was there. Everywhere—it was deserted." He looked like he was having a little trouble believing. "Ra truly is gone."

"Well, that's a good thing." Jack shoved his hands into flower-decked pockets. "Is there someplace you can send *us*? Nice as this is, we'd really like to go home."

"Home," Bes echoed. His gaze drifted away from them to the river. For long minutes, he silently regarded the water, its wildlife, reeds and floating rafts of papyrus plants.

"Bes, where is your home?" Daniel asked softly. "Do you know where your people are?" Ten thousand years was a long time to be away from home.

"My people are where they have always been," came the uninformative reply.

"Are you of the Nox?" Teal'c asked suddenly.

"The Nox…." Bes turned back to them. "The Nox are our friends."

"Well, maybe they can help you," Carter said. "We met the Nox on one of our missions. We could try to contact them again for you."

"Or the Asgard," Jack added. "Thor seems like a nice fella, I'm sure he'd be able to help you get home."

Suddenly, Bes smiled at them. "You are most generous and compassionate. Have you enjoyed your participation in the Trial?"

"Enjoyed?" Jack's eyebrows rose. "That's not the first word

I'd use."

"It has been a most challenging and illuminating experience," Teal'c said.

Bes nodded and gazed at the river again. Flocks of birds circled and swooped over the water as the day began to fade. The few white clouds in the sky were tinged pink from the sinking sun's rays, the sky itself turning a distinctive emerald hue.

"You have the courage to face what the demon has left inside you?"

The question hung in the air, not directed at any of them. After a beat of silence, Carter looked up from her flower-covered boots.

"Yes," she said quietly, avoiding the questioning looks from the men.

"You must know that even should those you love fall, your protection of them will never waiver."

At the undirected comment from Bes, Jack jerked slightly. "Okay," he said cautiously, accepting the statement was for his benefit.

Bes was silent again for a while, his back to the four, face turned to the sunset.

"Keep your heart open to those around you, and you shall prevail in your endeavor."

This little pronouncement seemed, like the others, without direction, until Teal'c straightened and inclined his head in Bes's direction.

"I shall."

Daniel shuffled his feet, obviously wondering—dreading—what would come his way. He caught Jack's eye, then looked quickly away.

"Alone, you will fail."

The soft words made Daniel flinch. He ignored Jack's quick glance and continued to stare at Bes.

"Remain with those who care for you, their strength shall be yours."

Jack knew exactly what Bes was talking about. He stared

at Daniel, watching that stubbornness swiftly rise on his face. He felt certain Daniel was formulating some half-assed plan to leave them and head off on his own to search for his family. Jack couldn't blame him for building some hope to cling to during the lonely nights, but he wondered if Daniel truly realized there was no way Jack would ever let him go off alone.

Daniel coughed, and sighed in defeat. He watched a cluster of ibis roosting in a leafy tree on the riverbank.

"I will."

His words carried gently to his relieved friends. Jack felt like planting a big kiss on Bes.

Far off in the distance, a low rumble of thunder underscored the dying light of the day.

"There will be no moon tonight," Bes announced, apropos of nothing. "My kindred come for me."

"They do? How do you know?" Carter stared around, not seeing anything different.

"More importantly, can they help *us* get home?" Jack said impatiently.

"It would delight me to return you to your home," a melodic voice spoke behind them.

They spun around to find a woman standing in the grass, as if she had been there all afternoon. Her auburn hair gleamed in the dusk light. An elegant white gown flowed around her body.

"You know, announcing yourselves would really be nice." Jack patted his flowered chest and looked suspiciously at the new arrival. "And you are…?"

"I am come for Bes. Long have we searched for our brother. The false one's concealment prevented him from calling to us. We are indebted to you all for freeing him." She glided over the grass to Bes and took his hand. "It is time to depart, brother."

"Wait, wait, wait." Daniel leaped forward. "We don't want to sound selfish, but can you help us get home? We can't stay here."

"Your path home is already set, dear one. We thank you,

again." She gave them all a dazzling smile and gathered Bes close to her.

"But—can you at least tell us who you are, how we can contact you? We could have a lot to learn from each other."

Bes reached out and brushed his hand across Daniel's chest. "Thank you, my precious friends."

With that, the two simply faded from view. SG-1 turned to stare at each other, perplexed and frustrated.

Jack glared up into the darkening sky. "So, what? That's it? What do we do now? Click our heels together and say—"

EPILOGUE

"There's no place like home"

"D'oh." Jack squinted as the bright light that had enveloped them faded away. A quick check for his team—Daniel stood next to him, Carter on his left, Teal'c closed up their standard formation on the far side. All of them were staring open-mouthed.

Seem to be doing a lot of that, these days.

They were still on the planet, but now some distance away from the buffet tables. The river flowed peacefully nearby, and in front of them rose a Stargate, shrouded in an aura of almost benevolent welcome. To one side a DHD squatted, its red crystal gleaming in the sunset. Beside it, sat four SGC-issue metal boxes; their gear, purloined by Bes many planets ago. Amazed, they wandered up to the Stargate, touching its warm, solid surface to confirm it was real.

"O'Neill." Teal'c indicated a cluster of severed black filaments protruding from the base of the Stargate.

"Huh. Carter," he began, but she was already heading to the DHD.

With practiced ease she popped the cover on the access panel and peered inside. Almost immediately she straightened up, a huge grin on her face. "They've been disconnected, sir. We should be able to dial out."

"We can go home," Daniel murmured in disbelief.

"Oh, you betcha." Jack was at the boxes in two bounds. Popping one open he ferreted inside, then sat back brandishing a backup GDO. "We may be covered in flowers but we're going home. Dial us up, Carter."

Carter had the first six chevrons punched in before they realized they had not yet identified the point-of-origin for the Barque of Heaven. She paused, and a seventh glyph — bearing the design of a simple circle, or perhaps a sun — depressed all by itself. The Stargate churned to life and as the vortex billowed backwards and then forwards, she smiled up into the sky and quietly called out her thanks.

Jack sent SG-1's ID code, then bent and helped Teal'c and Daniel pitch the four boxes through the wormhole. He straightened, for a moment drinking in the glorious sunset. Rays of deep golden light stretched up across an emerald sky, a fitting end to what had turned out to be not a bad day at all. He looked at his team: tired, healthy, covered in flowers but happy, and most importantly, alive. He gave them his cheekiest grin.

"Well, kids. It's been quite a ride. What do you say we go home?"

Teal'c inclined his head in silent respect and walked forward into the Stargate. Carter snapped off a parade-ground salute and followed Teal'c toward home. Daniel cast one look behind him, then turned and smiled gently at Jack. Jack waggled his eyebrows in response and ushered Daniel on. The Stargate wrapped Daniel in its light and swept him away. Jack also took a moment to look back and sent a jaunty salute of thanks before he too stepped into the Stargate and was gone.

The blue glow of the wormhole disappeared as the final rays of sunlight streaked up into the sky on the planet, named as Heaven by an alien known as Ra. Bes stood sadly bidding farewell to the prison that had been his home. The light died, signaling an end to the day, and to an era of slavery.

"I am ready."

He turned to look at the other. Smiling gently, she reached out and he met her hand with his, twining their fingers tightly.

She seemed to glow, her body losing its mortal form and turning to brilliant white ribbons of light. The ribbons wrapped around Bes, sharing her energy, rekindling his own. Tentatively, he loosened his hold on his mortal body and flowed into the form of pure energy he had never hoped to hold again.

Transformed and finally free, Bes ascended to the heavens.

About the Author

Suzanne Wood lives in Melbourne, Australia where she has been fortunate to spend many years working with her great love, books, in various fields of the industry, including libraries, retail, admin and bibliographic research. When not writing or reading the many books crowding her out of home, she finds inspiration in the beautiful bush of country Victoria with her beloved dog Molly leading the way. She has combined a love of mythology, Egypt and Stargate in this, her first novel.

http://heavenlybarquings.googlepages.com/

SNEAK PREVIEW

STARGATE SG-1: HYDRA

by Jaimie Duncan & Holly Scott

Daniel was third out of the gate, behind Jack and Bra'tac, so the scream of dismay and warning was shrill in his ears just as he cleared the event horizon. Not the first time people had run screaming when they showed up. Usually a little diplomacy meant SG-1 could talk their way into a friendship even with the people who'd become accustomed to getting nothing much but pain from the visitors stepping through the gate.

He shouldered his way past Jack, ready to perform the dance of meeting, greeting and getting information, and caught sight of a girl running fast back toward the village, slipping in the mud as she scrambled up the hill. She pulled herself mostly upright, half-crawling up the slope, but left her shoe behind. She was still shrieking. Nothing intelligible Daniel could pick out, just panicked noise.

"Well," Jack said, "that was quite the welcome."

Daniel glanced up at the village. The houses had steeply tilted roofs, much like Alpine chalets, but a bit less sturdy and whole lot sadder than the average tourist would find in any resort. Mountains surrounded the village, glaciers and snowfields dimmed to purple shadow against the blue of the sky, barely gleaming in the weak light of a distant sun. A few trees marked the wide skyline here, and far down slope the forest proper was a dark swath of unbroken green. The air was thin, but the voice of the girl carried clearly, sharp with fear.

"Yeah," Daniel said, meeting Bra'tac's stern, accusing gaze before stepping down off the gate platform. He turned and gestured to Jack, who thinned his lips and stepped down beside him.

"Carter," Jack said. "Take point." Bra'tac stepped out in front of them all and began striding up toward the narrow path. "Dammit," Jack said, and Daniel and Sam exchanged a quick smile as they followed.

Then Daniel looked up.

"Uh, I think we could just wait here," he said, pointing. A group of men streamed down from the village, half of them Jaffa in armor. Jack and Sam lifted their weapons and shifted into covering positions, while Teal'c moved sideways to cover their flank. Behind them, Reynolds and his guys fanned out, crouching and looking vulnerable in the absence of good cover. Daniel didn't move. If there were any chance of making sense of the accusations Bra'tac leveled, he'd need to be as conciliatory and open as possible.

"Stay mellow, kids," Jack said, elbow braced to level his weapon.

"Jack," Daniel said. "Let me take the lead."

The group of men was closer now, and they were running. Never a good sign. Daniel counted twelve, maybe fourteen, the girl lagging behind them. She slowed down and stopped in the middle of the road, watching the spectacle downhill.

"You!" one of the men shouted, pointing a long axe at Jack. "You will surrender your weapons to us now and step away from the kreis!"

To Daniel, it sounded like a German variant. "Circle," he told Jack, who didn't acknowledge him. The men – five Jaffa among them, staff weapons leveled at SG-1, Jack in particular – surrounded them. Daniel wasn't surprised, but he did note that the DHD was cut off, as well as the gate. Not a huge problem, and he knew Jack was already thinking them through it, but Daniel couldn't think of a way that wouldn't involve a lot of bullets. He'd have to find a way to prevent that.

"We mean you no harm," he said to the man who had spoken. "There's been some kind of mistake."

"The mistake was yours for returning to this place. After what you have done." The man's voice cracked with horror, and Daniel processed that, the utter finality in it. The man stared at Jack with haunted eyes. "On this day of all days, when we bury those you took from us. You, with your hands and your knives."

Jack said, "Daniel, you've got about ten seconds to—"

"I can see you believe we've wronged you, but it wasn't us," Daniel said urgently, stepping forward, hands outstretched. "We haven't—"

"You dare," the Jaffa nearest him said. "You, whose crime was worst of all. You stood by and did nothing."

"That's it," Jack said. Voice pitched just for his team, he said, "Daniel, stop talking and be ready to dial." He raised his voice to normal speaking levels for the benefit of the villagers, and Daniel glanced to his left. They were slowly encroaching on the team, backing them away from the gate. "Listen, folks, you've made the mistake, and we're going to go now. We'd rather do that without a fight, but—"

"Do not let them leave!" The girl's voice, high-pitched and plaintive, wavered down from the hill, and Jack said,

"Oh, crap."

They all moved at the same time, different directions in order of priorities – Jack, Bra'tac and Teal'c for cover, Carter for the DHD, Daniel with the same general purpose. Jack rolled to the side and crouched behind the gate's stone pedestal. The first staff blast passed so close to Daniel he could feel the hair on his arms singe, and he dove for cover, groping for his Beretta.

So much for negotiation skills.

Daniel scrambled into a low ditch, clumps of grass clinging to his face and hair like wet seaweed. He brushed them off and straightened his glasses. One huge staff blast shattered the frosty ground not ten feet away, raising the smell of boggy peat on a bonfire.

"Defend your positions," Jack's voice said, crackling out of Daniel's radio.

"Some position," Daniel muttered, as he scooped out a miniature trench for his arm to rest in, the better to aim at angry Jaffa. Goopy mud trickled down from the channel. He hunkered down against the shallow wall of the ditch, waiting for a chance to rise up and return fire.

Another staff blast gouged a hole in the side of the ditch right next to Daniel's head and he threw himself into the brackish standing water in the bottom of it to protect his face from the debris. Gravel and mud pattered down around him, sounding almost like rain.

He was inching his head up to ground level to get a look at the battlefield when a fresh cascade of gravel clattered down on his back, followed by the thud and splash of a body hitting the bottom of the ditch beside him.

Completely covered in the thick, grey mud, Jack rolled onto his knees, and straightened long enough to send a short burst of P90 fire over the edge of the shelter before hunkering down with his back against the sloping side of the ditch. "Clip," he said curtly, trying to wipe mud from his eyes with a gloved hand, and instead leaving more mud behind. "I'm out."

Daniel was, for once, grateful that Jack forced him to go into the field with extra ammo for any contingency. He lifted a magazine from his vest pocket and tossed it to Jack, who slapped it into place.

"What the hell is going on with these people?" Daniel demanded, slouching down and wincing up at the darkening sky. "I don't get it."

O'Neill only grunted and pulled out a telescoping mirror so he could get a look over the edge of the ditch. He grunted again and passed the mirror over. "See for yourself."

The field was churned mud. On the other side of it, Sam was strafing the treeline from the shelter of a blast crater, Teal'c beside her, reloading. A new clip in place, Jack popped up and neatly dispatched a Jaffa creeping up on their right flank. But there were more Jaffa coming. Many more. Daniel had only one more clip himself, and he wasn't feeling too great about using it on civilians.

"This doesn't look good."

"Oh, cheer up, Daniel," Jack answered. "I'd say we're about two steps past terrible. Far cry from hopeless." He got off two quick spurts of fire and then ducked down with a whoop as another staff blast sent up a fan of debris two feet away. Jack's teeth were white in his dirty face when he grinned. The grin had real, predatory amusement in it.

Daniel's radio let out a burst of static. "Daniel! What's your position?"

Jack's grin disappeared quickly.

Daniel's mouth fell open and he lifted a hand to point at Jack, like he could pin him to the dirt with the gesture. Then, with the other hand he keyed the radio. "Uh, hi. Who is this?"

"What? This is your commander, who is currently getting his ass shot to hell south of the Stargate!" Jack's voice was fuzzy with static, but recognizable. "Reynolds is in position. We're gonna make a push for the gate, so be ready!"

In the ditch beside Daniel, not-Jack gave Daniel a one-shoulder shrug. His mouth twitched up in an embarrassed grin. "Oops," he said, and in a second he had clambered over the edge of the ditch and onto the field. By the time Daniel had dodged another blast and the dust had cleared, Jack—or whatever was passing for him—had disappeared into the chaos of battle.

STARGATE SG-1: HYDRA

STARGATE
SG·1™

STARGATE
ATLANTIS™

**Original novels based on
the hit TV shows,
STARGATE SG-1 and
STARGATE ATLANTIS.**

AVAILABLE NOW

**For more information, visit
www.stargatenovels.com**

STARGATE SG-1: RELATIVITY

The past comes back to haunt Jack

STARGATE
SG·1

RELATIVITY

James Swallow

Based on the hit television series developed by
Brad Wright and Jonathan Glassner

Series number: SG1-10

by James Swallow
Price: $7.95 US | $9.95 Canada |
£6.99 UK
ISBN-10: 1-905586-07-8
ISBN-13: 978-1-905586-07-3

When SG-1 encounter the Pack—a
nomadic space-faring people who
have fled Goa'uld domination for
generations—it seems as though
a trade of technologies will benefit
both sides.

But someone is determined to
derail the deal. With the SGC under
attack, and Vice President Kinsey breathing down their necks, it's
up to Colonel Jack O'Neill and his team to uncover the saboteur and save the fledgling alliance. But unbeknownst to SG-1
there are far greater forces at work—a calculating revenge that
spans decades, and a desperate gambit to prevent a cataclysm of
epic proportions.

When the identity of the saboteur is revealed, O'Neill is faced
with a horrifying truth and is forced into an unlikely alliance in
order to fight for Earth's future.

STARGATE SG-1: ROSWELL

by **Sonny Whitelaw &
Jennifer Fallon**
Price: $7.95 US | $9.95 Canada |
£6.99 UK
ISBN-10: 1-905586-04-3
ISBN-13: 978-1-905586-04-2

When a Stargate malfunction throws Colonel Cameron Mitchell, Dr. Daniel Jackson, and Colonel Sam Carter back in time, they only have minutes to live.

But their rescue, by an unlikely duo — General Jack O'Neill and Vala Mal Doran — is only the beginning of their problems. Ordered to rescue an Asgard also marooned in 1947, SG-1 find themselves at the mercy of history. While Jack, Daniel, Sam and Teal'c become embroiled in the Roswell aliens conspiracy, Cam and Vala are stranded in another timeline, desperately searching for a way home.

As the effects of their interference ripple through time, the consequences for the future are catastrophic. Trapped in the past, SG-1 can only watch as their world is overrun by a terrible invader…

Order your copy directly from the publisher today by going to www.stargatenovels.com or send a check or money order made payable to "Fandemonium" to:

USA orders: $10.82 ($7.95 + $2.87 P&P). Send payment to: Fandemonium Books, PO Box 2178, Decatur, GA 30031-2178.

UK orders: £8.30 (£6.99 + £1.31 P&P). **Rest of the World orders:** £9.70 (£6.99 + £2.71 P&P). Send payment to: Fandemonium Books, PO Box 795A, Surbiton KT5 8YB, United Kingdom.

Or check your local bookshop — available on special order if they are out of stock (quote the ISBN number listed above).

STARGATE SG-1: ALLIANCES

by Karen Miller

Price: $7.95 US | $9.95 Canada |
£6.99 UK
ISBN-10: 1-905586-00-0
ISBN-13: 978-1-905586-00-4

All SG-1 wanted was technology to save Earth from the Goa'uld ... but the mission to Euronda was a terrible failure. Now the dogs of Washington are baying for Jack O'Neill's blood — and Senator Robert Kinsey is leading the pack.

When Jacob Carter asks General Hammond for SG-1's participation in mission for the Tok'ra, it seems like the answer to O'Neill's dilemma. The secretive Tok'ra are running out of hosts. Jacob believes he's found the answer — but it means O'Neill and his team must risk their lives infiltrating a Goa'uld slave breeding farm to recruit humans willing to join the Tok'ra.

It's a risky proposition ... especially since the fallout from Euronda has strained the team's bond almost to breaking. If they can't find a way to put their differences behind them, they might not make it home alive ...

STARGATE SG-1: SURVIVAL OF THE FITTEST

by Sabine C. Bauer
Price: $7.95 US | $9.95 Canada |
£6.99 UK
ISBN-10: 0-9547343-9-4
ISBN-13: 978-0-9547343-9-8

Colonel Frank Simmons has never been a friend to SG-1. Working for the shadowy government organisation, the NID, he has hatched a horrifying plan to create an army as devastatingly effective as that of any Goa'uld.

And he will stop at nothing to fulfil his ruthless ambition, even if that means forfeiting the life of the SGC's Chief Medical Officer, Dr. Janet Fraiser. But Simmons underestimates the bond between Stargate Command's officers. When Fraiser, Major Samantha Carter and Teal'c disappear, Colonel Jack O'Neill and Dr. Daniel Jackson are forced to put aside personal differences to follow their trail into a world of savagery and death.

In this complex story of revenge, sacrifice and betrayal, SG-1 must endure their greatest ordeal...

STARGATE SG-1: SIREN SONG

Holly Scott and Jaimie Duncan
Price: $7.95 US | $9.95 Canada |
£6.99 UK
ISBN-10: 0-9547343-6-X
ISBN-13: 978-0-9547343-6-7

Bounty-hunter, Aris Boch, once more has his sights on SG-1. But this time Boch isn't interested in trading them for cash. He needs the unique talents of Dr. Daniel Jackson—and he'll do anything to get them.

Taken to Boch's ravaged homeworld, Atropos, Colonel Jack O'Neill and his team are handed over to insane Goa'uld, Sebek. Obsessed with opening a mysterious subterranean vault, Sebek demands that Jackson translate the arcane writing on the doors. When Jackson refuses, the Goa'uld resorts to devastating measures to ensure his cooperation.

With the vault exerting a malign influence on all who draw near, Sebek compels Jackson and O'Neill toward a horror that threatens both their sanity and their lives. Meanwhile, Carter and Teal'c struggle to persuade the starving people of Atropos to risk everything they have to save SG-1 — and free their desolate world of the Goa'uld, forever.

O'Neill faces a nightmare from his past

STARGATE SG-1: A MATTER OF HONOR

**Part one of two parts
by Sally Malcolm**
Price: $7.95 US | $9.95 Canada |
£6.99 UK
ISBN-10: 0-9547343-2-7
ISBN-13: 978-0-9547343-2-9

Five years after Major Henry Boyd
and his team, SG-10, were trapped on
the edge of a black hole, Colonel Jack
O'Neill discovers a device that could
bring them home.

But it's owned by the Kinahhi, an advanced and paranoid people, besieged by a ruthless foe. Unwilling to share the technology, the Kinahhi are pursuing their own agenda in the negotia-
tions with Earth's diplomatic delegation. Maneuvering through a
maze of tyranny, terrorism and deceit, Dr. Daniel Jackson, Major
Samantha Carter and Teal'c unravel a startling truth — a revela-
tion that throws the team into chaos and forces O'Neill to face
a nightmare he is determined to forget.

Resolved to rescue Boyd, O'Neill marches back into the hell he
swore never to revisit. Only this time, he's taking SG-1 with him…

**Order your copy directly from the publisher today by going
to www.stargatenovels.com or send a check or money order
made payable to "Fandemonium" to:**

USA orders: $10.82 ($7.95 + $2.87 P&P). Send payment to:
Fandemonium Books, PO Box 2178, Decatur, GA 30031-2178.

UK orders: £8.30 (£6.99 + £1.31 P&P). Rest of the World
orders: £9.70 (£6.99 + £2.71 P&P). Send payment to:
Fandemonium Books, PO Box 795A, Surbiton KT5 8YB,
United Kingdom.

Or check your local bookshop – available on special order if they are
out of stock (quote the ISBN number listed above).

STARGATE SG-1: THE COST OF HONOR

**Part two of two parts
by Sally Malcolm**
Price: $7.95 US | $9.95 Canada |
£6.99 UK
ISBN-10: 0-9547343-4-3
ISBN-13: 978-0-9547343-4-3

In the action-packed sequel to *A Matter of Honor*, SG-1 embark on a desperate mission to save SG-10 from the edge of a black hole. But the price of heroism may be more than they can pay...

Returning to Stargate Command, Colonel Jack O'Neill and his team find more has changed in their absence than they had expected. Nonetheless, O'Neill is determined to face the consequences of their unauthorized activities, only to discover the penalty is far worse than anything he could have imagined.

With the fate of Colonel O'Neill and Major Samantha Carter unknown, and the very survival of the SGC threatened, Dr. Daniel Jackson and Teal'c mount a rescue mission to free their team-mates and reclaim the SGC. Yet returning to the Kinahhi homeworld, they learn a startling truth about its ancient foe. And uncover a horrifying secret...

Order your copy directly from the publisher today by going to www.stargatenovels.com or send a check or money order made payable to "Fandemonium" to:

<u>USA orders:</u> **$10.82 ($7.95 + $2.87 P&P). Send payment to: Fandemonium Books, PO Box 2178, Decatur, GA 30031-2178.**

<u>UK orders:</u> **£8.30 (£6.99 + £1.31 P&P).** <u>Rest of the World orders:</u> **£9.70 (£6.99 + £2.71 P&P). Send payment to: Fandemonium Books, PO Box 795A, Surbiton KT5 8YB, United Kingdom.**

Or check your local bookshop – available on special order if they are out of stock (quote the ISBN number listed above).

Series number: SG1-2

STARGATE SG-1: SACRIFICE MOON

By Julie Fortune
Price: $7.95 US | $9.95 Canada | £6.99 UK
ISBN-10: 0-9547343-1-9
ISBN-13: 978-0-9547343-1-2

Sacrifice Moon follows the newly commissioned SG-1 on their first mission through the Stargate.

Their destination is Chalcis, a peaceful society at the heart of the Helos Confederacy of planets. But Chalcis harbors a dark secret, one that pitches SG-1 into a world of bloody chaos, betrayal and madness. Battling to escape the living nightmare, Dr. Daniel Jackson and Captain Samantha Carter soon begin to realize that more than their lives are at stake. They are fighting for their very souls.

But while Col Jack O'Neill and Teal'c struggle to keep the team together, Daniel is hatching a desperate plan that will test SG-1's fledgling bonds of trust and friendship to the limit...

STARGATE SG-1: TRIAL BY FIRE

By Sabine C. Bauer

Price: $7.95 US | $9.95 Canada | £6.99 UK

ISBN-10: 0-9547343-0-0

ISBN-13: 978-0-9547343-0-5

Series number: SG1-1

Trial by Fire follows the team as they embark on a mission to Tyros, an ancient society teetering on the brink of war.

A pious people, the Tyreans are devoted to the Canaanite deity, Meleq. When their spiritual leader is savagely murdered during a mission of peace, they beg SG-1 for help against their sworn enemies, the Phrygians.

Initially reluctant to get involved, the team has no choice when Colonel Jack O'Neill is abducted. O'Neill soon discovers his only hope of escape is to join the ruthless Phrygians — if he can survive their barbaric initiation rite.

As Major Samantha Carter, Dr. Daniel Jackson and Teal'c race to his rescue, they find themselves embroiled in a war of shifting allegiances, where truth has many shades and nothing is as it seems.

And, unbeknownst to them all, an old enemy is hiding in the shadows...

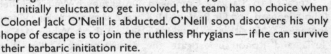

Order your copy directly from the publisher today by going to www.stargatenovels.com or send a check or money order made payable to "Fandemonium" to:

USA orders: **$10.82 ($7.95 + $2.87 P&P). Send payment to: Fandemonium Books, PO Box 2178, Decatur, GA 30031-2178.**

UK orders: **£8.30 (£6.99 + £1.31 P&P). Rest of the World orders: £9.70 (£6.99 + £2.71 P&P). Send payment to: Fandemonium Books, PO Box 795A, Surbiton KT5 8YB, United Kingdom.**

Or check your local bookshop — available on special order if they are out of stock (quote the ISBN number listed above).

STARGATE ATLANTIS: CASUALTIES OF WAR

The first victim of warfare is the truth

STARGATE ATLANTIS

CASUALTIES OF WAR

Elizabeth Christensen

Based on the hit television series created by
Brad Wright and Robert C. Cooper

Series number: SGA-7

by Elizabeth Christensen
Price: £6.99 UK | $7.95 US
ISBN-10: 1-905586-06-X
ISBN-13: 978-1-905586-06-6

It is a dark time for Atlantis. In the wake of the Asuran takeover, Colonel Sheppard is buckling under the strain of command. When his team discover Ancient technology which can defeat the Asuran menace, he is determined that Atlantis must possess it — at all costs.

But the involvement of Atlantis heightens local suspicions and brings two peoples to the point of war. Elizabeth Weir believes only her negotiating skills can hope to prevent the carnage, but when her diplomatic mission is attacked — and two of Sheppard's team are lost — both Weir and Sheppard must question their decisions. And their abilities to command.

As the first shots are fired, the Atlantis team must find a way to end the conflict — or live with the blood of innocents on their hands...

Order your copy directly from the publisher today by going to <u>www.stargatenovels.com</u> or send a check or money order made payable to "Fandemonium" to:

<u>USA orders</u>: **$10.82 ($7.95 + $2.87 P&P). Send payment to: Fandemonium Books, PO Box 2178, Decatur, GA 30031-2178.**

<u>UK orders</u>: **£8.30 (£6.99 + £1.31 P&P). <u>Rest of the World orders</u>: £9.70 (£6.99 + £2.71 P&P). Send payment to: Fandemonium Books, PO Box 795A, Surbiton KT5 8YB, United Kingdom.**

Or check your local bookshop – available on special order if they are out of stock (quote the ISBN number listed above).

STARGATE ATLANTIS: ENTANGLEMENT

by Martha Wells
Price: £6.99 UK | $7.95 US
ISBN-10: 1-905586-03-5
ISBN-13: 978-1-905586-03-5

When Dr. Rodney McKay unlocks an Ancient mystery on a distant moon, he discovers a terrifying threat to the Pegasus galaxy.

Determined to disable the device before it's discovered by the Wraith, Colonel John Sheppard and his team navigate the treacherous ruins of an Ancient outpost. But attempts to destroy the technology are complicated by the arrival of a stranger — a stranger who can't be trusted, a stranger who needs the Ancient device to return home. Cut off from backup, under attack from the Wraith, and with the future of the universe hanging in the balance, Sheppard's team must put aside their doubts and step into the unknown.

However, when your mortal enemy is your only ally, betrayal is just a heartbeat away...

STARGATE ATLANTIS: EXOGENESIS

**by Sonny Whitelaw &
Elizabeth Christensen**
Price: £6.99 UK | $7.95 US
ISBN-10: 1-905586-02-7
ISBN-13: 978-1-905586-02-8

When Dr. Carson Beckett disturbs the rest of two long-dead Ancients, he unleashes devastating consequences of global proportions.

With the very existence of Lantea at risk, Colonel John Sheppard leads his team on a desperate search for the long lost Ancient device that could save Atlantis. While Teyla Emmagan and Dr. Elizabeth Weir battle the ecological meltdown consuming their world, Colonel Sheppard, Dr. Rodney McKay and Dr. Zelenka travel to a world created by the Ancients themselves. There they discover a human experiment that could mean their salvation...

But the truth is never as simple as it seems, and the team's prejudices lead them to make a fatal error — an error that could slaughter thousands, including their own Dr. McKay.

STARGATE ATLANTIS: HALCYON

by James Swallow
Price: £6.99 UK | $7.95 US
ISBN-10: 1-905586-01-9
ISBN-13: 978-1-905586-01-1

In their ongoing quest for new allies, Atlantis's flagship team travel to Halcyon, a grim industrial world where the Wraith are no longer feared—they are hunted.

Horrified by the brutality of Halcyon's warlike people, Lieutenant Colonel John Sheppard soon becomes caught in the political machinations of Halcyon's aristocracy. In a feudal society where strength means power, he realizes the nobles will stop at nothing to ensure victory over their rivals. Meanwhile, Dr. Rodney McKay enlists the aid of the ruler's daughter to investigate a powerful Ancient structure, but McKay's scientific brilliance has aroused the interest of the planet's most powerful man—a man with a problem he desperately needs McKay to solve.

As Halcyon plunges into a catastrophe of its own making the team must join forces with the warlords—or die at the hands of their bitterest enemy…

Order your copy directly from the publisher today by going to www.stargatenovels.com or send a check or money order made payable to "Fandemonium" to:

<u>USA orders</u>: $10.82 ($7.95 + $2.87 P&P). Send payment to: Fandemonium Books, PO Box 2178, Decatur, GA 30031-2178.

<u>UK orders</u>: £8.30 (£6.99 + £1.31 P&P). <u>Rest of the World orders</u>: £9.70 (£6.99 + £2.71 P&P). Send payment to: Fandemonium Books, PO Box 795A, Surbiton KT5 8YB, United Kingdom.

Or check your local bookshop – available on special order if they are out of stock (quote the ISBN number listed above).

STARGATE ATLANTIS: THE CHOSEN

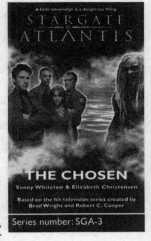

**by Sonny Whitelaw &
Elizabeth Christensen**
Price: £6.99 UK | $7.95 US
ISBN-10: 0-9547343-8-6
ISBN-13: 978-0-9547343-8-1

With Ancient technology scattered across the Pegasus galaxy, the Atlantis team is not surprised to find it in use on a world once defended by Dalera, an Ancient who was cast out of her society for falling in love with a human.

But in the millennia since Dalera's departure much has changed. Her strict rules have been broken, leaving her people open to Wraith attack. Only a few of the Chosen remain to operate Ancient technology vital to their defense and tensions are running high. Revolution simmers close to the surface.

When Major Sheppard and Rodney McKay are revealed as members of the Chosen, Daleran society convulses into chaos. Wanting to help resolve the crisis and yet refusing to prop up an autocratic regime, Sheppard is forced to act when Teyla and Lieutenant Ford are taken hostage by the rebels…

Order your copy directly from the publisher today by going to www.stargatenovels.com or send a check or money order made payable to "Fandemonium" to:

<u>USA orders:</u> $10.82 ($7.95 + $2.87 P&P). Send payment to: Fandemonium Books, PO Box 2178, Decatur, GA 30031-2178.

<u>UK orders:</u> £8.30 (£6.99 + £1.31 P&P). <u>Rest of the World orders:</u> £9.70 (£6.99 + £2.71 P&P). Send payment to: Fandemonium Books, PO Box 795A, Surbiton KT5 8YB, United Kingdom.

Or check your local bookshop – available on special order if they are out of stock (quote the ISBN number listed above).

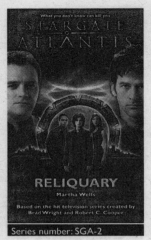

STARGATE ATLANTIS: RELIQUARY

by Martha Wells
Price: £6.99 UK | $7.95 US
ISBN-10: 0-9547343-7-8
ISBN-13: 978-0-9547343-7-4

While exploring the unused sections of the Ancient city of Atlantis, Major John Sheppard and Dr. Rodney McKay stumble on a recording device that reveals a mysterious new Stargate address. Believing that the address may lead them to a vast repository of Ancient knowledge, the team embarks on a mission to this uncharted world.

There they discover a ruined city, full of whispered secrets and dark shadows. As tempers fray and trust breaks down, the team uncovers the truth at the heart of the city. A truth that spells their destruction.

With half their people compromised, it falls to Major John Sheppard and Dr. Rodney McKay to risk everything in a deadly game of bluff with the enemy. To fail would mean the fall of Atlantis itself — and, for Sheppard, the annihilation of his very humanity…

STARGATE ATLANTIS: RISING

by Sally Malcolm
Price: £6.99 UK | $7.95 US
ISBN-10: 0-9547343-5-1
ISBN-13: 978-0-9547343-5-0

Following the discovery of an Ancient outpost buried deep in the Antarctic ice sheet, Stargate Command sends a new team of explorers through the Stargate to the distant Pegasus galaxy.

Emerging in an abandoned Ancient city, the team quickly confirms that they have found the Lost City of Atlantis. But, submerged beneath the sea on an alien planet, the city is in danger of catastrophic flooding unless it is raised to the surface. Things go from bad to worse when the team must confront a new enemy known as the Wraith who are bent on destroying Atlantis.

Stargate Atlantis is the exciting new spin-off of the hit TV show, Stargate SG-1. Based on the script of the pilot episode, Rising is a must-read for all fans and includes deleted scenes and dialog not seen on TV—with photos from the pilot episode.

Order your copy directly from the publisher today by going to www.stargatenovels.com or send a check or money order made payable to "Fandemonium" to:

<u>USA orders:</u> $10.82 ($7.95 + $2.87 P&P). Send payment to: Fandemonium Books, PO Box 2178, Decatur, GA 30031-2178.

<u>UK orders:</u> £8.30 (£6.99 + £1.31 P&P). <u>Rest of the World orders:</u> £9.70 (£6.99 + £2.71 P&P). Send payment to: Fandemonium Books, PO Box 795A, Surbiton KT5 8YB, United Kingdom.

Or check your local bookshop – available on special order if they are out of stock (quote the ISBN number listed above).